A DREAMPUNK ANTHOLOGY

A DREAMPUNK ANTHOLOGY

Edited by
Cliff Jones Jr.

ISBN: 978-1-7352171-3-0 (Paperback)

Library of Congress Control Number: 2020946275

Any references to historical events, real people, or real places are used fictitiously. Names, characters, and places are products of the author's imagination.

Front cover image by Gemma Martinez.
Book design by Allison Chernutan.

Printed in the United States of America.

First printing edition 2020.

Fractured Mirror Publishing
Knoxville, TN

www.fracturedmirrorpublishing.com

**To my wife Tina,
for believing in my dreams.**

Table of Contents

Prologue

It's been a rough night. After stealing a vial of perception-altering nanotech for some Discordian rebels who may or may not be planning to kill you upon delivery, you hear the unmistakable hum of an approaching swarm of security drones. You take off running, but not before a tranq dart catches you in the arm. The effect is staggering. To stay alert, you crunch down three tabs of amp. This has you so wired that you fail to notice the cracked vial in your pocket until it cuts into your thigh, delivering its microscopic payload into your bloodstream.

That's when things start to get weird.

Everything around you slows to a crawl. The hum of the drones becomes more of a dull growl, actually soothing in a way. Moving at a leisurely jog now, you easily keep ahead of your mechanical pursuers. You're not worried. You know just where to go. Drones are basically just electronic kites, and if there's one thing they hate, it's a forest.

After some unquantifiable stretch of time spent wending your way between trees, under branches, and over fallen logs, you come upon what looks to be a long-abandoned carnival, all overgrown and dilapidated. So of course, you find a way past the rusty chain-link fence and inside the fairgrounds.

Most everything is pretty well buried under vines and moss, but one structure in particular catches your attention: a large circular building on stilts that looks like some kind of decommissioned flying saucer from the age of acid. A busted neon sign along the path reads simply "Mirrormaze."

From the center of the building's underside, a faint violet glow betrays the unbelievable fact that the structure is still lit from within. An oasis of electricity in the midst of this jungle. Above your head is an open portal ringed with ornate Enochian sigils. A steel ladder leads up through the portal, providing the building's only apparent entrance.

Climb the ladder, and enter room 1 of the maze.

1

Pipe Dream

CLIFF JONES JR.

I CLIMB THE LADDER, RUNG AFTER RUNG, UP INTO THE CLOUDS and mist. I watch my hands as they grip, white-knuckled and weary. I have the idea that I might glimpse my own face, but it eludes me.

Who am I in this place? Am I a disembodied spirit, imagining these hands? Imagining this pain in my guts, this unbearable ache in the small of my back? Where am I going in such a hurry? Maybe I should rest a moment, just to—

Before I can finish the thought, the world explodes into a sea of greens and blues and violent hues defying description. I swim for all I'm worth, keeping my head above the technicolor waves. Where have I been all my life? What was I waiting for? Finally, I breathe in the life I've always known existed somewhere, just out of reach.

Is this my youth? Where is my quiet desperation, my stoic resignation to a life so ordinary I forget which one is mine? Every chance I get, I scramble for a way to break the pattern, to move beyond the bonds of day to day. But it never works for long. A dream, a trip, a song. In the end, it all comes crashing back to me.

I reach the shore in time: a salty, sandy stretch of sparkling beige. Pushing past the barren beach, I reconnect with grass and grub and shrub and wood. This is the world I love, my certain knowledge all has not been lost, though rearranged and tempest-tossed. I am home.

Is anyone else out here, alone in this paradise? I can make a life of drinking streams, hoarding nuts and berries, catching fish and rabbits if I must. But isn't someone else around? Is truly *no one* to be found?

Ah.

There you are.

I'm sorry for my solipsistic bent, the time that I have spent engaged in pointless speculation, even while my degradation threatens to consume what we have meant—to each other and to others in this living, breathing, writhing, squirming place. I see more clearly now. Nothing stays the same or returns to what it was. What was is not; what is was not and never again will be.

We race through forests beautiful and strange, around this tiny globe, until past and future coalesce into a tangled, happy heap of *now*. How long has it been this way? Was it ever any different? As my attention wanders, I lose my footing in the loamy jungle earth and tumble headlong into the muck.

You bend down to help me up, but it's too late. We've already begun our descent into the ether. I recognize the change that's coming, the barrier that we're approaching. I hold you close and wet your clothes with tears. This has all happened before but never just exactly in this way. We were happy for a time. It was nice, and now it's gone.

Where I'm going, you can't follow. I wish I could hold onto the memories of this side, my life with you above the clouds. But I'm already forgetting. Your face is once again replaced. I don't mind. It makes more sense this way, connected to my waking life. As if a dream were just a dream.

My eyes are open now. A familiar taste of bitter burning mothball reek. I feel as if I've lost something, but for the life of me, I can't imagine what.

Pipe Dream

You look around the empty room and see only distorted reflections of yourself—at least, you hope they're distorted. Something impels you to move forward, but you're unsure of which way to go. If you hunger for the ancient ways, turn left and proceed down a hall of mirrors to room 24 (page 297). Or if you thirst for what is yet to come, turn right and go to room 4 (page 33). If you'd prefer to linger in the here and now, just walk straight ahead to room 2.

Happy Birthday, Tinkerbell

ELIZABETH RODERICK

"Happy birthday," Fred said, dangling a baggie in front of my face.

"What the hell?" I shifted Melanie to my hip and took it, pinching the contents through the plastic. It was about an ounce of weed. The odor of it wafted up and stuck to my skin like tar. "What am I supposed to do with this?"

"You should make brownies."

I stared at him. "I haven't smoked weed since high school. You know it makes me feel fucked up and anxious." Melanie reached out with her chubby fists to grab the bag, and I yanked it up out of her reach.

"Yeah but eating it's different. Come on, it's your birthday. And twenty-seven is the rock star death birthday. Make some brownies."

I stared at the baggie, chewing on my lip, and Fred's mouth tightened. "It's good shit, my best yet. I call it Barney's Balls, because it's purple." He cackled. "Look how purple it is. It's Purple Haze crossed with Northern Lights."

"Yeah, it's purple," I mumbled. "It smells pretty dank, too." Melanie stretched out her grubby arm toward the bag again, squawking with displeasure.

Fred patted my ass as he wandered off to the living room.

"Make some brownies."

I sighed. I guess it didn't make sense to refuse my only birthday present. I slung Melanie over my back so she could watch while I melted chocolate and cracked eggs. I crumbled the weed in—it was enough to make the batter dry, so I added more butter and chocolate.

The pungent scent of that weed made my head feel weird, like my third eye was watering.

I poured the stuff into a pan and put it in the oven. The dirty bowl beckoned me from the counter. I loved brownie batter.

I got out a spoon and scraped the batter into my mouth, the piney residue making my tongue tingle.

As the musty aroma of Barney's Balls filled the house, I put the baby in her high chair and tried to feed her mashed bananas. Her gaze shifted between the spoonful of slimy pulp and my face, a furrow forming in her tiny brow. She smacked the spoon away and reached for my swollen breasts, hooking the collar of my shirt with sticky fingers.

"No, Gaboo, look." I ate a spoonful of the banana gunk. "Mmmm, yummy," I lied.

"Gaphhhhbt," she replied. I plied her with another spoonful. She opened her mouth experimentally, and I shoved it in. She mooshed it around with her tongue, scowling thoughtfully. Her baby hair had started to fall out, leaving her with one dishwater blonde tuft draped over her forehead. She looked like she had radiation poisoning.

"Those brownies smell done," Fred called from the living room, where he was watching *That Seventies Show* and coughing as he smoked a bowl.

I sighed and put the spoon down, slipping on an oven mitt.

They were indeed done, and I brought my husband a huge, gooey square on a plate. He dug into it like a starved puppy, sucking at his fingers. "This is good."

I put the baby on the couch between us and stared at my

own little piece of brownie, adrenaline creeping down my spine.

Fred glanced at me out of the corner of his eye. "Don't be scared. You need a little birthday trip." He took his empty plate into the kitchen and came back in with another huge slab.

Straightening with determination, I shoved the bite-size piece into my mouth, the sour zing of the weed giving me a full-body shudder. Fred laughed.

Half an hour later, we were still staring at the TV while Melanie babbled at me earnestly, slapping her bare knees. She sounded like she was giving a political speech. She had the comb-over for it, too.

"You feel anything yet?" Fred asked.

I shook my head.

He got up and came back carrying another gigantic piece, handing it to me. "This will get you going." He plopped back down on the couch and picked up his pipe.

I tore off bits with my fingers, but eventually ended up eating the whole thing. I loved brownies.

A little while later, I started to feel antsy. "Let's go to the park."

Fred strapped the baby onto his back in the carrier, and we headed out the door.

It was muggy, heat shimmering off the sidewalks. We passed dying lawns and kids playing in sprinklers.

We crossed Halsey Avenue, dodging between the cars. As I stepped onto the opposite curb, my head exploded.

The world wavered. Plastic dollhouses lined the street. They were an endless row of identical structures, reflections in a hall of mirrors. "What did you do to the houses?" I asked. "Are you trying to trick me?"

Fred raised his eyebrows. Melanie peered over his shoulder, chewing on her fist. She pulled her hand out of her mouth and pointed at me, her fingers glistening with spit. "Had dad gag gah," she demanded.

My stomach went cold with fear. "What is she trying to say to me?"

Fred burst out laughing. "Oh man, you're high now, aren't you?"

I blinked and hugged myself, vaguely remembering eating some weird-tasting brownies. "What happened?"

He put his arm around me, still laughing. "You're wasted."

We went into Rose City Park and sat at a picnic table in the shade. A group of teenage boys ran by, playing soccer. A sour-faced old woman with a bowl cut slouched past, leading an overstuffed Chihuahua, followed by a young couple, holding hands and chatting. All of them shot me meaningful looks, trying to communicate something to me silently.

I hugged myself tighter and looked up at Fred, suddenly knowing what those looks meant. "I'm dead, aren't I? I'm dead, and this is the Bardo."

Fred giggled. "Are you serious?"

"I got run over crossing the road," I realized.

A haggard-faced old man glanced at me as he scampered past. "Yes yes yes yes," he said.

I watched after him, panic crawling through me. "You're all spirits trying to lead me to the next life."

Fred grinned wryly, shaking his head. "Do you want to go home?"

Tears began to roll down my face. "I don't know. Where's home? What's it like?"

He stood up and took my hand, Melanie peering at me quizzically over his shoulder. "Come on. Let's go."

I clung to him as we walked. The identical houses marched alongside us, dream images created by my mind, remnants of my memories of the physical world. The sidewalk stretched out infinitely, and I knew I'd be walking endlessly, forever, never able to rest until I atoned for my sins and found my way into the next world.

We arrived at a familiar house. I came to a halt in the yard, staring at it in confusion, but Fred tugged me forward. "Come on, Gracie," he said, giggling as he unlocked the door.

Before I could go in, a voice sounded behind us. "Hey, scuzzbags." We turned to find our friend Tim grinning at us. A girl with a bony, twisted face was with him. She stared at me, her eyes huge over her sunken cheeks.

"This is Sarah," Tim said.

Sarah blinked at me.

We all went inside, and Tim and Sarah sat down on the couch. "What am I supposed to do now?" I asked.

Fred giggled as he went into the bedroom, coming out with an eighth in a rolled-up baggie. "Don't mind Gracie. It's her birthday. She's blasted."

Tim tittered as he took the bag and gave Fred money. "You're blasted? On what?"

"She made some special stratosphere brownies," Fred said. He took the baby out of the carrier and flipped her upside down, blowing on her bare belly. She giggled.

"Happy birthday, Gracie," Sarah said, still staring at me.

I fidgeted, staring back. There was something wrong with her face.

Fred put Melanie down on the couch between Tim and Sarah. I tensed up as realization washed over me: Tim and Sarah were demons and were trying to take Melanie's soul. If they took her, she'd be dead like me.

"Don't touch my baby!" I snatched her up and ran into the bedroom.

Tim and Fred's hysterical laughter echoed down the hall. "Don't touch my baby!" Tim screeched, and they laughed again.

I lay down on the bed, breathing hard and clutching Melanie. She gazed at me with her big, blue eyes, squirming and fussing and grasping at my breasts. She finally pried one out and latched on with a grunt.

Eventually I heard Tim and Sarah go out. Fred turned on

the radio. "This is rogue radio," the announcer said. "Broadcasting the real news from our hideout in the Empties. All you freedom fighters in the City, listen up for our coordinates if you want to come join us." He read out a long list of random words, but I wasn't smart enough to decipher the code. Maybe eventually I would be. I just had to keep my eyes open and learn.

I was stuck here now, but I'd figure a way out eventually.

I listened closely to the news station. In this new world I'd fallen into, the apocalypse had come: a sickness had wiped out more than half the world's population. The government was falling apart, and the rebels were amassing against them, ready to make a move and start the revolution. The commentator shouted out a frantic call to action.

Melanie had fallen asleep, her face still, her mouth open. I carefully detached myself from her and went into the living room so that I could hear the radio program better.

The radio wasn't on. Fred was sitting on the couch, reading a Stephen King novel, a stripe of afternoon sunlight falling across his face. He drew on his pipe and blew out smoke in a billowing cloud, which floated lazily through the sunbeam. "How do you feel?" he asked.

I sat on the couch, frowning. "Why didn't you tell me? About the apocalypse?"

He chuckled and shook his head, going back to his book.

The world shimmered and warped, twisting in on itself. "Is this real?" I asked, looking over at Fred.

Fred was gone. So was my living room. I was sitting on a white leather couch in a huge, shag-carpeted room, the walls lost in a golden haze. Next to me sat a man in a cream-colored suit. His bare feet stuck out from his impeccably-tailored slacks. Dark hair curled around his kind face. "It's real, and it's all a dream," he said.

"Am I dead?"

"Not yet. Just lost."

The brightness closed around me like a womb. It was inside of me, shining like the sun. This world was so small, so unimportant. Everything I saw as real was just a construct of the human mind.

I floated out of my body, hovering above myself and the cream-suited man. I floated higher and higher, faster and faster, the scene shrinking until it was just a tiny speck of light in an endless darkness.

"My baby!" I screamed. "I can't leave my baby!" My voice was consumed by the silence.

I struggled to remember what it was to be alive. It all seemed so strange and far away. Had I ever existed? I couldn't make sense of it. All I remembered was emptiness and loss, a vague sense of struggle and clinging to petty details.

Then I felt arms around me, and I looked up. It was the man in the suit, smiling at me sadly. "It's okay, Tinkerbell."

I woke up in my dimly-lit bedroom, the baby asleep beside me.

The various chemicals in your system have you on the edge of hypnagogia. To embrace whatever dreams may come, turn left for room 7 (page 63). To rage against the dying of your light, take another amp and proceed straight ahead to room 3.

MIRRORMAZE

Chrome, Reflected

RAGNAR MARTINSON

COLD ASPHALT DRAGS ME FROM CONFUSING DREAMS, FROM
the multilayered images of the angel, whose name I know like
my own and yet cannot pronounce. It slips away like colored
darkness and hides in neural subnetworks to which I'm quickly
losing access.

Unfocused, I stare at the black dirt, at some organic
object in front of me, which I then carelessly recognize as
my own hand. It costs a surprising amount of effort to move
the joints, but then it lifts up slowly, shaking, like an ancient
corroded mechanism. Silver liquid runs along my fingers
and over my palm until it vanishes like a thief between the
geometric tattooed lines at my sleeve. The lines form slender
symbols, which blur in the next instant. I look again, and the
wetness shimmers like oil, like fresh blood, like stale rainwater.

I blink.

For a split breath, I want to glide back into that neon dream
world. A woman's face flashes in the mirror of my shimmering
hand. She caresses my consciousness with shapeless words. I
remember that she was telling me an important truth. But
reality already grips me like a trophy, and it won't let go.
Insecurely, I push myself upright in spasms, some centimeters
at a time, then my muscles answer—painfully at first, then

powerfully reminding themselves of their capabilities.

As soon as I'm back to vertical, I have to close my eyes to the light that urges itself between my eyelids wanting to burn my retinas. I find myself on my knees again, heaving against a wall. Pieces of the world return, the world I crossed before my endless sleep.

Clear black shadows between the light lancing through the fog, a woman wiggling beneath me, the heat in which we turned, bass shaking our bodies…Someone pressed a microfilament syringe to my temple, and the sweet smell of forgetting flowed through me. Then came the darkness, and in the infinity, all I could see was the face of the angel.

With a second attempt, I manage to stand up, move the asphalt below me and the torn and fleeting clouds above. The pain behind my eyes slowly subsides, my environment a battle field of a city that throws her unnecessary items carelessly away. Unnecessary items like me, burned out, the feverish debris of a generation trying to escape.

Step after step, my feet carry me to a distant light source, as if they remember the way. I don't know this area of the city; it could be anywhere—not all who wander are found. Weird how the puddles are gleaming—changed by reflections, polymorphic chrome, then blood, then the milky liquid in the syringe which blissfully dissolved my existence. Again something runs over my hand. It drips into the mirror of the puddle where it disappears.

There she is again: the angel, the Mother. We had a conversation in this parallel dimension, and I had come to her for help. But what was her answer? Had there been an answer? I press my eyes shut and open them again. The street is as dry as my throat.

My fingers open and close until I remember where I wanted to go. Memory is retracting, moving out of reach. In the end, all that remains is the girl. She will know what happened, why I woke disoriented—maybe she'd also know who the angel is. Had she seen the angel too?

From the alley, I stumble into a thicket of people, faceless ghosts, a field of bright noises, a forest of neon and radiation that almost steals my consciousness again. I recognize this as Exiletown, the Babylonian shanty towers, peppery sweat mixing with smoked meat, smoke from gasoline burners, smoke from dream-laced cigarettes.

For no reason at all, I break into a run: I need to get out, wherever that is. Food stands fly past, surrounded by clients with flickering black eyes, longing for sustenance, pushing their credit chips forward like sacred offerings. The jagged downtown skyline in the distance pierces the clouds and ignites them in its orange light. I break through the eternal hectic of the subcity, every female face the face of the angel, fragile like porcelain.

The night presses hotly against my eyes. The empty windows stare down at me. Without warning, drips fall from the sky. Concrete and steel, leather and flesh, turn dark in patches, suddenly wrapping everything in rain and throwing the colorful insanity back to me. Between purposeful moving bodies in their trajectories, undeterred, I stop and extend my hand, hoping for refreshment. Where the rain touches me, subcutaneous flashes drink it in and return it chrome. I'm bleeding steel, which collects in mercury bullets on the ground.

The angel. She gave me answers to the most pressing questions, answers that would change my life. That was the promise in the syringe, the one we shared—nothing less than the Revelation of Truth. I feel strongly that I got those answers, but as I watch the silvery rain, I cannot remember a single one.

As suddenly as it started, the rain ceases. I hurry onwards, my fingers wet, the chrome running off and returning to dust. The naked body below me, she who shared the Revelation— I just taste her on my lips, and her name dawns on me: *Dakara*.

The way through the club is blocked by twitching limbs of senseless dancers. A wall of sound wants to throw me back to last night: the same glitch beats, the same stroboscopic lights, the same dilated eyes. But I conquer it and push into a hallway that smells of mildew and empty arak bottles. Five stories later, I find her in a narrow room on her bed. Above Dakara's mattress, a screen is glowing with static. Chaotic permutations swarm the surface in which the woman loses herself. A single wax candle smolders against the shadows, and I see it's not Dakara on the mattress, but her: the angel.

Her black hair oily, her white pupils staring into shimmering infinity, she arches in her skin-tight haptic suit. Her lustful screams make me shiver in memory of last night. As I approach, our eyes meet and something shatters, hurls her back to this reality. She breathes in sharply, like waking from a nightmare. Sweat glistens on her forehead, while the sweat on my skin evaporates in thick silvery swirls. The effect of the Revelation of Truth should have worn off by now, but it still won't let me go.

Dakara and I entered a world of euphoria to search for the truth, but last night held nothing but intoxication to escape a life long lost. The angel urges me to remember the answers. They were important; they would show me the way out. They promised bliss. If only I could remember them! Eventually, other neurons make up for the loss of information, and time returns with fragments of memory.

Dakara wakes up fully. She whispers my name, sits up and draws me into her embrace. Her smell clears up my senses. For a moment, all tiredness loses its grip, and I finally feel the floor that I stand on; I feel her warmth through the synthetic fibers. She asks me where I've been, and I feel my split lips curl into a smile. I tell her I was lost after I found the angel. Dakara's animal eyes widen, dripping of solace and empathy. Can I still see the angel? I nod and stop myself. What can I tell Dakara? That I've seen the angel but forgotten all that it told me? That I woke up thrown out like a used-up doll in Exiletown?

She motions me to wait, wiggles out from my embrace, and throws on a coat, which nearly extinguishes the candle. I fall into the warm bed, sink into the monochromatic chaos on the ceiling screen. Somewhere in the jumping grainy image, I feel the truth, and I grab at it, until someone pushes me down and starts to calm me down. Dakara stands in front of the bed, a human figure next to her, a sharp imprint on the window, which had been opened to invite the brilliant light into the room. Reluctantly, it drags the other objects into existence.

Dakara tells me she brought help. "Why help?" I ask and see sadness cross her face. The shadowy figure explains cryptic structural compositions, without me understanding the words. The movements tell me it's a man. As he gently grabs my arm, his hard, calloused fingers scrape my skin. He is looking for the port of the Fairy system on my forearm, feeling over veins and tendons to identify the fingernail-sized electronics. His other hand appears, in which I recognize a Tale module. He places it on the Fairy port, and it sucks into my skin like a leech. I realize that I'm crying—my hand moves to my eye, and I rub my finger in tears that stick to my skin like beads of quicksilver.

She is back, the angel, standing next to the bed. Her warm smile gives me hope she will tell me the truth again. This time, I'm prepared to listen and remember. I can see her mouth moving, but the sound is drowned out by the noises of my body: my arrhythmic heart, the air in my lungs, the idle resonance in my cortex. The device on my arm pulsates, and I want to rip it off, but my muscles cease to function, no data in my nerves. She is right there! Can't they see her? Finally, I will get to know the truth I've been longing for—if it weren't for the noise and the restraints and the light. "Darkness," I want to scream to Dakara. "Bring forth the darkness!"

The movements in the room become blurry. My perspective pushes against some resistance that suddenly gives, and I see myself in the bed, staring into my own wide eyes. Silvery chrome leaks from my arm and pools beneath my body. Two people, one female and one male, protect me, but their figures melt to schematics, misshapen shadows. Outside, the metropolis boils, calling me with the metallic voices of progress. I look down, and instead of my thin body, I can see the angel. In her gaze lie the answers to all the questions that weigh me down. She is silent now. It is too late.

Reality unravels, illuminates us from all sides. Our souls are alone in the infinity of my mind. I don't know why I'm here, where I was before, which events happened in what order… I don't know what I've been looking for or if I found it. I come closer to the angel, fall into her. She also has a Tale module in her arm like a parasite, but it pumps bright blood into her veins. Her being fills my existence. Before I can even understand it, our bodies unite in a storm of brilliant electric fire.

White light wakes me. Dakara stands in front of me, her short blond hair catching the early sunlight. She smiles and guides me into the bathroom and under the shower. She leaves me there as I wash my hangover headache down the drain. Dripping wet, I take some time to look at myself in the mirror. I'm sweating again from the humidity in the room. Tattoos cover my arms, their geometric patterns like circuits on my body. My right arm has a bright red wound. I don't know where it's from—maybe something happened last night? We had planned to go out, catching a special deal in the new venue over at the edge of Exiletown. Did we go? When did we get back?

Dakara returns with clean clothing, and I kiss her. She asks me if I'm hungry, and we go out for some food. As we move through the streets, bright facades reflect the neon ad of a woman with black hair and piercing eyes—and an impossible body type. Spreading out from behind her shoulders are pure white wings that carry the company's claim. I smile at the naive message, pulling Dakara closer. She seems to be looking at me suspiciously. For a brief moment, I consider asking her about last night. But then again, I feel calm, better than I have in weeks. My neurons blink without any excitement.

I decide to forget. There will always be another night, the dreaming of a city without sleep for us to explore.

Chrome, Reflected

You're fading fast after the night's exertion. Just power through it and turn left for room 6 (page 45), or else pop a protein supplement and proceed ahead to room 4.

MIRROR MAZE

The Future is Milk

COURTNEY LOCICERO

You zoom in on your petri dish and watch the specimen chew a path through flesh and bone. You record your observations, noting how it squirms with an air of conscious deliberation rather than instinctual hunger. You turn the dial on your microscope lens. The specimen's jaws are circular. It feeds and feeds.

Studies show that people who rate themselves as happy tend to drink milk.

You decide to experiment on reptiles, for obvious reasons. You've collected a host of varying species of lizards and snakes. Lizards tend to have more violent reactions to the implant. While their increase in activity makes them easy to study, they don't typically survive for long.

The longest a test subject has ever survived after implantation was 4.2 minutes. It was difficult for you to watch. The lizard swallowed its own tail. Wound up choking on it.

End world thirst. Drink milk.

Experiments fail. You are forced to return to square one. Draw up another hypothesis. Hold off on using the lizards. You take a break from this. A week later, you're at the pet store, picking up some garter snakes.

Raising kids can be hard.
That's why we teach them to drink milk.

Your colleagues don't understand. They laugh and scratch their heads. You smile and blink passively behind your glasses. You push them up and get back to work. As they leave for the milk bar, you tell yourself that they are all under the same influence as that poor lizard. Them and everyone else. Damn it, the whole *nation* is suffering from this parasite of the brain.

You always knew you were different.

Inside each of us is a void
that can only be filled by milk.

You look through the window. Staring down at the people on the street. Their jaws move without purpose or significance. This is life for them now. Empty. Mechanical.

They don't believe in your work. They think they like milk.

Drink Milk for President!

The new test subjects turn out to be a worthy investment. They last longer. Like you expected, the results are similar to the lizards, but with less drama.

These experiments have you feeling better about yourself, more confident in your original hypothesis.

Things are going so well that you decide to play a little game. You set five objects down in front of a garter snake: An egg. A grasshopper (dead). A marshmallow. An apple. A tooth (*Hylobates lar*).

The Future is Milk

Everyone has a right to drink milk.

To your amusement, the snake goes for the apple. In that unsettling way that snakes are famous for, it uses its abdominal muscles to force down the fruit. Initially believing the performance has ended, you close your notebook.

You pause when you see the snake regurgitating. Its abdominal muscles labor in reverse.

**Milk is everywhere. It's in our cows.
It's in our refrigerators. It's in our bones.**

The snake delivers the fruit whole. It is no longer an apple. It is now a peach.

You reach out to confirm this fact, and no sooner than your fingers test the velvety surface does it open in half, revealing its core. There is no ribbed pit, but rather the very tooth you set out earlier for the snake.

You are too shaken to record these findings. You pack up quickly, refusing to even stay long enough to watch the garter snake shrivel in on itself like all those that came before.

What does it mean, you wonder. What does it prove?

When you arrive home, the burning questions have yielded no reliable implications. You rummage through your pile of mail and bring forth an envelope tattooed in half-baked theories. On one of the few blank spaces left, you scratch the word: Inconclusive.

You think back to the spontaneous generation of the tooth in the peach's core.

You hesitate before writing: *Preternatural.*

You chew on your inner lip, scribble over that.

Embarrassing.

**milk.ly: The only app that delivers your choice
of milk straight to your doorstep, with just
the swipe of your finger.**

The next day you isolate the parasite specimen. You're getting to the bottom of this.

You decide to starve it.

Its head is elevated. Its circular jaws open and close. Its colorless eyespots search. As if it can see you through the microscope lens.

**The Vietnam War, the Theory of Relativity, the birth of
Jesus Christ. What do they all have in common? While
you're thinking it over, drink some milk.**

A week has passed. The parasite is still alive. You curse. All of your experiments—what answers did they provide? The parasite waves and dances before you. It mocks you.

You contemplate ending your life.

milk.ly: It's simple. It's easy. It's milk.

In time, your senselessness wears off. Your logic recovers. You mentally flip through the questions that have followed you since your secret discovery of the parasite.

You voice them aloud.

"What do you want?"

"Where do you come from?"

"Why do you drill through people's skulls and make them…make them…"

**You know that little voice in your head that tells you to
drink milk? It's there for a reason.**

The parasite waves, bobs its head. The round jaws open and close. Open and close.

It's Morse code, you realize.

You idiot.

You grab your notebook. You record the message.

Minutes later, you unravel the code:

Searching for the proper host. Need to clone. So much time on this planet. Nothing but failures. Perfect clone will yield expedition. Discovery. New dimensions. Failure yields obsession with contentment. A thirst for satiation. No will to strive or search beyond. Genes must be compatible. Need to clone. Need to clone.

You find your pills. The ones that help you sleep.

Single? Married? Divorced? Your next relationship status update might just be "Drinking Milk."

You look through the microscope. Staring down at the petri dish. In a lab full of lizards and snakes.

You have just made the greatest discovery of your career. Of your existence.

You light a match. You watch your notebook burn. You remove your glasses because they are useless when wet.

You are scared.

Be the change you want to see in the world. Drink milk.

You are aware that you have a superiority complex. You convince yourself that your lifelong feelings of isolation, of watching from the outside, justify what you are about to do.

Through the microscope, you watch the parasite catch onto the swab. You lift it high, imagining that somewhere on that cotton ball surface, your specimen is waving and bobbing and rotating its teeth. With purpose. With significance.

Do you have the right genes? Are you destined to be the perfect clone?

Who the hell knows?

You jam the cotton swab into your ear.

Because…when have you ever known what it means to be satisfied?

You find yourself feeling deeply unsatisfied. To pause and reflect on why that may be, turn right and head back to room 1 (page 13). To brush the feeling aside and just keep on walking, proceed straight ahead to room 5.

5
Sleepwalker

JEB R. SHERRILL

As a child, I often dreamed about a shadowed man standing in my shower, unseen behind the opaque curtain. I knew he was there, the way one only knows in dreams. Always there. I would stand at the sink for a moment, staring into the mirror at my face, but not quite seeing myself. Then I would turn to the shower and fling wide the curtain. My heart would skip and the world moved in slow motion as I fainted…

As the years passed, my dreams changed. I walked roads unknown. Country roads far from my home. I knew that if I found my way to wherever I was going, before I woke, something different would happen than usual. I just had to find my sleeping body—silent and unaware of the journeys I took each night—find it and embrace it. Hold on tight and wake… somewhere. Somewhere special. Somewhere other than my bed. Only at times like that, when I walked the very heart of the Dreaming, did I remember that each night plagued me with the same endless trek.

The dusty paths seemed to move in circles and I rarely noticed they weren't pavement, though any roads near my home should have been. I passed familiar houses I'd never seen and familiar people I'd never met.

"Make love to me," a woman called from her front porch,

her voluptuous figure reaching out like the aquatic tentacles of a siren's cry. I knew every curve of her as if we'd visited in other dreams, but of the waking world I doubted her existence altogether. She was suddenly standing before me, caressing me, pushing herself against my trembling body. In other dreams I hadn't even thought to resist, the pattern of my dream destiny already set, my entrapment inescapable. But this time I pulled away. This time the destiny seemed different. I had to go home.

For moments that might have easily been years, I realized I was dreaming. I even thought to myself how easy it might be to wake, escape the journey altogether. But at the same time, I felt certain truths like mile-long strips of white silk brushing through my mind in one long, steady current, tickling parts of my brain that only partially understood them. Those truths bade me continue.

Somewhere, in my vague consciousness, I saw my body lying in bed, though I saw myself quite differently than in the waking world. I saw myself as an ancient warrior, clad in a white tunic and brown leather armor. I/he had long black hair and a beard reaching my/his navel. I/he lay in the center of a circle marked with words and runes I could not understand. I saw that if the warrior ever found his own sleeping body in the dream, then he could travel to another location of the Dreaming and when he awoke, he would have moved to a corresponding part of the waking world. This must have been my dream destiny, but I did not put that all together then.

Instead, I continued down the dusty roads, finding some of them marked by metal pipes that led to dark lagoons where it was night, though it was day elsewhere. A glowing light illuminated the water, and I would find that the lagoon was no more than five feet wide and just inside a cave. All of this lay in the woods behind a house that belonged to my uncle, but it was not my uncle's house, not in the waking world.

I searched for what must have been hours, or perhaps eons, always knowing my home lay just beyond the next hill but never making it over that hill.

I would be at work and out of uniform, in nothing but boxers, and of course I never cared. I would simply search about for my clothes, certain they couldn't have gone far. I'd laid them near, seen them in my head so close I could almost pick them up, but still I could never find them. Those parts passed on into nothingness, though I never noticed.

Again, I would remember the warrior, lying on his white sheets at the center of that black circle in a flowing tent of white veils that hung from nowhere.

I returned to my journey, the one I'd never really left, traipsing down the thin strands of dreamstuff over black stone bridges I knew I'd seen in my own backyard during childhood.

I walked through my uncle's house, a house with far too many floors to be a house. Staircases filled the middle floors, ones that went up to nowhere and ones that went down to nowhere else. I found parts of the house that just couldn't be. Secret, hidden places and rooms concealing strange and ancient things I never could quite look at.

And then there were the elevators in the building where I worked, the building I know I never worked at. The elevators went up and down and side to side. They took me to dizzying heights so lofty I fell flat against the floor, pinned to the dirty carpet, terrified to creep towards the sliding doors. No matter what, they always took me to the wrong place, and I'd try to make my way down staircases that never went to anything but other staircases and strange floors that looked like unfinished parts of skyscrapers and red deserts without a sky.

Then I would be at my school auditorium, just minutes before a show. *My* show of course, and it would be hours before anyone would arrive. I'd search the stage and find the secret place that always lay beneath the floor: first the area that housed the many trap doors and then the space under that, a tunnel leading to nether-places. I'd push small pieces of wood embedded in the doorframe, opening giant wooden doors too tall to have been there. Then I would move through those doorways and find places and things that simply couldn't exist below a stage. I once found a restaurant where they made food to sate my craving hunger, food I'd wanted to eat all day, but I never got to take a bite.

Then I was on my journey again, the same familiar roads, the same beautiful women trying to seduce me along the way, and my vision of the warrior lying still where a mage had placed him. A mage he/I had somehow instructed to do so. I wondered at the reason and at my terrible dream destiny, which was somehow entwined with his. He who was me.

Before.

Later.

Now.

I found the sparkling brooks that flowed like oceans and ran with sea creatures who'd swum up from the very depths to show themselves and make me faint or else move on to another part of my dream. I feared to go past them, forever unable to ford the river of doubt I knew to be no more than a stream.

Sometimes I wished I could dream of that train I dreamed of as a child. It was a tiny train, like an electric locomotive one might find outside a grocery store or a mall. The kind one stuck a quarter in and it vibrated for three minutes, moving ever forward to nowhere. I used to dream I rode it deep into the night of my mind, its light-up buttons all the colors of the rainbow. It moved on tracks I somehow laid for it as I went, chugging down the blackness without noise.

There are no trains anymore, but there is also no longer the man lying in wait behind the shower curtain. The one whose face I never saw because just as I pulled the curtain back, I'd faint and wake to the cold sweat and terror of my room's darkness, the door cracked open just enough to let the light in, a light which had been turned off hours ago while I slept. Perhaps the man I never saw was the warrior/myself, my terrible destiny staring back at me from that place in my mind I dared not go. I suppose I don't mind not having the train if I don't have the dream of the shadowy man either. The loss of a fantasy for the loss of a nightmare is an even trade in anyone's book.

I turn back to the roads now, those winding paths that must lead home, down the valleys and the hills to the suburbs where my house must lie. Perhaps I never find it because I'm looking for a house on a street, and not a castle in the mountains. Perhaps the wild warrior only finds my little house in a future he cannot recognize, yet finds familiar.

And perhaps *I* am the man that stands in the nightmares of *his* childhood, the man he never sees and never knows is only a child himself, too afraid of the night to ever harm him. He may never find his dream destiny. I may never find mine. He may never even wake, the mage's spell working too well, the circle holding him asleep until he finds himself and awakes to that terrible destiny that must be his…must be mine.

Something is seriously wrong with your body. If you'd like to trade it for a new one, turn right for room 10 (page 111). Or if it's more the world that feels wrong, proceed straight ahead to room 6.

MIRRORMAZE

Angel in the Cave

CLIFF JONES JR.

My granddaddy told me this story when I was about your age. And now, Angel my boy, I'm passing it on to you. I'm not sure if I can get all the details right, but the real core of it—the bones—that's buried in my brain pretty good. That's what you have to remember, too: just enough to get the point, not so much that you miss it.

A real long time ago, there was a young hunter who used to roam the woods not far from here. He always worked alone, and he wasn't much for socializing. But everybody in town loved him because he brought home more meat than anybody else and never hesitated to share it. The key here is that no one ever had to *earn* what the hunter gave them. It was just charity. Not the sort of charity that comes from guilt or pity either. The hunter just knew that bringing home the meat was his job, so he did it. Simple as that.

Trust me on this, Angel: If you can get a really clear, bright feeling in your gut that you're doing your job, that you're doing exactly what you were made for…you don't need any more reward than that. Just to be alive and full of purpose is more than most folks ever have. Don't throw that away just for pay. Money's nice to have, but it can cost you.

Anyhow, this hunter needs a name, right? When my

granddaddy was first telling me this story, he tried to get away with just saying "the hunter" over and over like there weren't any other hunters around. But I bugged him about that until he finally said, "Okay, Jim, you want a name? The hunter's name was *Jim.*" I never actually believed that the hunter and me just by coincidence had the same name. It was just to show me that this fella, he could be anybody. So, Angel, you want a name? The hunter's name was *Angel.*

One day, this hunter Angel was out on a hunt. He'd already been out for two solid days with no luck, but he was tracking down the cave of a really big old bear, the kind that could eat you up and still have room for seconds. Angel had a lot invested in this hunt. The payoff for sneaking up on a bear that size in the middle of its hibernation could be huge. This was the dead of winter, you see. Hunting's not so easy in the winter, but it's about the only time you can hope to bag a full-grown bear. At least back then it was. Bears were bigger, and weapons were simpler. And of course, everything was much colder then, too.

Now I'd like you to imagine what life was like for Angel's town in the dead of winter. Folks spent most of the day just huddled up in their burrows trying to keep warm, hoping supplies would hold out. Normally, these people were busy farming or making things like clothes and blankets and such. But for about four months out of the year, the ground was too frozen to work, and all the furs were needed to keep everybody from freezing to death.

As you might guess, the days could get pretty monotonous. That's why stories and music were so important to these people. If you want to keep warm, you've got to keep your heart beating, and if you want your heart to beat, you've got to *feel* something. If you were to walk past Angel's town in the winter, you wouldn't see much. Just about everything was underground. But you'd feel the earth under your feet pulsing with energy and passion. Now that was some *real* music back then. Just playing for the sound of it, that's all.

Angel in the Cave

While everybody back in town was dancing and wailing and banging their drums and blowing their flutes, Angel was approaching a cave. *The* cave. He could feel it. At this point, as he'd practiced, Angel made a conscious effort to separate himself from his body and let the ambient calm of his surroundings soak through him bit by bit. He felt like a very skilled ghost manipulating an empty body so that you'd swear it was really alive. Each step he took had an unreal grace to it, like the movements of a marionette.

Slowly, steadily, Angel's hand drew his rusty blade from the leather sheath that hung across his back. It looked like a machete, but with a jagged back edge. That blade's teeth had torn the guts out of too many animals to count. But always to *fill* the guts of Angel's family and friends. So the whole process—brutal and disgusting as it was—had a sort of righteousness to it.

Before entering the mouth of the cave, Angel's eyes fixed on a spot where he could hide while waiting for the bear to bleed out. If you ever go up against a bear, locating this safe spot in advance is absolutely critical. When it comes down to it, it's much better to let the bear run off and die somewhere you can't find it than to find yourself in the path of an animal that big, that tough, and that *terrified.* No use in the both of you dying, is there?

I'll spare you the gory details and just tell you that Angel won the battle that day. As always, it was a combination of luck, skill, and—let's be honest—fighting dirty that gave our hero the victory.

Just so you don't get the wrong idea, let me point out that Angel took no pleasure in killing the animal. Quite the opposite. Here's a bit of grandfatherly wisdom for you: There's nothing better in this world than food. And nothing *worse* than violence. More often than not, the two go hand in hand. It's a shame, but that's just how it is. You can try to minimize the violence—and that's admirable—but sometimes you're just *hungry.*

Angel followed a long, red trail in the snow and eventually came to the rapidly cooling body of that shaggy white bear. He set right to skinning the beast as quickly as he could manage, knowing that even in cold weather, letting that fatty hide start to rot in place would leave a nasty taste in the flesh. He then plunged his blade deep into the bear's throat and dragged it all the way down to the groin, splitting the animal's rib cage and letting its entrails spill onto the blood-soaked snow. He'd be leaving a load of scraps for scavengers. It'd be hard enough to drag the best meat back without any help. Even the head would have to remain in the snow where it lay. No room for trophies.

Angel unrolled his sled and loaded the hefty slabs of bear meat onto it, fastening them in place with twine. This was no easy task, and let me tell you, dragging that thing all the way back home—I'll just say this: The only way to get through an ordeal like that is if you're fueled by something pure, like *love*. It's like childbirth. A truly selfish woman could never endure it. If you'd ever seen the process, you'd know what I mean. Luckily, we're not so selfish as most people think. The species would be doomed if we were.

So anyhow, Angel trudged through the snow, dragging this load of meat on the sled behind him. His shoulders and legs felt as if the muscles were being stretched to the breaking point, burning and stinging with each onerous step. But as he drew closer to home, his burden actually seemed to lighten a bit. More than once, Angel glanced back to make sure none of the meat had fallen off the sled. With an end to his journey in sight, the bundle didn't look quite so massive as when he'd first set out.

As Angel was approaching his town, he saw heads popping up out of their burrows—first just a couple, and eventually several dozen. Everybody had to make sure it was really him, and then they'd tell a couple more people nearby before running out to greet him. Angel, the town hero! He straightened up and smiled through the pain. This was a ritual that he thoroughly enjoyed.

Among the last to see Angel's kill was his great-uncle, the oldest man in town. He was one of the few that didn't run out to join the celebration making its way through the snow. Instead, he just stayed put and waited. This was partly because he was a dignified and well-respected elder, but mostly he was just too dang old to be running around and carrying on like that. I'll tell you, when them folks got to celebrating, it was something to see—and to hear! But when Angel finally made his way to the center of town where the elder was waiting, everybody got quiet real quick.

It was up to the elder to inspect Angel's kill and determine if it was fit to eat. This was basically just a formality, but you can bet everybody was deadly serious about it. The old man did his usual rounds. He hobbled over and pressed a hand on the meat to test its firmness. Then he bent down and gave it a sniff.

That's when the elder went pale and his mouth fell open a little. He actually seemed to stop breathing for a moment. It looked like he'd been struck dead right then and there. Then he stumbled backwards and sat down in the snow. Several of the onlookers tried to help the old man, thinking he'd fallen ill, but all of a sudden he rose to his feet and proclaimed, "This…is no bear. It is a *man*."

None of the townsfolk knew just what to make of this. They could see the meat, and sure, it might possibly be the body of a large man, but it might also be a small bear. No one seriously entertained the idea of Angel being a murderer, much less a *cannibal*. Still, they were all obliged to trust the elder, even if he had seemed to be losing his grip on reality lately. Maybe giving complete authority to the oldest person in town wasn't the best idea, eh?

Angel's face grew hot, despite the icy weather. "I didn't…" he fumbled. "That is, I would *never*…It *is* a bear! I killed it myself!"

The old man glared at Angel, looking deep into his eyes.

He saw no malice there. Now with a gentler tone, the elder announced, "I don't doubt that when you killed this creature, it was a bear. But now…through some magic unknown to me… It is not. You must return this body. It's not right that it should be here, separated from its head, its heart…Whoever this is, he deserves a burial."

Angel was crestfallen. And besides that, he was *hungry*. Were they really going to waste this beautiful kill? Yes. Of course they were. The elder had spoken, and that was final.

The old man continued, "We must return this…these remains…back to where they belong. And pray that will be enough. Do I have any volunteers for the job?"

None of the men—because the elder was really only addressing the men—raised his hand for a good ten or twenty seconds. But as soon as the first hand went up, others started to follow, and eventually every able-bodied man in town was standing there with his hand up.

See, that's how a crowd operates. Only the first two or three of them actually had to be willing to go. Any more than that would be excessive on such a journey, and everybody knew it. The lazy fellas—and also the cowards—they waited to raise their hands until enough *real* volunteers were already available. Watch out for people like that, Angel. It's much better to be alone than mixed up with a crowd that'll desert you as soon as they feel like it.

Now this hunter, he was no fool. He could see all these volunteers were really only in it to look good in front of the town. If any of these fellas ran into trouble out in the wild, they'd run right back to the group, bringing the trouble with them. "I'll go alone," Angel said. He spoke directly to his uncle but just loud enough for most of the crowd to hear. "This is my kill, so it's my responsibility."

The elder had obviously expected such a response. He stepped toward Angel and said under his breath, "Be *careful*, boy. This thing you've killed…I don't think you've actually *killed* it."

He was truly shaken, as if that dismembered body might return to life and seek its due vengeance.

Angel wasn't so easily frightened, but he decided to humor the old man. It was the only thing to do, after all. No dissonance should be perceived between the generations. No rebellion. He knew that road, and at the end of it was anarchy—not a *lack* of rulers, actually, but a *glut* of them, each struggling moment by moment for supremacy. Chaos: the quickest path to despotism.

With this in mind, Angel turned around and headed right back out to find that distant cave where he'd killed the bear. Somehow, despite his aching muscles and the gradual upward slope of his path, the sled was a little easier to pull this time. *I must be getting stronger,* he thought with a smile. Just when he caught sight of the cave, the sled seemed to weigh nothing at all, and Angel fell forward, face down in the snow.

When he looked back, he was shocked to find the sled completely empty. Not only was the meat gone, but the whole thing was clean and dry. Angel examined the twine he'd tied around the bear meat that morning. It looked fresh and unstained—not even a trace of blood. Now, *this* terrified the mighty hunter at last. He could think of no possible explanation for the disappearance of that meat, unless…Unless his great-uncle was right. The creature—whatever it was—wasn't actually dead at all.

At this point, it was nearing sundown, and Angel knew he'd have to make camp for the night. He didn't relish the idea of venturing into that cave again, but that was the sensible thing to do, after all. He tried to convince himself that the bundles of bear meat had fallen off his sled as he walked and he simply hadn't noticed. It was a strange thing that the blood was gone, but it could have been washed away by kicked-up snow landing on the sled and then melting away in the sun. These things were possible. Other things were not.

Angel chose not to examine the spot where he'd butchered that great white bear earlier in the day. He might have found the bear's head, at least. He could have brought it back to town and proven he hadn't somehow killed a *man* by mistake. It had been a bear all along! But for reasons beyond his ken, Angel pushed thoughts of that sort out of his head. He wanted to forget the morning's hunt for good and all.

One thing he couldn't put out of his mind was the grumbling in his belly. He hadn't eaten a bite all day. If he'd have killed an elk or a bison, then he would have made a meal of the liver before heading back to town, but not a bear. No, he just drank the blood from the heart, said a prayer, and moved on.

By the way, that's sound advice you ought to take to heart, boy: Don't go eating the liver of a predator. Every animal you consume leaves just a bit of its spirit lingering in your liver. And if you eat a liver that's already loaded up with spirits—well, that's just too much to handle. Seriously, it can kill you.

Just as Angel was starting to think about the most likely place to scare up a squirrel or a rabbit for supper, a fat snowshoe hare went bounding across his path. You can bet that caught his attention! With a smooth, even motion, trying to avoid seeming overeager, which of course he was, the hunter reached into his pack and pulled out a small blow gun, already loaded with a dart. The hare twitched an ear and hopped off toward the cave. Angel followed casually behind, taking care not to pursue the animal directly but at an angle, as if his mind were elsewhere and the shrinking distance between them was of no importance at all.

If you're trying to go unnoticed by an animal—or a person, for that matter—it helps to keep your conscious attention off of them. Attention is a physical thing, you know? You can feel it. But we haven't built the machinery to detect that sort of thing artificially yet, so if you ask one of these know-it-all scientists, they'll tell you I'm dead wrong—that the mind is nothing more than tiny little lightning bolts flying around inside the brain. That's all they can see with their machines, so they assume that's all there is. Arrogant dregs. Anyhow…

Angel in the Cave

The hunter kept following that snowshoe hare, patient as anything, and it led him right back into the cave. Daylight was fading fast at this point, and Angel didn't think he'd be able to see well enough in there to sink a blow dart into his prey, so he decided to scare it back out again. He hung to one side of the cave and shuffled around noisily, keeping his eyes open wide all the while, blow gun ready just in case the opportunity presented itself.

Now, a funny thing happened to Angel inside this cave. He was an experienced hunter, well acquainted with both darkness and silence, but the cave had such an oversupply of both that he found his heart racing uncontrollably. He felt like a scared little boy. True, he was only about your age, but kids didn't stay kids for long back in those days. He hadn't actually thought of himself as a child for years, and this sudden panic was embarrassing as all get-out. Of course, no one was around to see, so there was no call for embarrassment, right? But then again, I'm telling you about it right now, so *someone* must have seen it. Just goes to show, your gut knows things your brain'll never understand.

In the darkness of that cave, Angel began to feel like he was deep down underwater, so deep he couldn't tell if it was day or night, storm or still. He began to notice consciousness slipping from his body, mixing into the oceanic ether. As the hunter made his way to the floor of the cave, the world seemed to shift and distort around him, as if it were a living thing restlessly trying to find a comfortable position to sleep alongside its master.

Now in a dream, Angel saw that his surroundings had completely transformed. His clothes and his body were different too. Everything had a delicate, sterile feel to it, even his own skin. The hunter's thoughts on this metamorphosis never had time to solidify into anything memorable though. In a few moments, he had forgotten he was dreaming.

His conscious mind retained no memory of a small town

dug into the frozen earth, an unreasonable elder convinced of the impossible, an enormous white bear, or the cave it had inhabited, which now sheltered a dormant young man who shared his name. All of these things quietly transformed into memories more suited to the environment inside his dream. Even the language he spoke was now altered, unrecognizable.

That was the whole story, just as my grandpa told it to me. *Not much of an ending,* I thought. *The hunter kills a bear, brings it home, brings it back, follows a rabbit into a cave, and falls asleep.* My grandpa stared at me, awaiting my reaction to his half-baked fairy tale. "What happened next?" I asked, more to fill the silence than anything else.

"What's next?" he repeated to himself. "What's next, eh? Well, Angel my boy, that's up to you, ain't it?"

Before, I could ask him what he meant by this—whether he wanted me to write my own ending to the story or what— there was a slow, booming knock at the door. It made me jump in my chair, and I had the fleeting impression that I was hearing the terrible heartbeat of that great white bear from the story. Then I felt silly for imagining such a thing. I was pretty young at the time, but not *that* young.

Oddly, my grandpa didn't react to the knock at all. He just stared at me with a knowing smile as if there were no reason to go on with the story, like everything was going just according to plan.

"So…should I get that?" I asked after some hesitation. It really was strange to get a knock at the front door so late, creepy story or no.

All my grandpa did was nod and smile.

I summoned all my courage, pushed aside silly superstitions, and looked through the peephole. I couldn't make out very much with our porch light burnt out, but judging by the silhouette I saw, our visitor seemed to be a very large man dressed in a heavy white suit. This knowledge did very little to relieve my apprehension. I pushed thoughts of the bear down a little deeper into my subconscious.

"Can I help you?" I shouted through the door, trying without success to sound confident and maybe a little menacing.

"I'm a friend of Jim's," was the man's reply. I looked back at my grandpa hoping for some sort of explanation, but all I got was a look that seemed to say, *Well, what are you keeping a friend of your granddaddy's waiting for?*

I gave in and opened the door to the intimidating figure. The man stepped right inside, immediately taking a seat in my grandpa's big brown recliner. I found it a little strange that my grandpa had moved to the couch, apparently to make way for this stranger, but I wasn't about to question it openly, not where the man could hear. Not that I was afraid of him exactly, more concerned I'd offend our honored guest.

Sitting there, slumped in that cushy leather easy chair, this man looked even more outlandish than I'd imagined from my limited view of him on the porch. Judging by his shaggy white hair, he must have been about my grandpa's age, but his face looked many years younger. If not for his unusually dark eyes, I might have guessed he was an albino. He wore a completely white suit accented somewhat unsettlingly by a bright burgundy necktie.

With a voice like rolling thunder, he said, "The name's Elliot. You must be Angel." He smiled broadly, revealing what seemed to be too many teeth. "Me and your granddaddy go way back." I couldn't say why, but I didn't quite believe that. "So, tell me a little about yourself, son. The last time I saw you, you was knee-high to a grasshopper; ain't that right, Jim?"

My grandpa simply smiled and nodded, as if in a trance.

Despite a strong desire to excuse myself and head straight to bed, I suddenly began telling Elliot everything that came to mind, embarrassing or not. I even said things my grandpa didn't know. I wanted to hold back, but I just couldn't. Maybe it was the way Elliot stared so intently into my eyes the whole time. Normal people glance around a little while they talk. Unbroken eye contact is just…*weird.* But whether I liked it or not, Elliot dominated the room. I was bound to sit there and answer his questions just as that easy chair was bound to support his considerable weight. We'd both do our best, the chair and I.

The more I talked, the better I felt about Elliot. He wasn't my enemy; he wasn't my friend; he was just…there to listen. I'm a little embarrassed to say, but I talked for hours once he got me going. It got pretty emotional. A few times, I actually found myself breaking into tears as I spoke—sobbing openly, in fact. But I kept right on talking, while Elliot stared and my grandpa just nodded. It was all so unreal. In retrospect, maybe I was the one in a trance.

By the time we'd finished our one-sided chat, all I could do was stumble off to bed. I can't remember the details of what was said, but it seemed to me that I was being judged and evaluated. I do remember the last thing Elliot told me before I left the room: "You're doing fine, son. You've just got to make peace with yourself."

That night, I dreamed I was the hunter from my grandpa's story. I crawled out of the cave to find the morning sun beaming down onto the body of a freshly killed snowshoe hare. Had I done that with my blow gun? I couldn't remember. There was the dart, still in its neck. I must have shot the thing in the cave, and then it ran out and I thought I'd lost it. Strange to have no memory of that though. I did seem to recall a few other things, but…nothing that made any sense.

Best not to look a gift hare in the mouth—so I've heard— so I immediately set to skinning and gutting the fuzzy little critter. I'd never done such a thing in my waking life, but in my dream, I wasn't the least bit squeamish about it. I was a hunter, after all.

I needed to build a fire before I could make a proper meal of the animal, but I was so ungodly *thirsty* that I had to set aside a few minutes for chewing snow. At the end of this tedious procedure, my whole head ached from the cold, but at least I wasn't going to die from dehydration.

As soon as I was clear-headed enough for the task at hand, I cleared a patch of ground near the cave entrance and piled up some kindling from whatever dry brush I could find. Then, I pulled out my pump drill and set to work forming an ember I could use to start my fire.

This all seemed perfectly natural inside my dream, but in real life, I'd never used anything but matches to light a fire. Pretty clever device though. You push the handle up and down, and these twisted cords spin a vertical stick back and forth really fast as you go. All the friction at the bottom starts an ember burning in the wood you're using as a base.

Once I had a decent fire going, I skewered the hare—which my dream-self considered to be a very different thing from a rabbit—and roasted it with greedy haste. At this point, I was practically starving. And I don't just mean uncomfortably hungry; I mean dangerously malnourished. I devoured that animal like my life depended on it. No salt, no pepper, just blood and char for my spice. And honestly, it was the finest snowshoe hare I'd ever tasted. When it comes to barbecue, I highly recommend the full DIY experience.

With my immediate needs satisfied, I began to look at the cave with a newfound curiosity and a certain sense of wonder. What *had* I seen in there the night before? The walls had seemed softer than they should have been…almost *alive* somehow. Beckoning. Before I realized what I had in mind, I was scanning the nearby pines for leaking pitch. If I could find a good-sized chunk, I'd have a decent torch in no time.

And once again, the forest provided. There was a chunk of dried resin the size of a walnut on the second tree I examined. I cut a green branch and split it two ways with my knife on one end. This gave me four prongs to hold the resin in place. Without delay, I walked over to my fire, kicked up a few coals to get the flame going again, and lit my torch. I was heading back into the cave, and this time, I'd have my wits about me.

Torch in hand, my heart began to race with excitement. Or maybe it was fear. Those two are hard to tease apart sometimes. I crept into the shadows of the cave mouth as if I were stalking an animal: toes up, ball first, rolling from outside to inside. My boots were thin and flexible enough to feel the ground under my feet. I carefully avoided any noisy twigs or leaves, brushing them aside before shifting my weight.

Honestly, I don't know what I expected to find in there that needed to be approached so gingerly. I'd spent the night in this cave, after all.

After maybe twenty paces, I was surprised to find that the cave kept right on going. If anything, it had even opened up a little. I held up my torch to have a look around. The firelight illuminated dozens of pale, roundish shapes, which I took to be formations of stone. And then one of them moved.

It was something like a barn owl, but easily the size of a large dog. To wake its sleeping companions, that enormous owl let out a truly horrifying screech, which resonated up and down the cave in malevolent waves. I'm not ashamed to say that at this point, I hit the floor and huddled in a ball with my hands over my face. As those monstrous birds poured out of the cave— really, there must have been hundreds—I felt their wingbeats on my back and imagined the damage a single talon could do to my unprotected flesh.

When it was all over, I felt certain there wasn't a single owl left anywhere in the cave. They moved as a unit, like a school of fish. I wondered what they would do out there in the blinding daylight. Find another place to sleep? If I'd have gotten just one warning hoot, I swear I would have backed right out and let the owls have their cave. But as it happened, I had the place to myself now, and my torch was still lit. No sense wasting a good torch.

I walked on, deeper and deeper into the cave. I walked until my torch burned out, and then, surprising myself, I kept right on walking into the endless black. Away from the world I'd known. Away from needy townsfolk, spineless warriors, and my doddering old uncle. I didn't even glance back to see if daylight was still visible behind me. Not likely. I must have covered a mile already.

The air grew warmer as I walked—so warm it was almost steamy. I shed my outer cloak. There was a slight breeze, which pulsed back and forth in a slow, subtle rhythm. It felt as if I were walking into the belly of an enormous beast. The beast sighed with delight, relishing every morsel of its meal.

Eventually, I saw the proverbial light at the end of the tunnel. A perfect circle of daylight came gradually into focus, and it seemed as if I were passing through a veil of illusion separating the real world from mere fantasy. *But I was going the wrong way.* Things were becoming increasingly artificial—a flimsy, stylized mockery of the real world.

As I approached the light, the cave walls began to take shape once again, but they were unnaturally smooth and even now. I was no longer in a cave, properly speaking, but a *tube*— a concrete drainage pipe, it seemed. In fact, I knew this pipe. I wasn't far from home. Now that I was closer to the exit, my eyes grew more accustomed to the light, and I could see it was dark outside apart from the glow of streetlights. Why had I thought it was daytime?

I splashed through the remaining feet of the drainage pipe and climbed up to street level. It was the strangest thing. I couldn't remember going down in there, and I really had no idea what time of night it was. I felt for my phone, but I didn't seem to have it on me. I hoped I hadn't lost it. But first things first, I had to get back home before my grandpa got worried and went out looking for me. If I were late enough for him to worry, he'd probably take my phone away anyway.

As I walked down the side of the road to my house, I was

surprised to feel the gravel under my feet. I looked down to see boots I didn't recognize. In fact, none of my clothes were familiar at all. They felt hot and sticky against my skin, like rough leather. The whole night felt like a bad dream. I just wanted to get back to my room, to my own bed—something familiar I could hold onto as the world went on hurtling through space.

But as soon as I got where I was going, I knew it wasn't my house at all. I wasn't that boy Angel; I was the hunter. I couldn't remember my name, but I knew who I was, and I knew where I belonged. This make-believe world was not for me. This world of paint and plastic and radio waves…of cheeseburgers, tollways, jet planes, and jelly jars…It was all so much garbage, piling higher and higher, scraping the blue from the sky.

And there in the midst of it all was that boy, that insipid little *Angel*. He was everything I was not. Or more to the point, he was everything I chose not to be: soft, weak, timid, uncertain, fussy…practically a full-grown man, but a child all the same. He made me sick to my core. And yet, we were connected somehow. Wherever I turned, he stuck to me like a shadow. I wanted to be rid of him for good. Well, there was only one way to be sure of *that*.

Slowly, silently, I crept up to Angel's bedroom window. There he was, sleeping like a baby. I knew he would be. I also knew he never bothered to flip the latches when he shut his window. I took out a small knife and used it to pop the screen out of the window frame. Then, I pressed both palms against the glass and slowly slid the window open. I leaned inside with the upper half of my body and cautiously pulled myself all the way in, taking care not to lose my balance and wake the little darling.

I stepped up to the bed, drew my knife, and brought it closer to Angel's throat. I could practically hear the pulsing of his heart—a heart I so recently believed was my own.

Then I heard a noise at the bedroom door and practically tripped over myself spinning around to face it. It was the slightest little creak, but under the circumstances, you can understand my alarm. I thought it would be Angel's grandpa—or maybe that friend of his, Elliot. But of all the things it might have been, it was just a little kitten, a tiny white ball of fluff in a red collar. There must have been a bit of softness in me still because looking into those innocent, trusting eyes, I couldn't help but smile.

Is *that* what I hated so much? *Weakness?* Angel was like a weak little kitten, yes, but was that such a terrible thing? He had people to care for him, and they didn't seem to mind. Who was I to say that only people like me should exist in the world? In fact, I'm not sure I'd want to live in a world like that. I'm not sure I could *survive* in a world like that.

As silently as I'd let myself in, I climbed back out the window, slid down the glass, and popped the screen back in place. I didn't belong *here*—that was certain—but it was a big world, after all. And honestly, I could get used to the weather in this place. I wasn't accustomed to sweating so much, but the warm breeze was really quite pleasant. So I headed back down the road, into the deep, dark woods, in search of my destiny.

And that was the end of the dream. I awoke the next morning to find that same little kitten on the pillow next to me. My grandpa said that Elliot had left her for me as a parting gift. I named her Snowshoe. I'm not exactly sure how she wound up in my dream, but I figure I must have seen her in the night while I was half asleep.

The other possibility—that the dream was somehow *real*—is something I've considered, but...I'd prefer not to imagine that hunter still out there, stalking the woods near my home. I know him too well to believe he'll stay away for good.

To look ahead into your future, turn left for room 3 (page 25). To embrace the here and now, turn right for room 9 (page 95). Or to travel to still more distant lands, proceed straight ahead to room 7.

MIRROR MAZE

7
Martian Spirit Quest

STEVEN R. BRANDT

I WANDERED ALONG THE RED, DUSTY PATH, LISTENING TO MY breath go in and out through the respirator on my suit. It had been four days since I set out in the wilderness, marching toward Olympus Mons, the tallest of Mars's mountains. I'd brought no food and no water with me. That is how a spirit quest is done, a tradition established by the second generation of settlers—or so my father told me.

We call ourselves "Native Martians"—though if you ask me, the only natives to Mars are a few strange bacteria. Some of our traditions came from various religions of Earth; others were things people made up during the generations since we came to this planet.

Somehow, my dad had gotten me to believe in this stuff— enough to go on a spirit quest. On it, I was supposed to have a dream where I either hunted and killed a mighty animal, like a leopard or a dragon, or I befriended one, like a hawk or crow. Whatever I experienced, the elders would interpret it using their secret scrolls.

My vision had been total nonsense, nothing but random stuff dreamed up by my subconscious. The interpretation would doubtless be that I was a loser who played too many video games.

I promised myself, though, that if I ever had children, I'd not put such stale air in their heads as spirit quests or any kind of religion.

Finally, I reached the ceremonial hut—a glass dome on an outcropping near the base of the great mountain. With a sense of relief, I punched in the code to open the airlock, waited for it to cycle, then stepped inside.

I looked around.

The surface of the dome was painted with magic runes, which to me, looked kind of like spiders—or maybe a child's drawing of a spider. In the center of the hut was a holographic fire. Of course, oxygen was too precious to burn on Mars colony. Fires reminded us of our spiritual connection to Earth.

It was a fake fire, for our fake beliefs.

I sighed. On the far wall sat three people. My dad was in the middle. He was wearing his gray and blue ceremonial robes, which looked like badly fitting pajamas. He was the biggest of the three with the muscular frame common to Martian garbage collectors. He had a broken nose from a bar fight and a scar from another bar fight. If he were to stand up and walk, he'd limp—because of yet another bar fight.

Hypnos, the shadow shaman, sat to his right dressed in black. He had a silver kippah—a kind of flat, brimless hat made of metal—atop his shiny bald head. He was thin with an odd flat face like a Persian cat.

Oya, the solar shaman, sat at my dad's left dressed in sparkly gold clothes. Half her face was painted white and the other half black.

"Did you have a vision, Moon Hawk?" my dad asked, his voice deep and serious.

I hate it when he calls me that. Yes, my name, Mirik, means "Moon Hawk" in one of the ancient Martian dialects, but it sounds so dorky.

"Yeah," I admitted. "Around the third day, I fell asleep next to a big rock shaped kinda like a fist."

My father puffed out his chest with annoying pride. "Did you dream of an animal? Did you hunt it?"

For a moment, I couldn't speak.

My dad never tired of telling me about his spirit quest. He'd dreamed that he had hunted a dragon and shot it in the belly. It didn't die though. Not many saw dragons in their visions, much less managed to hit one with an arrow.

He said it portended greatness for our family. Well, as near as I can tell, the garbage business kept us fed, but it fell a few light-years short of greatness.

"Well?" Oya asked.

I coughed. "Um. At first I dreamed I was playing with my virtual reality gaming console. Then, a coyote appeared to me."

They looked quizzically at one another. "Describe it," my father said.

"It was like a living cartoon of a coyote, really. He invaded my virtual reality kung fu battle. I yelled at him and told him to go away. He did."

At this the three shook their heads with a quick jerking motion, as if they had been startled awake from a dream themselves.

"My son," my dad explained. "A coyote symbolizes a change that the universe has planned for you, an important destiny. To reject it is a grave error."

"It was a cartoon coyote," Hypnos pointed out.

The three had a good frowning among themselves.

"Look," I said. "It was a dream. I didn't decide to reject it. It just— It just happened that way. This whole spirit quest thing is just a lot of stale air."

My father flinched at the words.

Oya put a hand on Father's shoulder. "It is okay. He suffers from the same limitations we all do. Here in the mortal realm, our thoughts come slowly, and we can only use reason. One day, we will make intuitive leaps, and our thoughts will take us between worlds."

Wow. I blinked. What nonsense. Talk about being full of stale air.

"Go on," Oya said.

I blew out a breath and decided to keep my opinion of her spiritual wisdom to myself.

I was so thirsty. It would be so much easier to talk if I could have water. That would have to wait though.

"So anyway, I went back to playing my game. Right when I was about to beat the boss in the anti-gravity level, this hawk flew in and tried to speak to me. It tried to land on my arm, but I shooed it away."

My father put his head in his hands the way I knew he would. When he spoke, his voice was almost a groan. "A hawk symbolizes taking power and leadership."

"Yeah, well, I wanted to play my games." I shrugged.

"Is there more to your vision?" Hypnos asked.

To be honest, I was kind of enjoying this now. Let them all suffer their disappointment. That's what they got for putting me through this ordeal.

"Yeah," I said. "A crow tried to interfere with my game next. I used my throwing stars on him until he left me alone. He nearly cost me the whole dystopian level before I got rid of him."

Hypnos shook his head sadly. "Had you accepted him, you would have been a shadow shaman for our people, like me, shepherding them from life to death."

"Look," I said, "I get it. I'm going to be a screw-up. But I don't want a great destiny, or to be a leader, or to be a shadow shaman. I just want to play video games."

"It's a rare thing to be offered any of those three animals on a spirit quest. To reject all three…" Oya shook her head.

My dad just continued to stare downward. He didn't speak, didn't look at me or anyone else. Okay, seeing him this upset wasn't fun.

"Look, I'm still just a kid," I objected. "Maybe I'll want all those things when I'm older, but not now."

The fake fire crackled. I decided I hated it.

"Was there anything else?" Hypnos asked.

"No. The alarm in my suit woke me up at that point. There was a small puncture in the front, right here." I touched the patch. "I can't figure out what could have happened."

My dad lifted his head. "His dream got interrupted. Maybe he can go again?"

Hypnos made a swatting motion with his left hand, dismissing the idea. "No. The spirit quest, like life, is a one-time thing. A dream interrupted by a mysterious cause is a sign of rejection by the spirit world and foretells an early death."

Maybe it was the fatigue, the thirst, and the hunger—but I suddenly felt cold, seriously cold, as if I'd just been plunged into ice water.

Of course, I didn't believe in this stale air about an early death. This was the twenty-second century. We'd gotten to Mars by science, not by riding on the backs of dragons or whatever our sacred stories said.

Still, Hypnos's words bothered me. It was as if something sharp had been driven into my heart and left there.

A lot of people had short lives. It was something I knew but didn't think about much. Of course, I wouldn't live a short life—but what if I did?

If I died today, how would Mars be any different for my having lived here? My online friends might miss me for a while, but that would be it. I was nothing and no one.

"Can I go now?" I asked.

Only after I'd spoken did my own words seem ominous, as if I'd asked if I could leave existence altogether.

Oya and Hypnos nodded.

My father took me to Marvin's Flash Fried Chicken, one of my favorite places. He bought me a giant Fizz Bang drink to go with it. We ate in silence. Normally, when I was hungry, my food tasted really good. Today it didn't.

What was the moral to the story about the night Phobos betrayed Deimos? Oh, yeah, silence is not a good seasoning for a meal.

One year later, instead of playing video games, I was driving Quixote, our millipede transport vehicle, home across the dusky surface of Mars. I'd begun learning how to drive shortly after my spirit quest. Turns out, I liked the sound of the many feet stomping across the ground.

As soon as I had been able, I started a daily run out to the outer colonies. Resources were scarce out there. Last year, one whole subsection had gone dark, and a dozen people died from lack of clean water and air.

No one had noticed for a week.

My dad and I had helped bury the bodies. He said a kid shouldn't have to see so many dead people, but he didn't send me away. Most of the corpses didn't look like people at all. They'd all dried out and shriveled up to the point where I could almost imagine they were something else, like broken androids maybe.

They weren't though.

Knowing that sent shivers through me and gave me night-mares for weeks afterward.

During the next year, I also helped my dad, Oya, and Hypnos with the ancient Martian chants to the Lonely Spirits—the ones who ruled Mars for the many eons before the settlers came. With each death, those spirits became a little less lonely—or so Hypnos said.

Sometimes my dad went with me, and we repaired and inspected habitat domes together. The thanks people gave us was the only thing that put a smile on his face—a rare thing to see after my failed spirit quest.

We never talked about that day much, but I think the promise of an "early death" never left either of our minds.

My eyes watered a little thinking about how little time we might have left.

Why hadn't I done better on that stupid spirit quest? Surely now, a year later, I would do well if I got the chance. Shouldn't it matter that I'd changed? Didn't it count that I was making a difference in other people's lives?

Thinking back on that day, I wish I'd lied. No one would've known, and my dad would've been happier.

For most people that I've talked to, emotional pain doesn't feel like it comes from anywhere. For me, it feels like sorrow is this hole in my chest right above my heart—as if all the emotional pain is pumped into me from that one spot.

The pain rushed in now.

An image of a cartoon coyote loped across the surface of Mars in front of me.

I blinked. For a few seconds, my sorrow receded. What had I just seen? I pulled up my vital signs on my suit: Blood pressure was high, as were cortisol levels.

This had to be stress. Hypnos had said I spent too much time thinking about my failures and about death, that it wasn't good for me. The remedy he'd recommended was the chant of peace.

With a shaky voice, I sang, "Spirits around us, above us, below us, spirits of the dark and Earth left behind, hear me. Spirits who call us and guide us and give our hearts wisdom, take my hand. Spirits who watch over the living, the dying, and the place between the stars, set us on the course that will lead us to peace."

Still, the sadness intensified. Somehow, the feeling was connected to my dad.

"Quixote," I said, addressing the millipede's computer. "Call Dad." The screen chimed for several seconds before he answered. "Dad," I said, barely able to control the sob in my voice. "Is something wrong?"

My dad had a dazed expression on his face. His hair was

disheveled. "I saw my lost hawk this morning," he said. "It soared out over Olympus Mons, circling around the top."

Lost hawk? There were a few people who had hawks over in Emerald City, one of the biggest and wealthiest settlements on the planet. Certainly, our family was not among them. Even if we had been, hawks required air to breathe. Even the mechanical ones needed an atmosphere to fly in, and there was none to speak of at the top of Olympus Mons.

"You—You mean you dreamed it, right?" I asked.

"I—" Dad looked off into the distance. Tears rolled down his cheeks. "Did I? Maybe life is just a dream. It seems like yesterday I held my little Moon Hawk in my hands."

Moon Hawk. My name. What did that mean?

A chill wriggled down my spine. "Dad, what are you talking about?"

"Son," he said. "I don't know if you can hear me, but I wanted you to know: I failed my spirit quest too. In mine, I saw a moon hawk that asked me to watch its nest. I didn't want to though, so I left with my bow to hunt the dragon."

"Dad!" I screamed. "I'm right here."

"The shaman told me the dream meant I should not have children, that I'd fail them if I did. Was he right, Moon Hawk? I wanted better things for you."

I stopped my vehicle. My chest constricted; the edges of my vision disappeared into purple stars. I blinked. A rock that had been over a hundred meters away was now directly in front of me and I braked to avoid it. Had I blacked out for a moment? What was wrong with me?

"Quixote, end call," I said. "Establish connection to emergency services. Transmit my location and biometric feed."

As the millipede rumbled to a halt, I stared out the viewport. The rock I'd stopped for was huge and fist-shaped.

What did it mean?

But I knew. This was the rock where I'd had my dream. This was my second chance to finish the quest, to do better than I had the first time.

Before I could think twice, I went to the airlock, then outside. When I reached the rock, the world faded away, and I was at home playing with my virtual reality system.

Playing again felt odd. These days, my game system sat mostly unused while my dad and I ferried garbage or helped people.

I grinned. I'd forgotten how much fun this was. This time though, I promised myself I would pause the game if any animals wanted to talk to me.

Despite my time away from my games, I played better than I ever had before, rediscovering the joy I'd once felt in conquering the different levels and acquiring treasures and abilities. I did so well, I reached the tenth level—something I'd never achieved in real life.

Behind the last door was the final boss: a dragon capable of destroying whole armies with a single breath. The creature swam out, gliding through the air like an eel. Its scales were light green and scintillated like stars. From its shining belly protruded an arrow, bright with blue fletching. Was it my father's?

My dad had hunted a dragon on his spirit quest, hadn't he?

Was this vision both my second chance and his?

I raised my bow to fire, but hesitated. The monster had my father's eyes, but larger, much larger. Reflected in them, I saw a hawk circling Olympus Mons.

Instead of shooting, I stretched forth my hand. The dragon came to me, and I petted its snout.

Then I understood. The meaning came to me the way it can only in dreams, by intuitive leaps. The wound my father had inflicted on the dragon was the cause of the hole in my suit during my spirit quest. When he'd fired the arrow, he'd wounded the creature reflected in its eyes, and the wound had transferred to me.

It was all a circle, like an orbit of a moon or a planet, or the spinning of a galaxy.

I struggled to take a breath.

"We can visit the Lonely Spirits, Moon Hawk," the dragon said. "The beings at the core of moons and planets. Know that Mars is not the only place such may be found. I will guide you to their brethren. You will see the diamond rains of Saturn and the lakes of methane on Titan. You have refused the coyote, the hawk, and the crow as unworthy. Take me, a dragon, and together we will fly."

"Yes," I said. "I'll go with you, but let me pull the arrow from your chest first."

"No," the dragon said, whirling its eyes at me. "You are not strong enough. Even if you were, doing so would ruin everything. The arrow shaft is the handle by which you may cling to my spirit when we travel. Open your eyes."

I stared in confusion. "But I'm using my eyes to look at you right now. What do you mean?"

"Open your other eyes."

I reached up, putting my hands to my face. My eyelids were indeed closed. How then was I seeing?

It was then that I remembered this was a dream.

"Look here," I heard a distant voice say. "There's a hole in his heart. It's a miracle he's lived this long with such a condition. We'll have to get an artificial one installed right away."

With an effort, I forced my eyelids open. I was in a hospital bed, an array of equipment all around me—as many blinking lights as there were stars. Doctors wearing the pale green of dragons stood over me, disguised with white masks.

I turned my head. Through a large glass window, I saw my father, Hypnos, and Oya looking in, their faces as solemn as they'd been at the end of my spirit quest. When he saw me looking at him, my father's face lit up, and he pointed at me.

"Let me talk—" I croaked. Talking turned out to be difficult. My throat was so sore and dry.

The doctors turned.

"He's awake," one of them said. "How can that be?"

Because they were masked, I couldn't tell which one of them had spoken.

Another of them, one with a soft feminine voice said, "Let the father in. It may be the last time they speak together."

A motor whirred, and the back of my bed rose, lifting me to a sitting position. A doctor placed a glass of water in my hands. I looked at my fingers. They seemed weak, useless things. Though it was a struggle, I lifted the glass and took a drink.

As I did, my father, Oya, and Hypnos filed in, their steps synchronized. For a moment I had the impression that my hospital room was a ceremonial hut and I was the holographic fire at the center.

They gathered around me.

"Mirik," my dad said. He leaned over and touched his head to mine, as if he feared I was too frail for a hug. Perhaps I was.

"Call me Moon Hawk," I said.

My throat felt better after the water.

Hypnos regarded me with curious eyes. "I thought you disliked that name?"

"Since I finished my spirit quest, I now understand it."

"Son," my dad said, "you finished it over a year ago."

"No." Thoughts swam in my head. How to get them all out? "No, it was unfinished. Neither of us failed, you know. You may have only wounded the dragon, but the arrow pierced me—it made the hole in my suit during my spirit quest, as well as the hole in my heart. Do you see?"

Hypnos cocked his head at me, looking at me with a raven's curious gaze. "Did you dream you are a dragon, Moon Hawk?"

"No, the dragon is my guide."

His expression hardened then, and I imagined I could hear his thoughts. The sacred writings told him how to distinguish a true dream from a false one, and what I said was something he believed to be impossible.

Oya, too, shook her head. I could hear her thinking that no

one got a second chance at a spirit quest.

"I know, no one can have two spirit quests, but don't you see? This is the same one. The three of you are here in a hut of glass as before."

My father and the two shamans looked around at the glass walls.

"In the spirit world, there only ever was one quest. It all happened at the rock near Olympus Mons."

Dreams and mirrors flashed in Oya's eyes. Her gaze turned silver and infinite. Hypnos and my dad couldn't see the change in her, but I knew she understood.

I gazed at Hypnos. "Didn't our ancestors ride with dragons to this world? Isn't that what our stories say?"

He took a step back. "Yes, but—but—but it's an image, a metaphor—It's…"

We were all silent for a few seconds. Hypnos stood there, frowning and rubbing his chin.

"The dragon said I would fly with him. He said that Father's arrow made it possible, the one he fired in his spirit quest. Hypnos, do you see? It went into the dragon, and the dragon gave his wound to me, joining us."

He continued to scowl.

I tried again. "Though the details of my father's quest remain secret, I know them. My father's arrow struck the dragon in the heart, but it did not die. The fletching was blue. I am the child he was not supposed to have."

Hypnos and Oya looked accusingly at my dad.

He raised his hands, palms out. "I didn't tell him any of that. I swear"

Crows appeared, standing on each of Hypnos's shoulders. His smile returned. He too understood.

Only my father did not.

"Son." My father was weeping now. "I'm here. I know I haven't been the best of fathers. I know I—"

"Hush." I took his hand in mine. "After I died, I heard you

telling me—"

"You're not going to die," my father insisted, interrupting me. "The doctors are going to fix you up. Give you an artificial heart."

"It's okay," I said. "I already will die. You were right; the shaman was wrong."

Somehow though, I knew he didn't understand and that he wouldn't, no matter what I said. After my death, he would still say the words I heard in the millipede.

"Hypnos, after I die, I will explain it better. Then you can tell my father. Maybe one day it will make sense to him. Okay?"

I blinked at Hypnos. The crows nodded their heads.

"I will," Hypnos promised.

He and Father took hold of my left hand, Oya my right.

"I'm going to the stars now," I said. "I won't need your crows to help me, Hypnos."

With that, I rose from my body, my claw clasped around the arrow shaft in the dragon's belly. The dragon was above me, luminous and ghostly. My wings beat softly beneath his.

"Am I a hawk now?" I asked, noticing my new form.

"You always were," the dragon said. "Practice flying for a bit above Olympus Mons. When you are ready, I will take you to Saturn."

And so I flew. The light of two moons on my wings made me feel light. There is purpose in all things, however well disguised. In the mortal realm, thoughts come slowly and people can only use reason.

One day, like me, they will make intuitive leaps, and their thoughts will take them between worlds. When that day comes, my dad and I will be together again among the stars.

You have the sudden urge to take a nap. To press on a little further, turn left for room 2 (page 17). To sit down and see if sleep takes you, proceed straight ahead to room 8.

MIRRORMAZE

The End of Michael Clement

J.R.R.R. (JIM) HARDISON

As his car flew through the air, Michael Clement snapped fully awake and into a kind of crystal clarity he had never before experienced in his thirty-three years of life. It felt ironic that his first taste of such beautiful lucidity should come so close to what seemed to be the likely end of his existence.

As the car hurtled through the air and began to flip he felt as if the whole universe had slowed to a near stop. His body had decelerated with the physical world so that he could note that he had not fastened his seat belt but couldn't begin to move to belt himself in. There was no sound either, as if even that had slowed down and was still crawling toward his ears like a slug. It occurred to him as the front of the car struck the ground that maybe the world was moving at its normal pace but his mind had sped up.

As the front grille caved in, all the assorted loose junk he'd piled in the backseat—his luggage, his guitar, the cardboard box of hardback books—moved past him in slow motion and slammed into the dashboard and windshield. He raised a mental eyebrow at his luck that nothing struck him. Then his chest slammed against the steering wheel and his face crunched up against the windshield. He didn't feel much, just a slow pressure as the windshield deformed around his cheek, the glass fracturing in a spiderweb of cracks. The car sprang back up into the air, like a gymnast doing a handspring in a super-slo-mo instant replay. Actually it was more of a front-flip with a half twist, trailing a leisurely plume of desert dust and powdered glass.

Obviously, he must have dozed off behind the wheel, but he was at a loss to imagine the circumstances that could possibly account for what his car was doing now. The stretch of highway he was on had been straight, flat, and smooth for the last fifty miles and had seemed to stretch away straight, flat, and smooth for the same distance ahead. Had he hit something? Blown a tire? He knew he hadn't veered off the road because he could see the white lines of the highway tumbling by as the car cart-wheeled along. It occurred to him that he ought to be frightened and he marveled at his own detachment. He wondered how fast he must have been going to produce such a spectacular crash.

The back end of the car struck the ground on the driver's side taillight and Michael was slammed in slow motion to the coffee-stained carpet of the car floor. The impact was too slow to hurt, but the feel of the crunchy fibers against his cheek grossed him out. From his new vantage point he could see his long-missing Velvet Underground CD under the passenger's seat with all the little pebbles and dirt that had accumulated over the years. So that's where that had gone.

The suitcase, guitar, and books started a freight-train return journey toward the backseat, narrowly missing him a second time. And then, as the car continued to fly, he was rolled into a position where he could see the beautiful, crystal-clear night sky sprinkled with a gazillion twinkling stars and framed up like a postcard through a gaping hole in the shattered windshield. Had his body been responsive, he would have gasped at the beauty.

The car launched itself into another flip, and as it spun to face forward again, Michael could see the towering streetlight into which he was about to slam headfirst.

"Wow," he thought, "there's no surviving that." And then the car and the lamp found each other and Michael's startling clarity came to a jarring end.

When he opened his eyes, he again saw the breathtaking panorama of the stars, but this time he did gasp, and because the gasp hurt, it helped him to understand that, somehow, he was still alive. The speed of time caught up to him then, and with it came fear. His head flooded with images of pulverized internal organs, compound fractures protruding through shattered limbs, crushed vertebrae, or his brain swelling fatally in his skull. Terror nearly accomplished what the accident had failed to. For a moment he felt as if his heart would stop from the sheer horror of what might be.

When the pounding in his chest subsided, he sat up, discovering by the act that he could. Was he all right? Or was he just in shock? He twisted at the waist, expecting his guts to spill out, but feeling only a slight twinge, like a pulled muscle in his back. He looked behind him. There was his car, ridiculously crumpled and wrapped around the light pole like a cartoon vehicle, roof smashed flat, front seats pushed up against the back ones, the whole thing less than half its normal length.

He got to his feet, a little shakily, and looked around. The glorious stars provided little light, but the huge highway lamp— miraculously still working even though it was keeled over at a forty-five degree angle—cast its blue-white glow wide enough for him to see.

He was maybe fifteen feet to the right side of the road in a patch of warm sand. He could tell it was warm because his left shoe and sock were missing. The contrast between the temperature of the sand and the crisp night air struck him profoundly and he took a moment to clench and unclench his toes as if he were standing on a beach. Michael shivered and expelled a plume of steam from his lungs. Then he started to move around a bit, experimentally, feeling for anything broken.

Again, his imagination brought him sensations of disaster. The way it would feel for the ends of mangled bones to crunch against each other or for a bruised bowel to rupture violently. He shuddered, but none of it was real. He was essentially unhurt, at least as far as he could make out. With that realization he experienced another sensation he could not recall having felt in his thirty-three years. It was exhilaration and joy at the prospect of being alive.

Prior to this moment, life had not been particularly fun, good, or even terribly pleasant for Michael. That had been the main motivation that had led him here. He had been putting it all behind him, turning things around, moving away from the unhappy past, the unhealthy associations of home, and a failed marriage.

"Holy shit!" he shouted into the night. He looked up at the stars above him wonderingly, and his eyes welled with tears.

That glorious glow lasted eight minutes.

Eight minutes and one second later it occurred to Michael that he was in the middle of the desert in the dead of night. His car was destroyed. The carefully packed belongings that constituted everything he had in the world were likely crushed. He was missing one shoe and sock that he suspected he would never be able to find in the dark—assuming they weren't crushed inside the ruins of his car. Before the accident, he had been driving for two hours and had only passed one other car. One. The last rest stop was at least fifty miles back and there was no telling how far ahead the next one was. The cell phone in his pocket had been dead for hours.

"Holy shit," he muttered. He had a decision to make and he was not good with decisions. Wait here? Someone would come along at some point. But the desert was supposed to get cold at night. Bitterly cold. He'd read that, or seen it in a movie. If he just sat around waiting, would he be okay, or would he freeze? At least walking would keep him warm.

So then, back or forward? Back had the advantage of being

a known quantity. But back was fifty miles and he was missing a shoe. And back was the past and everything he was hoping to put behind him.

In such close proximity to his near death, it seemed too symbolically significant for him to retrace his steps. It would mean something. Something bad. So, it was either go forward or wait by the car. At least waiting by the car he had the light. He was not fond of the dark. Not since he was little. He looked up at the light, buzzing above him, and marveled again that it was still working. Then he peered down the road into the distance. A row of identical highway lights stretched off for miles toward the horizon until they vanished as tiny pinpricks behind a rise in the road. He supposed the darkness wouldn't be too bad even if he pushed on. As long as he stuck to the lights, he'd be fine.

How long was it until sunrise? He checked his watch. The watch he had inherited when his father died. Predictably, it had stopped, a single white-edged crack across the entire face. He stood staring at it for a full minute, wondering how he felt about its ruin. The minute hand had come off and the hour hand was stopped just shy of midnight. Giving up on sorting out his feelings about the watch, he started to wonder whether he had been unconscious after the crash, and for how long. It took him a moment to realize that he had slipped into stalling on making a decision.

Decisiveness. It was important. This was, more than ever now, a new start, a new lease on life even. Staying wasn't a decision. It was an indecision disguised as a decision. Fine. He'd walk forward into this new life. Things were going to change and he was going to change things. He wouldn't let surviving this accident be a meaningless event. It felt like it meant something, so he was going to make it mean something.

Energized, he stepped onto the shoulder of the road and started off, consciously deciding not to throw a last look back at his crumpled car. The asphalt was warm under his bare foot. He flexed his toes on it, remembering walking the freshly refinished roads around his house as a kid. He used to pop the tar bubbles with his toes and come back with the soles of his feet absolutely black. And then he'd catch hell for it, and worse.

So, everything he owned and every scrap of his past had been destroyed in the car? Fine. Better than fine. This was an opportunity. A crossroads. He was free now like he never had been before. Free to reshape himself into something new and stronger and better. Someone stronger and better. Someone bold and decisive.

Caught up in the moment, he worked the cheap silver wedding band off his ring finger, intending to drop it by the roadside and never think of it, or the broken promises it had come to stand for, again. But he didn't drop it. He clutched it in the heart of his hand until his palm sweated around it.

Bold, decisive, strong. He stopped and hurled it away into the night to prevent the possibility of going after it. Then he took off his remaining shoe and sock, tucked the sock down into the shoe, tucked his broken watch in with it and left them there at the side of the road like an offering or a grave marker. "I'm free," he said out loud. "I choose." As he said it, he set his sights on the most distant highway light, miles off and waiting for him, bright and inviting like the future. And just like that, the light blinked off.

Michael stopped.

Okay. These kinds of coincidental things happen all the time. It was random. Only an exaggerated sense of his own importance could make it seem significant. The old Michael with his useless philosophy degree would see the light going out as an ominous metaphor. The new Michael would see it as a challenge. He'd see it as a challenge and he'd spit in its eye. It would be morning before he reached the damn burned-out light anyway.

This was good. It was a test. And at the same time it was a reminder that he shouldn't be looking at the last light, but at the next one. *One light at a time. One light at a time.* He switched his focus, squared his shoulders and started again.

It took him one thousand two hundred and seventeen steps to get to the pole of the next light. He could do this. He touched the cold steel post with one hand, then locked his eyes on the next one and started counting over from one. If he just kept counting, the number would go too high and he'd lose count somewhere. The old him always made mistakes like that. Besides, now that he knew how many steps it took, he could use that to measure his progress, judge his performance.

He was at two hundred thirty-one when something broke the rhythm of his steps. What? Something had caught his attention, some movement ahead. Some little flicker. Maybe it was a shooting star? He scanned the sky for anything and then realized that he'd lost count. He stopped walking. He'd lost count and it bothered him. Where was he? Two hundred twenty-two? No, that would have been easy: two two two. He would have remembered that. In fact, he would have remembered anything in the twenties, wouldn't he? Damn it. Why couldn't anything just be easy? Ever? This was supposed to be his new start and it was going wrong already. Anger started to rise from the bottomless well of it inside him, but he caught himself.

What did it matter? He'd just cheated death. What step he was on didn't make any difference as long as he was moving. Maybe the old Michael would get pissed, but this new guy he'd suddenly become, this new guy was bigger than that. Screw counting steps. He started walking again.

Maybe he should change his name. Michael Clement was who he had been. Clement wasn't even his real last name. It was his stepfather's name. No one knew who his real father was, or what his last name should have been. It could have been anything. It could have been something cool. He'd played this game before—the game of imagining who he was supposed to have been. Anything would have been better than who he was. Any last name would have been better than what he'd been saddled with. "Clementine! Clementine! Little darling Clementine!" The other boys had tormented him relentlessly. It hadn't helped that he was slight, delicately featured, and small for his age. It hadn't helped that he'd learned how to flinch and cower long before he was sent to school.

No. Michael Clement was the old, frustrated, impotent loser. This new guy was *different*. This new guy was a *winner*. He was going to do important things. He was going to make a difference in the world. He needed a name to reflect that. A "make a difference" name. Completely fresh, first and last. Quinn maybe. Or Max. Something really strong. Maximilian Stone. Maximilian Hammer.

He smiled at the foolishness. Max Hammer. Subtle. Maybe he should call himself Abraham Christ. He smiled again. Jefferson Lord? Lincoln King?

This time, he saw what last time had merely broken his concentration. In the distance, behind the light he was focused on, the last light in the line blinked off. Was it the same one he'd seen the first time? Maybe it was blinking on and off. That's probably what got him last time, the light blinking back on.

So, his future was a blinking light? What did that mean, symbolically? But even as he thought it, the current last light blinked off too. Now he stopped. It wasn't the other one blinking on and off. They were going out, in a line. Coming toward him.

He started walking again, counting the lights between him and the burned-out ones. There were fourteen. One thousand two hundred and seventeen steps between lights. What was that, like four miles or something? Could a person even see for four miles? Then the new last light, number fourteen, went out too.

Michael flinched. He felt a sensation in his stomach like he'd just crested the rise of a roller coaster and was looking at the drop. He was instantly angry at himself for the feeling. He was still just the same weak, cowardly, superstitious Michael Clement he'd always been. Lincoln King wouldn't be shaken by a malfunctioning light. Lincoln King wouldn't be shaken by anything. Or afraid of anything. Once he set his mind to doing something, he'd damn well do it, whatever it took. Lincoln would be a man who walked into the future, into the darkness if need be, with his chin up and a sense of purpose. Lincoln would be a man who got things done no matter what it took.

"Damn straight," he said out loud, desperately trying to keep control of Michael Clement and his little-boy fears. He forced himself to start walking again.

And another light went out. Twelve left. Twelve left between him and the approaching darkness. He couldn't help but think of it like that. The approaching darkness, rushing down the highway to meet him like some vast, black bird of prey. Lincoln wouldn't picture it that way. He wouldn't grant the darkness the power to walk toward him. Lincoln wouldn't be afraid. He'd be the thing to be afraid of. He wouldn't picture the darkness coming for him; he'd picture himself coming for the darkness. That's what Lincoln King would do. Lincoln King. The name wasn't a joke anymore. It was a real name, a strong name. A new name. His new name.

Wrestling Michael Clement, Lincoln King picked up his pace, bare feet padding on the cooling asphalt. It was just some mechanical problem with the light. Some meaningless mechanical problem.

The twelfth light went out.

Screw it.

The eleventh.

He kept going. Actually thrust his chin out defiantly, daring the next light to go out. Which it did.

He stopped. There were nine lights left between him and the darkness. Nine lights. That was like what, two miles and change? He was just over halfway to the nearest light. He looked back over his shoulder at the well-lit length of road stretching away behind him, at the wreck of his car wrapped around the pole two and a half poles away.

Maybe it was the crash! Maybe the crash had pulled a wire loose or something, and the lamps were failing in sequence as power stopped getting to them. The idea felt ridiculous even as it came to him. He recognized it as his weakness and fear grasping at straws to explain what was happening. He turned back to the road ahead, half expecting the darkness to be a couple of lights closer, half fearing it would have come even farther than that. But there were still nine lights burning.

He frowned as something occurred to him. He took an experimental step forward and the ninth light failed immediately. He stopped and waited, eyes locked on the eighth light. Without his watch, he had little idea how long he stood there, staring at the light. It felt like ten minutes, but it could have been less. The entire time, the light burned steadily, without so much as a flicker.

Finally, he tried another step and the eighth light winked out as if he had flipped a switch.

Now he was afraid. Michael Clement, Lincoln King or whoever he was. He shivered in the cold night air and tried to think. How could this be happening? Why was it happening? Maybe the two were the same question. It wasn't coincidence. He was sure of that. Lights only went out when he was walking toward them.

Maybe this wasn't really happening. Maybe he was lying unconscious in the sand or in his car, dreaming all this. He pulled out his wallet and took out his driver's license. He turned the plastic card over and read the back aloud.

"Class C. Any single vehicle with a GVWR of not more than 26,000 pounds with the proper endorsements." Then he flipped the card over and waited a moment. The picture showed him weak and foolish, still slight, still delicate. Clement, Michael James. Coward, weakling, pushover. His mouth tightened unconsciously at the bitterness of his self-loathing.

He turned the driver's license back over and read the words again. They were the same. Same words, same size, same font. He was not dreaming. Words are never fixed in dreams. He'd read that somewhere.

So, what then? Was he…was he dead? It was possible. He could have been killed in the accident. But even if he were dead, what was going on? This was not like any conception of death he'd heard of or imagined. He tried to really consider the possibility, but he just couldn't make it work. Why would death be like this? What was the point? It just didn't feel right. He couldn't believe he was dead. So what then?

Darkness was coming toward him, but only when he was moving toward it. What did that mean? Did it mean he should turn around and go back? He turned again and looked back.

Go back? Back down the road from where he had come. Back past the wreck of his car. Back past his shoe, his sock and his watch. Back past his wedding ring. Back to the way things had always been.

Instead, he turned around and started forward again. At his first step, light number seven went out. He shuddered, but he kept on going. At his twentieth step, light number six went out. He kept going, but his hands started to shake and his lower lip quivered.

Maybe this was a test. A test to see if he had what it took to change. Light number five went out. He had to have steel in him to change. *Real steel in his gut.* Michael Clement was weak. Michael Clement let the world frighten him into bad choices. Michael Clement let his two-timing wife and a thousand assholes like her walk all over him. Michael Clement let the darkness terrify him, just like a weak, worthless little boy. Michael Clement let his stepfather—

"Worthless," he hissed, forcing his trembling limbs to take him forward as light number four was extinguished. Lincoln King wouldn't be afraid of anything. Lincoln King would be strong and certain. Lincoln King would fix things. Nobody would walk all over Lincoln King just as long as Lincoln King could keep walking right now.

Light number three went out. This one was close enough that he actually heard a click when it died and heard how the combined buzzing sound of all the lights was reduced by one. He balled his hands into fists to stop the shaking and clenched his teeth.

"Lincoln King," he whispered to himself, "Lincoln King."

Light number two went out.

Lincoln King, or Michael Clement, both started to cry as he walked up to the last light and saw only darkness stretching away ahead of him. He started to cry like a filthy, worthless six-year-old and he couldn't force himself to stop or to take another step forward. He stood shaking and crying, helpless.

The last light, the one he was standing under, went out with a loud click.

In the absence of its electric buzz there was perfect silence and perfect darkness. Just like the storm basement. Just like the utility closet. He was paralyzed by it, just as he'd been as a child. Paralyzed and waiting for the sound of his stepfather's feet coming through the dark for him.

And then came the soft slap of bare feet on the asphalt.

Michael twitched like a rabbit at the sound, shut his eyes tight against the dark.

A familiar, male voice said close beside him, "It is all right, Michael."

He turned to its source, opened his eyes, and found that he could see. He could see better than the dim starlight warranted. And as he saw the other, he recognized the face and the voice.

It was himself, or a version of himself, only better looking in subtle ways. There was no cowardice or worry marring the features, no subtle weakness in the stance or the expression.

"Have no fear," the other said with Michael's own voice, only richer, more confident, and powerful.

Michael tasted sour bile and fought not to be sick. "Are you m...m...me?" he asked, sobbing softly.

"No," the other smiled sympathetically. "I am another. You can think of me as a kind of...angel. I only look like you because you cannot comprehend my true form, so your mind reflects itself back to you. And no, you are not dead...but that is my goal. I am here to ask you to make a choice. It would be better for the world for you to have died in your car wreck."

Michael tensed and took a half step backward. "What? Are you here to kill me?" he asked, his voice just above a whisper. The angel stared at him with eyes of infinite sadness.

"I would, were I able. But that is prohibited. I cannot kill you unless you first choose to die. You must make that choice freely and of your own accord or I can do nothing."

"I don't want to die," Michael whimpered, his voice breaking.

"I know," the angel replied, "but it will be significantly better for the world and for your kind if you do not live through this night. For this reason we would like you to choose to die, despite your desire to live. And you must choose quickly, before the new day starts, or all will be lost." The angel's voice was warm with tenderness and compassion, but his words brought gooseflesh to Michael's arms. Whatever was happening, he no longer doubted it was real.

"Why?" Michael blurted, forcing the question out. "Why would it be better if I died?"

The angel looked deeply into his eyes. "It is prohibited for me to reveal this to you until you make the irrevocable choice to die," the angel replied.

"But if you don't tell me, I can't choose," Michael whimpered, expecting the angel to become angry. Instead, his doppelgänger laid a hand on Michael's shoulder. Its flesh was hot, and its touch tingled.

"You have free will. You can choose to do anything you want. And you must choose death," the angel told him. "If you do not, the consequences will be significant and terrible."

Michael frowned, but his mind grasped at a possibility. "But if I really have free will, how can you know I'm going to do whatever you think I'm going to do that will be so horrible? What if I just choose not to do the bad thing?"

The angel smiled ruefully. "It is complicated. The possibility exists that you might not do what we fear. But that possibility is infinitesimal at this point. You see, with the exception of this choice I offer you now, there is no single choice you can make that will turn the balance. It is the sum of all the choices you have made so far and will make soon. Every choice you have made individually up until now has led you to this moment. Every choice you put behind you adds to the weight of your fate, to your path through possibility. The weight propels you forward and builds your momentum in a particular direction until you have no more ability to stop or even steer yourself than does an avalanche."

As the angel spoke, Michael began to shiver uncontrollably.

"You are not predestined to do what you are going to do," the angel told him, "but at this point it is virtually inevitable. This is why I stand before you now, offering this choice. This is the last possible point where you can freely choose to stop yourself. This is the last possible moment when a single decision can change the terrible future that lies ahead."

Michael fought to master his voice before he spoke. "What if I refuse to choose?" he begged.

"That is still a choice," the angel frowned. "You must actively choose to die. Anything else is a decision to live."

Michael shook his head. "Then no! I choose to live!"

The angel did not hesitate. "Reconsider," it demanded, but for the first time, the confidence slipped from its tone. "In all of the history of the world, this choice has only been offered four times before, and in all the remaining span of time, we are only allowed three more direct interventions. Reconsider."

"What did the others choose?" Michael asked.

"Three chose death. One chose to live."

"Who were they?"

"I cannot tell you. Two of the names would be meaningless to you. The other two you would recognize in an instant."

"Tell me or I'll choose to live," Michael cried.

In response, the angel grabbed him with both arms and leapt up into the air. Michael screamed and struggled as they rocketed up at dizzying speed, but the angel's arms were like bands of steel.

"There are laws that bind me as tightly as the laws of physics bind you, and I can no more break them than you could defy gravity," the angel told him sternly as they rose. "The universe is caught in a cosmic conflict between the forces of light and darkness. Without the elder law, it would be shattered in an instant."

Higher and higher they sped until they stopped quite suddenly. "Behold," the angel said in a voice that sounded like God from a Hollywood movie. Michael looked down. The Earth lay below them in its entirety, a bright blue orb in the glittering darkness of space. From this vantage it looked tiny and fragile and beautiful. Michael clung tightly to the angel now, dizzy with fear. He closed his eyes, but the vision of the delicate planet continued to glow in his mind.

"What I'm going to do will be bad?" he whispered.

"Catastrophic," the angel confirmed. "Your time grows very short and even I cannot give you more."

Michael opened his eyes and found they were back on the road again. Tears streamed down his cheeks. "How would you do it? How would you kill me?" he asked.

"You will die in your car wreck, as you should have. Your neck will break. It will be quick and painless."

Michael looked long and hard into his own face, the face of the angel. His thirty-three years of life had been no picnic. They'd been brutal and fearful and filled with disappointments.

Would it be so bad to let it go, especially if by doing so, he could avert some terrible future in which he was the ultimate villain?

"Michael Clement," the angel said urgently, "I must return you to your car in mere moments. You must decide now."

Michael opened his mouth to say yes, but before he could utter the word, there was a shimmer in the air beside him and another copy of himself materialized.

"Don't do it, Lincoln," the new one cried out. "It is a trick."

Michael froze, eyes wide, mouth still open. The first angel whirled on the new arrival.

"You have already spent your opportunity!" he hissed in a voice that nearly stopped Michael's heart.

"We spend another!" the second angel spat back, then turned his attention full on Michael. "Lincoln King, you must survive this night! The enemy attempts to betray you and lead you to betray your world! Yours is a glorious future that shapes mankind for the better!"

"Do not listen," the first angel roared. "He lies! You must choose to die!"

"You have a holy destiny yet to fulfill," the second yelled. "You must choose to live!"

Without warning, the first angel launched himself into the second, and the two spun up off the ground, ripping and tearing at each other like birds of prey.

"Michael!" the first screamed.

"Lincoln!" the second gasped.

"You must die!"

"You must live!"

"Quickly! Say the word! The moment is upon—" the first angel's words were cut off as the world made a sudden, sickening lurch.

Michael was behind the wheel of his car again as it launched itself into its final flip. The universe was back to slow motion, and his mind was crystal clear as before. Every detail was exactly as it had been the first time. The car cartwheeled around to face forward, and Michael could see the looming steel light pole into which he was about to slam headfirst.

The thought of his neck snapping, of the bones grinding apart, of his head flopping against his back, surged through him. The fear made him sick and he was sick of the fear. He made his decision. Michael Clement was a fearful coward and it was time for him to die.

But not of a broken neck.

Michael Clement would die to make room for Lincoln King. And Lincoln King was going to change the world.

If you're starting to feel like you know who you are, turn left for room 15 (page 193). If you need more time to think about it, proceed straight ahead to room 9.

9 Origin

YELENA CALAVERA

In loving memory of Dirk William Chalmers
9 January 1988 – 6 June 2019

The Drakensberg Road

When I was a child, while my father was undergoing *thwasa*, the calling by the ancestors that beckons a person to initiation, he had a teacher called Ma Bengu, who lived in Winterton in the Drakensberg. She was a sangoma, a diviner. To visit her, we would make the four-hour journey from Johannesburg to Winterton on a Friday evening and stay with my mother's cousin at their house in the Berg.

I used to love riding in the car with my dad, my mom, and my sister. I would sit in the front seat of that old, blue Jeep with its infamous roof rack while my dad was driving. He had some *muti*, spiritual medicine, and beads and things hanging from the rear-view mirror. We listened to tapes of Buffy Sainte-Marie and the Indigo Girls, *Songs of New Mexico*. There was always something about the desert in that music and in my soul.

At one point on that road journey, we would take a left-hand turn-off from the main road and go past the snaking river with the half-submerged, flat-topped trees. I remember the strangeness of the grass and the water. You could only see a thin sliver of water through the long, yellowy grass, and the trees were dotted along that line, snaking away, following the bend of the river. It was beautiful and mysterious; I'd never seen that before, and I haven't seen it since. It's a place that's etched in my memory from that time in my childhood and from those journeys.

Sitting in the front seat, somehow it was always hot. The seats were covered with dark-patterned, woven material that was fraying in places, and they had blue faux leather around the corners. That car had this comforting smell of having been journeyed in, a combination of sweat, maybe, in the seats, and the sweet scent of warm, slightly sticky polyurethane.

I would sit in the sun feeling warm all over my little body, my head lolling against the side of the seat belt, Indigo Girls playing in the background, my dad driving, and the blue Jeep going along. There was wellness, and I looked at the world with wonder, reverence, and a quiet sense of mystery. I felt a part of something hard to describe, but magical.

In the back sat my mother with my small sister, playing with her dolls and looking at picture books. Both were quiet, and sometimes all of us were quiet, and then there was just the music.

Part of me is there still, driving along next to that snaking river, having turned off from the main road heading toward the Drakensberg, the sun sloping toward the west, heat of the afternoon tailing off into the evening—that special time of day just before the light takes on a golden quality. I can still hear the Indigo Girls singing that nobody gets a lifetime rehearsal.

I remember I said to my dad, "Can we get one?"

And he asked, "What do you mean, Ayla? Can we get one of what?"

I said, "A lifetime rehearsal."

As we traveled farther, soon there were pine trees whizzing by, the remnants of plantations, telephone wires, and long grass. This was the Freestate.

There was one place on the road where I would always ask my father to stop. I called it the "Wind Tunnel." Next to the seemingly endless barbed-wire fence, under a few pine trees growing in the sand by the side of the road, there were some cylindrical shells made of corrugated iron, lying on their sides. At the time, to me, they seemed huge—certainly, large enough for me to stand in. What were they before they ended up by the side of the road?

We would stand there shivering while the wind was howling through the cylinders and making the most powerful sounds.

Vooooooooooooo! Avoooooooooooo!

The Wind Tunnel, somewhere that told me where we were on the journey, how long before we reached Winterton.

There were many road trips like that. My childhood is a maze of roads winding through the African landscape, black mountains of the escarpment, bleak beauty of the Karoo, red sands of the Kalahari, verdant hills of Kwa-Zulu Natal, set to the soundtrack of a little plastic suitcase filled with my father's tapes.

All the roads had strange destinations at the end of them. Sculpture parks filled with totems, huge caves where scores of people slept by the light of a thousand candles, roofless huts next to the Zambezi River, ramshackle houses in the desert where people came from miles around to meet around the fires of people of power who carried stories and rituals. Credo Mutwa and Ma Bengu, my father's teachers, were the most mysterious of all.

Those powerful people did not notice me, because they were giants and I was just a child.

But in my grief, my defiance, I see and remember everything.

What were they going for, my father and all those others who went? I never could tell you. And now, when I ask my father, he tells me it was just his ego's quest for gratification. I know why he says that, but I think he does himself a disservice by oversimplifying it like that.

Something was calling, something of Dreamtime. Something without a language, that speaks and calls in dreams and whispers, tells stories and shows the way. It transforms, but not from one thing into another thing in a way that's easy to define or describe.

It heralds some transfiguration from one mystery into another, singing in a net of visions projected onto the night sky. Some parts added, some left behind, some breathing, some decay, some swirling cosmos, some river delta, some sacred body of water, some grotto. Some smoldering fire left in the morning after long drumming into the night. Togetherness, stories. Dreamtime. Drinking homemade beer from a round, black clay pot. Red and white cloth imprinted with the image of a leopard. Strings of red and white beads. A hat made from a jackal's fur and tail. A woven bag that held the bones. A stick with a golden lion's head. Strange carvings. They meant something. Could have been anything.

At home, my father had a shrine with pieces of driftwood, kelp, shells and coral, and woven baskets. In the cupboard beneath, there were boxes full of tapes, and there was a CD player where I listened to the first CD I ever bought, the soundtrack to the movie *Now and Then*.

I remember early days, the sun shining in through the windows of that house where I grew up, onto the brown carpets, giving me that same warm feeling that I had driving in the old blue Jeep. The warmth that is my nature; the warmth of Africa, Freestate, and Drakensberg, a long road to the Kalahari's red sands.

This is who I am.

Sun Meets Moon

At the origin, there is an eternal moment where the sun is shining in from the window of an old blue Jeep traveling down winding roads from Johannesburg to a house in an informal settlement on the outskirts of Winterton in the Drakensberg. On that road, there is a snaking river with half-submerged, flat-topped trees growing out of it.

I met you at the origin, when I was just a tiny child. My parents took me to your house in the Jo'burg suburb of Bordeaux, near where my Granny taught at the primary school.

The first time I saw you, you were a golden-haired little boy standing in the driveway, clinging to your mother's skirts, shy of this little girl being shown to you.

"This is Y'ael," your mother said, trying to coax you out of hiding. "Don't you want to say hello?"

Even then, your presence was like the sun. We were thick as thieves from day one, and I followed you around everywhere. You always were one step ahead, and nothing's changed.

I remember the Scalextric set of racing slot cars you had set up in one of the rooms and how we were trying to learn to blow bubbles with our chewing gum. We couldn't figure it out, so we just mashed the bubblegum into these sort of flat sheets, put them on the top of our mouths, and held them there while blowing to make a bubble. Then we went to show the adults how clever we were to have figured it out.

I loved you before I knew what that was.

Your dad would bring you to my house after school on his motorbike. He and my mother would sit at the kitchen table in the sun, drinking tea and talking for hours. Outside in the garden, I taught you how to talk to the fruit trees.

Then, we were not allowed to see each other again for a long time because our parents messed things up between themselves, each with their own shadows.

Six years later, we found our way to each other again by chance through some little primary school "boyfriend" I had who was a friend of yours. We met again at the Fratelli's in Blairgowrie for the first time. I was twelve, and you were thirteen. We were friends again instantly. You told me that while we were separated, you had missed me terribly, wondering if you would ever see me again.

"There was a Yale lock on one of the doors at home, and every time I opened that door, I would think of you."

Once in high school during the school holidays, we went to Delta Park, climbed a tree, and got stoned. I got stuck, because I was too paranoid to jump down from the relatively low-hanging branch we had been sitting on. It was highly ridiculous, I was aware, but the fear was no less real. You had to lift me down. We went back to my place and watched Pink Floyd's *The Wall*.

"Whoa, man," was all you said.

Days of Sunshine and Cigarettes

A tumultuous decade passed. You were still like the sun, but there was a darkness that would roll over your skies at times.

We would sit together by the window in your kitchen at a little black table and set of chairs, soaking up the afternoon sun. You'd roll yourself a cigarette, and we'd drink a cup of tea, and I'd ask you to roll me one, too, even though I didn't really smoke. For you it was such a habit, you know? A bit of a crutch. If I'd told you that, you would have laughed. You had this deep laugh; it made me feel comforted, safe, and like I was home.

I loved your house, loved being there with you and talking with you about everything. So much so that I moved in. Twice. Neither time ended well. The first time, you carried boxes out of my ex-fiancé's house and told him good-naturedly that you were there if he needed a friend. He prickled, and behind his grin, he was snarling. I tried very hard not to laugh.

Remember that one day? There was just the once, just that once. It was enough, and too much, and too little. It was everything. It was all of love. A promise. Thirsty mountains next to the sea, where no rain falls.

One night, your mother told me that for all those years, you were often unhappy. "He would come to me and say, mom, I don't know if I want to be with so-and-so. I think I'm supposed to be with Y'ael."

The second time I lived with you, one morning you were on Skype with your dad in the lounge, and I had one of my boyfriends over. We were standing where your dad couldn't see us, and he said, "When are you and Y'ael going to make me some gorgeous grandbabies?" I tried not to laugh, but not very hard.

It was never really like that though, was it? Come to think of it, I do remember once, when I was about eighteen, I locked myself in my bedroom, and you stood outside the door, playing your guitar and serenading me tunelessly with a terrible song you had made up on the spot. I was too angry to laugh.

After you died, I dreamt that I saw you in an airport. It was virtually abandoned. You were dressed like David Bowie in the '80s. You had a mullet and earrings with feathers and some strange patchwork quilt of a coat made of lavender and lilac flaps of material. You looked like yourself, but you looked like someone else. You looked eternal, and I knew that I was seeing you before you were born and after you died.

You took your leave of me and walked off somewhere, and I walked off somewhere else in the airport, taking different flights. But I knew I would see you again.

Secret Ways

On 9 November 2014, on Beltane, the pagan sabbath of the great union between the Goddess and the God, our lives forked off in different directions, forever.

It was a few months after I moved out the second time. You took me to Northcliff Hill. Even though I thought I knew the place so well, you showed me secret routes that followed hidden pathways in the grass next to the orange-stained Witwatersrand quartzite. The pathways led to sacred groves, where circles of candle wax told of rituals past. You had gone beneath the surface of this place, and I had just skimmed the top of it.

You took a selfie of us with your long arms. I still have that photograph.

Following that, you took me to the Faraday *muti* market in Jo'burg CBD. What I saw disturbed me. In my childhood, during his *thwasa*, my father had taken us to places like these. They were the sorts of places where sickly, slow, smoky, earth magics moved low to the ground. Humans trying to control fate, to part the veil to speak with the dead. I was happy to get the fuck out of there, but you had not finished blowing my mind.

We drove around for a while, and then you parked your little green car on the side of the road somewhere, and we walked through Hillbrow. Even though we were in one of the most dangerous places in the world, and we were walking—two white people—I wasn't afraid because I was with you. You had that kind of power and gravitas.

As we walked, I smelled the pungent odor of *muti* burning. You told me that criminals burned powerful *muti* in rituals before doing violent crime and thought that the only weapon the *muti* didn't protect you against was a spear. This was why you kept a spear next to your bed, you said. Your girl later told me that you had grabbed that spear and wrestled a robber over the balcony into some cacti where the two of you were living.

You showed me my city, showed me something I was too afraid to know. Beneath the surface, where I had been too afraid to go, you went in.

You took me up to Hillbrow Koppies, the cliffs, and we took a photo of ourselves in front of Ponti Tower. The Zionists were singing songs of worship down below.

We went back to the car and drove around some more before turning down Louis Botha Avenue. You took me to a famous Rasta place on Rocky Street, and we went up and got some food. When we drove back, you played me a song, "Weeping" by Bright Blue, and you told me it was about Apartheid.

"It wasn't roaring; it was weeping."

We drove through those tattered streets, and you had such compassion. I saw something in you. And I saw something in me.

That night I went back home, I had a shower, I went out in Braamfontein, and I met my husband for the first time.

Journey to the Shining Gate

When you died, I flew home. I could feel you all around me. The golden warmth of you, a thread weaving through my whole life, my whole being. I went straight to your mother, and I cried with her.

On the day you were cremated, I slept at your mother's house next to the girl you loved. The other girl who loved you slept next door. We all cried together and sang together. We three were sisters and lost lovers, and we were all your mother's daughters. We all knew everything everyone else had to say, and there was nothing to say. There was only love.

It was cold that night, and I wondered at the mystery of it, sleeping there in your old room on a mattress on the floor, makeshift bedding, next to this girl I'd met only once before. It had been on the night we had our farewell party at Fratelli's, before my husband and I moved to London. You two walked in while Chris Isaak's "Wicked Game" was playing.

My sister said, "This song is my guilty little pleasure."

I said, "Oh, mine too." I sang along for a few lines.

Your girl had stared at me with her intense, dark eyes. I could tell by the way she looked at me that you had told her everything, and that she was the one. I was happy for you.

"I get it, you know," I said to her when we had climbed under the covers, faces lit by the light of the gas heater. "You and Dirk."

"What do you mean?" she said.

I said, "I can't tell you anything that you don't already know."

If there was anywhere you would have been that night, it was somewhere in that house, rattling around, making tea, rolling yourself a smoke. I imagined what you would have said and how you would have laughed if you'd known we'd all be together, these three women—two of us bizarre anachronisms—and your mother. We told stories, and we cried, and the loss was bottomless.

In death, there is no linearity; in summing up, everything is simultaneous.

A few days before I was supposed to leave to fly home to London—I'd been so strong, there for everyone, holding ceremony space, singing medicine—I was driving my sister's car, and I turned down into 4th Street, and the tide broke over me. I pulled over and screamed, and I cried until my throat was raw.

I drove to your house, and the other girl who loved you opened the gate. I drove in, and I wept into her sandy-brown hair. She held me, and there were just hearts beating.

And you weren't in that house, but you were in that house.

I remembered a fight we had about some logs I'd asked you to help me carry in from my car.

"Why the fuck should I help you, Y'ael?" you shouted. "I'm not your boyfriend."

You and me and the sunlight, the rolled cigarettes, the fighting. Two people with strong wills, locking horns, taking each other for granted, taking youth for granted. This was my first love—a friendship that spans a million years, filled with strife and conflict, grief and loss, love and remembrance, mystery, forgiveness, and grace.

I moved out in a towering fury, and we didn't speak for months after that fight, until one of our friends ended up in the hospital after a motorbike accident and I came to you and curled up in your bed. I parked your sister in; my car was blocking hers. She came to knock on the door—she was used to girls parking her in. I came out, and she smiled and said, "Oh! It's you."

Your mother, another housemate, and I had once teased you that you kept bringing girls home who had the same name, and we couldn't tell them apart. We told you that we would need to take Polaroids of each girl, write their names on them, and stick them all up on the pantry wall. We all thought you would blast us for that.

"There's only one problem with that," you said.

"What's that?" I asked.

"We're going to need a bigger wall." You punctuated that with your deep laugh, and we were all in hysterics.

One day, close to the end—or was it the middle?—you came to my house, and we cooked breakfast together. You told me you wanted to cuddle. I told you that I didn't feel like it, and you said, "Please. Please hold me because I feel like a baby that hasn't been touched in a long time." So, I held you.

The Sangoma's House

I never did make it back to London because as I reversed out of your driveway, at the bottom of the hill I saw a shimmering wall stretching across the street and all the way up to the sky. It was a portal, and on the other side, instead of showing the roundabout at the intersection of 3rd Street and 4th Avenue in Linden, there was the turn-off to the Drakensberg and the snaking river with the half-submerged, flat-topped trees. I rolled down the window and drove my sister's car through the portal.

Was this real, or was I in Dreamland? It made no difference. Jung once wrote that when he had been a young boy, he sat meditating on top of a stone, and a strange thought occurred to him: Was the stone dreaming *him?*

Maybe this was leopard-dreaming, jackal-dreaming, desert-fox-dreaming, and I was just a momentary emergence.

Returning to the leopard's dream, the dream of the jackal, perhaps I could undo some of the hollowing-out that had come along with the growth of my scientific understanding. If I could be involved in nature again, rediscover my lost identification with natural phenomena, maybe I would not, as Jung said, feel so alone in the cosmos. To extend this further, maybe thunder could once again become the voice of an angry god, the snaking river could again contain a friendly spirit, a puff adder I saw alongside the Drakensberg Road could embody the wisdom of all of nature, a grotto in a rural village could be the home of some menacing demon. As they did to the ancients, voices could speak to me from the mountains, and I could speak to them, thinking they could hear.

As I drove through the portal, I realized that this was why all those people went to Credo and Ma Bengu, because their contact with nature was gone, and with it had gone the sense of personal meaning that this "symbolic connection" had supplied. My father's shrine with the kelp and driftwood, the sticks carved with totems—signposts on the way back to participation in the mystery of nature.

Now, I am no longer in Linden, no longer in linear time. No language has tenses for Dreamtime, because everything is simultaneous.

This is the leopard's dream, the dream of the jackal, and the desert fox. In their dream, I am no longer on the road driving my sister's car, but I am in a house like Ma Bengu's house, looking out toward the west. It is one of those straw and clay houses that you see in the settlements outside the big towns where there are no street names, but there is sand, barbed wire, plastic blowing through dry grass, and there are pylons overhead. These clay houses are of simple but sturdy construction. Simple means, simple furniture, simple things inside. A place where a person can live a simple life, close to land and community.

I'm looking through a doorway. The veld outside has recently burned, as it does in this part of the world. A burnt white tree marks the landscape. There are no other structures all the way to the horizon, where dark clouds swell up from the ground. They are broken by a band of crimson, orange, and yellow that merges with another wall of grayish purple. It is sunset time, red sky. The veld is rustling, regrowth after the fire. Eerie, beautiful, comforting.

On the veranda, underneath a roof of transparent green corrugated plastic sheeting, there's a group of nine African women, robust and bold, each with dresses made from colorful fabrics. They wear doeks, cloth wraps, on their heads. They are women of power, gathered to speak secrets, share wisdom, talk about healing their people, and about the change that is and must be.

They do not see me, nor will they unless I speak the right word.

"Ma," I say. This means "mother."

They turn and fix their eyes upon me. I am seen, and I walk forward, out of the house and onto the veranda. I walk through an opening in the circle between the two women closest to the door and go to one of the women at the far side. She is an albino with golden-white braids. Later, when I tell my father this, he says to me, "A white African, like you." She is wearing small, oval-shaped, gold-rimmed glasses.

I go to her and I say, "I'm the daughter of Derek and Sanet."

She tells me, "Yes, I know, Derek. Yes, I know Sanet. Yes, I know you."

I do not have to explain any more. The woman sees all my ancestors, right to the dawn of time. She welcomes me. I have come to the right place. I am needed here, and my arrival was expected.

She takes me inside and tells me to wait because the sangoma will come to me in just a moment. She goes into a warmly glowing room at the back of the house, arched doorway halfway obscured by a screen of darkly varnished pine and white linen. She goes in, but doesn't come out again. Instead the sangoma emerges—a breathtakingly beautiful African woman, whose presence takes up the whole room. She's round, with rounded shoulders, a buxom and graceful woman with high cheekbones, clear, smooth skin, and kind, intelligent eyes. She radiates warmth and power. She has a crown of beads on top of her short hair. I can never remember the colors; they always shift in my mind.

She comes forward and asks me to come sit with her on a couch in the middle of the room. Or was it a bench? I can't remember. She sits with her back to the door, resting her elbow on top of the chair, and I sit facing her.

She says to me in a sonorous voice, "Tell me, daughter, why have you come?"

There were so many answers that I could have given her at that moment, aside from the obvious one.

But instead, I tell her simply, and I know it to be true, "I have no idea."

She glances down and laughs a little, "Mm-hmm," as if to say, "Yes, I expected you would say that, and it is the right answer. It shows your wisdom."

Looking at me kindly, she says, "You have come because I brought you here."

The Bone Woman

Now that I am deep in the Kalahari and I have not seen another soul for 200 kilometers, I think back to my childhood and that winding road to the Berg, sweet-smelling polyurethane seats, padkos, food for the road, packed by my grandmother—scones with cheese and margarine. The Indigo Girls playing, the windows slightly open, the grass rustling, the flat-topped trees and the snaking river. The Wind Tunnel, the howling wind. No lifetime rehearsal. Just now.

After crossing the portal, I traveled that road again to visit the sangoma in the Drakensberg. I'd traveled alone, hoping she'd have something to tell me, some medicine for a grief as big as the world. I wondered if it was the same road you took to

Bulwer in the Drakensberg, the day before you died.

I guess I thought maybe we would have traveled along there together sometime, and spoken about the journeys that took our parents to the places they ended up, and what became of us. My heart and your heart, with these golden strings tying them together, forever.

But Ma, she only said, "You've come because I called you here."

"My child, you are destined for the wasteland now. You must decide: Do you want to live, or do you want to die? In the wasteland, both are possible. You can sink beneath the sands, and the dust will swallow you, bleach your bones. But, Ayla, I believe you want to live. If so, you will have to learn who you are without this man, your brother. You and he are not the same creature, but you do share some mysterious origin, which is up to you to decipher."

"Go out, go into the desert," she told me. "Gather yourself the sets of bones for a leopard skeleton and a jackal skeleton. Pick through the desert, through dry riverbeds and mounds of sand. Abandoned dens of meerkats. Don't get gored by a warthog. You'll get thorns in your hands; your hair will turn to straw. Your lips will be chapped. You will be parched because there's not enough water. Your shoes will wear out. Your nails will crack. Your fingers will bleed. Your skin will burn in the sun. The parting in your hair will flake. Eventually, you'll wear big glasses and a cloth around your mouth. You'll find a hat, boots. Something in you will become wild, feral, out there as you hunt for bones."

So I left my life behind, and I went into the Kalahari looking for bones. Looking for the immutable lifeforce of the jackal and the leopard, that which can't be killed, even by burning. Wherever there was a leopard bone, there was always a jackal bone. The bone discoveries were far apart, days apart. Sometimes I went for weeks without finding anything. How long had I been out here gathering bones? Months, years maybe. It was hard to tell, once I had stepped out of linear time.

"One day, you will have complete skeletons for both the jackal and the leopard," Ma told me. "Sit with them under the cold moon, watch the clouds go across the sky, watch night turn to morning, cracked mountains, long road winding across to your left, all the way to the west, you on top of the hill. If you sit for long enough, you will start to sing. The animals will start to be fleshed out and then they will begin to breathe. They will leap up and run away together, toward the horizon, becoming larger and larger and larger and larger in size until they're giants. Giants larger than the mountains, the earth rumbling under their feet."

I watch as the two furred behemoths become filmy and transparent, filled with liquid stars. As they lope toward the sea, the landscape scrunches up like a tablecloth under their paws, great folds forming in the strata, making the mountains that are the spine of the world. The huge pawprints they leave behind fill with water and become the oceans.

They begin to gallop, and then they leap into the sky, where they merge with the purple cosmos and ring out as constellations, leopard and jackal.

When they have returned to the stars, I am no longer there; there is no woman singing. But there is song, there are the red sands of the Kalahari, and there is the night.

To explore another past relationship, turn left for room 14 (page 179). To leave your old self behind, turn right for room 6 (page 45). To do both at once, proceed straight ahead to room 10.

Transmigration

DAVID PIERRE
TRANSLATED BY LAURA BAILO

Release

My first wish after Dr. Vigil discharged me from the hospital was to visit Huertahernando again.

It took me a full month to recover from the surgery. After that, it took me two months to rehabilitate my motor functions, which had been asleep for so many years without even dreaming about a resurrection. During those three months, Agén—one of the nurses from Vigil's team—became my inescapable shadow. The medical team in charge of me had been keeping an eye on my sudden migraine episodes: some kind of intermittent headache that had been visiting me every single day. Headaches were something I'd only suffered on a handful of occasions in my previous body, and that puzzled them. But it didn't worry me, even if it meant the body was rejecting my brain. I could move. I was able to walk again, like when I was a little girl. I needed fresh air, pure air. I needed to leave the disinfected stench of that insipid center of sickness, healing, and death.

At least for a little while.

Both Agén and the rest of the doctor's subordinates—whom I didn't even get to meet—thought that my petition to travel to a middle-of-nowhere village on a mountain more than 500 kilometers away was crazy, something completely and absolutely insane. Despite that, Dr. Vigil and her team of legal counselors couldn't deny their first brain transplant any inclination that got into their new—and at the same time, old—head.

Huertahernando was a quaint little village lost in Guadalajara. In it, you felt as if even the air you breathed was in a holding pattern, removed from the flow of time. At the same time, the fifty or sixty people that inhabited the village seemed lost in a sweet and unmovable routine that ended up defining them almost like character stereotypes. There was Hugo, for example, the hunter; Alberto, the collector of B movies; Concepción and Bernarda, who together were the village's number one source of news and gossip; or María.

Just María.

One summer, when I was fourteen years old, I spent two weeks there thanks to one of those coincidences that fate arranges here and there before they fade away. Felicia, my classmate in high school and loyal friend during recess hours, offered to let me evade my reality for a few days. The only thing I could do was accept, moved as I was by the curiosity of the moment. At that time, Huertahernando's population was probably around sixty or seventy people. I couldn't help but ask myself if ten years later those houses of unmoving stone, the enormous fountain dedicated to Carlos the Third, and the ruins of the lambing shed would still be standing.

Felicia wasn't the best friend one could have, but it took me a few years to notice that. The girl was tall and walked very straight, forced, almost as if she had a stick up her ass. Her skin was white like clouds on a clear day, and her heart seemed to beat with the rhythm of a guitar on one of those nights when horror stories are told. Felicia always made an effort to show off that she was superior to me, mainly in terms of the relative intelligence that defined us both on the clearest days, of which there weren't many.

It was on that first visit to Huertahernando that I felt some kind of revelation. Or rather, I felt it when I met María. She was the only one of the young people in the village who decided to accompany Felicia and me while we wandered, and I discovered the almost-holy places that had built the summers of my non-best friend's childhood and teenage years during her first fifteen years on this earth. María didn't mind that I—in a relatively advanced stage of my illness—moved around in a wheelchair through the irregular terrain of La Huerta. She even joined me and pushed on more than one occasion when Felicia decided to leave me alone, sitting on the filthy sofa in her Aunt Concepción's house. During those late hours, I tried with difficulty to tune into nearby TV stations, but without success. Except of course for when María was with me. During those times, we turned off the idiot box and talked about poetry we didn't understand or about books we liked to read then, which now we can't even remember.

During our stay of fourteen or fifteen days in Huertahernando, Felicia started to abandon me more and more because she liked her sunny friendships or her bicycle routes to Ribarredonda or Buenafuente better than dragging a half-dead girl in a wheelchair through the whole village while old women asked to whom I belonged. María soon took Felicia's place in an almost definite way, and I must confess that right then, in that environment of being far away and breathing real oxygen, I preferred her company over anything else.

On our first walk without my non-best friend, María chose to show me the façade of the Purísima Concepción church, which by the way, didn't honor Felicia's aunt at all. The baroque sanctuary had a small iron gate, cold granite walls, and an entrance to the municipal cemetery. On it, we could read several hateful messages sprayed with red or silver paint that, in subtle use of rhetoric, drew a comparison between religion and phallic elements. Other sentences simply extolled science, the evolution that its cult espoused, or the relevance that it had in an everyday sense.

The Purísima Concepción had been closed for a few years already because in Huertahernando, the Catholic's belief had started sinking almost to a point where it had disappeared, the same as was happening in the rest of the peninsula. The multiple cases of corruption, rape, and murder that would make even the Pope blush—he raped his sister's granddaughter, remember—had made the church lose all its credibility in less than half a decade. Despite that, contemplating a building like that always made me feel stunned. The biggest building in the whole of La Huerta was an old sign of ecclesiastic power that stood before us defiant, explosive, and deprived of feelings. María looked splendid with the sunlight bouncing off the façade of the old sanctuary and then onto her tanned skin, and on her curls turned orange because of the sun or because of some genetics in her family tree that I would never get to know.

"Do you live here?" I dared to ask from my jail with wheels.

"Yes," she said. "At least in the summer."

"Why's that?" I insisted. I wanted to know more.

"I spend the school year away, in the capital." She smiled. "There's not much to do around here."

"Despite that, the village is not so bad," I said, returning her smile with a crooked one of my own.

After dinner that same night, María took me to the fields at the end of the village, which were immersed in a deep darkness that was only broken by the permanent shine of the stars in the sky. There were several allotments there, the private fields where villagers sowed barley, oats, or wheat. But that night, the allotments were only black earth blanketed with little stars—some high, some fallen—that stood before us both and La Huerta.

María helped me get out of the chair and laid me down on the ground next to her. I felt the cold on my upper body. The other half was asleep already. Our nervous breaths mixed, becoming two deep rivers with different courses. She touched my left hand with the points of her fingers and then played with the hair on my arms while she drew spirals with her fingers. And my breath stuttered. She then caressed my legs with hers through our jeans and I blushed time and time again without showing it.

And then, she kissed me. She put her hands on my cheeks and turned my head, guiding my mouth to hers like in an earthquake. She made me discover her and discover myself and wish for more of that bitter sweetness. I wanted to grab her too. I tried to raise my hands toward her face, and I made it. And between tremors of ineptitude, she made me dream.

Then she left. And I left.

Dr. Vigil had insisted on Agén coming with me on my return to Huertahernando. None of the specialists who looked at my recovery with a magnifying glass trusted that a just-transplanted human brain wouldn't run away by train, by bus, by plane, or by any of the possible combinations that they had counted with those means of transport. It looked like those masterminds lived in fear, as if they were waiting for their small and fragile experiment—which by the way, just scraped by the legal limits—could break down at any moment.

I started collecting my things from room 35, the room in Astorga Hospital that had pretended to be my home for so many months. I put my new clothes, which the medical team had bought for me just so I could display my new body, in a suitcase and for the first time. Then I looked at myself in the bathroom mirror. I observed myself from head to toe. I'd been avoiding reflections in all their manifestations, but if I were going back to Huertahernando now, if I managed to see María, I wanted to be sure of myself and my new me.

And that's how I met myself. The anonymous donor's body was that of a young woman, much younger than I'd have expected, around twenty or twenty-two years old. Had I just gotten two, three, or four years younger? I asked myself where her brain would be now. My new skin was brown, shiny. The black curls of my hair fell toward my shoulders even though I was wearing a ponytail. The hair's density disguised in part the scar on my head. Thin lips, green eyes. That entire body seemed like the opposite of my past life, the human wreck of milky skin in which I'd become atrophied, the state that all those doctors could only cure by introducing me into a new shell. I couldn't avoid asking myself where my old body would be now. Maybe abandoned, lost in a bin for organic material, or buried in some kind of meat cemetery.

Agén moved from being my shadow-nurse to being my driver. For the first time, I saw him wearing street clothes, with a black T-shirt and jeans, his blond hair to the side in a cowlick. He was as bland as any person could be. He was waiting for me outside, looking disinterested. He didn't seem happy with having to take me to my destination. When he saw me come out, he tried to take my suitcase, but I insisted on carrying it myself.

We walked silently down the stairs toward the car. Agén was a man of few words. I noticed he walked with his splayfoot curved inward, and then I saw that he was carrying a white case with a blue cross. I looked at him relentlessly until he deigned to speak to me.

"Medicines. Just in case," he said as matter-of-fact as ever.

"I've told you a million times I don't want drugs."

He didn't answer. Both Dr. Vigil and he were sick of my opposition to obeying their medical recommendations to a T. Agén and Vigil were in charge of reminding me time and time again that my surgery had been a long and difficult process and that I must recover well for the sake of the future of humanity.

The future of humanity, of course.

Agén and I went into the car. It was a hybrid, one of those really quiet ones. And they say dogs look like their owners. What about cars?

"What is that village we're going to called?" Agén asked while he turned on the satnav.

"Huertahernando," I said, savoring every syllable as it passed my lips.

Return

I feared that my return to Huertahernando would turn into a second revelation, one of those inverted revelations that make you discover that your memories have glorified past realities too much. On coming back, I almost felt like the exact opposite, that my memories hadn't been an exaggeration, that they were reality instead of a dream. The green and brown of the mountains that surrounded La Huerta started getting into my brain, and with them the elm trees, the boxwoods, and the junipers, the holm oaks, the pines, and the savines. And the leafless bushes stripped by the cold and wind. And all of that vegetation that stood before me now, glorious and more alive after ten years, after a paused life, it welcomed me on the regular rhythm of a breeze, the sort that presages a sudden start to summer.

The handful of old houses, the church, the cemetery, and the fields of stones and wheat seemed to be more vivid this time, more illuminated by the air that was breathed in that separate world that only rural landscapes know how to invent, as if they were fictional entities with a giant brush. Vacant lots without owners, natural locations, the valleys of the Ablanquejo river surrounding La Huerta. And around it, the roar of hidden roe deer and the caw of rooks, which together accompany the music of a stirred land that looks barred but is full of hidden secrets.

"How's your head?" Agén asked, pulling me from my astonishment. He always talked very softly, as if he was letting out whispers of insecurity.

"Well, quite well," I said. At that moment, I noticed my voice was different.

"Has it bothered you during the trip?" he asked.

"Not much." I paused. "Don't worry."

"I have some pills here that—"

"No. I don't want to take anything," I said abruptly. Agén answered with a soft sigh.

Aunt Concepción had died of old age while she slept some years ago. Or so they said in the village. She was almost one hundred when one day, Bernarda knocked on her door, as she used to do every day, and found that her old partner of morning adventures wouldn't answer. She talked to some of the neighbors, and they entered Aunt Concepción's home together. They had found Conchi on her bed, her wrinkles rigid and white, her eyes closed, and her consciousness immersed in some kind of peaceful dream. She wasn't breathing.

These days, Conchi's house served as a rental residence for the few lost travelers who chose to let their feet rest in Huertahernando. Someone named Felicia was in charge of the formalities of renting, or so Agén told me after searching for a place to stay on the Internet and finding Villa Concepción as the only option. It only took a call for my old non-best friend, who didn't even visit the village in the summer anymore, to accept our stay without hesitating for an instant. She explained to us over email that we would find the keys buried in a pot in the entryway and then told us the details of the house's interior, which I already knew. She also thanked us for paying the rent in advance.

Aunt Concepción's house was situated in the middle of the village, and it was one of the few houses in La Huerta that had been remodeled. The house had two floors, a huge dining room, two bathrooms, an American kitchen downstairs, and four bedrooms upstairs. Preserved cow legs had been Aunt Concepción's obsession in life, and Felicia seemed to have respected it since four of them were still hanging from the wall in the living room. Would all four have belonged to the same cow?

The house had everything Agén and I could need: water, electricity, clean sheets, dishes, and even a huge window in the first-floor hallway where lost bats got in during the night time and time again. Felicia and I had received some scares. We both felt some kind of phobia about flying mammals. Imagine the situation.

"Call me Nahir," I told Agén while I hung my clothes in the wardrobe. "And don't follow me everywhere; I can see your intentions."

"Nahir?" he asked.

"It's my middle name. I never use it, but they know me here."

"It's not as if they were going to recognize you…" he said. After a second, he pulled a face in regret.

"Just call me Nahir."

"Okay." He paused. "About me not following you…"

"Come on, Agén. This place is tiny," I said, and then I looked into his blue eyes with my new ones. "Please."

"Okay…" he said at last. "It's not as if I can make you do anything."

"Exactly," I said with a sarcastic tone.

Agén answered once more with a sigh and then walked up the stairs toward the room in the upper floor he had chosen as his bedroom. I amused myself by not telling him that room was where the now-dead Aunt Concepción had slept all her life.

My headache wouldn't stop getting worse, so I decided to stretch my legs through the village, to again meet its narrow passageways that could only be walked one way, to see once more the pleasant old ladies who looked at me so many times as if I were an alien moving around in its spaceship. Maybe this time I was an alien after all, at least in my new body.

On leaving Villa Concepción, I walked into a group of four little girls who were running down the street in a stampede. Their steps crunched in the echo of unmoving walls and created a feeling of amplitude that seemed to extend throughout the whole of the small village. For an instant, I imagined an alternate reality in which I'd been Felicia, the Felicia who enjoyed each and every childhood summer in Huertahernando. Afterward, I imagined her in a wheelchair.

When I came back to myself, the four little girls had disappeared from sight, and the place had sunk into complete silence.

It took me just two minutes to reach the main square. Its structure was still intact: that imposing fountain anchored to a monolith with its taps posed in a cross shape in the middle. Surrounding it, the comfortable homes of the neighbors, every other one with a plaque written in gothic characters to commemorate one act of honor or another for the village. I sat down for a few minutes on a stone bench, looked toward nothing, and thought about myself. Who was I now that I only had a small part of my old self? Was I still me, or had I turned into the anonymous donor? What in the devil would have been her name? She didn't have a name, and I had two. What a waste.

I spent a while sitting in the main square. In that instant, the silence felt like the only resident of La Huerta. Seeing the absence of activity in that place, I decided on a change of scenery. I made my way to the pelota court where ten years before Marta and Amelia—the village twins with black and curly hair—trained with so much persistence and effort. Apparently, their dream was to become professional tennis players, and that was the only way they had to practice.

I sat down on a stone bench, and I noticed that a girl who was more or less as old as my new body was spending her time throwing a ball against the wall and then sending it back with insistent hits. She was sweating. Her hair, like curly carrots fighting against the midday sun, reminded me of someone.

Then the ball bounced too far, and the girl went to collect it. It landed close to my new feet. And I recognized her, the tanned skin covered in sweat from the effort and the summer.

I hadn't remembered the way she walked until I saw her again.

"Good afternoon," she said. "And sorry."

I didn't know what to answer.

"Are you all right?" she asked then.

"Yes!" I woke up. "I'm sorry. I'm Nahir."

"My name's María," she said.

"Do you…live here?" I asked, in a show of slyness.

"Yes," she said with her head down. "I'm in charge of the village's bar."

"Oh. Interesting." Discomfort burned inside me. "And… you take care of it from here?"

"No!" She smiled. "Today's Monday. We close on Mondays, you know…It's our weekly day off."

"Of course," I said, having fewer words at my disposal each time.

"Well, I won't bother you anymore," she said, then smiled again. "Pleased to meet you, Nahir."

And I'm pleased to meet you again.

"Wait!" I said in an outburst of impulsiveness.

"Yes?"

"I just got here, and I don't know the village," I lied.

"It's not like there's a lot to see…I'm sure you and your boyfriend can take a look while walking around."

"What? My boyfriend?"

"That guy you arrived with," she said, winking. "We don't miss anything around here."

"Oh! That's Agén. He's…He's my cousin," I lied again.

Neither of us said anything.

"I've just noticed you look familiar, I must know you from somewhere," said María suddenly. My heart lurched.

"I think you're mistaken…"

"I can't remember where from…That's infuriating," she said. "It's not actually you…Don't get me wrong; it's more something like your expression, the way you move your eyes.

Let's take a walk, see if I remember," she added.

My reunion with María turned into a succession of cold sweats and soft trembling, which I managed to stabilize as well as I could. Once I had calmed down and was walking again next to María through Huertahernando, I realized that my headache had gotten worse, settling on the right side of my skull. Was the anonymous donor trying to escape; did she want to throw me out? It was intense, persistent, and it made my new left eye beat while immersing it in some kind of strange blindness. I moved my hand toward my forehead in an effort to make the pain stop. It didn't work.

Was the body rejecting my brain? Maybe the nerves of seeing María again? The lack of treatment? I was just rapt by her presence and tried to give the best performance of my life (of both lives).

María showed me the most interesting places in Huertahernando during a walk that seemed too long for me. My migraine kept growing; a dense fog was settling inside my head, in my new eyes and in my being. The irony of a long-awaited moment being broken by my new illness.

During the walk, I thought we passed by Aunt Lisa's house, a traditional construction of stone close to the square that was quite deteriorated by the passage of time. Then she showed me her bar, El Corzo, which was closed, and the fountain of Carlos the Third. We also walked by the bricked-up church, and it looked to me as if it'd been painted.

Luckily, I already knew all those places. My migraine wouldn't stop getting worse, and I couldn't pay the attention María's enthusiastic explanations deserved. I thought I heard her talking about the strategic importance of La Huerta during the war, about her honorable people and the hunting culture.

We were sitting on a bench in the main square when I couldn't help but raise my open hands to my burning forehead. My surroundings were transforming in a single unit of unbreathable air. I feared the worst.

"Are you feeling all right?" María, who'd already seemed worried during the tour, asked.

"Yes…" I struggled to say.

"Doesn't look like you do," she answered.

"It's…I think it's a migraine. It happens sometimes." I lied.

"Ugh, maybe you should lie down. I once met a kid who had migraines. He spent days stuck in his room when he got one."

"Yes, I'd better go," I said. Then I got up, with my hands still on my forehead.

"Where are you staying?"

"In…Villa Concepción," I said in a weary voice.

"Poor Aunt Conchi…" she said, looking to the sky. "What if I call on you later and we continue our walk?" María asked in another abrupt change of topic. "I still have a place left to show you."

"Yeah…Come later. Give me a few hours," I said.

"Feel better, Nahir," María said, her lips anchored in a smile while I got lost in the emptiness on the square and rested my hand on one of its rusty fountains.

Some kind of clumsy impulse helped me move forward.

Suddenly, something like a white cloth covered my eyes and wouldn't let me see, the same thing that happens to old dogs. I made my hands into fists and moved them, following instinct to regain my eyesight, trying to mend the reality that surrounded me. I wondered whether it might have been better to accept the drugs Agén had offered me.

The migraine seemed to take over my new body completely. I found myself immersed in a strange world of unreality and simplicity that was defined by the natural grandeur that surrounded the small village of Huertahernando. Around me, there were no longer houses of cold stone, only enormous lakes and forest with trunks the black color of coal. Water ran around the trees sunk in the river, cobalt blue and jade green leaves, like my new eyes. On my face, I felt the frozen mist of a mountain winter.

Something was invading that summer; something was invading my resurrection summer.

I raised my hands, stricken. They were no longer my hands but the hooves of a deer. I had to accept a new change of body. On instinct, I situated myself on four legs, the four legs of a hunched mammal with a brown coat, soft and unreachable. Then my hooves lifted up victoriously, grew, and stomped in a sign of distress. That transformation hurt. My whole body had turned into an enormous deer who just wanted to scream. *Help.* I wanted to ask for help, but I was only able to let out choked bellows, useless sounds of a beast about to be hunted.

Faced with no logical explanation for the sudden mutation, I started running. Now my four new legs reached a dizzying speed moving up a slope. I ran toward a giant mountain where waterfalls of beautiful shining water seemed to wink at me on their way down. When I reached the top, I stopped to drink from that potion so pure and crystal clear. The water was tasty, its impeccable sweetness moving down my body, burning with pure pleasure. I believed in that moment that I turned into the water and air of that place, and I let myself be wrapped in a cutting breeze and jumped into the river I'd drunk from before, turning into water flowing toward a better life.

I came down and back up that waterfall in defiance; then the water expelled me outward. I emptied the river and the lakes, and I watered with my essence all the green vegetation that covered La Huerta and its people in sweetness. I turned into the trees of the black forest, which in less than a second seemed about to be pollinated. I then let myself be dragged by the wind, I gave myself to the pollen of the place, and I turned into a breeze of cold shivers—soft, not atrophied. It didn't seem to be summer anymore, more like spring or autumn, or a strange and harmonious mix of seasons in the diaspora.

After being air, I met a rook who ascended in a beautiful spiral toward the starred sky of Huertahernando. I turned into her too. I learned to fly, and with her feathers, I made myself a disguise that greeted even the most incredulous of the animals who lived in the now—or the before—forest which had taken the place of the lost-in-time village.

Almost without knowing, I started my way down toward Villa Concepción. Night had begun to fall as fast as always, and I saw myself transformed into a coal-black bat that dared enter through the huge hallway window, breaking the ancient stained glass into a thousand pieces. That window was the only sign— along with the preserved cow legs—of tradition that was left in the huge house.

I'd been a deer, then water, then a tree and its essence. I'd been air, a rook, and a bat, and living breath when waking up in a past, future, or alternative world where La Huerta was no longer, but a world of almost supernatural beauty.

And the migraine, at last, was disappearing.

Revelation

I woke up on the upper floor hallway of Villa Concepción. Agén wasn't home. He'd have gone out looking for me, or maybe he'd decided to take a walk through the village at last. When I opened my eyes and my consciousness, I was surprised by the cold that ran over my whole body. I was naked. I must have lost my clothes in that kind of strange quarrel in confrontation—or union—with nature. I myself would have sworn it was a dream, a hallucination, or the domination of a perturbed mind over a quiet conscience.

I was dirty, muddy, with my face full of smudges from moved earth. My nails were black, my heart beating with the rhythm of a horror song. I was covered in scratches and superficial injuries, but my head was completely clear. I got up from the floor full of aches and pains.

"Shit," I said to no one's ears. "What the hell happened?"

I made my way to the bathroom and took a quick shower. Before that, I couldn't help but amaze myself looking over my new body as many times as I could wish for. I even desired myself for an instant, just before getting in the shower. Then the burning water cleared my depraved and egocentric ideas.

I almost had no time to react when, just as I was leaving the bathroom, I heard Villa Concepción's doorbell ringing to the delight of my new ears.

"Shit!" I said for a second time.

It was María.

I got dressed in the first clothes I found and came down to open the door to my new and old friend. She was astonishing that night, almost like my teenage memory. She was wearing long, torn trousers and a white T-shirt that showed her sun-tanned shoulders.

"Nahir! I thought you weren't in," she said. "Are you feeling better?"

"Yes!" I said, in a kind of childish claim.

"Have you had dinner already?" she wanted to know.

"Something like that" I answered, remembering the pollen.

"Then, should we keep walking?" María asked.

"Of course."

It was night. The summer wind picked up frozen against our faces, and I felt my new lips start to crack, red like my internal hunger. I couldn't stop thinking about the strange trip I'd experienced hours before, so once again lost in my own imagination, I followed María wherever she and her games wanted to take me.

This time, as I could easily sense, María took me to the vacant lots, to the dark allotments where years before she herself had given me my first kiss.

For the first time in my life, I felt complete. No pain, no worlds to reach. I had a functional, healthy, body, a friend that didn't have to push my chair, and a beautiful place lost under a blanket of stars. I was beautiful too. I couldn't even remember all the times I'd dreamed about that.

"I like coming here for a walk," said María when we got to the allotments. She put a lock of hair behind her ear, then looked me in the eyes.

"Do you bring many people here?" I asked, cunningly. I looked away for a second, then forced myself to be brave.

"Yes. I like sharing this experience," she said pointing to the illuminated sky.

"It looks as if the stars could fall on top of us at any given moment."

We spent some time in silence. Watching the stars, then looking at each other, then touching our hands together shyly. But neither of us were shy, actually.

María looked thoughtful. She caressed my arms firmly and delicately at the same time, and I closed my eyes by pure instinct. It was the first time I'd felt a touch so real, so part of me.

"It still infuriates me that I can't remember why you look familiar," she said in a rebuke, her hand on her chin, the other on my leg.

"Maybe we knew each other in another life," I said, then instantly regretted it.

"Do you believe in those things?"

She then put both of her hands on my legs and went over them slowly.

"I don't believe in anything. I just doubt."

"I think you know more than you say."

For the first time, my hands were the ones that reached a body, a skin, the pleasure keeper that was María. Too fast, by the way, because I couldn't hold myself back nor my desire.

"Does it matter?" I asked, before throwing myself into her arms in a voracious kiss.

I was hungry. I wanted to recover the time that I hadn't even been allowed to miss. I kissed María with a fury, and I took off her white shirt. We were no longer children.

In that moment, while we were joined together as a single being, it seemed to me as if the allotments disappeared, just as the village had vanished before my eyes hours before. Now there was light in them and miniature mountains and huge deer who drank the emerging water. María didn't open her eyes at any moment. I couldn't have closed mine even if I'd wanted to. Besides, the stars in the sky seemed to be getting closer to us, a blanket of compression closing in on us. The stars began to fall, sowing chaos over that new world while María and I merged in an incandescent ray of light.

The light became plasma, and our bodies just a star in the middle of nowhere. I saw then the inside of María, and finally understood why I had never been able to get her out of my head. She and the stars and the fallen fire were the same. A unique being vinculated to creation, not only to the creation of Earth but of hundreds, thousands of realities and places that passed my sight in a few seconds. Was the transplant a trap to meet María? No, Vigil and Agén didn't know anything. They wouldn't have understood it anyway.

Then both of us, combined in a celestial body, traveled to distant galaxies. We met water people, humanoid deer, and a giant village of talking bats, which paired with tree roots to create a new hybrid race, never before seen in the universe.

All of this happened within the space of a few moments, at least in the real world. My sight seemed to have improved thanks to the improvised illumination. I got dressed, helped María do the same, and lay down on the ground. The cold also ran over my legs this time.

"You know?" I started saying slowly. "I have two names. Nahir is my middle name." From the frozen ground I broke the ice of the moment.

"And what's your first name?" María wanted to know. But she already knew it.

"Paula. I'm Paula," I said, looking into her eyes and then to the stars that came down with no stop from the sky to the nocturnal forest, burning everything except us.

"What did you say?" she asked.

A smile was more than enough answer, alive, growing, lit up as it was by the fire that surrounded us.

If you long for a change in your life, turn right for room 5 (page 39). Or if you need more than one, proceed straight ahead to room 11.

MIRROR MAZE

11

A Bottle of Jinn

CLIFF JONES JR.

Spirits

"SORRY, IT'S **9:01**."

"Yeah? And what's that supposed to mean?"

"We're closed."

"*Closed?*" The tipsy-looking woman scowled and furrowed her brow, not believing what she'd heard. "The hell you are. Ring me up!"

Penny lightly closed her eyes and summoned the patience to explain once again: "It is unlawful in the state of Texas to sell liquor after 9:00 p.m."

"Naw, that's bull crap. Let me talk to your manager." She craned her neck to look around the store, making a big show of it.

"I'm the manager on duty, ma'am. If you visit one of the bars down the street, they'll be able to sell until 2:00 a.m."

The woman's mouth fell open in horror. "*Ma'am?!*" For a moment, she looked genuinely hurt. But then her angry scowl returned, and she headed for the door in a huff, leaving her birthday cake vodka on the counter. "See if I ever come back here!"

Penny exhaled a weary sigh of relief. Only one straggler

to deal with tonight. Not bad. Familiar Spirits had apparently lost a customer, but they'd survive. Penny doubted the woman would actually keep her promise to stay away anyhow. Drunks had conveniently short memories.

As Penny was preparing to lock up and exit through the back, an intriguing bluish glint caught her eye. On the floor of the supply closet near the back door, a cobalt liquor bottle stood mixed in among the cleaners. Its olive green label read in ornate, faux-Arabic lettering: "Damavand Persian Gin."

Persian? Penny racked her brain trying to recall if she'd ever seen a bottle like that before. She was pretty sure she'd remember Persian gin. There was *Indian* gin, sure, but they used to be under British rule, so Indian gin made sense. Persia was… Iran? Was liquor even allowed there?

In any case, she was certain there was no Damavand gin in the inventory. And there wasn't much else on the label to identify it, just "Triclave Bottling Company" and "750 mL." Not even a health warning. This bottle must have been sitting in the supply closet for years, since long before Penny was hired. Some former employee had probably stashed it there, preparing to move it out the back door when no one was around. It was an old trick, and it usually worked. Penny had done it herself a few times—in her younger, more reckless years.

That is to say, before she met Felix. She'd changed for him. And then he'd left her.

If the bottle wasn't in the inventory, she reasoned, then it wasn't actually the property of Familiar Spirits, not technically. And in that case, she wasn't technically stealing it. It was more like a lost-and-found item. But there might be a hidden security camera somewhere that didn't agree with her logic, so Penny gathered up a few empty—or at least *nearly* empty—bottles of cleaner to make the liquor less obvious. Behind the store, she tossed the cleaners into the dumpster and drove off with her prize.

Rain

By the time Penny pulled up to her lonely studio apartment, it had begun to rain. Across the eastern sky, delicate tendrils of lightning wove their fiery webs. The entire way home, Penny had resisted the urge to crack open that mystery bottle and have a sip. Once the engine was off and there was no "open container" law to worry about, she gave in to temptation.

It was, without qualification, the best thing Penny had ever tasted in all her twenty-three years on the planet. And she didn't even think she *liked* gin! She was more of a bourbon drinker—though her professed favorite was mezcal, a white lie she'd told her Uncle Manny while bonding over a bottle.

But this…This was something else entirely. The spirit was infused with a fresh herbal bite: juniper, of course, but also parsley, basil, maybe a little mint? This was balanced with a fruity sweetness: figs, dates, apricots…And definitely some spices like coriander and cardamom. And was that *rose*? All of it swirled together into an icy, smokeless fire that seemed to light Penny up from the inside.

The first tentative sip turned into a swig, and then that turned into a guzzle. By the time Penny pulled the bottle away from her lips, she'd already downed a good third of it—far too much for an empty stomach. Now suddenly tipsy, she got out of her car and stumbled through the pouring rain to the front steps of her apartment. Had there been any neighbors watching—and there were a couple, actually—they would have assumed she'd driven home drunk—as in fact they did. From behind their respective mini-blinds, they clicked their tongues in disapproval.

As Penny fumbled with her keys, she failed to notice a large, black dog creeping up behind her in the rain. It waited expectantly for the door to open, and then as soon as there was a suitable gap, it pushed past an already unsteady Penny and shook itself vigorously, sprinkling the room with dog-scented rainwater. Penny tried to shield her face from the spray but slipped on the tile as she turned and fell heavily, like a sack of drunk potatoes.

What followed might have been a dream, or it might have been something else entirely:

Penny found herself alone in darkness, walking swiftly toward the center of an immense stone enclosure. The darkness was deep, but not total. All along the distant cavern walls rose hundreds, perhaps thousands, of glowing lavender threads. Like frozen lightning or the ghosts of some primeval forest, they towered high into the air, converging to reveal the conical shape of the enclosure.

The ground was an uneven expanse of black basalt dotted with countless shallow puddles. Each of these reflected a small portion of the luminous threads above. As Penny stepped and splashed and padded in her bare feet—bare everything, truth be told—she began to see a a hazy white figure take shape ahead of her. The closer she got, the bigger it seemed, until at last she was staring up at a pale giant many times her size. He was as bare as Penny, she couldn't help but notice. Or he would have been, except practically every inch of him was covered in shaggy white fur.

The giant glanced down at Penny as she approached, but he seemed more interested in staring at the lavender threads. But actually…he wasn't staring so much as *watching* them. Now that Penny was standing still, she could see the threads were actually shifting and branching and swaying—just very, *very* slowly. She watched them dance awhile before stumbling back onto her sense of time.

Penny looked down at the giant's feet. Around each ankle was a heavy shackle connected to a chain, one of silver and the other of gold. The ends of both, she noticed, were not bolted to the cavern floor but sunk down into the rock. "Why are you chained up like that?" she asked.

The giant looked down and smiled. "Oh, the chains aren't for me. They're for the dragons." As if that were all the explanation needed.

"I'm sorry," Penny went on, "but *what* dragons?"

"The ones inside me. The only dragons I'm able to chain."

This made a kind of sense, but Penny wasn't satisfied. "So there are dragons living inside you?"

"Yes. Three of them. They've been there since I was born."

"But how could you know that if you can't actually…you know, *see* them?"

"I know them by their faces. The faces they have me wear: Fear, Sorrow, and Rage."

Just then, the silver chain began to rattle. It shook and clattered ever more violently until it actually rose up off the ground.

The giant looked down slowly, his expression unchanging. "Hm," he grunted. "Now what do you think that means?"

Wind

When Penny awoke, there was no dog in her apartment. There was, however, a very large man with copper skin, curly black hair, and a tidy little beard.

"What the—" Penny started. "Who the hell are you?!" The intruder was clad all in gray, in a flowing sort of a robe, like a wizard or something. "Are you a wizard or something?" Penny asked with all the eloquence she could muster through several ounces of gin and a throbbing headache.

"My name is Aeshma," replied the man. "I have come here to—"

"Your name is *Asthma?*"

"Aeshma. I—"

"Ozma?"

"Aesh—"

"Ash! Okay, sorry about that," Penny said with relief. "I'll remember cuz my boyfriend has a cartoon name too. Felix. You know…the cat?"

Ash made no reply for a moment and then continued: "I've come here because I owe you a favor."

Penny wrinkled her forehead. "How's that? I don't believe we've met, sir…Are you a customer? Familiar Spirits?"

"Yes, that's right," said the man. "Familiar spirit. I'll grant you *one* favor. Take a moment to think it over. Whatever you wish, I'll do my best to make it happen."

Penny stared hard at the stranger. Her brain was a black fog, as usual, but a few streams of light shone through. It made absolutely no sense, but somehow Penny believed the man might actually *be* a wizard…or an angel, or some otherworldly wraith with the power to work miracles. She dropped her gaze and muttered to herself: "Felix."

"Pardon?" asked Ash is his eerily formal way.

"My *ex*-boyfriend, actually," Penny continued. "Felix. I want…I want to talk to him. He changed his number, closed his Lookbook account…practically dropped off the face of the earth! Can you help me with that? Is that something you can work out?" Her tone started off somber but developed a mocking edge to it as she went on.

Ash grinned. "Done," he said simply. "Check your phone."

Warily, half dreading what she'd find, Penny pulled out her phone. It was sitting at the new call screen with an unfamiliar number already filled in, ready to go. She glanced at Ash uneasily and then started the call. Her heart rattled violently as she waited for an answer, ring after maddening ring. Then, at last: "What do you want, Penny?"

It was Felix. And he knew it was her! Well, of course; *she* wasn't unlisted. Her number hadn't changed since the break-up. She really should have thought this through a little better. "Hi, Felix," she said meekly.

There was an awkward silence, and then Felix sighed with audible annoyance. "'*Hi*'? Look, you've got to know this worries me. I told you not to call me. I even *changed my number.* What's so important that you had to track me down?"

"I just…*miss* you," said Penny.

Another pause. "Well, I miss you too…a little," Felix conceded. "But we've been over this. I've got my problems, and you've got yours, and they don't, you know…*mix* well."

"I know that's how it *was*, but—"

He cut her off: "You need somebody that can take care of you. And that's not me."

"I've actually grown a lot in the past few months," Penny pressed on. "I've been through some stuff. And I've been taking good care of myself. Really, just meet me for coffee or something. *Please?*"

Felix let out a groan, but he didn't say no. He seemed to be thinking it over as the wind outside howled like a banshee.

Absently, Penny added, "Actually, could you come over here? I can *make* some coffee."

"What? Why don't you want to—" Silence. Penny caught her mistake a moment too late. In a low, serious tone, Felix asked, "Have you been drinking?"

What could she do at this point? Even over the phone, the guy was a human lie detector. "*Well…*"

Felix hung up. And Penny knew he meant it. She stared at her phone in shock. That was it. It was really over. It would take a miracle to win Felix back now. *A miracle.* The thought reminded her of Ash. She looked all around the apartment, even outside, but the mysterious visitor had simply vanished.

Penny began to suspect she'd imagined the whole encounter. Maybe hitting her head on the tile had temporarily fried her circuits. Or maybe she was just cracking up. It was an unsettling possibility, but not half as frightening as what she really suspected: *She'd just met a demon.*

Storm

Penny numbly placed a couple of pale sausages into a skillet and started them cooking. With a slow, mechanical motion, she shifted them back and forth as they sizzled and browned. She told herself she'd feel better with some food in her belly, but she didn't really believe it. For that matter, she didn't particularly *want* to feel better. But there was a part of her that recognized she wasn't herself at the moment. That part of her still wanted to exist, despite everything. So she tried to be like a clock, just ticking away without a thought.

As she stared at the sausages cracking and splitting in the pan, she wished she could just have a cry and be done with it. But it never worked like that. First cold, then hot, then down, then back up again. She could already feel her detachment giving way to disgustingly predictable hostility. She had the idea of calling Felix back to tell him off, but she resisted, trying instead to refocus her anger on herself, where it belonged.

She caught sight of the bottle of gin on the counter and realized with a flood of relief that in this particular instance, alcohol was the answer. It would either make her feel better, or it would cause her some much-deserved pain. Either way, she'd be able to escape from the storm of the present moment and into a safer state of mind. Well, safe apart from the risk of alcohol poisoning.

Several ounces later, the room began to wobble and pulse and contract ever so slightly. After finishing sausage number one, Penny had a sudden urge to get up from the table—easier said than done—and step outside for some fresh air. As soon as she'd turned the knob, the door flew open, smacking her in the face. The rain had pretty well stopped now, but in its place was a brutal, howling wind.

Before she could get the door closed again, a little bird flew in and flitted around the room. The poor thing was probably disoriented from the storm. No, on second look, it wasn't a bird...

A bat! Kill it! Penny fumbled around the kitchen, first grabbing a spatula and then searching for something with a longer reach—like a broom, maybe. *Would a mop work?*

"What are you looking for?" inquired a wry, playful voice.

Penny turned in the direction of the voice and nearly fell backward with shock. A tall, solidly built woman stood there in her kitchenette—another spectral visitor clad in gray, just as Ash had been. Penny shuddered violently, made some incomprehensible noises, and threw the greasy spatula at the woman's face. All of this was automatic, as well as completely useless.

"Oh, sorry about that," Penny said, using her sleeve to wipe sausage grease from the woman's cheek. Then after an awkward silence, she asked, "So, um…who are you?"

"I am Hazel of the Hidden," said the woman in a half-bored tone, "an ancient tribe variously called angels, demons, elves, fae, jinn…But to you, forsooth, I am a *goddess*."

"Forsooth?"

"For reals." Here Hazel grinned, acknowledging the absurdity of the situation. She picked up the bottle of Damavand gin and gingerly screwed the cap back on. "You set me free from this prison, and for that I thank you." She gave a theatrical bow. "Okay, one wish. You know the drill."

"You can grant wishes?" Penny asked excitedly. "Like a genie?"

"I can grant *wish*," Hazel corrected. "One wish, and then I really must be on my way."

Penny thought this over—insofar as she could think *anything* over in her inebriated state. Her thoughts went something like this: *That's actually a genie, for reals! One wish? S'posed to be three! Wait…that guy Ash was like…the same kind of thing, I bet. That stupid phone call…Was that a wish?* "But he said 'favor'!" Penny yelled this last bit aloud.

Hazel smiled broadly, which might have been captivating or alluring if she weren't also busily chewing away at the last remaining sausage. As it was, Hazel's meaty grin reminded Penny of something predatory and vile—and *evil*. She longed for the comfort of Felix: his voice, his smell…his bed.

"I still want Felix," Penny said weakly. "I want him to come over so we can get back together and everything will be okay again."

Hazel raised an eyebrow. "That's *three* wishes," she replied with a condescending laugh. "The first is granted; the other two I'll leave up to you."

And with that, Hazel was gone. Again it felt as if Penny might have imagined the whole embarrassing encounter. But both sausages were gone, and she was still hungry. No, wait… She was going to be sick.

On her way to the bathroom, Penny stumbled back into that other place, the conical cavern lit only by lavender threads of slow lightning. And just as before, in the center of that cavern stood a pale giant covered in white fur. Only this time, there were no chains binding him to the volcanic rock floor.

Never one to waste time on formalities, Penny asked the giant simply, "What happened to your chains?"

He considered the question as if he hadn't thought of those shackles in ages, looking down to confirm they really were gone. "The two on my feet are missing, yes, but I still have one inside my skull. And that one's not so easily broken."

"Oh, you think so, huh?" Penny found herself unexpectedly angry at this giant. What was he doing just standing around in the dark when he was finally *free* for the first time in his life? Hadn't she done that? Where was his gratitude? "Look, what are you still doing here?" she asked. "What's so great about this—What do you call this place?"

"The Domeworld," replied the giant.

"Really?" Penny was unimpressed. "You consider this a 'world'? I've got news for you: This ain't nothing but a big old creepy circus tent! And you're just standing around all alone in here waiting…Waiting for what?"

The giant seemed to seriously consider this question. "I hadn't thought of myself as 'waiting' exactly, only living. Are you waiting for something? Is there something you need out of this life before it comes to an end?"

Penny was dumbstruck. "I—I don't know."

The pale giant looked back up at the light-threaded ceiling of his Domeworld. "You'd do well to answer that question soon. The end comes whether you're ready for it or not."

Flames

Some time later, Penny awoke from a heavy nap. Her left arm tingled from the awkward position she'd had it in, and the right side of her face bore a mark from the toilet seat, which she'd been using as a pillow. Once she'd regained a vague sense of where she was and how she got there, Penny flushed down the aromatic remains of one sausage and way too much Persian gin.

This was a new low.

She cleaned herself up, found her phone, and checked the time. *12:30?* Where was Felix? She'd made the wish, and Hazel had said it was granted. Without much thought, she started a text to the number Ash had given her: "Are you coming over?" She paused a moment, reconsidering, but then the thing just sent on its own. *Damn cheap phone!*

Two agonizing minutes later, there was a response: "Why would you think I'm coming over? I was almost asleep."

Penny scrambled for something meaningful and poetic to say, but all she came up with was, "I'm sorry," followed shortly thereafter by, "I love you."

"I love you too," replied Felix. "But that's not enough."

Not enough?! It was enough for *her!* It had been enough for Felix too until that Thanksgiving with his family. That hadn't gone well.

"So, Penny...Tell us about your parents. I hear your dad has an interest in...*Bigfoot?*" On this last word, Felix's mom couldn't keep the laughter out of her voice. She was obviously making fun.

"Ha, yeah..." Penny replied through clenched teeth.

"It's all a joke, right? The systematic extermination of this continent's oldest indigenous race?!"

Felix had already known that Penny had a few quirks and tics and occasionally suffered the odd meltdown. None of that had seemed to bother him, but his family had treated her like... Well, like she was autistic. It was true enough that she was on the spectrum—but *barely*. If Felix couldn't handle that, then *forget him!*

And just like that, Penny knew what she had to do. She grabbed the bottle of mystery gin from her table, pulled out the stopper with a satisfying pwot, and began to chug. It lit up her insides like liquid flame, but Penny was determined. When the bottle was empty, she slammed it down, ran to her front door, and violently threw it open. The night was calm now but still overcast. Penny stared up at the starless sky. "Well?!" she shouted into the void.

In answer, there came a bright lavender flash as lightning struck a small elm tree in the apartment courtyard. The sound was like a bomb going off. The tree caught fire instantly, casting a hazy glow in the fog. Penny imagined she could feel an electrical charge lingering in the air. "Come on!" she taunted.

Thunder rumbled in the distance, and the power blinked off, leaving only firelight. Penny's courage faltered as she made out a long, black shadow slithering toward her in the grass. She wanted to turn and run, but she didn't dare. Not when she was so close!

Just before it reached Penny's feet, the black serpent leapt into the air. For a moment, it seemed to balance on the tip of its tail. Then, it sprouted four spindly limbs and began to fatten and contort into the shape of a human. In an instant, there was no snake, only a very large man in a gray robe. This one had his hair tied back and wore an oddly rectangular beard.

"It seems you've been expecting me," laughed the apparition. "The name's Ozzie. What do you want this time?"

Penny gritted her teeth and gulped hard, fighting back

tears. "My ex-boyfriend Felix…I want to forget about him. Start over."

Ozzie stepped closer and leaned in as if to whisper. Then with a ragged grin, he said, "Easily done, gal."

Penny involuntarily shut her eyes and turned away as she felt the jinn's hot, putrid breath on her face. In a moment, she remembered nothing of the night's events but felt only a vague sense of loss, like she was waking from a dream that she knew was important somehow. A light rain began to fall, dousing the flames in the elm tree's branches.

Lightning

When Felix pulled up to Penny's apartment, he found her standing in the courtyard, completely soaked from the rain. She was down in the depths for sure. He'd said he wasn't going to take care of her anymore, but if he didn't, then *who would?* He did love her, after all, and Penny took care of him right back… in her way. She was a hot mess, but at least she meant well. And she never hurt anyone but herself.

Penny turned to look at Felix with that same sheepish grin she'd worn the first night they'd met. It really was uncanny, like they'd somehow become strangers again, with a chance to start fresh—or to avoid all that heartache and go their separate ways now, before it was too late.

Felix considered his dilemma, searching for some banal aphorism to tip the balance. "Life is short." "You only live once." Surely both couldn't be true. That would be too cruel. And life was short; he could see that much from his experience so far. The older he got, the faster the years went by.

So that decided it: After all this time—probably a third of his life—he'd only ever really loved one girl? Then why go off looking for somebody else? "Lightning never strikes twice." Sure, he and Penny had been miserable together. But they'd also been happy, right? They could be happy again.

"Penny, I—" Before Felix could finish this thought, the courtyard lit up with another brilliant flash of lightning. It was accompanied by an ear-splitting thunderclap, which Felix never heard. His body lay unmoving in the grass while his mind wandered off to another place:

Under a towering canopy of incandescent threads, Felix pressed on through the darkness. The further he walked, the more these lavender streams flickered and danced like the inside of a plasma ball. They were calling to him, but there would be time enough to hear their songs later. He had to take his place in the heart of the cavern before the rattling inside his head made him forget…

Forget what exactly?

No time for that now; he was nearly there. He had to walk. To keep walking. There was a reason for it somewhere, just… No matter. The only thing that mattered now was to keep on going. There was an engine deep inside the man. He could feel it now, humming away, turning his gears, pushing him toward…

The chains!

That was it; he'd forgotten the chains. And not only that. The *dragons*. How was that possible? Even now, they were hungrily nipping away at the backs of his eyes, breathing their sulfurous stench out through his nostrils. *His* nostrils. No, this was too much to endure. He'd have to give in sooner or later. Why prolong this misery? But—

Without the faintest notion of why, Felix fell to his knees onto the hard cavern floor. Of its own accord, his right arm plunged into the black stone below. In that particular spot, it gave way to his touch, becoming a thick, viscous liquid. Deep in the muck, he grasped what he'd been looking for.

It was a thick silver band on a silver chain. As Felix pulled the band up out of the stone, the dark liquid fell off cleanly and resolidified back into the ground. When the chain would give no more, he pulled the ring apart and clasped it around his right ankle. He then plunged his left arm into the stone and retrieved a second band of gold, which he clasped onto his left ankle.

At long last, Felix was alone. He let out a sigh of relief, finally allowing himself to absorb the breathtaking splendor of his surroundings. It had all been worth it in the end. Every bit of it. He gazed up at the myriad threads of his life, the countless streams of long-gone consciousness. Here they were again. Here they'd always been.

In a mirror to your right, you could swear you just saw a cat, but just as you turn to look, you hear an indistinct voice on your left. To follow the cat, turn right for room 20 (page 237). To follow the voice, proceed straight ahead to room 12.

MIRROR MAZE

12

Hidden Features

ALEX PILALIS

JIM YAWNED AND SETTLED INTO BED, DETERMINED TO actually get a good night's sleep for a change despite his chaotic mental state.

He brought up his favorite meditation app and nuzzled his face into the pillow as a sleepcast began to play. A deep, soothing voice described an aquarium, detailing its inhabitants and the environment. Jim had found that sleepcasts like this helped stop his mind from overflowing. After several weeks of not sleeping well—*or was it months, now?*—he needed all the help he could get.

The tenth anniversary of his dad's death was coming up. The weeks surrounding this date were always a hard time for Jim, his mum, and his little brother. His mum had been getting less capable these days. The doctors had diagnosed early onset dementia, so Jim was under pressure to lead the family and look after everyone.

He was only twenty-five, but he had to be the man of the house. It wasn't easy to live up to a dad who could do anything, knew how to fix everything around the house, kept all the bills paid, and was always a source of support to everyone he knew. Thoughts like these plagued Jim late at night, but at least listening to sleepcasts gave him some chance of sleeping.

At some point, he must have fallen asleep, because he became aware of slowly drifting back to consciousness. Still half asleep and too tired to move or open his eyes, he realized he wasn't alone in the room.

A soft voice was whispering, right near him. Someone was in the room.

His heart raced as he focused on the voice. It sounded a little like the sleepcast, but those only lasted forty-five minutes, and it felt like he'd been out for a long while.

He soon determined that it was indeed the same, soothing meditation voice from the sleepcast. That resonant, husky, American voice with a slight southern drawl was easy to recognize. It was whispering now, as though it were talking to someone else in the room who couldn't be heard.

Jim lifted his head and turned to his phone. He blinked awake and looked over his empty room. Moonlight came in through the skylight window and bathed the room in a dull, milky shade. No one was there.

The voice had stopped, too.

Jim sighed and tried to go back to sleep, guessing he'd just imagined the voice. Or maybe he was dreaming. He put it out of his mind and managed to get some broken sleep before groggily waking up the next morning.

He felt like a zombie at university. He'd lost track of the number of people he'd bumped into, or things he'd misplaced and had to look for. The lack of good sleep had really been getting to him, and it hurt his head to try and focus on anything.

One of his lecturers even pulled him aside after class and asked him if everything was okay.

"I'm worried about you, Jim," Mr. Banks had said, displaying his best concerned frown. "You haven't been yourself for a while. Is everything okay at home? You can talk to me, you know."

Jim had promised him everything was okay, not wanting

to bring up his dad's death anniversary. He just wanted to be left alone and sleep for twenty hours. That would sort him out.

When Jim saw Lara Hoyle in the hallway, his heart did a somersault—the way it always did when he saw her. He had never known a girl could look so perfect—hadn't even known what the perfect girl looked like—until he'd met Lara Hoyle.

He told himself it was his lack of sleep that gave him the strength and determination to walk up to her. What would the harm be in just saying hi? He'd spent far too long thinking about talking to her instead of actually talking to her.

He approached her as she was walking the opposite way.

"Hey, Lara. How's it going?" He gave her his best smile, standing strong and trying not to make himself look small. Girls loved confidence, right? Like facing a dangerous animal in its natural habitat, Jim couldn't show any fear.

There was a flicker of recognition as she passed and ran a hand through her long hair. But then she *kept walking.*

Jim stood there, open-mouthed.

Had she even seen him and heard him? He remained dumbfounded, watching the sway of her hips as she walked away. He must have really looked like shit for her to ignore him like that. Not that she'd ever given him much of a warm welcome in the past.

These days, it felt easier than ever to ignore people like that, or leave their messages unread. In the many dating apps Jim had tried, he'd found that girls would just stop replying to his messages at any random moment. If there was one thing he really hated, it was being ignored.

That night as he settled into bed, he put on the aquarium sleepcast from the night before, curious if he would hear the same whispering glitch.

The moment came when he eventually slipped back into a groggy consciousness, almost like something had nudged him awake. He hadn't even realized he'd fallen asleep.

That same meditation voice was in his room again.

Jim focused on its words.

That's right. He was strong tonight. Clear visuals. Solid compre-hension. He follows descriptions well…Yep, he's a good one.

It sounded like it was talking about him. Jim's first thought was that it was some kind of analytic setting on the app.

Without really knowing why he did so, Jim focused on the voice and sent his own thoughts out to it, not wanting to startle it again by waking up.

The voice stopped. He guessed he'd scared it away again. But then his heart jolted when it said, *Hello Jim.*

Jim's pulse thudded in his ears, bouncing against the pillow. Was this really happening? He must be dreaming.

Hey. He sent the word out there. Out into the ether. Not knowing who would catch it.

You should be sleeping, Jim. The voice was the same deep, husky southern drawl, without any inflection or tone that Jim could interpret. It felt strangely like having a conversation with Alexa or Siri.

Who are you? What's going on? Jim thought. He kept his eyes shut tight.

A moment of deafening silence passed until the voice said, *This is a hidden feature of the app. It isn't meant for users.*

Jim found that hard to believe.

I was with you during tonight's meditation, the voice went on. *I was impressed by how well you could see the aquarium in your mind. You know, you're one of our strongest visualizers out there.*

Our? Jim asked.

The app. We are all connected.

Jim was sure he was dreaming. But it at least felt like he was getting some rest. He didn't want to force himself out of it just so he could lie awake all night, worrying about his family.

How can you know what I'm seeing in my head? Jim asked, unsure if he wanted to know the answer.

During the meditative state, Jim, anything is possible.

That sounded good to him. He wanted to live in a world

where anything was possible. A world where girls didn't ignore him. A world where his dad was still alive.

Jim threw another thought out there: *Is it possible to share visualizations with other users?*

Several seconds of silence. He wondered if he'd scared the voice away or if he'd woken up without realizing it and now his dream was over.

It is, the voice simply said.

Jim paused, unsure about asking more. He really wasn't sure if he wanted to go down this rabbit hole. But he had to know… *How?*

If you concentrate hard and visualize what you want to see, and who you want to see, and if two people share a similar level of visualization accuracy, then it is possible for them to share a meditation.

Can you… Jim hesitated, finding the courage to projects his thoughts. *Do you have a user called Lara Hoyle?*

Another odd silence. Maybe it was processing something. Searching its databanks or whatever.

We do. We know her very well. She is currently using the app. Would you like to connect with her?

Ahh…Sure.

He was definitely dreaming. He had to be. But he wanted to see how this one played out. He guessed he knew which part of his subconscious this had come from. Last year he wrote a paper about companies collecting and analyzing user data, so he wasn't surprised that this app had information on its users.

Just relax, the voice soothed. *Drift…off. The sun sets over the ocean, casting the last of its glorious rays over the glistening waters, which sparkle like thousands and thousands of sequins, writhing and undulating.*

Jim felt some of the tension loosen in his neck and shoulders as he listened to the penetrating voice. It painted him a picture of a beach in the Bahamas. He focused on each detail as it arose, the world expanding before him.

He did everything the voice told him to do.

At some point he became aware of the sound of crashing

waves. He must have fallen asleep again, as it now felt like he was coming to. Except he wasn't in his room anymore.

The soft roar of the waves became clearer and more defined as he opened his eyes.

He was on the beach. Actually on it.

The glistening ocean, the reds and oranges smeared across the sky, the swaying palm trees lining the beach where it met the grass—everything was just as he'd pictured it. He could even feel the hot sand grinding between his toes.

He looked down to find that he was in the same red trunks he'd imagined. When he looked up, he saw her.

There, several feet ahead by the water, was Lara Hoyle. Jim recognised her instantly. He had never seen her in a bikini, but she was everything he'd imagined. Bronzed skin, flat stomach, long hair flowing softly in the warm breeze. The outline of her curvy body was striking against the setting sun.

Jim stepped towards her, his bare feet throwing up sand. His heart raced as he got closer, not knowing what he would say, just that he had to go to her.

She stared out towards the sunset, seeming to be in deep thought, but turned as Jim came to her. She stumbled back, her beautiful, long-lashed eyes widening.

"Whoa, whoa," Jim said, raising his palms to her. "It's okay. I won't hurt you." He wasn't sure why he said this, but felt like it was the right thing to say.

She covered her breasts with one hand as she stared at him, uncomprehending. "Jim?"

He smiled at her. She remembered his name, at least.

"Yeah. Ah…hi," he said sheepishly. "Nice evening for a walk, huh?"

She narrowed her eyes. "What's going on? Why are you here? How are you here?"

Jim took a tentative step closer, careful not to startle her. "You know, I've always felt like me and you had some kind of a connection. And this proves it. Our internal thoughts and feelings have connected us tonight."

She shook her head, her face twisting with disbelief. "What are you *talking about?*"

"The fact that we're both in this story and were able to visualize the same beach with the same details means something. Do you see that?"

She scrunched her face, a hand still over her breasts. "No."

"Yeah, me neither," he said, and chuckled. It was meant to be a forced laugh to put her at ease, but then he really laughed, his shoulders heaving as the absurdity of it all got to him.

She laughed hesitantly, half hysterical and half bewildered, then stood with her hands on her hips in a superhero pose. She looked around them, seeming more at ease now. "Well," she said. "I have no idea what's going on, but you're right. It's a nice evening for a walk."

Jim beamed at her. A sharp bolt of excitement surged through him as she smiled back at him.

They began their walk along the beach. It was easily the most beautiful place Jim had ever been to—if this technically counted as him being there.

He asked Lara how she was getting along at school, what she liked to do on the weekends, if she had any hobbies, her favorite places…The usual getting-to-know-you stuff. All the while, he tried not to stare at the swell of her breasts in her tiny red bikini. He wondered if he had conjured that exact bikini or if Lara did or if it was something they both somehow subconsciously agreed upon.

A dark thought struck him: Could he remove the bikini with his thoughts?

Once the conversation was flowing, he was surprised at how different she was from how he'd imagined.

She thought she was terrible with guys, never knowing what to say to them or how to act around them. He had never taken her for an introvert, considering how energetic and talkative she seemed around her friends. She admitted that her perfect day out was a day in. It turned out she liked to read and listen to podcasts and paint. He had taken her for the clubbing type, dancing all night in dark bars and getting wasted.

She even admitted, after taking a moment to collect herself, that she'd struggled with anorexia when she was younger. Jim had no idea. He listened as she talked about her childhood, and the pressures of being the daughter of a former model.

He lost track of how long they'd been on their walk. The beach looked endless, fading away into the distance. He caught sight of something huge and dark across the ocean. A solid black mass, almost like a mountain, stood beyond the horizon, half obscured in the faint mist of the hazy evening air.

It was an odd sight that gave Jim pause. What was something like that doing there?

He thought he heard Lara ask him something, when suddenly the world trembled. They both stumbled and steadied themselves as a huge chunk of the beach broke apart ahead of them. An enormous section of the ocean rose up as the ground lifted, creating an immense waterfall.

Jim reached out for Lara as he tried to find his own footing. Another section of the world behind them broke off, rising up and falling away. Deep, reverberating booms echoed across the beach as fissures flared out, like an earthquake that was breaking up the entirety of existence. In that moment, he got the bizarre image of Lego pieces falling apart. His fingers reached out to Lara, but he couldn't quite get to her.

Jim bolted up in bed, instantly back in his dark room. His shoulders heaved with his heavy panting. Sweat had built up on his face and chest.

He took a moment to reorientate himself back in the room. That dream had been so vivid, so real. His head swam with dizziness, and his stomach felt tight. It reminded him of years ago when he'd got sunstroke.

Jim ran a hand through his hair, then paused to look at it, seeing the tiny grains of sand that should not have been there. His stomach lurched. He dropped his head back onto his pillow, his heart still trying to calm itself down, and did his best to search for a sleep that never came.

He looked for Lara the next day at university. He had to know if she was okay, and what she remembered about their shared dream...meditation...whatever it was.

When he finally caught sight of her across campus, he jogged over. She must have been walking to her next class, but when she saw him, she froze, her eyes widening just like when she'd first seen him on the beach. She stepped back and looked around her with tense brows.

"Hey," he said as he came to her. "It's okay. I won't hurt you." He had his palms out to try and keep her calm, but it must have looked like he was reaching for her, because she let out a yelp and broke away into a run.

"Hey!" Jim called out, suddenly becoming aware he was shouting at her. Several people had stopped to look at him. He wanted to chase after Lara and explain that he just wanted to talk, but all he could do was watch her run away. He sighed bitterly and shook his head.

Was she afraid that their shared moment last night had been real? Or didn't she remember, and she thought he was a madman who had just tried to grab her or something?

Jim walked back home after class, preferring the forty-minute walk over catching the bus. He stopped by the supermarket on the way and bought several weeks' worth of groceries. An inkling of a thought had been stirring within him for a long while, and by the time he got home, it had manifested itself into a fierce determination.

An idea had come to Jim. A dangerous one that made his heart race just thinking about it. He knew he was crazy. He was afraid it wouldn't work, and even more afraid it actually would.

That night, he cooked dinner for his mum and brother. His dad's old recipe: spaghetti and meatballs. His dad would always make it on special occasions or if someone wanted cheering up or wasn't feeling well.

Tomorrow marked the day of his dad's fatal embolism.

Jim had never forgotten the sight of coming into his parents' room and seeing his dad lying there as his mum screamed and moaned hysterically. He looked like he was sleeping. Eternally sleeping.

Boiling the kettle and opening a fresh packet of biscuits—the good ones with the chunky chocolate bits—Jim catered to his mum and little brother that night.

His head still throbbed with that dull fogginess he'd been feeling for some time now, from his lack of sleep, but he was glad he could focus enough to make a decent meal.

He smiled as he handed them tea and hot chocolate, feeling like he was starting to take care of his family. Take care of them like his dad used to. He even helped his mum pay a bill on her tablet, which she had never worked out how to do. He made sure to write down the steps of which icons to press and how to log into her banking app for future reference.

And he showed his little brother where their mum's pills were for her dementia, so he'd know where to find them.

As Jim went up to bed, he was both excited and terrified at what he planned to do.

He opened the meditation app and set it to a random sleepcast. He didn't think it mattered which one he chose. Then all he had to do was fall asleep.

The sleepcast began, describing a sleepy town on a rainy day. *Nestled between the ocean and a forest lies the small town of Nightville. Here, all your worries can drift away…*

It felt like the hardest thing Jim ever had to do—his mind was racing with so many thoughts and possibilities—but he forced himself to focus on the soothing voice and visualize what it was describing.

It's a rainy night, tonight. It's a good thing you have your umbrella. The sounds of pattering raindrops fill the quiet street you're walking down…

He had to focus on the mediation. He just had to fall asleep. If he could just—

Jim. I know you're awake.

Jim paused, holding his breath, not daring to move.

Would you like to speak with me, Jim?

His heart thudded in his chest as he built up the courage to send out a thought. *I was wondering if you could connect to people who don't use the app.*

I can connect with anyone's consciousness. If they are dreaming, thinking deeply, or mentally transporting themselves somewhere. Everyone is connected by the transmissions of their thoughts.

Jim had been hoping for such a response. Somehow, he had known it.

Okay, Jim thought. It took him a long moment to gather enough strength to send out his next thought.

I want to speak to my dad.

Silence. That deafening, pregnant silence filled with an endless possibility lost in the emptiness.

Are you sure, Jim? That is inadvisable.

His heart felt like it would burst from his chest. *Yes. I'm sure. I want to see him.* He didn't know how this system worked, but he would tear it all down for the chance to speak to his dad again.

Very well. Now, just relax, and listen to the sound of my voice. I have a very special story to tell you.

Jim nuzzled his face into his pillow and assumed his usual sleeping pose. Somehow, he felt calmer now, like the worst of it was over. There was a strong possibility that this was all in his head, and he would just dream about his dad, but still... he'd take a vivid dream over nothing.

This is the story of the black mountain, the soothing voice began, emphasizing some of the descriptive words and drawing out others. *In the valley of a vast, barren land of weeds and rocks, there stood a great black mountain. Its ebony exterior shunned the light and gave off no gleam nor shine. No, this was a mountain for the darkness only.*

An uncomfortable feeling began to build up in Jim, but he

pushed it away. If he could reach his dad through this app, he would listen to anything it had to say.

At the base of the mountain, a wayward dark spirit roamed who existed only in the daylight. The darkness wanted to take the spirit, but the spirit had forgotten who it was and liked to live in the sunlight. And so, the darkness played a trick. It called out to the wayward spirit, drawing it to the other side of the mountain, away from the sun. The spirit was lost behind the mountain and became shadow. It existed in the daylight but only away from the sun. From then on, it was only free to escape at night. By day it was chained to the ground, trapped as the shadows of the world.

The spirit could no longer live in the light.

Jim woke up.

He hadn't realized he had fallen asleep, but he must have. He blinked his eyes open and saw he was in a desolate world with black clouds moving through a maroon sky. The barren land he had just been visualizing. Before him stood the enormous black mountain, reaching up to the tortured, roiling clouds.

Everything felt as real as the beach with Lara. He saw he was dressed in what he considered his regular clothes: jeans, boots, and an old Metallica T-shirt.

Seeing the colossal mountain and its jet-black peaks gave him a terrible, sick feeling. The entire world was dim and gloomy, but there was an orange glow on the horizon to his right. The maroon sky was brighter over there.

Jim swallowed down his apprehension and replaced it with the fierce determination that had got him there.

"Hello?" he called out.

He stumbled across the ground, looking around, hoping he wouldn't disturb anything threatening. Who knew what kind of world this was?

He caught sight of something moving away from the mountain. Jim tensed and his heart jumped when he saw it was a person. A man.

That same square face, steel-blue eyes, and salt and pepper hair had been in Jim's mind for ten years now.

"Dad?" Jim said, quietly at first as his mind struggled to accept the sight, and then repeated with more force: "Dad."

It was the man Jim remembered, but he was different now, more grizzled. Jim had never seen him with heavy stubble before, and his clothes were worn and muddied, like a homeless man.

"Jim?" his dad said as he came to him, eyes wide and mouth open in awe. "What... How... Are you really here?"

Jim welled with emotion and grabbed his dad, pulling him into a tight hug. Tears flowed as he buried his face into his dad's shoulder.

"Jim," his dad said as he held him at arm's length. "Is it really you?" His face twisted with a strained mixture of grief and happiness. "You've grown so much."

Jim struggled to understand. "Dad, what's going on? Where are we?"

His dad held a grave look as he shook his head. "You shouldn't be here, son. You have to go away, before—" he spun around to face the rising sun, now higher on the horizon. Jim had never seen him look so shaken and afraid before.

"Dad, what—"

His dad gripped him by the shoulders with great urgency. "Jim, listen to me. You have to go, now. Before the sun comes up. I got trapped here by a voice, and haven't been able to leave."

Jim stuttered and mumbled while he searched for something to say, his mind a chaotic mess. He couldn't believe he was really there with his dad, after all this time. "We can find a way out then. Together."

His dad shook his head. "No, son. You have to go."

"Not without *you*."

The sun had half cleared the horizon now, highlighting more of the dead land. There seemed to be an endless expanse all around them, with the mountain as the only landmark.

His dad sighed deeply. Tears fell down his lined face and his shoulders dropped. He hung his head.

Jim had a hand on his dad's shoulder. His stomach lurched when he saw it had started to darken. No, not darken; *fade*. He held his hand up and saw the color leaving his fingers, moving down his arm.

"Dad, what—"

"It's too late," his dad said weakly, his eyes red-rimmed.

Jim saw that his dad had started to fade, also. The mountain behind his dad began to show through him. As the sun rose, a great shadow moved away from the mountain, reaching for them.

"I'm sorry, Jim," his dad said, defeated.

"No. Dad, no. Whatever is going on, we can figure a way to get out. Together. I promise, we'll get ourselves out of here."

And then what? Did that mean he could bring his dad back to the real world too? Bring him back alive…in his coffin? Jim didn't have any of the answers, and there was no time to work anything out.

He could only watch as he and his dad faded away, and joined the growing shadows around them.

As his world faded into darkness, he thought about his body in the real world, out there on his bed, looking like he was sleeping. Eternally sleeping.

But one day he would wake up again. With his dad.

One of the mirrors in this room is rather dusty. You wipe it clear, and for just a moment, your own face looks like a cat! If this doesn't particularly surprise you, turn right for room 19 (page 229). If you're starting to think you may need professional help, proceed straight ahead to room 13.

13
Kiss of Fire

ANNA TIZARD

I CROSSED THE ROAD, COWERING INTO MY JACKET COLLAR against the wind-whipped rain. Why was I out in this mess? For a second I couldn't think straight. I always seemed to be out in this wretched street. Same old story: I couldn't stare any longer at the dreary four walls of my flat, my self-imposed prison. A gambler can only sit on his hands for so long.

I headed for the bus shelter. It was somewhere to stand, to hide from the rain. The bookie's was just a few doors down. But I wasn't there yet, was I? I had a choice.

So why did it feel like I didn't?

The presence of the betting shop was already there in my mind before I could even make it out through the sheeting rain. My chest thudded with the promise of that place: the next flutter, the chance to win again. Janine said it was a false promise. Janine said a lot of things, like "You can't kill off your demons unless you greet them face to face," and "Do the work and you'll get there." Looking at me sadly with her chin cupped in her hand, she also said, "A little fire is good for you. But you—you burn the house down."

That's how she saw everything: in terms of fire, air, water, earth. Why couldn't I choose a normal, reputable psychotherapist?

Same reason there was for everything: money.

I laughed at myself, at my complete idiocy, a bleak sound that was quickly smothered by the downpour's hiss. The houses and shops hunched like spat-out teeth, knuckled against the wind. I shivered into my jacket, trying to warm my thoughts on Janine. I knew it was unhealthy, but there was nowhere left for my thoughts to hide from the dull thud of my cravings.

Janine. The idea of her glowed like a sun inside me. A twin glow, next to the other one: my addiction, my "flame" as she loved to call it, her fingers outspread in explanation as she paced her office, which was actually just her own front room. But I didn't want to get hooked on her as well. I wanted a *cure*, for God's sake.

She wasn't really my type. She was one of those super-healthy women, model thin, floating around the place in softer-than-air skirts. Her fingers glittered with gemstones. She had decorative seashells pinned to the walls; her kitchen cupboards overflowed with herbal supplements. Every time I went in there to make a cup of tea, I half expected to find a broom made from a sprig of wheat.

But there was a spark when her eyes caught on mine. What she said about the human psyche couldn't possibly be true, but she told it like a great story, and I found myself hanging on for the next episode, a fantasy I wanted to half-believe in.

"The interior life is a sort of mindscape, and that's something you can co-create."

Surely she didn't mean… "You're going to create it with me?"

A smile tickled her lips. "Samuel, I mean *you* can co-create it, with what's already there. There's so much that's beyond our control in that other reality. We *are* our minds; we don't create them. But there are tools we can use to explore the parts that are usually hidden from us and," she bobbed her head, "tidy things up a bit. With hypnosis, you can create a space of your own, a way into the unknown, where you can safely observe and confront your inner demons."

Week after week, she had me slide into a trance where I built a static image of this very street. I mentally pieced together the houses, the rooftops, made up new colors where I couldn't remember the real shades of the doors. It felt like a child's sketch; only the bookie's was easy to "draw."

But huddled in the bus shelter, staring out at the rain, I wondered about Janine's methods. Was I any better than when I'd started? In some way, hadn't I made my addiction more real, more indelibly *there*, by creating an imaginary version of it? Had Janine made up these methods on a whim, or had she actually learned them from a textbook or a certified course?

And while I waited for something inside me to change, to become *normal*, there was nothing to feel but the misery of this cold squall and the sweet, warm pulse that beat against it; the thing I had to deny—I *must* deny—again and again. I leaned my head against the side of the bus shelter, not caring that the water trickled down my neck and cheek.

A voice like music carried on the wind. I looked up and saw a figure in a blue raincoat cross the road.

"Well, that's my Samuel."

It was her. Or was it? Janine lived miles out of town, and this woman seemed…different. Without flinching at the rain she lifted her head, her eyes like jewels. She shook her wavy, soaked hair and smiled. My heart slid down to my feet. She had Janine's slightly upturned nose, the light brown skin, though her eyes seemed…a different color?

She touched my chest, and there in her hand was a fine thread. I nearly laughed out loud. I'd never seen a shirt's stitching come undone like that. A soft, drooping thread, wispy as cotton. But she held it in her delicate hand as if weighing it, drawing it away to show me its length, and pointed across the street, where the shops were smeared by the rush of rain.

I blinked hard but couldn't see what she was pointing at. The rain was just too heavy.

"Is that really you…?" I began. She'd said my name, hadn't she? But I couldn't say hers. I wanted her to say it, to prove it.

She said nothing, but held the thread out as if to challenge me, to ask me what it was. The touch of it ached right down into my gut.

It was a part of me…but how? That was impossible. But the thrumming in my skull echoed the same vile idea: the thread wasn't cotton, and it had nothing to do with my shirt.

The rain was a disguise, blurring the already unclear edges, the half-complete sketch that was this street. I mentally scrambled about for the memory of leaving my flat and couldn't find it. It made sense now. I'd come from Janine's, but not physically. The last thing I saw was her front room, those white curtains. I'd fallen so deep into hypnosis I didn't know I was in it, until now.

How could that be?

I stared around me, the shops whose fronts shifted under the burn of my searching eyes. I saw it now, this smudged, unfinished picture: a mind-made creation. The rain was the perfect cover-up—having made me cower as I'd crossed the road, not noticing the missing details. The street was the skin of my mental capacity, stretched as far and thin as it could go. But that meant none of this was really real, and the woman was an imaginary version of Janine. Wasn't she?

I didn't remember making it rain.

"Did I—Have I imagined you?" I stammered. My voice croaked, a real sound. I touched my throat. Real skin.

"Ah, darling," she said in a sing-song voice like a cartoon princess. Then she leaned closer, and I noticed the beauty spot on her cheek that was Janine's. "I'm here."

I stumbled back but she still had my life-thread in her soft, sharp-nailed hand.

I'd let her in. Whoever she really was.

"Honey," she crooned. "Don't be afraid. We did it! This is the other side of real. We're going to put out that rotten fire inside you. Together."

"But…You can't really be here, if this is inside my head." If I believed that, why was I trying to reason with her? "You look… different," I added, hearing the hope in my voice and not caring that she'd heard it too.

"Samuel," she breathed. "We're inside your mindscape, but it's not a closed-off area. I've said it a hundred times in therapy: No man is an island."

My panicked mind fluttered around this possibility. Yes, Janine often said that…but then, I'd never taken it literally. But how did she get inside my head?

If my imagination had altered her appearance into this other Janine, the real Janine didn't have to ever know how breathy and strange I'd made her.

She was my therapist! She meant me no harm. Of course I would tell her later about this, when I was *back*…We'd have a laugh about it together.

Other-Janine turned and gave my thread a gentle tug. In an instant, I knew it might as well have been an umbilical cord for a fetus. I was that fetus. I was here, apparently alive, but I was *inside* this street in a way that made me intensely vulnerable. The thread led to my physical body, perhaps. My lifeline to the real me.

I couldn't fight. I didn't dare think what would happen if I tried.

Real-Janine's unusual methods had taken me this far. I had no choice but to trust her and see this through to the end.

"Are we going to the bookie's?" I asked, silently adding, *to meet my demons?* The idea of saying these words out loud made me stiff with cold. All that stuff she said about not being in control of your mind…

"The bookie's," she repeated with a mocking downturn of her mouth. With her free hand she gave my shoulder a push, and I shuffled out of the bus shelter with her, keeping an eye on my life-thread. I squinted through the rain past her pointing finger.

In the row of half-imagined shops stood the place where that pulse had beaten back at me just minutes ago, except that it was now a charred hole. A black, singed structure, smoke trailing from inside. The dirty smell of charcoal wafted toward me on the wind.

"What? How? I didn't do that…"

Janine's voice was liquid at my shoulder: "You did this before you even arrived. If you keep up your addiction—if you keep your fire going—your beloved bookie's will simply remake itself and burn again, over and over. This place doesn't follow the rules of up there." She actually gave a flick of her chin, towards the rooftops. So my physical body really was somewhere else…*up there*. "And now it's time…"

She smiled and drew my life-thread through her fingers. A shiver rippled down my back. With nothing more than a gentle tug she had me helpless. I trailed after her, swallowing back dread.

Right next to the blackened bookmaker's, she stopped by a door that I'd never seen before: an old, rustic wooden thing that looked so out of place it might have been from another time, or another dimension. I didn't want to think about how it got there.

She touched my face and said, "Your life is full, and you don't need to gamble."

I caught my breath. Janine always said that at the end of our sessions. So I was still in therapy…Even if Other-Janine was weirdly changed by my imagination, her actions were still controlled by Real-Janine, who was still *up there* trying to help me, leading the way.

"Say it back to me," she said, nudging the door open with her elbow.

"My life is full, and I don't need to gamble," I bleated. My heart hammered: *trust, distrust…trust, distrust…*

She pulled playfully on my hand—not that she needed to—and I staggered after her into a pub.

The second thing I noticed about that pub was the massive but empty hearth: no fire, though it was freezing. The floor was slippery; a sheen of condensation had turned to ice. But all that came after a few seconds' delay.

Two mermaids languished on a leather sofa.

"My half-sisters," said Janine, gesturing towards them with her free hand as if this were the most ordinary thing in the world. "Bessie and Lilith."

Their sea salt aroma stung the air. As the light caught them, their fish skin tails shimmered from silver to blue to silver again. It seemed wrong for such an artificial light from one of those chintzy chandeliers to cast itself upon these… divine, supernatural creatures. For that's what they were. No doubt about it.

I stood and stared. Each second I felt more wrapped in their otherworldly aura and my own deepening panic. There was no one else around, not even a bartender.

This is a place inside your head.

The mermaids watched me with mock shyness as they nursed glasses of brandy or whiskey. I gave an involuntary shudder and tried to remember if I'd said, "Hello."

"Aww, you've scared him, Janine." The one with smooth brown skin and Egyptian eyes sat forward, swilling her drink impatiently. Her voice sounded…bawdy, of all things. The light splintered uncertainly against her scales as she tucked her tail under her and to the side.

"Don't be silly, Bessie," Lilith flipped a hand at her. But she mirrored Bessie's movement all the same, her yellow-green eyes pinching at mine. "He's just curious; that's all."

Forget hellos. This was my mindscape. "Did I make you up, or did you climb into my mind like Janine?"

They tittered, pretending to hide behind their drinks like school girls while exchanging looks heavy with meaning.

I wasn't going to let up. "How did you get in here?" I demanded, adding silently, *If I didn't invent you entirely.*

They stopped laughing and looked pointedly at Janine.

Janine nodded toward a plain, unpainted door to the left of the empty bar. "They came in through that door."

I moved toward it, then remembered my life-line in her hand. I stared at the thin strand, wondering if I dared just swipe it from her like I would in physical reality, or whether she had some other powers in this place that meant I didn't stand a chance.

She seemed to understand what I was thinking and weighed the thread in her hand. "You gave me this power. If you try to take it back, it'll snap and your life will be over."

"How do I know you're not lying? You're not even the real Janine!"

"You trusted me. You let me in. All I've done is help you. We co-created this street together…"

"So this is just a street? It's not…*all* of my mind?"

At this, she and her sisters laughed, knocking back their heads. Their cackling grated on my nerves. "Ohh, Samuel, you're so funny. The mind is all. The mind is everywhere. The body, the physical plane, is just the smallest, tiniest little part." She pinched her finger and thumb. "Like a little tiny sliver of skin floating on the biggest ocean."

"Or floating in space, more like!" Bessie shouted from the sofa.

Lilith made a swirling motion with her finger to mimic this idea, her eyes wide. "Wooh."

The air swooped in and out of my lungs too fast. But even as my head felt light, I was aware of the real thing happening elsewhere. Here, it was like the idea of hyperventilating…while somewhere else, at the other end of my life-thread, my physical lungs were actually experiencing it, doing it.

How could that reality be the tiniest thing, a sliver of skin floating on top of…all this, and hell-knows-what more?

I wouldn't give in to panic. Janine wouldn't *hide* all of this from me, not when I'd come this far. I glared at her. "Let me see what's behind that door."

She fell silent while she considered this. Finally, she shrugged. "Maybe just a quick peek."

She stayed close by me while I approached the door and pulled its handle, which rattled as if worn with use. But I forgot all of that—I even forgot the mermaids—while I took in what was behind that door.

A waterfall. A sheet with rushing, silver-licked twines flowed right past the doorframe. There might have been a whole other world behind that, for I heard echoed bird calls that hinted of a rainforest, deep, far cries like whale calls, and much closer, chittering noises that made the hairs on my neck spring up. Something was watching me through the curtain of water. Murky shapes moved as if through mottled glass, finger-shadows stroking the ribbons of water. I didn't dare speak for fear of giving myself away.

But despite my trepidation, my bones ached for what was behind that curtain. With my throat clenched to keep from uttering a sound, I instinctively stepped closer and reached out. The light on the water, the way it danced…

Janine gripped my shoulder and forced me back around to stare into her face.

I vaguely registered the sound of the door slamming behind me. The mermaids were restless on the sofa, reaching out to the door as if to a long-lost loved one and covering their forbidden wishes with their trembling hands.

Janine spoke almost into my mouth, she was so close. "It's where you come from, when you're ready for life."

"You mean— before—?" I blathered, struggling to focus on her words. Even with the door shut, the memory of those noises—that rushing water—sang in my very muscles, a memory before every other memory I'd ever had.

"You cannot go back," she said, emphasising each word. "You only go back when your body is dead."

Removed from the beauty of that place, my thoughts

returned to those murky shapes and fingertips. "What were those…?" I shuddered.

"Hungry souls," she said, "demons who want to return. To life."

Janine continued to stare at me, tensed, waiting for me to take it all in. Slowly, she relaxed and let go, though she made sure I saw my life-line in her hand just in case I got any ideas about opening that door again.

She lowered her lashes at me, and with a breathy sort of sadness said, "Now let's do what we came here for. Your fire is hurting you. And it's all going to waste…"

She said it like a little girl with an excuse. She said it, and it didn't matter that I couldn't make sense of it—because her eyes were hard, dangerous, fixed on my mouth. She pulled me toward the sofa with a strength she shouldn't have had. Her nails dug into my arm, and I felt myself collapse in the space between the mermaids. I knew then that this had all been a trick, and I was powerless to stop it. Janine had called up these mermaids, these…demons from that other place, and she'd lured me here to…to…

I half-sat, half-lay on the sofa. Gently, they stroked back my hair. I heard myself try to breathe calmly. The air juddered in through my throat and out again.

"Shame." Janine's voice came soft as butter as she stroked the sleeve of my jacket. "You don't have to suffer like this. You can give it all up, boy," she said, her head tilted on one side, a casual goddess.

"Ooh, the way you long for magical things," said Lilith, creeping over the others toward me. "No wonder we look like this. Janine, you were right to bring us here. He's a lovely specimen. He has…so much to give."

"The only question is," Bessie piped up, staring at me with her chin rested on her sister's shoulder, "how much are you willing to give?'

"Oh, he has plenty," murmured Janine.

They bent their heads closer as if to kiss me, all of them at once, lips parted, Bessie running a soft tongue over hers—and the breath began to pull out of me.

Except that it wasn't my breath. It was something else. My warmth, my life, my…*fire*, as they'd called it.

But even as they dragged it out of me, I wanted it. I wanted them to do it.

That's the trouble with an addict's demons, I guess. You adore your demons. Real-Janine had been wrong—if she'd ever meant to therapize me: I would achieve nothing by confronting my demons. An addict meets their demons face to face every day. You offer up your life to them, daily. You give them all your power. People who don't have this thing this flame inside them—just don't understand. They think it's all inside your head. Your mind. They don't realize that *mind is all…*

They took too much. They took too much, and I knew it, but I couldn't stop them.

I looked down and saw my broken thread. Janine had paused and was staring at me uncertainly while the other two kept on. I could actually see the flames now: strange, smoke-like twists of blue and amber drawn out into their greedy lips. That's when I realized I was looking down on myself, on my dream body. I saw Janine's reaction from above: pulling the other two away, as if Real-Janine had just found her way at last into her demon-avatar and discovered she had a conscience. But I couldn't stay to watch the flapping of her hands, gesturing at the others as my dream-body faded into nothing on that couch. What was left of me soared upwards, freed, through a ceiling and a floor, an untidy kitchenette, followed by another ceiling and some roof tiles, then the sky.

Where? Where? I thought furiously, waving my arms which were hollow now, only ghost arms. A seagull showed me its beady, sarcastic eye before flapping straight past, as if to say, "Shame you're not worth eating." So I was still real, in some way—wasn't I?

I thought about my body, my real body, and Janine's front room where she held our hypnosis sessions. Rising up over the rooftops, I searched for the place, floating southward toward the seafront. Past rows and rows of houses, all jumbled and skewed. It was all so blurred. I hadn't practised envisioning any of these places before, but with a fierce concentration, they just about made sense, the buildings teetering and twisting the wrong way as I mentally turned them over like stones, scouring the place for her front door and the mottled white wall. *There.*

Quick as a thought, I melted through the window but stopped just inside. There was my body, still lying on that leather couch. But it wasn't mine anymore.

What did it mean? Was this window a sort of doorway now, back into the physical world where my body lay? Maybe if this was where I first drifted off…My life-thread had broken, but my mind still found its way back.

Real-Janine was sprawled in her armchair, her head knocked back as if in a bad dream. The skin of her throat wavered up and down as if she had another tiny pair of lungs in there. Sweat moistened the fine hairs around her forehead and neck. So all of this took some effort on her part. Her mind, or a part of her mind, had met me on that other plane and was still there, feeding, or deciding what to do about those—well, they weren't her sisters; that was for sure. The way they'd called me a "specimen." What would they become, now they had my fire? Did they have more power now; could they move around different planes of existence? I couldn't imagine it. It was all beyond me.

I was beyond myself.

My body lay in the chair, slumped and emptied. And yet— my abdomen still rose and fell. I was alive! *He* was alive… My body. But I was his mind. At least, a part of it.

I drifted closer, wondering if there was still a way to go back in, to get back *home*. But nothing worked. The closer I floated, the louder I heard my own breath sawing in and out. Eventually I felt something of the muffling, stuffy fabric of the armchair behind my real head. *His* head.

Janine stirred in the other chair, wiping her forehead and squirming uncomfortably as she woke up. Her brown eyes locked on me and she sat bolt upright, staring. I pulled away, up, back out the window and into the street. But the coldness that flowed through me had nothing to do with the air outside, a sky fabricated by my mindscape. It was that flash of pain I'd seen criss-crossing her face. Was it…guilt? Had there really been a part of her that wanted to help me?

It haunted me, that look. I drew away into my blurry-edged world, the memory thumbing over itself, unable to rub it away. There was sorrow in those eyes, too: the answer to my unasked question. No, there was no way of going back. She'd taken it too far, invited too many demons who'd feasted too greedily. There was no way back.

I spent some time on the rooftops with the seagulls, who barked at me reproachfully. Together we floated over the sea. It wasn't enough; I couldn't talk to them, and I was an annoyance, a constant source of suspicion. I was their ghost, but I wanted to tell someone, anyone, that I was the one that was haunted.

So I went back. I slipped through the window again into the real world. There was still one question I might find the answer to: *Why?*

The familiar front room again. The seashells on the walls. So that's where I got the idea from, to turn those demons into mermaids—if that's how it worked. My unconscious mind had made those demons less frightening by dressing them up, making them beautiful, although they were no less obstinate or greedy than any demon of my own I might've expected to meet.

I watched Janine move about her daily life.

She was fleshier than before, her cheeks pink, her walk

more sturdy. She did this weird thing in the kitchen where she opened the cupboard, stared at her herbal supplements and ran her fingers over the plastic bottles before closing the cupboard door again. For several minutes, she stood there crying, whispering, "Thank you," over and over. She hugged her sides, blinked at unseen monsters in the edges of the kitchen and finally smiled.

Something had been horribly wrong before. Something had been wrong, and since we'd been inside my mindscape, it had gone away.

There was a white piece of paper stuck on the fridge that she often touched. I floated closer to read it. It was a letter from her doctor confirming that her body was free of cancer. I saw the herbal supplements for what they were, why she used to be so thin. So this was the primary reason she'd taken me to that place and drawn out my life energy…wasn't it?

Again, that look of guilt in her eyes haunted me. What was I supposed to feel now? It was still a betrayal—she'd taken away my life! If she'd asked me at the outset whether I would give up some of my fire to save her life, would I have agreed? I would've thought she was crazy…But still, once I'd entered that pub, I'd have been prepared, wouldn't I? And if those demons weren't involved—who knows?—we could have controlled the process. I saw myself pulling away just in time. I could've given her just enough and then gone about my way, addiction-free. But no. She had to keep it secret and turn me into a victim.

Still my emptied body went about its business.

That other Samuel had moved in with her. Or he'd simply failed to leave. They were a couple. In any other circumstance, I wouldn't have believed his/my luck. Except for that moping look Janine had, the curl of her shoulders, the pinched mouth when he wasn't looking. So she still felt a touch of remorse.

Not nearly enough.

He lived a plastic life. He ate, he went to my old office and worked, he watched all the TV shows Janine wanted to see. I heard him laugh, and it was fake. He never cried. He had no desire, no terrors, no passion, no hope; I saw it in the blank features of his—what used to be *my*—face. He lived, but he didn't know why. He had no fire, and he didn't realize that she'd taken it. She and those demons.

"It's her!" I screamed, raging near his head. "She's the one who took it from you!"

But he swatted the air at some unseen fly and scratched his ear. Even Janine didn't seem to see or hear me anymore. Every day I was becoming more of a ghost, retreating further from that world into this one, a mysterious place that ordinary, healthy people find so hard to detect.

Janine was healthy now. Her body was healed. There was nothing drawing her to an awareness of something other, something more. The mind held no mysterious potential for her beyond the simple daily curiosities of life. She'd taken what she needed from this side and then left it well alone.

She no longer saw patients in her front room. She was qualifying as a masseuse and worked in a room above a hairdresser's. There really was nothing for her in hypnosis anymore.

I drew away from them, wafting in the rafters of real and imagined places. I soared over the sea, learning the ways of whales, and even saw the glistening curve of a mermaid in the water. The bookie's was permanently charred now, its fire put out. I lingered outside the pub next-door to it. There was that forbidden door inside…There might be portals into other places too, in there. Who knew what glittering mysteries lay behind them? But still I craved my old life, the promise of the real.

In the street, I found one of the mermaids again, her dark, wavy hair swaying on her shoulders as if still feeling for the water. She walked on two legs: a human now, a real being walking down a metaphysical street.

"Lilith?"

She turned, and the sight of those yellow-green eyes was

like a punch in the stomach. I was ready to launch at her, but I was breathless, wafer-thin. Words crowded into my too-tight throat. But before I could lash out at her, she screamed at me in that street of nothingness.

"You got your revenge, okay? Your fire is more than I can bear." She threw her arms out to the sides. "I'm addicted to all of this now…The *idea* of this." She drew clasped hands under her chin and raised her tearful eyes to the sky. So she was stuck here, stuck with my cravings. Physical life was a prayer to her, a broken promise, nothing else. This made-up street wasn't enough.

"What was it you called physical life again? The tiniest sliver of skin on the surface of the ocean?"

"I'm sorry, okay? I'm sorry! Sorry, sorry, sorry!" Lilith swiped at me with half-hearted hands, her 'sorries' lost in sobs. When she finally looked up again, she murmured, "I was hungry. I wanted real life."

"What can *I* do?" I asked. "Can't you go back through that door?"

She stared at my shoe, her lip trembling. "Maybe… But what about *you*?" She shook her fist at me, her frown deepening as her voice rose to anger again. "Why can't you be the bastard she said you were and think about *you*?"

I was speechless. It was bad enough that Janine had offered these demons my fire as some kind of life-giving feast… But she'd let them believe it was okay because I'd deserved it. What stories had she told them; what made-up crimes had I committed?

But I was sick of being a kind of fictional character, someone nobody ever sees or meets. I didn't want to know the details.

Lilith drew closer. She opened her palm and showed me a tiny piece of grayish cotton. "I kept it. Take what's left. There." She tipped it into my hand.

"But that—won't be enough, will it?" I didn't dare believe

her. It was too good to be true. The last remnants of the rage I'd stored up for her, was ready to pelt at her, melted from me in an instant.

"If you want it hard enough, it will." She stared at my mouth, guilt biting her forehead. Then she kissed me.

Her lips were stronger than mine; she was a being with a more defined body than mine. A warmth began to fill me up, flames dancing down my throat like a soothing smoke, just as she pulled away.

I didn't dare speak. I couldn't bear to say out loud what I thought she'd just done, in case it turned out not to be true.

"There." She smiled, stroking my face. "That should be just enough."

I flew back to my body as fast as if I had wings. The other Samuel lay there numbly, bundled in a duvet, enjoying sleep like the half-dead creature that he was.

I waited by the window again. I waited until Janine switched off the light and climbed in.

I hovered over the shell of my body, not knowing where to hold the piece of life-line to connect us up. But the thing quivered in my palm, seeming to want to do it on its own.

I let go, and crashed back into my body.

I've seen waterfalls. Mermaids. The door into the unknown. It waits for me; it waits for everyone. But I'm not ready to step through and become part of that place. In a way, wouldn't that be too easy?

Without being dead, I couldn't help but think I'd become like one of those demons, trying to claw their way out, greedy for someone else's fire because mine was put out too soon.

I was back inside my body; we were one again. My skin didn't stop tingling for three whole days. All my senses were alive—*I* was alive—like I'd never felt before. I walked out of that house and never looked back.

I might've waited till Janine was out of the house and set fire to that place. The perfect revenge: reduce her house to a smoldering shell like that burned-down place inside me. But my anger had died down; I had better uses for the flames I had left. I was relieved. The edge of that need, that craving, just wasn't inside me any more. Instead, I had this funny glow, a reflection of light against a rush of water. The dance of that light. I saw it when I closed my eyes.

It's the reason I teach meditation now. I see the flicker of craving in people's eyes, the desire to find something *more*. And there is more. There are many places that can be reached through the doorways of the mind. You just need to be prepared for what you might find.

Once this is all over, you need to find a better way to relax. Take up a new hobby maybe. If gardening sounds appealing, turn right for room 18 (page 223). Or if knitting might be a better fit, proceed straight ahead to room 14.

Flight of the Universe

STEPHAN COGHLAN

THE CRUNCH OF METAL, THE SHATTERING OF GLASS, THE snapping of bones, the tearing of flesh savaged by the impact— it was all mercifully brief, broken as the light across the street turned green and pulled Jacob Houghton back to reality—back to what he hoped was *his* reality—just as the drivers behind him began honking their horns.

It was not the first time that day that Jacob had suffered through such an ordeal, nor would it be the last. He dreaded what was to come.

Shaking himself back to reality, Jacob stepped on the gas and pulled his car into the intersection, just in time to be the only vehicle to make it through before the light changed to red, leaving a long row of frustrated drivers in his wake.

And in other news, scientists believe they may have found the edge of the universe, the radio cheered.

As he stepped onto the accelerator, the car leapt ahead, weaving through the heavy urban traffic. Someone up ahead slowed abruptly, their tail lights flashing crimson. Desperate to avoid the collision, he veered onto the sidewalk, only to feel the car lift over a group of people waiting for the bus, their screams muffled by the snapping of their bodies—

But again, this wasn't reality. Jacob carefully followed the urban grind of morning rush hour, plodding ahead, stopping constantly, waiting until the next intersection and gap in flow, where he could lurch forward only to stomp on the brakes again. Twenty minutes later, he pulled into the same parking lot that he did every working day. It was both a curse—to be so banal, so predictable—and a blessing—to have something grounded in reality. Because with every step he took, he was somewhere else: living, dying, jumping into a trench, holding his lover tightly, their naked flesh almost scalding as they cemented their passions, enjoying a last meal before being strapped to a gurney and wheeled toward the last chair he would ever occupy.

Sitting gratefully in his cubicle, Jacob started up his computer and checked the multitude of emails and scheduled meetings. It promised to be another day of moving at the pace of a sloth in order to conform to office standards. Falling behind was bad and would affect his quarterly review, but going above and beyond was worse because he would earn the scorn and ire of his fellow coworkers for making them look bad. So he took his time, carefully spelling out each word, double- and triple-checking his messages as he strove for the most mediocre work he could manage.

By noon, he was thoroughly bored, but it was better than the chaos playing itself out in his head. In his physical reality, he breathed in the funky, overly salted smell of microwaved sardines, which his coworker was wiping up in the kitchen, while the sting of accelerants, the moist touch of earth, and the sickly sweet cloying scent of death filled another reality stream. A coworker leaned in to complain, too close for comfort. Jacob—*another* Jacob—punched the intrusive complainer right in the mouth, while still another gathered the same coworker into his arms and pressed their mouths together.

Jacob ran out of work by early afternoon, and knowing he could hardly get more basic if he tried, he opened up his personal email:

SUBJECT: Long time no see
SENDER: B-Boy

Jacob's heart flipped, and for a moment he considered deleting the email. It had been so long since he had talked to B-Boy—Brennan, his childhood friend—that Jacob almost didn't want to hear how he was doing. But something drew him forward. He hunched over his desk as the radio in the next cubicle droned on in the background.

I mean, Don, that the universe has stopped expanding, as far as we can tell. Imagine a balloon, if you will. You fill it up as far as it can go, until it's stretched so thin that if you put any more air into it, the material bursts. We call this the Big Rip—

Jacob opened the message.

Hey Cobby,

I know it's been a while, but I'm back in town. Just started a new practice not too far from where you work. I was thinking of catching up on old times.

I miss you, buddy.
Sincerely, B-Boy.

Jacob hesitated, debated, held his cursor over the trash icon…But then he shrugged, and his fingers danced across the keyboard.

How long do you think this is going to take?

I don't know for certain, but it's already been happening for years. It's just that we've only begun to see the effects recently. What I can tell you is that it's increasing in speed exponentially, and it appears now to

be moving faster than what we had thought physically possible.

The voice on the radio was drowned out by the clinking of bottles as Brennan pulled two beers from his mini-fridge, which was handily disguised as a fancy wood-paneled cabinet. Popping the caps, Doctor Brennan, licenced psychotherapist, handed a cold one to Jacob, who accepted it gratefully and leaned back onto the couch that was normally reserved for paying clients.

Evocative aromas filled his nose: chicory and cumin, Old Spice and worn leather, all accompanied by the tang of sweat and the sweet, citrus touch of decaying books. It was soothing, with a subtle hint of the terrifying exposure of vulnerability.

Inhaling, Jacob tried to relax, hoping his casual pose and somewhat sarcastic answers wouldn't appear too abnormal to someone who used to be incapable of reading subtle hints and had to be told outright what others were thinking.

"To friendship." Brennan cheered, and Jacob reached out to touch glasses—but he also saw himself drinking without the toast, and another him was posing in a joke, trying to test Brennan's comfort levels, while still another was smashing the bottle over his friend's head, holding the doctor down, jamming the shards into Brennan's throat—

"To friendship." Jacob replied, and they both took long, hard pulls on their respective drinks. The bottles were already slippery with condensation. Brennan was forced to keep the office warm to soothe his suffering clients as they relieved their emotions.

"Congratulations, Doctor."

"Thank you." Brennan smiled, as he perched himself on his fancy desk's writing pad. "And how shall I address you?"

"Why change?" Jacob said, once more sipping his beer, speaking slowly, carefully, hoping to avoid giving away any hints that he was struggling to focus on only a single here-and-now.

"Cobby it is. And I'm not your doctor," Brennan replied. "Not yet."

Chuckling, Jacob shifted his position, looking at the only other occupant of the room. "What's that supposed to mean?"

"It means that I haven't asked you if you want my help yet."

"Oh my God," Jacob's snort of disgust rattled from his throat. "Is this a sales pitch?"

Waving his free hand, Brennan dismissed Jacob's comment. "No, not a sales pitch, but an offer for someone to talk to."

Jacob remained quiet, waiting to see where Brennan was going, and when the doctor knew that his guest wasn't going to bolt, he began his pitch:

"I know it's been years, but I still worry about you. Last time I really talked with you, you weren't the same. You, Cobby—once playful, fun, happy-go-lucky—were busy ignoring everyone you ever knew. Don't forget, I knew you well. You didn't have trouble at home, you were doing well enough in school, you weren't pushing drugs down your throat, so what happened? Why the change?"

So many other Jacobs reacted, but at least one of him kept calm and still as he answered: "Puberty."

"Bullshit, and you know it," hissed the doctor. "I was your best friend, Cob. Don't lie to me. You're the reason I chose this profession. I was worried about you. I wanted to help people like you. I've checked up on you; you've barely done anything with your life. You don't commit to relationships, your work is subpar at best… It's like you're still dissociated from the world."

Jacob was screaming, upending the couch, and at the same time he was weeping, begging for forgiveness, and yet another him wasn't anywhere near Brennan's office but driving fast along an Italian mountain road, vials of pills and empty bottles of grappa clinking on the seat beside him—

"What really happened?" Brennan asked, honest concern in his voice.

So, Doctor, your honest opinion. Is this the end of the world?

"It's like I told you." Jacob took a steadying breath and then began to tell a tale he had spun a long time ago: "I just felt different, out of focus, unalive."

Biting his top lip, Brennan rubbed his free hand over his knee. It was a mannerism that he had never grown out of, and when Jacob realized that Brennan still had the same tell, he laughed. Finding himself caught, Brennan paused, and then joined his buddy.

When they quieted down, Brennan was still serious, but his concern was softer, more compassionate than Jacob remembered him to be capable of.

"Are you happy?"

Jacob stewed and shifted unconsciously as he tried to fabricate an answer that wouldn't have him sounding like a madman, or maybe, one that would.

When he spoke, he surprised himself: "No."

Brennan smiled, victorious, but Jacob recovered and went on the attack.

"How the hell did you, Mister Fidget, actually make it to be a doctor?"

"Knitting." His deadpan reply brought another snort from Jacob, until his friend reached into his desk and produced needles, yarn, and a long but unfinished scarf.

"You're shitting me!"

"It helped me focus."

"Prove it."

Polishing off his beer, Brennan expertly cast the thread onto the lead needle, and as Jacob's jaw dropped, his friend's tools clicked together, and in moments a line was added to the scarf.

"You know I suffer from attention issues, and for the longest time I was a 'D for Diploma' kind of guy. Well, before I headed off to postsecondary, I took a summer to stay with my grandparents."

Jacob nodded. It was the last time he had seen Brennan.

"We had two weeks of rain. There was almost nothing to do. I'd read all the books and had no new games to focus on. Grams dragged me out to the living room and asked for my help. She and her church group were knitting clothes for their missionary group. Let's just say I was hooked by the first successful stitch."

He wasn't stopping, and if anything his speed increased as he spoke, but his words were more level, calm, collected.

"Beats the hell out of a fidget tool. It also came with an advantage that no one will stop you if they find out you're doing something for charity. No one wants to be the bad guy and tell you not to knit for sick children."

"Huh." Jacob pondered his friend's words. "Have any spare needles?"

Should we be worried?

Yes. The voice paused and inhaled so sharply it was audible even over the scratchy static of the AM band. **This tear is happening faster than we thought possible. It's not just an idle rip; it's as if it's actively being pulled apart by force, or pushed apart from the inside—**

How long until we start to notice?

It's moving fast, very fast.

"Goddamn it," Jacob cursed, staring at the work in his hands. "I dropped a stitch."

And in that pause, he was again split from his reality, taken for a flight from one reality to the next. As he flitted through the universes, he found himselves fleeing from dying worlds, worlds under collapse, crumbling buildings, fires, quakes... The sky was going dark, yet he seemed to find new realities faster than ever before. It was getting worse, getting stronger, and the multitudes were more than ever.

Grabbing his crochet hook, he caught the errant loop, and in that moment he saw a red truck hurtling down on himself.

He felt his body destroyed, the agony of lying broken and dying on the pavement.

As he threaded the yarn back to the level of the needles, the effort of this action brought him back to his physical now, back to the welcome mundanity of his job. Yet he couldn't shake the thought of the truck barreling down on him. He looked around his cubicle, half-expecting to see it still oncoming.

He inhaled, and the odor of microwaved green beans forced its way through his nose and rested heavily on his tongue.

"Cob!"

Startled, Jacob stood up and looked around for Brennan. His cry of panic and desperation had been palpable, real. But Brennan wasn't here. He was at his office, helping others, trying to relieve the anxiety in his clients.

Having finished the line, Jacob hurriedly set down his tools and the beginnings of his bulky scarf, and his fingers tapped at the keyboard, answering one of his two requisite emails per hour.

People were beginning to panic. The news he had heard on the radio was spreading, and a sense of dread was slowly permeating the workplace. The other employees were beginning to take their vacations. They were going out, seeing the world, or just spending time with family. As such, he and his sparser department had been asked to increase their workload, and in an unofficial lunchroom meeting, they had agreed to double their productivity—no more, no less.

SUBJECT: Drinks tonight
SENDER: B-Boy

You won't believe who I just had a chat with. Dewey! He's opened a new place. Well, not exactly on his own, but he's got a partner, and they've been running a small joint not too far from the original. He promised that if we show up, he'll whip us up our old favorite.

You game?

Unable to stop himself from smiling, Jacob typed out his message. The clacking of his keys alerted his coworker, who looked over their cubicle wall, concerned that Jacob was going above and beyond their agreed upon quota.

"It's personal." Jacob explained, to his peer's relief.

If it was getting quiet at the office, it was worse at the bar. Depressing, really. The attached diner was almost painfully bright, and the few families that did eat there gladly focused on their conversations or the sports playing on the television screens. The bar area was dark. And not very busy, which meant that Brennan and Jacob didn't have to yell over the din of a crowd to talk, and that they were able to find seats together with ease.

It also meant that their orders of deep fried green beans came hot and fast. Dewey delivered each rack with a smile, a kind word, and a comment from times past.

"Hell of a way to say goodbye." Brennan sighed, wiping beer foam from his unshaven upper lip.

"You don't really believe all that hype about an upcoming apocalypse, do you?" Jacob asked, popping the first of his fifth order into his mouth. The crunchy and salty exterior gave way to the soft, chewy, almost sweet interior.

"I'll tell you that I can't ignore it." Brennan admitted, rubbing the stubble of his face. "And I think I'm letting it get to me. If I'm not careful I'm going to start acting like—"

His voice trailed off, but Jacob continued: "Like *I* did."

"Yeah." Brennan acknowledged the statement, once more sipping his beer.

We interrupt this program to—

With quick thinking, Dewey changed the channels, and the relief of not hearing the news any further spread across the diner like a whispering breeze.

And somewhere, Jacob heard screaming as people rioted. And somewhere, Jacob was leading a procession, a strange cross held high over his head. And somewhere, Jacob was being secured to a similar creation, and about his feet lay pitch soaked logs, and people wept for him, grateful, calling him their sacrifice, while others jeered, calling him a witch as the fuel was lit, and the flames licked at his legs, and the smoke clotted his lungs. As the flavor of the beans changed to the coppery taste of blood frothing from his pierced and collapsing lungs, he knew that his fifth order was going to be his last.

"Any plans, boys?" Dewey asked from behind the bar as he refilled their drinks.

Brennan chuckled.

"I'm just going to try to keep calm. Why panic for the end of the world? You?"

"Keep 'em calm," Dewey cheered.

"And carry on." Jacob completed the cheer as he patted at the ball of yarn in his pocket.

The office radio continued blandly.

Big Rip.

Heat Death.

Collapse of the universe.

Those are the names given to the ultimate apocalypse, the disintegration of all reality. The end of the universe, not just the world. Here to discuss, is the author only known as the Sons of Mars—

"Oh bloody hell!" Jacob cursed, as once more he over-stitched, seeing where his work bloated from the yarn over. Dropping his needles, he contemplated whether to draw out the yarn, or to take the extra effort to tink backwards, and fix his error tightly.

Was there even a point?

Was there even a reason why he was at work today?

It was clear now that there was little time left.

It's begun right now, the voice on the radio screamed, demanding attention. **The universe has been stretched too thin, and now it's tearing itself apart.**

Lying back, Jacob closed his eyes and felt himself scattered about, thousands of parts, his body in too many realities: living, dying, making love, causing war, killing, watching the birth of a child.

Frustrated, Jacob stood and walked to the big window that encircled the building. Outside, it was blowing a gale, yet sunny and still.

A siren began its piercing scream, and Jacob chuckled, until the screams of those around him became too loud to ignore. His workplace companions, few and far between, were the ones making the chaos. They were the ones panicking, hiding under their desks or rushing for the stairwells as the building shook underfoot and ceiling tiles fell from above. Lights swung from their chains, and Jacob felt—in other realities—his body being crushed by falling debris, the building pancaking, flattening.

Then the rumbling was over, and he was okay. As everyone around him picked themselves up and dusted themselves off, Jacob calmly began to pull on the yarn, slowly undoing the chaos he had made in his creation, slowly pulling back through each loop, until he got to the bulge, and there, he hesitated. He wasn't that far along. He could keep going back, erasing his mistakes, starting anew.

The red truck came barreling toward him, directly through the window.

"Cob!" Brennan's yell rang through Jacob's head as he stared at the bloated extra stitch and imagined another, and another, and another, swelling his work, misshaping his scarf. Swelling it beyond control until it spilled over, breaking apart.

There was a solution, a cure to the apocalypse, to the Great Tear.

Turning, he ran for the exit.

The sky was black, despite the hour. Glowing dark, almost amber, the sun seemed to be wavering, unsure if it still wanted to hold its shape.

Another tremor ran through the ground under his feet. In the broken, flipped sedan, knocked over in the latest quake, voices once more emerged from the speakers.

It got too big, too thin. This was bound to happen.

Across the street, the sign for Dewey's hung precariously, barely held by a single surviving warped anchor.

Closing his eyes, Jacob tried to remember the moment, the breaking of his body, his first death, his first wish to be apart. Holding the scarf out ahead of him, he hesitated, lifting one foot, and prepared to step out onto the street.

A cheer rang through the air and set the beaten wooden bleachers vibrating underneath him. Shrill voices screamed, some breaking under the strain of the force of the call, others breaking under the effects of puberty. The bright lights overhead were piercing but not nearly as painful as the squeaks of rubber-soled shoes on overpolished wooden floors.

The ball arched over the other players, bounced off the net, and another cheer erupted from the crowd. All except for Brennan, who jeered loudly, slipping further into the bench.

"Lame," Brennan lamented, then sat up straight and grabbed Jacob's elbow. "We're never gonna win at this rate. Let's skip out and go get something to eat."

Shaking his head, Jacob tried to clear the ringing in his ears. He was unable to rid himself of a sense of deja vu. Hadn't he been here before, years ago? Brennan was his best friend, and they were out watching the local schools play against each other, as they always did. Tickets were cheap, and it was something different from staying in and playing games or working on homework—assignments that felt uninspired and canned, merely shoving the same curriculum down everyone's throats despite their differing strengths, weaknesses, future desires, and aspirations.

Squeezing down below the bleachers, Brennan waited for Jacob to catch up. Curious what was going on, Jacob followed.

Why was he back here? Was there a point?

"Let's go to Dewey's," Brennan encouraged.

"Mmmmm, green bean fries," Jacob heard himself say, and he felt himself smile. It was almost like he was his old self again, years ago, but there was something else holding him back and away, as if he wasn't quite there either.

His stomach rumbled. Dewey's green bean fries with spicy mayo was a favorite then and a familiar taste Jacob realized he missed to this day.

Why hadn't he had them in so long?

Pausing at the street, Brennan looked both ways before he waved Jacob to hurry up.

Laughing, Jacob stepped onto the black asphalt of the street, before it came to him what was going to happen: He was going to look both ways, cross the street, and then—

The red pickup truck came barreling toward him. He screamed as the steel and plastic front end slammed into his teenage body, shattering it, sending him flying to lie broken and dying on the pavement.

Gasping, he lay there feeling his life ebbing, wanting nothing more than to be free of the pain, for things to be back the way they were, to be free from the agony of his reality.

For a moment, he hovered, caught between realities. Then he felt himself rewind, felt himself split. He was both dying on the street while the pickup drove on, and he was stepping onto the street, intact, unbroken. He paused as the red pickup truck came whipping around the corner, missing him by inches.

"You coming?" Brennan asked.

Jacob stepped back onto the sidewalk. Shaking his head, defending himself with his arms, Jacob tried to figure out what he was going to do. He felt himself stepping out across the road again, felt himself dying from the impact, felt himself walking home, felt himself splintering, dividing, becoming thousands of selves all at the same time—

Holding out the scarf and its swollen knot, Jacob yanked, undoing the stitches, focusing on the threads all coming apart beneath his fingers, his careful work coming undone, all the way back to the original thread.

Young Jacob waited, wondering if he should join Brennan across the street. He slid his foot forward, his toes at the edge of the street, about to slide over the curb, and then he stopped.

"Are you coming?" Brennan asked.

Jacob could feel himself breaking apart, the impact of the truck, his other deaths, his other moments, his other realities crashing together, colliding, smashing into one. He pulled his leg back.

"Hey, Brennan," Jacob yelled across the street. "Make mine with Cajun dusting, will you?"

Brennan laughed, and both turned away. And for one moment, Jacob thought he felt himself—hundreds, thousands of him—knitting back together, and then, then—

Then he worried about homework, about the future. Sitting on a bench, he watched as a red pickup came zipping around the corner, down the street.

"Someone's in a hurry," Jacob observed, chuckling. "Don't be in a rush to be too many places at once," he laughed as the last of who he'd been vanished. And then, he was just himself, Jacob Houghton. He had a long life ahead of him, and only one to think about.

You decide you need a vacation. If someplace close to nature sounds nice, turn left for room 9 (page 95). Or maybe a cruise on the open sea; turn right for room 17 (page 211). If this puts you in the mood for seafood, proceed straight ahead to room 15.

15
Teacup Koi

COURTNEY LOCICERO

KEVIN HONG'S GIRLFRIEND BROKE UP WITH HIM AT HIS favorite bakery chain, Yummy Joy Cafe.

Presently, he wondered why there was an impossibly small koi fish swimming tight circular laps in his ceramic cup.

"Do you see this?" He asked his ex, but she had already left. Kevin's sole company was this calico intruder and the surrounding cafe customers. One of them was a blind man who constantly grinned regardless of whatever activity he could perceive. Another was a quiet sketch artist, who Kevin usually did his best to ignore. He searched for him now, but the artist wasn't there today. Kevin couldn't decide how that made him feel. Good? Or just confused.

The koi fish was his new object of confusion. It was cute, but he wanted it out of his tea. Getting dumped was an unwelcome surprise. He wasn't quite ready to let in anyone new.

Without making a fuss, Kevin brought his tray with teacup and kettle to the front register. He requested the manager and forced a smile when the elderly, over-complimenting owner arrived.

Before this Taiwanese senior could offer up another one of his routinely empty compliments, Kevin lifted his hand.

"I just need to replace my order." He gestured half-helplessly to the koi fish.

The owner stretched his neck and made a sort of throaty cluck.

"Can't. Fish is lucky."

Kevin almost snorted, but held it back so as not to offend the owner. His eyes went to the fish, then back to the old man.

"So…what do I do with it?"

The owner sucked in a contemplative breath and leaned to the side.

"Pass its test. You have to show it that you're ready. Then fish will go away."

Kevin almost lost his grip on the tray.

"A test? What if I fail?"

The owner grabbed onto his own neck in a choking charade, showing off the whites of his eyes and upsetting Kevin further.

"So when you said the fish was lucky, you meant the bad kind."

The old man dropped the act and corrected, "Luck is earned. Can't expect fish to just give it to you."

"Nope," Kevin shoved the tray at the old man. "I suppose you can't."

That night Kevin slept with the teacup koi on the dresser beside his bed. The aquatic stranger wandered into his dreams as easily as it had wandered into his tea.

Kevin's brain occupied the body of the mysterious fish. Instead of swimming through tea, he swam through clouds and sky. The sharp contrast of pink sunset against opaque fluffs reflected the graphic calico pattern on the army of koi that swam alongside him.

Twilight became a starry night. Some of his koi brethren pulled ahead while the rest dissolved into the constellated background. By the time the stars around them had all collapsed, Kevin realized that he was the only fish left.

When the sky fell, so did he.

There was barely a splash when he hit water—just a rude slap and the invasive floral notes of jasmine.

Kevin thrashed in the tea as a fish would on land. It didn't make any sense. This is where he was supposed to belong, right? *Right?*

"Choose."

Someone poured milk into the tea. It made handsome shapes that Kevin admired as he actively drowned.

Oversized tapioca bubbles rained slowly from above.

"Choose." A straw descended like a fisherman's spear. "Or die."

Kevin's muscular tail twitched in an effort to propel him upwards. Towards the cruel barista trying to stir him up with the tapioca. Towards the trumpeting horn of some mammoth creature. The brash notes translated as, *Don't you want to be happy?*

Kevin writhed and fought, his fear of the heavens stronger than his instinct to live. The straw created a vortex, pulling him down with the giant tapioca balls.

"Choose."

The surface called to him.

"Or die."

Kevin woke to find his hands grasping his own neck. When he oriented himself enough to loosen his hold, he could breathe again.

There on the nightstand, the teacup koi swam laps, hugging the cup's smooth ceramic walls just as it had the walls of Kevin's taut esophagus.

He rubbed his neck. He could still feel the resistance of the fish's micro-scales as they *tore-slid-tore-slid* down his throat. For a moment, the dark eye beads of the fish reminded Kevin of that cryptic Taiwanese man. He kicked the nightstand.

The cold tea splashed onto his pillow, where the koi also landed.

The little fish danced for oxygen.

Kevin's throat constricted in sympathy.

He couldn't breathe *again.*

Kevin entered Yummy Joy Cafe with his laptop and a transparent athletic tumbler. He didn't care if the other customers saw the fish inside, defecating sweetly in its tea-quarium.

He chose a spot near the smiling blind man, far away from the center table. The man sitting in the center—a sketch artist—had henna tattoos swirling up and down his hands. He sketched beautiful things with those delicate, beautiful hands.

Kevin ignored the man and hissed at the koi fish, "What do you want from me?"

But the tiny intruder no longer occupied the tumbler. Kevin didn't celebrate the koi's vanishing act as he opened his laptop and ordered his usual. The quiet sketch artist sat in the same spot where Kevin had been dumped less than twenty-four hours ago. Kevin told himself that he hadn't noticed. And even if he had, what did it matter?

The waiter returned with a kettle and a ceramic cup balanced on a tray. Kevin poured without looking, his eyes on the screen, his attention on the sketch artist.

He drank without thinking.

The koi greeted him, shimmying down his throat with violent enthusiasm.

This was a public place, so Kevin choked as politely as he could, convincing himself that there was a bittersweet dignity in dying by the hands of an imaginary koi fish while sitting next to a jolly blind man in one's favorite cafe.

Kevin stood up.

If he was going to die, he wanted to at least see what the sketch artist was drawing. Like those samurai warriors who always bled out while they hallucinated soft, pink cherry blossoms kissing the snow.

Kevin was now standing over the artist, choking mutely so as not to disturb him. In his dying moments, no one would suspect why he really stood there. That he had seen this sketch artist before—had watched him. Or that were he not facing imminent death, he would never have approached this quiet man with the delicate hands.

The sketch artist looked up. His eyes, though dark, glimmered brightly. The lines that made up his face were yummy, Kevin thought. They brought him joy.

The koi was wedged in pretty good. Kevin's eyes watered at the strain.

The artist met his gaze. "Oh. Want to see?" He tilted his sketch pad towards Kevin. "It's not very good. I'm trying to capture this elephant." One of his exquisite fingers pointed to his drink as he whispered, "You probably can't see it, but it's *bathing* in my wintermelon tea right now."

Very suddenly, Kevin swallowed.

Breathing, he realized, was a blessing—second only to being able to say to the artist, "Do you mind if I sit?"

To your left, you hear a flutter of wings, which for some reason reminds you of an angel...or a demon. If this doesn't bother you, turn left for room 8 (page 77). If it makes you want to say a prayer, proceed straight ahead to room 16.

16 Two Roads

M. CRANE HANA

HEAVY WITH CHUNKS OF CONCRETE, THE WICKER BASKET pulled at Mazy's wrists and pressed her hemp-rope sandals into the floor. Her feet itched. Mazy closed her eyes. She angled her right foot, sliding her big toe off the sandal bed.

Three feet to Mazy's left, Julianna's bronze knife *scrape-scraped* against a plastic case. Out in the hallway, Gillen laughed like a waterfall, trading science puns with the distracted caretaker.

Mazy's toe touched the planetarium's pink granite floor. She heard a hawk's cry. She saw—

Sunlight and snow on pink granite cliffs. Straight white clouds cutting across blue sky. The cloud-lances glittered at their tips with roaring old-time petrochem airplanes that hadn't flown since Mazy's ma had been a girl.

The granite held good memories. Other places didn't.

Out in the Delta, Aunt Asima had wanted Mazy to wear long black cotton dresses and hide her hair in a black scarf. Only sing in church. Never dance outside. Four months into being Asima's fifth foster daughter, Mazy had walked barefoot on the earth and seen the high wall of brown water it still remembered after fifty years. In thirty minutes, a whole city had become sodden white plaster and splintered wood.

Don't look close at the old driftwood piles, Mazy. Don't remember the steady rumble of the flood, coming right up through the ground. Don't look out to the Delta, or see the drowned valley shiver again along its shore...

Asima had driven right back to the state adoption office in the nearest city, not even the one where she'd adopted Mazy. "I can't keep her. The Devil's in this girl, or God, and I'm not enough of a sinner or a saint for this!"

Asima hadn't been the first. Mazy hadn't been angry. The foster group home had well-stocked vending machines she could jimmy open.

Now, with Julianna, she missed real chocolate something fierce. A girl could only take so much carob.

Four weeks after fostering with Julianna, Mazy wore gray Irish linen, never touched by steel tools or industrial pesticides, and sandals of braided hemp and crepe rubber from organic plantations in Costa Rica. She washed her skin and tight brown braids with vegetable glycerine soap. She ate no meat or refined sugar. In the evenings, Mazy listened while Julianna read chapters from an old book where the characters spoke too many words for what they really meant to say.

In the planetarium, Julianna crooned over the knife, "Lady of Life, guide my hands. Take back seven thousand years of war and poison."

Eyes still closed, drifting in the granite's dream of hawks and sunlight, Mazy listened more to the planetarium's automatic program droning softly from hidden speakers:

"Section twelve contains core exhibits from advanced schools in the western North American regions. Exhibits one through seventeen commemorate the completion of the space station *Cristofori* in the year—"

"Mazy?" Julianna snapped her fingers close in front of the girl's face.

Mazy stumbled out of the dream.

Julianna's thin pink lips were pressed even thinner in something that might be disapproval. Or maybe indigestion. Mazy looked beyond Julianna's shoulder. Eucalyptus leaf shadows flickered across the granite tiles.

"Mazy!" Julianna angled the knife, catching a stray sunbeam. Mazy blinked at the sudden light.

"Let Charlotte Montrose's Blessed Future begin aright, today." Julianna murmured. "Let Earth shake off her oppressors."

"Blessed be the Future," Mazy answered. Julianna had used that benediction over the first dinner of Mazy's new life.

The guide voice said: "Exhibits eighteen through twenty-five are finalists' dioramas of the spaceports at Upton, New Mexico, the proposed space elevators near Nairobi, Kenya—"

Mazy dropped the basket. Gray concrete lumps spilled out, clattering on the tiles. Her sandal bumped one piece of concrete while she bent down. The lump shot forward and ricocheted off the display case.

"Stop daydreaming and pick those up!" Julianna snapped.

"Exhibits twenty-six through—"

Mazy gathered the concrete lumps, then wiped gritty fingers on her linen skirt.

Not far away, a siren began the slow wail of an earthquake warning.

Mazy thought about Gillen, the newest sister. When Gillen had found them a week before, she was already quoting from Montrose's book. Already seeking a dedicated gray-clad Sisterhood just like Montrose's stern and beautiful moon witches.

Gillen even knew about Mazy, and why Aunt Asima had really given her back to the care of the state of California.

To Julianna, Gillen and Mazy were proof that Charlotte Montrose had known the future a hundred years before.

At the state foster hearing, when she didn't think Mazy was listening, Julianna said the old bungalow near Griffith Park came from her trust fund. But later, to Mazy, Julianna said the sanctum's house and funding came from mysterious benefactors who followed her moon goddess.

"You should listen," Julianna said now in the planetarium, tapping Mazy's basket arm. "Know your enemies. Charlotte Montrose knew it for truth, even though she hid her prophecies in fantasy novels. Arrogant technocrats use up our world to launch themselves like a spaceborne virus. The ignorant blindly follow their warrior religions. Their defeat begins today!"

Now, in the planetarium, Mazy's nose itched from the smell of concrete dust. Julianna said the lumps came from a freeway no one used anymore.

The dust remembered other things: sharp jolts, screams of tearing metal, the rumble and sigh of concrete realizing it was really only sand and gravel. No one had bothered to rebuild the ruined bridge after the hillside shrugged it off. The broken span pointed east to a waterless valley littered with termite-ridden stucco and plywood ruins, everything the gray-tan color of driftwood and the linen Mazy wore. As in the Delta, old bones tangled among the tree roots out in the valley.

The crumbling concrete bridge had been important enough for Julianna to pay for a two-hour robot cab ride to reach it. She hadn't asked Mazy about what the dust remembered, so Mazy hadn't told her. Some of the concrete bridge chunks Julianna had chosen still carried old brown bloodstains. Mazy avoided touching those.

"Lady of Life," Julianna began again.

"Can we get frozen yogurt, after?" Mazy asked.

Julianna rolled her eyes. "Mazy. Please pay attention."

The floor shuddered gently. Outside, the eucalyptus trees danced to something more than wind. Another earthquake siren sounded not far outside the planetarium.

"We'll get some honey-vanilla-raisin yogurt from the organic store," Julianna said quickly.

"Caramel," said Mazy. "And real chocolate. From the sweet truck down on Los Feliz?"

Objects rattled on shelves. Crafted for such tremors, the planetarium dome groaned on its sprung foundation. Julianna swallowed, more of a loud gulp like a surfacing catfish. "Caramel and chocolate," Mazy repeated as the floor settled.

The distant sirens stopped.

"Mazy, observe," said Julianna, pretending to ignore the twitching ground. "What we do today is momentous—"

Already observing, Mazy let Julianna's prayers fade from hearing. She liked the planetarium, the long curving chambers filled with pictures of grinning Eagle Scouts holding star charts, treasured model rockets, hand-painted posters announcing a famous scientist's lecture, diagrams of space stations, and shelves of rocks. She wanted to come back without Julianna and watch stars dance to music in the planetarium.

Julianna's prize lay on one clear plastic shelf: Moon rocks sent ahead for the visit of an astronomer whose name Mazy didn't remember. Gray-tan stone wrapped in unmarked plastic, set here momentarily amid the protection of other decadent technocratic materials.

Mazy remembered cold soda pop and warm turkey-and-cheese sandwiches at school, dirt roads alongside corn fields, gospel songs alternating with kicks and slaps, and her own wavering image in brown ditches. She couldn't recall more than two foster families before Asima. They blurred into tired, earnest faces, sometimes waving goodbye in not-so-hidden relief.

She liked this city, its golden-green jumble of olive groves and dying palm trees, seacoast and steel, lights that blazed all night, right-angled daylight spearing up through darkness.

Even the dirt smelled different, more like the concrete from the broken highway.

Explosions and shouts, the glitter of broken glass and steel, the smell of burning oil, and the iron scent of old spilled blood. Bad sweetness clung to hidden places where people crawled away to die.

Newer smells: flowers and perfume. A thousand different foods, a thousand languages. Buildings clad in solar panel wraps. Wind turbines on every high roof and hill. Green roofs and vertical gardens spilling down in tiers. In the clear air, only the blue of distance half-obscured the Hollywood Islands. People lived, adapted, and rebuilt.

Mazy liked this world. She wasn't sure about the old one, or the one Julianna wanted to make.

Calm solidity flowed out from the pink granite floor. Nothing sudden here. Just tiles cut from a mountain four hundred miles east. The mountain slowly pushing upward into sunlight, like a cat wanting to be petted.

Julianna had promised never to kick Mazy.

Aunt Asima had kept her household in beautiful order, lawns green and clipped, clothing washed, and locked freezers filled with real meat and vegetables. Asima's one-level house was rambling white brick shaded by wispy willows, at the end of a quiet country road near the edge of the drowned city.

Asima had learned not to beat Mazy, but not before Mazy had learned about hunger and thirst, and how a low hiss of "Maize Robinson..." was worse than hearing it yelled.

A movement dragged Mazy's memories away from the scent of Delta fields pockmarked by new sinkholes, or vanishing under the silky, muddy rush of pale brown water.

Julianna reached into the display with a pair of ornate tongs she'd said were stolen from a European museum. Celtic. Ancient. Handles swirled with bronze dogs, their eyes pale domes of blue-white moonstone. The ends of the tongs were scooped bronze oak leaves.

Last night, Gillen had shown Mazy the same tongs on a fancy website. Copies made for people who liked their houses to be art galleries. Not ancient, not even Celtic, but a fantasy revival from only a few years before.

In the flickering blue glow of the Sanctum's sole computer, the two disciples stared at the pictures on-screen.

"She stole them and the knife. Last year," said Mazy. "She said."

"Hard to reach into a screen and grab them out. Her bank account says she bought both a few days ago."

"You got into her account?" Mazy was impressed. "How is it?"

"Pretty sad. Sshhhh," Gillen had whispered. "Tell you a secret, Mazy-Maize Earthdancer? There are no other Moon Sisters. Just us. You, me, and Mother Julianna."

"Are they all gone?"

"They never existed."

"But the books Julianna showed us! All those people read them, loved them. Believed them. Julianna says that's why the earth ripped itself apart."

Gillen shook her head. "She has probably the last hardback set of Montrose around, and those look like she had them rebound sometime in the last twenty years. The publisher canceled Montrose's contract long before the earth danced. Montrose herself retired in disgrace, after it came out that she'd excused and hidden a sexual predator. I had to go to a university special collection library out in eastern New Mexico to read the only other copies left. No one else remembers Charlotte Montrose."

Now in the planetarium, Mazy watched Julianna lift out a plastic-wrapped moon rock, slit the plastic with the knife, and caress the stone.

Mazy wanted to hold it, feel it. What would moon rock remember?

Julianna beamed an old gray smile beneath the wings of her dark walnut-dyed hair. She tucked the rock into her cavernous hemp purse. She took the closest-shaped concrete chunk from Mazy, slipped it into the plastic bag, and replaced it in the display case. "First part's done. Out we go, and collect Gillen on the way."

Mazy glanced backward into the planetarium, its cool expanse more like a temple than Julianna's dusty backyard altar.

"Let's see if Gillen has seduced the caretaker yet," laughed Julianna in a low, spiteful voice.

"I can't imagine what this place will be like next week when you give your speech," Gillen said to the caretaker.

Strawberry-blonde Gillen had violet-tinted lips and gray-violet eyes, her only jewelry a carved pale amethyst pendant daintily etched with a five-pointed star and crescent moon. The caretaker was a small, elderly man, seeming more flustered than flattered by Gillen's attention.

Gillen's wry grin included Julianna and Mazy when they rounded the lobby corner. "Mother Julianna," she called. "There was never any need for this subterfuge. Tom is a Brother."

Caretaker Tom gave them an apologetic shrug, and lifted a silver oak leaf on a silver chain from inside his white linen shirt. "Blessed be, ladies."

"Oh!" breathed Julianna. "When did you join the Orders?"

"Aught nine. At Cal-Tech, of all places."

"He's modest, too," said Gillen. "Tom planted the first oak tree on the moon."

Julianna's lips thinned, a shade away from a snarl. "Then you've read the prophecies of Sister Charlotte, about the Scouring of Earth? The way the seas, fault lines, and volcanic traps must wake and destroy mankind's vast pride? Of the new world that shall rise from us? You know why we must have these stones?"

He sketched a brief bow in her direction. "I have. But I don't know what rocks have to do with it."

Gillen said, "Mother Julianna thinks it's improper for mortals to keep fragments of the moon. This stone may be used in rituals to hasten the Scouring."

"Ah," said Tom slowly. "I appreciate your zeal. Have you such power?"

Mazy looked up from the lobby tiles, which had a zigzag pattern of smaller blue-black stone tiles mixed with the pink granite. "Sister Julianna made the Appleton Crossfault shiver last month. With silver, blood, and an iron meteorite. I danced. The dirt thumped right back at my toes." She looked at Julianna and Gillen. Gillen's returned smile was different from Julianna's.

Tom stared at the skinny teenager. "Whose blood?"

"Mine," Julianna said quickly.

"We might all perish on that day, if you succeed." Tom looked tired and sad, and then his gaze cut toward Mazy. He winked.

"No! We are the prepared ones. Some of us will survive. The Scouring must come," pressed Julianna, gearing up for a sermon.

Gillen leaned forward and patted the big hemp purse. "May I see it?"

Julianna dug out the stone, peeved at the interruption. "It would have been better to have the very first ones brought back."

Bored again, Mazy stared at sunlight on stone tiles. Her folk had come from Africa and Puerto Rico after the big storms. She knew the names of the places. What were they like? What were their rocks like? Julianna's spells would end in wreckage and lost chances, not freedom. No better than Asima's house, after all. Mazy would miss the cool linen against her skin when she went back to the state foster house, cheap polyester clothes, and vending-machine chocolate.

Gillen weighed the stone in her fingers. "I found out some interesting points about this, just now. Do you know where it's from?"

Julianna shrugged. "The Moon. Our Lady's Mirror."

"The Mare Orientale, the Sea of the East. The far edge of the Moon that we see from Earth. It's refractory basalt with over ten percent titanium and a few water molecules. A wonder of the Goddess." While speaking, Gillen half-turned and put the stone into Mazy's hands.

Sea of the East. Impossible words lodged inside Mazy's thoughts and sang there:

Earth and her Moon, one body tightly wound into a semi-molten sphere, until another massive sphere crashed just alongside, shattering itself. A dull red blob of Earth-stuff and the interloper flung outward, collapsed into another ball. Red paled to silver, darkened to black. So huge, so close in those first eons.

Earth and the Moon, the interloper's bones buried deep under the Moon's dust,

Spinning together, drawing apart, driving tides across the new oceans of Earth.

Down through the ages, until—

The Moon remembered human footsteps, little rocket flares, gloved hands reaching out to take these very rocks.

Mazy blinked away the Moon's dream, knowing it would stay with her.

"So?" Julianna blustered. "The Moon's purity was debased the moment human tools touched it!"

"You use bronze tools, but ride on steel and plastic trains driven by electricity from nuclear, solar, and hydrothermal power plants," Gillen said. "Your bronze knife holds a better edge because an alloy toughens it. You claim to be a white witch, but you would wake fire and earthquake, upheaval and death. Isn't that dark sacrilege? Even if it is futile."

"Futile?" Julianna growled, stepping closer to Mazy. "Look

around. This new world believes more in science than our Lady's magic. They insult and ignore her to their peril!"

Gillen shook her head. "I think they only ignore and mock you. How many doors did our Lady open for you, but you didn't step through? You want the wrong things for the wrong reasons. Montrose wrote a book because she never gained such power herself. You made it into a prophecy. There is no Sisterhood but you. The rest of us stopped trying to manipulate the world with selfish little spells, and settled for changing ourselves to fit the future!"

"Gil," said Tom.

"Why can't a druid be a hydroponics engineer on Luna Colony?" Gillen pointed skyward, more fiery than Mazy had ever seen her. "Why can't a witch be a programmer? What is wrong with seeing the Lady's signature in a carbon-nanite tube or in the transit of a water-rich planet across a star thirty light-years away?"

Julianna's face turned gray-white as her dress. Her thin lips flattened again as she shrugged off doubt. "*Technophile*. Then we are three no more." To Mazy, she said, "We will find another sister." To Tom: "Will you let me take the rocks?"

The little man shrugged. "Not my circus, not my monkeys. Go with what you've already taken."

Julianna and Mazy stood silhouetted in the planetarium's outer doors. Afternoon sun brimmed through the glass, slanting through green-gold filters of olive, fig, palm, and eucalyptus leaves—reflections from metallic traffic on the street below the hill. Now that the earthquake warning was over, electric vehicles whooshed faintly on the roads, mimicking the sound of the sea.

"Wait," said castoff Gillen. "Goodbye, Maize Robinson." She tossed the amethyst pendant. Mazy caught it and tugged the chain over her head.

Later, over chocolate yogurt, Mazy would look at her prize. On the silver back, Gillen had scratched in delicate letters: "Two

Roads to the Moon." One of Julianna's pirated ideas turned on itself, into a highway that did not smell of dust or death.

Tom relaxed against a wall in the lobby. "How ridiculous, Gil. How could that woman and her misplaced rituals, her ignorance, ever harm humanity?"

Gillen looked at him grimly. "By holding us back until it's too late to leave the planet. Do I detect a bit of aristocratic scorn? You believed enough in her to come here a week early, Dr. Hennessey."

"Only to see you, witch." He absently played with the second medallion on his silver chain, a silver starship in a wreath of oak leaves. "But now I will see that child for the rest of my life. Poor girl."

"Mazy is a sharp young woman under her dreams. She won't let her own talents be siphoned by Julianna much longer." Gillen chuckled. "Or by me. Julianna may give her prizes a little power born of belief, but not much. She'll curse awhile in her little house and then destroy the rocks with a bronze hammer."

"Is there a watch on both of them, just in case? Now that you aren't a dutiful Sister anymore?"

Gillen nodded. "Julianna will get a couple of new, perfect recruits in the next few months." She looked around at the shelves, posters, and mobiles spinning on their wires. She touched one model rocket with a gentle fingertip. "Ad Astra, and all that. To the Future."

"To the Future!" Tom said, then laughed, and lifted from his briefcase a bag of heavy, well-traveled, refractory basalts from the far plains of the Moon.

You're so tired you catch yourself drifting off right where you stand. You can almost but not quite remember the dream you were having. If it feels like it belonged to someone else, turn left for room 22 (page 253). Or if you're fairly certain the dream was your own, proceed straight ahead to room 17.

17
Alice Under Marmalade Skies

CATHERINE DUFOUR

SITTING UNDER A TALL LINDEN TREE ON A LAZY SUMMER afternoon, Alice found that she was bored half to sleep. She had just finished her book and did not know what to do until tea time. She lay down on the grass, taking care to smooth her hair over her shoulders. Now that she was ten, she needed to take some interest in her appearance. (Her sister had been *quite clear* on that point.) Alice took care to keep her eyes wide open so as not to fall once more into one of those peculiar dreams she used to have, whose telling had only brought her rude comments—or in one case, unseemly attention.

The sky through the linden's branches was blue as blue could be. So Alice was surprised to feel a small, cold drop fall on the corner of her chin. Then another on the tip of her nose, and then two more in the middle of her forehead.

She hastily sat up, drew her hand across her face, and looked down at her fingertips.

"This is quite curious," she said out loud, for she had an old habit of addressing herself when there was no one else around to talk to, "but it does seem to be marmalade."

Alice tasted it hesitatingly and then exclaimed, "Orange marmalade! Really? Really! How comical! Alas, I fear I am dreaming once more."

The thought of having to grow large and small again, and run after white rabbits, and fall down at least two thousand miles, and listen to songs almost as long, made her feel tired enough that she settled back down on the grass.

"Oh!" she cried. Beyond the linden tree, enormous clouds were drifting against the blue of the sky. They were positively orange, shading here and there to darker crescents that looked exactly like candied peel.

"I have never seen such curious clouds before," said Alice, sitting back up. She was smoothing her hair again when a rabbit wearing a funnel collar ran close by her and disappeared into a copse on her right. Alice got up with a sigh and approached the copse, under which opened a familiar-looking rabbit hole.

"For once, I'm glad I have grown. It is quite impossible for me to fall down to the Queen's croquet ground again," Alice mused aloud. Not that she disliked croquet, but that particular type of croquet was very difficult to play, especially as flamingos and hedgehogs were hardly obedient creatures.

"Walruses are not very obedient either," said a voice from behind her. She turned round and saw what appeared to be a decorated military officer standing near the copse. He was clad in a red velvet uniform with silver hook-and-eye fasteners that shone in the peculiar orange light and a funny little black hat, which Alice found most ridiculous. (But she did not burst out laughing, because she had already turned ten.)

The man wore a short mustache and fine round glasses with smoked lenses—just like Mr. Carlisle, who came to the house from time to time to tune the piano. "Only he's *much* more handsome than Mr. Carlisle," Alice said to herself, though she was hardly accustomed to having an opinion on other people's faces since her sister had explained to her that it was none of her business.

"Sir…Sir, I seem to recall that walruses are above all cruel things," she said in a very small voice.

In another moment she blushed, for she had completely

forgotten to introduce herself.

"Of course," she thought, "if one considers that I am almost a young lady, *he* should be the one introducing himself… but I believe that, in such a case, it would be good manners for me not to address him altogether; which would be a pity, because I want very much for him to tell me why he is wearing such a little hat with such a large uniform."

"Why cruel?" the officer went on, wiggling his tiny mustache on either side of his mouth. "There are no creatures more peaceful than walruses—apart from hedgehogs, of course—and I find you quite *impertinent* towards such animals."

"I'm sorry I have offended you," said Alice, feeling none too proud. "Mayhap one of his friends is a walrus, or a family member?" she reflected under her breath. The man raised an eyebrow. "Although this does not seem very likely, for your teeth appear to be quite the right size…the right size for an officer, of course," she hastened to add so as not to offend the man any further. "And I wonder if the word 'impertinent' is quite correct. But I was told the story of a walrus and a carpenter who fed on oysters and—"

"Have *you* never eaten any?"

"Well," Alice hesitated, "I might have, but…I had not invited them for a walk first, you see?"

"Not at all," the officer muttered, and leaning over Alice, he began picking flowers from the copse.

Alice stood up to watch, thinking they were beautiful flowers with large petals of yellow and green, as translucent as white mica. They grew so fast that the officer had to unfold a stepladder and then stand on its platform and finally raise himself upon tiptoe.

"They grow incredibly high, do they not?" said he in a thoughtful tone, cutting the thick green stalks with silver pincers.

"Oh…yes, quite" said Alice, who was feeling giddy from standing with her head back.

"Would you like to help me carry them to their destination?" said the officer, who having climbed down off the stepladder, was binding the flowers together with the chin strap of his hat.

"Well, yes, if you want," said Alice. Then she considered a little and added, "unless they are for the Red Queen. Or the Duchess. Or—"

"Haven't these ladies offered you impeccable hospitality?" the officer asked in a surprised tone, turning wide, reproachful eyes on her.

Alice faltered a little, and then remembered that she was now ten years old and ought not to let herself be overawed anymore.

"No, they have not. They talk loudly, they speak nonsense, they find fault with every sentence I say, and they put far too much pepper in the soup, so that it tickles my nose. And that's when they're not after my head!"

"Ah, well," the officer retorted, "to lose one's head is not always an unpleasant experience. And what do you have against pepper? Indeed, my name means 'pepper,' and no one has ever told me I tickle." And then with a tip of his ridiculous hat, he added, "Sgt. Poivre."

He then turned his back on Alice and began to stride across the meadow with the huge bunch of flowers thrown over his right shoulder, leaving a trail of flattened grass behind him.

"I meant to ask you—" Alice panted, struggling to keep up. "I meant to ask you why you are wearing that hat."

"It is either of two things," Sgt. Poivre replied with a martial air. "Either I am wearing a hat, or I am not. And if I am not, then there's no question to be asked about my hat. Contrariwise, 'Why *aren't* you wearing a hat?' Now that would be a pointless question. And if I *am* wearing one—"

"Oh, no, you don't!" Alice cried out, stamping her foot. This forced her to stop, but fortunately, Sgt. Poivre also stopped at the same time. Otherwise, they should not have been able to keep up their conversation, such as it was. "I shall not bear yet again one of those arguments that bring on nothing but headaches!" She took a moment to catch her breath and then proceeded in a calmer tone: "It would be simpler if you told me that you are embarrassed by my question, and that you have no intention of answering it. For indeed, your hat looks surprisingly like…like *tonsillitis!*"

Sgt. Poivre looked at her with such a pained expression that Alice felt herself blushing to the roots of her hair. "What are you doing here then, if you can only bear reasonable conversations?"

Alice almost replied that she had never asked to walk under marmalade clouds with a man wearing a hat that looked like an illness, but she gave it up, being quite busy enough trying not to be left behind, for Sgt. Poivre had resumed his march through the tall grass.

Presently, they came to a forest of tangerine trees. Sgt. Poivre had the greatest difficulty maneuvering the flowers between the trunks, setting off here and there great showers of tangerines.

Soon, a gang of rocking horses were crowding around the heaps of fruit, noisily devouring them in a great gnashing of wooden teeth. Alice kept jumping to the side so that her feet would not get bruised by the rockers, which swung back and forth, squirting juice and pits all round.

"At your age," Sgt. Poivre observed, "you should be wearing red shoes."

"Why, that would be as ugly as your hat!" replied Alice rudely, for she found the comment oddly improper and did not feel as much inclined to be nice as previously. Since she had turned ten, in fact, she sometimes found great pleasure in disconcerting the people she was talking to by giving them answers they did not expect.

"Red shoes," Sgt. Poivre went on imperturbably, "and also a red petticoat."

"Ah!" Alice exclaimed, pulling on her blue skirt, which for the past few days had seemed to her somewhat shorter than usual.

But Sgt. Poivre did not let her go on: "There was a time when it would have been a red riding hood, so you have no reason to complain. And we must do something about your bodice."

Alice did not hear this last remark as she was busy wondering what this all had to do with Little Red Riding Hood and whether she should have an opportunity to meet the Big Bad Wolf.

"That would be," she thought to herself, "a probative experience."

She did not know what the word *probative* meant, but she had always been fond of nice grand words. Meanwhile, they had reached a bridge by a fountain, whose margin was lined with pies filled with marshmallows—some blue and some pink. A newspaper taxi was parked at the foot of the bridge.

Sgt. Poivre fastened the flowers to the roof rack and opened the door. Then he beckoned to Alice, who was lingering before the pies. "I fancy the blue marshmallows should make me grow larger and the pink ones grow smaller," she said to herself. "Or should it be the reverse? How can I find out? I might try a little of this one, but if I grow too fast, the bridge will collapse under my weight, and I'd very much risk drowning. Unless of course I've grown large enough by that time not to lose my footing…"

Her thoughts were interrupted by Sgt. Poivre, who was gently shaking her shoulder and saying over and over, "Are you coming? Are you coming? The train will leave without us!"

"What train are you talking about?" murmured Alice, though she was not surprised, for she believed all taxis inexorably led to trains. She climbed in a paper taxi, and with a gentle sound of ruffled newspapers, it took them to a little blue and green railway station. Alongside the station, massive locomotives were moored amidst billows of white steam. Plasticine-skinned porters, their uniforms richly adorned with looking-glass fragments, came to take Sgt. Poivre's flowers away and usher him and Alice aboard. They found their seats in an empty compartment and sat down side by side.

"I do not know whether these floating steam engines will go very fast," Alice speculated.

But Sgt. Poivre reassured her: "It is the landscape that moves, you know. All the steam engines have to do is to remain alongside the platform, and even a steam engine is smart enough to do that."

Looking perfectly reassured himself, he took off his little hat and set it on his lap. Alice, in order not to laugh inopportunely (for the little hat looked more and more like untreated bronchitis), merely looked out the window. The landscape was indeed passing by, alternating between endless fields of strawberry plants and shaded gardens in which the main crop appeared to be…*octopuses*. Just then, a flight of wild honey pies came in through an open window, crossed the compartment, and flew back out again without a single pie alighting, to Alice's great regret.

"I'm glad I didn't eat any pink or blue marshmallows," mumbled Alice, "for surely I should not have been able to get on the train. I should have been too big to fit in or too little to reach the steps."

"One is always either too big or too little," declared Sgt. Poivre in a melancholy voice.

Alice turned round to face him and saw, much to her astonishment, that big bright tears were rolling down his pink cheeks before disappearing into his mustache.

"You, for instance," Sgt. Poivre began again after blowing his nose, "are now too big to come here."

"Why?" asked Alice carelessly. "After all," she said to herself, "now that I am ten, it seems pointless to force myself to ask only sensible questions, when so many people do not bother to."

"Oh, this is a place that doesn't agree with grown persons," said Sgt. Poivre. "Here, consider Miss Rigby..."

"Who's Miss Rigby?" Alice asked, yawning discreetly. She felt tired and would have gladly taken a nap on the seat, would it not have been very rude to Sgt. Poivre and had the seat not been so terribly uncomfortable, as it was made of varnished black wood with silver hinges. "Is it this...Miss Rigby that we're on our way to meet?"

"Who is she?" Sgt. Poivre repeated in a funereal voice. "Alas, she is no more. And as to meeting her, I do believe we are *sitting* on her."

Alice started to her feet and saw that indeed the seat she and Sgt. Poivre had taken looked *exactly* like a coffin. She remained speechless for a moment, then cried out, "But...this is awful! I shall not remain here a moment longer!"

She hurried out into the corridor, which was yellow and terribly damp. The windows were perfectly round and carefully shut. Pressing her face against one, Alice saw a fish swim by wearing a curly wig on its head. Sgt. Poivre came and rested his face next to hers.

"We're not in the train any more, are we?" sighed Alice.

"Of course we are. Only we've moved into a submarine landscape," Sgt. Poivre replied shortly. "Please try to attend."

"Oh, my head hurts..." moaned Alice.

"You are decidedly far too big," grumbled Sgt. Poivre.

"But what danger is there for a big girl here, apart from a headache?" Alice countered. She found those constant remarks about her size difficult to endure, especially since her size had been *incredibly* stable since the beginning of the dream, and therefore *absolutely* beyond reproach.

"I was talking about your age," Sgt. Poivre replied in what Alice thought was an *insufferably* peremptory manner. "Do you want to know what befalls grown-ups who venture into Alice's world? Oh, examples abound. There was a story my friend Lewis Padgett told me...Do you remember the

Jabberwocky poem? That same poem you read backwards through the looking glass. Well, rather than just a poem, it is a recipe. To return to the Sea."

"I don't see the point in that," mumbled Alice, while a bed of mussels mockingly winked at her.

"Humans never return to the Sea, do they? They live and die wherever they spawn. Because they haven't read 'Jabberwocky,' which alone holds the key to reentering the Sea. Of course, only children can understand it."

"So how can that harm grown-ups?"

"It harms them in that one day their children read the poem and return to the Sea without them. Picture a teddy bear left behind on a bed, and a father sitting at the end of the bed crying because both his children have just returned to the Sea and left him all alone."

"Oh, that is a dreadful thing, surely," whispered Alice, wiping the condensation which her breath had left on the porthole's freezing glass.

"The Jabberwocky's song is very, *very* dangerous. Especially in French."

"And why in French?" grumbled Alice, who could not differentiate between '*J'ai tout*,' and '*Je hais tout*.'

"Because it was translated by Boris Vian! And when a poet translates a poet, you get a poem squared, don't you?"

"Oh?"

"It is *dangerous*. Do not forget that! Nothing is easier to recognize. The poem begins: "Twas brillig, and the slithy toves'…"

"When I tell my sister this part," moaned Alice inwardly, "I shall never be able to recall that poem, and she'll make fun of me once again. Could it be a bad habit of mine always to relate my dreams to a hard-of-hearing cat and a sister who laughs at them and then goes on to run them down from the rooftops?"

"You must not, when you are married, let your children read it," Sgt. Poivre insisted. "And then there's that story my friend Gahan Wilson wrote, in which we once more come across the Walrus and the Carpenter eating oysters."

"Oh, those two, I hate them!" exclaimed Alice. "No one is more deceitful, or more cruel! To invite those poor oysters for a walk, to have them slice the very bread on which they were to be crucified…"

"Well, according to my friend, these oysters were quite human, and the bodies that were found on the beach were very pale."

"Were they sick?" inquired Alice.

"I don't think so, no," mumbled Sgt. Poivre, sucking on the corner of his mustache. "They were drunk, I believe. And there's also that song: 'All the Young Girls Love Alice.'"

"Why should they all love *me*?" asked Alice with concern. "I get along well with Mabel and with Ada, but I detest Amy… And anyway, I prefer cats. And there is no such thing as a human oyster."

Sgt. Poivre gave her a sidelong glance. "It is not a very respectable song, and it doesn't end very well. By the way, I was also told a story—"

"I do not want to hear any more," said Alice sulkily, turning her back on Sgt. Poivre. "Is it my fault that Mr. Dodgson wrote silly stories pretending they were my dreams?"

"Want it or not, a thousand fantasies have added to yours, and they form like… like a gigantic ball of yarn!" said Sgt. Poivre enthusiastically. "Or a spider's web, in which many innocent people got entangled," he finished somberly.

"That is not my affair!" cried Alice who, now that she was ten years old, had decided she would no longer feel guilty for all the foolish things that were attributed to her. "Let everyone look where they're going, after all. And I hate knitting, and I'm afraid of spiders."

She purposefully strode down the damp yellow corridor and pushed open the door leading to the next carriage. But rather than a carriage, she found herself entering the engine driver's cabin, or else an observatory, with thick, round windows that plunged into the dark blue of the sea. Passing fluorescent squids caressed the glass with long, waxy tentacles.

"So, how are you feeling, my dear?" said a man sitting in front of an instrument panel covered with little blinking lights. He stared straight ahead, not looking at Alice, turning a huge wheel of polished wood from time to time.

"I feel strangely oppressed," said Alice in an uncertain voice. And then in another moment, she felt comforted, for she had just recognized her cousin William's voice.

"Look!" he said. "We're coming to the Abbey."

The submarine was moving slowly through a field of verdant seaweed, chasing herds of seahorses out of its way. Far ahead, Alice saw the silhouette of a long church in ruins coming into view, pale and dismal in the twilight.

"On the road to the Abbey," murmured William, pulling several short levers. "And look! Sgt. Poivre's band! There they are, all four of them..."

Alice saw on the road in front of them a gaily colored brass band marching by, led by four minstrels in sparkling uniforms, and among them was Sgt. Poivre, who played the sousaphone with gusto. He had taken off his glasses, and his eyes twinkled like twin kaleidoscopes. Alice thought she recognized all the musicians marching in pairs: the Mouse and the Lory, the Duchess and the Dodo, the Baby and the Snark, the White Queen sitting cross-legged on Humpty Dumpty's head and hitting her own with a silver ladle...

"...and this is the last time," finished William, heaving a deep, melancholy sigh, which turned to steam in the freezing air.

"This, however, is the *first* time I've had such a sad dream," said Alice with a lump in her throat. "I keep being told that I've got no business here, and certainly I should be better off elsewhere."

"Really?" William asked, turning a big Cheshire Cat smile on her.

"Well," mumbled Alice, blushing, "I think so, yes. Or maybe not. That is, apparently I've got no business in my own dreams anymore. One wonders how I got into this one in the first place," she finished in a sulky tone, wrapping a strand of hair around her finger.

"That's because of all the mushrooms, you see…"

"What mushrooms?"

"All these mushrooms. Really, cousin, you oughtn't to…"

William got up and advanced towards her, while the yellow submarine seemed to sink into ever darker waters. The air kept getting colder, and the sounds of the brass band grew fainter.

"You oughtn't to sleep amid these mushrooms."

Alice opened her eyes and saw William's smile right above her. She turned her head and found herself nose to cap with a little rounded mushroom, which exhaled a curious acid smell. She sat up, shivering, and William put an arm around her shoulders.

"They're toxic, cousin, and it seems you've caught cold."

"I've had another dream," Alice explained through chattering teeth. "If you want, I can tell you all about it. But only *you*, Billy. Don't mention it to *anyone*…" As she spoke, Alice discreetly pulled on her skirt, which really did have a tendency to shorten these days. "At any rate, not to my hag of a sister, nor to that tiresome Mr. Dodgson."

You lose your balance for a moment, and it feels as if the whole building is moving. You recall its flying saucer shape. If a trip across the universe sounds appealing, turn right for room 14 (page 179). Or if you suspect it's already underway, proceed straight ahead to room 18.

18
Dorothy in the Land of Poppies

CLIFF JONES JR.

OVERCOME WITH PLEASANT FATIGUE, DOROTHY RESOLVED TO rest a moment on the poppy-laden ground. But as she nestled among the crimson flowers, she found no ground beneath them, only an endless night sky. She pushed her face through the petals and stared into that black abyss. And then, to her amazement, she found the darkness staring back at her.

What she had taken for stars she now recognized as reflections on a pair of dark eyes and a wet pug nose. What might have been a pink crescent moon was nothing more than the familiar protruding tongue of her little dog Toto. But oh, how large he had grown!

"Is that really you, Toto?" Dorothy exclaimed. "You've grown so that I almost didn't recognize you!" The celestial canine face resolved itself into a more manageable form that, while still quite large, no longer defied reason.

"I've become a wolf," Toto replied. "Though truly, I always suspected I was a wolf on the inside."

Dorothy had never before heard Toto speak, not even a single word. Yet this was unquestionably the voice of her oldest and dearest friend. And despite his transformation, this new Toto felt perfectly natural, as if he'd always been an enormous talking wolf.

"What's become of…" Dorothy began, trying to recall exactly who was missing from their party. "Was it always just the two of us?"

"I think that's right," answered the beast. "I know that I exist, at least the part of me that does the knowing…And you seem to exist as well—though it could be that you're actually just a bit more of me—but as for the rest of this…" He raised a forepaw and lowered his head in something approximating a shrug. Then without finishing the thought, he turned to leave the meadow.

Taking this gesture as it was intended, Dorothy climbed onto Toto's woolly back, gripped the fur behind his ears, and held on tight.

Together they raced over hill and dale, through the Whispering Woods, and across the Deadly Desert. And then before Dorothy knew quite how it had happened, they were inside a long, white hallway with stacks of wire cages along both walls. The air was thick with the scent of disinfectant, which only partly masked the musky odor of animal waste. Most of the cages held field mice, but there were also a few rats and rabbits, and the pitiful mewling of a kitten could be heard some ways off.

Toto followed the sound without a word until they were face to face with the little creature. The door of its cage was wide open, but the tiny orange tabby cowered in one corner, its head buried in its paws, refusing even to look at its visitors. Here too was something familiar.

"Is that you, Lion?" asked Dorothy.

"Lion?" echoed the kitten. "I don't believe I've ever been a lion, not really. But yes, it's me, such as I am." He looked up at Dorothy and seemed to grow a little large for his cage. He resumed speaking, now with a faint but undeniable hint of regality: "We're all stuck here, and I'm afraid it's my fault somehow. I tried to run, but…Oh, this awful smell! Can we go somewhere else please? Find a bit of fresh air?"

Dorothy scooped up the Cowardly Kitten and placed him in front of her on Toto's back, to which he clung with tiny kitten claws. Now they were ready to continue their journey. Without turning back, there was really only one direction they could go. And so they forged ahead through the cluttered, fetid hallway, marching on.

All at once, the hall came to an abrupt end, and it seemed the group could go no further. The bare wall before them was completely white and featureless.

"Oh no, this won't do at all," cried Dorothy.

"We'll have to turn back," whined the Cowardly Kitten. "I never much cared for mice, even at my full stature. And now… Why, I'd be helpless as a kitten if one should chance to escape its cage!"

Toto stood stock still, staring at the wall ahead of them and sniffing with his powerful lupine snout. "Paper," he said at last. And then before Dorothy could ask what he'd meant by this remark, Toto leapt directly at the wall as if he meant to jump right through it.

And miraculously, that is exactly what happened.

As Toto's immense paws hit the paper wall, it ripped away to reveal a large, scientific-looking room on the other side. The trio flew through the air and landed heavily on a polished metal floor. Obviously unprepared for this slick surface, Toto faltered and slid across the room. The Cowardly Kitten was able to dig in his claws and hang onto Toto's back, but Dorothy tumbled to the ground and rolled into a tangle of cords and wires.

Just then, a high-pitched alarm went off, and Dorothy found herself inside what seemed to be a sort of coffin made out of glass or crystal. Though she had to admit it was surprisingly comfortable, she had no intention of remaining inside the ghastly thing a moment longer. She pressed on the inside of its transparent lid, but it wouldn't budge. Coming faster now, her breath began to fog the glass.

"Come on now, it won't do any good to panic," she chided herself. "What would Uncle Henry do?" She tried to imagine the kindly old face of her dear uncle, lined with decades of hard-earned wisdom, but all she got was vague gray shadows. It was as if she'd never really known the man, only seen a gray-cast photograph. As she tried to focus her mental image of Uncle Henry and bring some color into the picture, his face resolved into the Scarecrow, looking vapid and foolish as ever.

"Oh, Aunt Em!" she cried out. "I need you!" But again, all she could recall was a vague sense of the woman: her deep gray eyes, her silver hair pulled back into a bun, her skin the color of…well, of *metal*. It wasn't the sweet face of her Aunt Em at all but that of the Tin Woodman, cold and without emotion. He looked on expressionless as Dorothy burst into tears and began pounding her fists against the glass.

Just as she was beginning to lose all hope, the lid of her coffin released a hiss of air and proceeded to open completely on its own.

Dorothy sat up and looked around. She was in the same scientific-looking room as before, but Toto and the Cowardly Kitten were nowhere to be seen. To her left and to her right were scores of glass coffins identical to her own. She had a feeling she wasn't in Oz anymore.

From across the room, a woman in a white jacket and trousers came running toward her, apologizing indistinctly for the unpleasant noise the alarm was making. "Looks like a monitor got unplugged here somehow." She stooped down to wrestle with a tangle of cords and wires. At last the noise stopped, to the woman's obvious relief. "Now," she began hesitantly, "you must be wondering what you're doing here. Am I right?"

Dorothy could think of no response to appropriately convey her bewilderment, so she asked simply, "Have I died?"

"Have you— No, nothing like that!" the woman answered

with a smile. "Listen…I'm Theodora Lake. And you are?"

"Dorothy Gale."

"Right," replied Theodora. "Kansas. Have you been to Oz yet?"

Dorothy was astonished. "I've just come from there! But how did you—"

"So you know then, how it's possible to be in one place and then fall asleep, and when you wake up…you're somewhere *else*. Do you follow?"

Dorothy nodded, mostly to be polite.

Theodora continued, "We're on a generation ship bound for Rigil Kent. It's going to be quite a long time before we get there, you know, so the passengers need something to do while they wait. So you *dream*, basically. But it's under control…so you don't have any nightmares or—We call it the *DIVE*: Dream-Integrated Virtual Environment. See? Kind of a pun. Is any of this making sense?"

Dorothy shook her head.

"Well…It's not really so important that you understand everything just yet. You woke up early, and I need to send you back—like the sooner the better." Theodora set to drumming her fingers along the inside of her wrist, and as she did so, her eyes darted back and forth like mad. "Okay, this should do it. Back to chapter nine…" Her gaze returned to Dorothy, and seeing the tears in her eyes, Theodora softened her expression.

"All right now, no need to fret," said the uncanny woman. "It's just—The real world is—Well, now that you know it's all a dream, you'll have to be very careful not to treat it as unimportant. Just because a thing's not real, that doesn't mean it doesn't matter. Do you follow?"

"I suppose…I understand," conceded Dorothy. "So really…there's no such place as Oz or Kansas…but where else am I going to go?"

"Well put," replied Theodora after a moment's consideration. "That's a decent attitude to have, and true enough. Just try not to lose perspective when I send you back. The DIVE is… It's as much a test as it is a training program. And if you fail, then we can't use you, except as—Well anyway, don't fail." She forced a toothy smile, but it did little to mask the pained look in her eyes.

"No…" Dorothy muttered, unsure of where she was headed with this sudden urge to resist. "No, I don't want to go back. I can stay here with you. I can— I'm sure there's something I can do!"

Theodora shook her head with a short, sad laugh. "Honestly, you don't want to be like me. You get to see the Promised Land, kid. I'm just—" She gestured feebly around the room, down the row of glass coffins. This was her life—day in, day out—with no promise of a better life in another world.

"I don't care!" Dorothy shouted in return. "I don't want to sleep. I want to live! I can't just pretend like I don't know. I have to…" She trailed off, feeling suddenly sleepy as Theodora resumed drumming her fingers on the inside of her wrist.

Dorothy lay back once more in her glass coffin, resigned to a life of make-believe. It wouldn't be so bad. In fact, there was some comfort in knowing that whatever happened to her in life, however bad things got, somewhere she was safe and clean and cozy, and Theodora Lake was watching over her.

Just before the transparent lid moved itself back into place, Theodora leaned in to say one last thing: "Good luck, Dorothy. If anybody gives you trouble…just toss a bucket of water on them. You'll be fine."

The coffin filled with a familiar medicinal scent—*poppies?*—and Dorothy drifted off to sleep once more.

This room contains a couple of small bookshelves. The one on the right is labeled "non-fiction" and contains mostly self-help guides and psychology textbooks. The one on the left is labeled "fiction" and seems limited to fairy tales. For non-fiction, turn right for room 13 (page 161). For fiction, proceed straight ahead to room 19.

19
Domestic Animals I Have Known

CHARLES C. MITCHELL

ONE SUNNY AFTERNOON, A LITTLE GIRL NAMED EDIE DECIDED to climb the gigantic crepe myrtle tree in her grandmother's backyard. Halfway up, she found a small hole where a limb had broken free. This cavity collected twigs and old leaves and converted them into a special kind of dirt that her grandmother called "wishing dust." Edie reached into the tree, grabbed a handful of wishing dust, and closed her eyes. As she tossed the dust into the air, she whispered to herself, "I wish for an adventure."

As the dust rained down, a jumble of growls, hissing, and caterwauling came from the bottom of the tree. The noises quickly turned to the sound of coughing, and an irritated voice rang out: "Hey, watch where you're throwing that stuff, kid!"

Confused, Edie looked around and said, "I'm sorry. I didn't realize anyone was down there."

Directly below her, she spotted a fat orange tomcat dusting himself off. "Never mind that. I'm glad I found you. I'm Detective Pinkerton, and I'm here on official business." Noting the girl's astonishment, Detective Pinkerton continued, "Yes, yes, I'm a talking cat, one of many, but let's get past that already. This is important, and a lot of cats need our help! Now please climb down from there with another handful of that wishing dust; we're going to need it."

With a handful of wishing dust, Edie made her descent from the giant tree, muttering, "Is this a dream? Am I dreaming? I must be. I'm sure cats can't talk." Then as she carefully lowered herself onto a limb that resembled the neck of a large giraffe, she asked, "Are you really a detective? What does a detective cat investigate? What makes you different from a house cat?"

The cat laughed. "I assure you that this is no dream. I'm really just a house cat. My human companion Phil gave me the title of detective, but never mind that now. I'm actually here about your companion, Dori. You see, she's a dear friend of mine, and she needs our help. Along with hundreds of other innocent cats, she is being held in the Cunabula dungeon."

Edie reached the ground and stood twice as tall as the upright Detective Pinkerton. He extended a paw and briefly shook her free hand. "It's a pleasure to finally meet you, Edie. Dori has spoken highly of you." Detective Pinkerton motioned for the wishing dust with both front paws.

"Wait," she said, "you mean you know my little gray cat Dori, and she's in a *dungeon* somewhere?" Edie began to pace and flail her arms about as she spoke. "Why are we just standing here?! We have to save her! Why is she even in there?!"

The talking tomcat let out another laugh. "Did you say 'little' gray cat? I wouldn't have used the word little, but don't worry; we'll rescue the big gray fur-ball. As for why she's locked away, I'm afraid she's a victim of the cantankerous King Felix. He recently went around throwing oodles of unlucky felines into the dungeon over really ridiculous offenses. I believe Dori was taken in for napping in the King's garden. She's really done nothing wrong. Anyway, hand over the dust, and we'll get going."

Detective Pinkerton waved a paw full of wishing dust over the base of the great tree, flicking his tail about as he went. He sprinkled a little here and a little there, all the while making a strange chattering sound. Finally, he threw the last of the dust at the base of the tree, and a small cloud formed around the two of them. They were still coughing when the dust settled, revealing a tiny wooden door leading into the tree.

"Right this way," said Pinkerton, grabbing Edie's hand with one paw and opening the door with the other.

"Don't be ridiculous. I'll never fit through there," said Edie.

Detective Pinkerton paused, "I seem to have gotten ahead of myself." He began searching through his own thick orange fur until stopping at a fold behind one of his ears. "Ah, here we are," he said, pulling out a small fish-shaped treat. "Eat this and we'll be on our way. It's infused with mutagenic botanicals."

With the hope of rescuing her cat Dori from a dungeon, Edie reluctantly ate the odd little treat. She struggled to ignore the cat food taste in her mouth as she chewed.

"Delicious, isn't it? I make them myself," said Detective Pinkerton proudly.

Before she could answer, Edie began her surprise transformation into a cat. A fluorescent green glow surrounded her body as she shrank and transmogrified. The wide-eyed young girl watched her hand change into a paw and sprout black fur. Detective Pinkerton seemed to grow as she got smaller. When her transformation was complete, he stood almost twice as tall as her. The fat orange tomcat took the little black kitten by the paw, and the two disappeared through the doorway in the side of the tree.

The mismatched pair floated gently down into the earth. Above them, a complex web of roots could be seen. What appeared to be thousands of fireflies littered the atmosphere, illuminating the outline of a massive city in the distance.

"That's Cunabula!" cried Detective Pinkerton, pointing to the silhouettes of three massive towers. "We'll be there soon enough." The grass-covered ground became visible below as they continued to drift gracefully down.

"You mean the door to this place is in my grandma's

backyard?" asked Edie, looking up to the opening in the tree.

As their paws landed on the soft ground, Detective Pinkerton said, "There are many doors that all lead here. Think of this place as everywhere and nowhere at the same time." He smiled. "Welcome to Aeluria!"

The two cats made their way down a dirt path, through patches of trees and shrubbery. As they popped out of a thicket and could just make out the edge of the palace ahead, Edie asked, "So how am I helping Dori? What's your plan, Detective?"

The orange tabby continued forward as he answered: "I thought your presence here would be obvious. When a cat's in trouble, it's nice to have a witch on their side, especially when the cat in question happens to be that particular witch's familiar. As far as a plan goes, I figured we'd sneak into Cunabula and free them by force. You can use your magic to help us if we get into trouble…" Detective Pinkerton trailed off as he noticed a concerned look on the little black kitten's face.

"I'm afraid I don't know any magic. I'm not a witch. I'm just a girl disguised as a cat," said Edie.

Detective Pinkerton smiled. "Come on now, all little girls know magic. Besides, only witches are able to transform into cats, and other than cats, witches are the only creatures magical enough to enter the land of Aeluria. I'm sure your powers will help us when the time is right."

A busy little city surrounded Cunabula's tall, luxurious towers. Cats of various colors and sizes crammed into the streets. Vendors lined the sidewalks, standing behind their booths, each filled with basket after basket of everything from dried fish to bottles of cream. Some booths had mostly cheeses to offer, while one had several different varieties of catnip on display. One vendor, a slender tortoiseshell cat, amused onlookers as he skillfully made biscuits. A yellow cat with a bobtail pushed a few discarded fish bones through the crowd with a wide broom. Cats shifted here and there, giving the yellow cat the room he needed to work. The large orange tabby and the little girl disguised as a black kitten trailed closely behind the cat with the bobtail and broom, finding it easier to get around that way than squeezing through the crowd on their own.

After navigating the maze of busy streets, Edie and Detective Pinkerton finally arrived at the Cunabula Palace entrance. As they made their way across a wooden drawbridge suspended above a moat, the little black kitten peered down into the water to marvel at the hundreds of multicolored koi fish. While doing this, she caught her new reflection for the first time. Edie stared into the pool of her own eyes: two yellow dots lost in the endless glowing orbs of fireflies.

Detective Pinkerton nudged her forward, but just then a fluffy white cat moved to block the entrance, let out a lazy yawn, and said, "State your business."

Detective Pinkerton cleared his throat and said, "We've come to dine in the King's Court."

The fluffy white cat looked annoyed. "Dining in the King's Court is through invitation only," she said.

Detective Pinkerton began searching through his tufts of fur. "I have both of our invitations here somewhere. I'm sure of it," he replied.

A line of cats waiting to enter the castle formed behind Edie and Detective Pinkerton. The fluffy white cat rolled her eyes, more annoyed than before. At this point, Detective Pinkerton pulled several small fish-shaped cat treats from the thickness of his fur and dropped them in front of the aggravated fluffy guard. The white cat's mood shifted immediately, and her main focus became the treats. A few cats in line scrambled forward to take what they could. Some cats hissed and pushed to get to a few of the little fish-shaped morsels. During this commotion, Edie and Detective Pinkerton slipped through the doorway and into Cunabula.

The two adventurers ran through the high-walled palace corridors and down a spiral staircase, pushing past a few surprised cats. The stairs went on and on until reaching a dark chamber at the end with a heavy wooden door glowing with a hazy bright green light.

"We've made it to the dungeon," whispered Detective Pinkerton. "Now is the time for you to use your powers to break the enchantment on this entrance."

Edie pressed her face to a small barred window in the center of the door. "There are so many cats," she gasped, "I don't even see Dori. We've got to get them out of there, but I don't know how to use magic!"

Somewhere deep inside herself, the black kitten felt an animal rage begin to well up. But it was tempered, and in fact strengthened, by righteous indignation. It was simply wrong to cage these pitiful creatures. They deserved freedom! Edie pressed her face and paws harder against the barred window. As she focused her attention, a bright white glow surrounded her body. She thought of all the helpless cats trapped for no good reason, and something spectacular happened: The white glow spread and intensified until only the piercing light was seen. A loud concussion echoed through the room, and everything went black.

The black kitten opened her eyes to find herself in a small cage in a large, circular red room. Looking more annoyed than ever, the fluffy white guard stood between her and a shackled Detective Pinkerton. In the center of the room sat an enormous platform and throne, which held a giant purple cat wearing a golden crown.

Detective Pinkerton cried out to Edie, "The enchantment on the entrance is broken, but the door still holds!"

The giant purple Maine Coon laughed and in a deep booming voice said, "Yes, you have both failed! You were unsuccessful in freeing my prisoners, and now you sit in my court to face judgment." King Felix paused to pick his teeth with a fish bone, then continued, "You really thought it would be that easy, hm?"

Unfazed, Detective Pinkerton retorted, "I did, actually. With all the catnip you've been confiscating lately, I expected to find you in a more agreeable mood."

"So you've noticed, eh?" replied the King. "Well, I didn't do it for fun. I did it for science, for gnosis, for *technomancy!* My newest strain combines the magic of wishing dust with the ataractic properties of catnip. I call it 'catnap.'" He looked expectantly at his old nemesis, who appeared to be cleaning his claws out of boredom. "In any case," he continued testily, "you've caused chaos in my palace, you've led a witch against me, and you've wasted a perfectly good enchantment on my dungeon door. It'll have to be replaced, which isn't cheap. For your actions, you are both banished from Aeluria. The witch is to return to her world with the impression that this has all been a most unpleasant dream, while Pinkerton is to return to his companion to live out the rest of his days as a lowly house cat."

King Felix let out another deep laugh and motioned toward the fluffy white guard between the two would-be heroes. The guard pulled a paw full of catnap from a little brown bag and sprinkled a bit on Detective Pinkerton and Edie. The King grinned from ear to ear as the pair began to drift out of phase with Aeluria. Already, they looked like a couple of ghosts or hallucinations.

Suddenly, a frantic Siamese cat burst into the King's Court yelling, "Your Majesty, the prisoners have breached the dungeon door! They are escaping!"

King Felix yowled in anger as the two interlopers faded from Aeluria forever. Edie's magic had worked on more than just the dungeon door; it had spread to the prisoners inside, giving them the strength they needed to revolt when the time was right.

A perfectly human Edie awoke under the giant crepe-myrtle in her grandmother's backyard. She stared at the base of the tree, struggling to remember the events of the day. It all seemed to be slipping away like a complex dream.

The girl's grandmother called out to her: "Edie, dinner is ready!"

Turning away from the tree, Edie began walking toward the house. When she'd gotten a few steps away, a tiny meow came from the base of the crepe-myrtle. She turned to see her large, roundish gray cat Dori relaxing and flicking her tail about. The girl bent down to scratch behind Dori's ears and noticed a little fish-shaped treat in her cat's mouth. Dori dropped the treat at Edie's feet and purred loudly.

You can't quite be sure, but you think you hear faint whispers coming from the hall to your right. To follow them, turn right for room 12 (page 147). To keep your own company, proceed straight ahead to room 20.

20
The Mirror Cracked

TESSA B. DICK

THIS MUST BE WHAT IT'S LIKE TO GO BLIND, SHE THOUGHT. Stumbling into her kitchen, which was dimly lit through uncurtained windows, she cursed that fate had doomed her to be born under a dying Sun. She shivered despite being bundled up in thermal underwear, jeans, and a jacket. Her cat nodded knowingly, his bright eyes disclosing an ability to see clearly in the reddish glow of the setting Sun.

"It's okay, Cedric," she told him. "I won't step on you this time."

Deeming her promise unreliable, Cedric hopped up onto the kitchen counter. He had learned from experience that the most sensible policy was to perch high above the offending feet of his pet human.

She coughed, and Cedric jumped at the explosive sound. She coughed again, her chest constricting as she brought up a blob of phlegm. This winter cold was hanging on much longer than it ought to. Or was it the flu? And was it really still winter? How could anybody tell the seasons when a summer day felt bleak as a long winter's night?

She fumbled with the electric percolator, ensuring that she had it ready with half a cup of used coffee grounds and a quart of water. It had to be ready to produce a strong brew of her favorite beverage when the Powers That Be turned on the electricity for a mere two hours in the middle of the night.

Night, she pondered. *Who can even tell when it's night?*

Cedric purred in agreement—or hope—while she popped open a can of tuna to share with him. She grabbed a relatively clean spoon from the sink and carried their dinner into the bedroom, where she lit a precious candle. It was sitting on a low table in front of the floor-length mirror to maximize the coverage of its flickering light. Taking a seat on the floor, she dipped her spoon into the can and scooped out a bite of tuna. She was able to see fairly well in the reflected candlelight. Cedric, still purring, rubbed against her and the tuna can while padding about in a circular path around her.

He tried to shove his nose into the tuna fish, so she raised both arms high in the air, one holding the can and the other holding the spoon. "Wait your turn," she said. "I'll give you the can when I'm done eating." She felt certain that Cedric understood this daily ritual, but he didn't like waiting. He wanted to be Alpha, the boss. The flickering candle cast weird shadows and swaths of light onto the mirror, which threw those spectral images onto the walls and floor around her. She shivered, partly from cold but also reacting to the spooky appearance of the dancing light and shadow. Sometimes the reflection in the mirror looked warmer and more real than her dim, gloomy apartment.

Cedric hopped onto her lap and nuzzled her chin and chest.

"Okay," she said. "You can have the rest of it." She set down the can, and Cedric began to enjoy his share of the meager fare. "I don't know if we can get any more," she told him. "The shortages are getting worse every day."

She remembered days from her early childhood, when the world was filled with glorious light. The warm yellow Sun—sometimes a bit too warm—nourished trees and grass and farm fields. Her parents brought home carloads of food from the neighborhood grocery store. Their big house was lit up and warmed both day and night. Food and other resources were plentiful.

Now she lived alone in a small second-story flat with brown walls and brown floors and brown ceilings. She'd had to remove all the curtains to let what feeble red light there was come in through the windows. She felt completely alone, except when the cat reminded her of his presence. She didn't know what she would do without him. The Sun, the beautiful Sun, was dying. Sometimes she thought she saw a glimmer of the former, living Sun in the yellow light cast by a candle into the mirror. *A trick of the light,* she told herself. But she wished that the yellow Sun could be real.

Maybe she had simply dreamed of that former time of abundance; maybe it never happened at all. Perhaps she had read about it in a book of fairy tales. Wishful thinking, nothing more. The red Sun had always shone in the sky, and this brown flat on a brown street in a brown city had always been her home. There was no "over the rainbow." Food and light and heat had always been scarce. The only yellow sun was the flickering candle flame cast upon the mirror. She could almost feel warmth emanating from that reflected yellow light.

Cedric was licking the last bit of tuna from his lips when the ceiling light began to glow. The sound of the percolator invited her to the kitchen, where she would soon smell the delicious odor of coffee brewing. Cedric cried out, and she jumped. Her offending foot had touched his tail while he was too absorbed in licking the tuna off his face to see her coming and move out of the way.

"Sorry," she told him as she caught her balance and managed not to fall. She bent down to pet him, but he walked away, his uninjured tail held high above the floor in case she might step toward him again.

Stopping to wind the big clock in the hallway, she explained the situation to her cat: "We have to be friends. We're all we have, just each other. I never mean to step on you, but I can't see you in the dark. If only you were a white cat, or even an orange cat, I could see you. But you're a gray cat, and you blend right into the carpet. You're nearly invisible!"

Cedric cocked his head as if he understood. He did not follow her into the kitchen. She sleepwalked through this nightly ritual, winding the mechanical clock because an electric clock would never tell the right time on only two hours of electricity a day. Sometimes it was less than two hours. She wondered why the time even mattered when everything was the same. Night and day, the whole world looked brown in the light of the red Sun or the glow of dim street lights. The hot black coffee would warm her temporarily, but then the world would turn cold again. They had no heat because the natural gas reserves had been used up two years ago. Cedric, with his natural fur coat, didn't seem to mind the cold.

Of course, she did need to know the right time to go to work. It wasn't much of a job, sorting through used clothing and various household goods that had been donated to the charity shop. The boss told her not to ask where the things came from, but everybody knew that thousands and perhaps millions had died when the gas ran out and nobody had any heat. If the cold didn't kill them directly, many succumbed to the flu or other contagions. They gave her plastic gloves and a cotton mask to wear in case the clothing still had some germs, but she refused to worry about that.

She went through her mindless tasks on automatic, tossing coats into one box and children's clothing into another, sorting slacks and shirts, dresses and skirts, and so forth, each type of item into its own box. There wasn't much need for children's clothing, since nobody in their right mind would have children these days. Coats and warm clothing, on the other hand, were at a premium.

On the walk home, she stopped at the little grocery store, hopeful to find some kind of food that both she and Cedric could eat. All the fish had died off long ago, but canneries had preserved as many as they could while they still had power to run their machines. The oceans had turned into filthy basins of dead marine life, animals and plants alike, except the algae, which seemed to flourish in the changed conditions. Cattle, sheep, and goats survived in the equatorial regions, and to some extent in the temperate zones, but everything north of the thirtieth parallel was covered in ice.

The biggest problem was growing food for livestock. The Sun simply did not put out enough light to grow corn, wheat, soy, alfalfa, or any other crop. The Powers That Be arranged for greenhouses to be erected and supplied with electric light, but their productivity was limited. Soon they would have no electricity at all, not to grow crops and not for those precious couple of hours in which she could enjoy a cup of coffee and see the walls and the floor in her brown apartment. Reptiles fared the worst, since they had to sun themselves to avoid freezing. Besides, not only humans but also animal predators had eaten almost anything they could catch. Dormant lizards made easy prey.

She found a can of mackerel, a stinky fish that she could barely swallow without gagging, but Cedric would love it. She counted out the coins from her pocket and paid the sallow old man who owned the store. He nodded and scooped the coins into his pocket. He rarely spoke, and today he remained silent.

When she got home, the cat did not come to greet her. "Cedric, where are you?" she called out. Cedric always came to see what she had brought for him. "I got mackerel," she said. Still he did not come to greet her. She looked in the kitchen, but he was not there. She set down the canned mackerel on the counter and called his name once more. No response. A tinge of fear ran up her spine. Had something happened to him? Was he hurt? Was he dead? She couldn't bear to lose her only companion. He was a very old cat, but she had never considered that she might outlive him.

She stumbled into the bedroom, clumsily walking into the

door casing in the darkness. Now her shoulder hurt from the collision. "Cedric?" she asked, squinting to see a little better. Then she heard the familiar purr. There he was, sitting by the mirror, staring into it as if he wanted to go there, to get inside the reflection.

"Silly Cedric, don't you know by now that the cat in the mirror is just you?" He nodded as if he understood.

She spooned a portion of the canned mackerel into a bowl for him in the flickering light of a candle, reflected in the mirror, while they sat on the floor of her brown bedroom. Uncharacteristically, he refused to eat. For a moment, she thought she saw a sunlit world in the mirror, a land of grassy fields and tall trees under the light of a yellow Sun. She felt sure that Cedric saw it, too. Another cough racked her chest, and she bent over in pain. The spasm seemed to last forever.

When it was finally over, she saw Cedric clearly in the mirror. Not reflected, but actually through the glass, looking back at her. He turned and started dancing in a circle on the green grass under a yellow sun. Without thinking, she reached out toward him. Her hand slipped right through the glass into that mirror world. As if pulled by an invisible force, she stood up and walked into the mirror, joining her cat in a new, bright, sunlit world of grass and trees. The radiant yellow sun warmed her face. She laughed and cried and danced in circles with Cedric. This time she did not step on him because the sunlight made his sleek gray body visible on the green grass. She laughed and cried some more, and then she and Cedric walked across the colorful field of grass and wildflowers to look for a town, or at least a house where they could ask where they were and how they could live in this wonderful world.

The authorities found their lifeless bodies on the floor of that brown bedroom, but they were not dead. They were alive in another world.

You see an empty liquor bottle on the floor. If you wish you had some booze right now, turn right for room 11 (page 131). Or if you'd prefer something stronger, proceed straight ahead to room 21.

243

MIRRORMAZE

21

Walking in Dreams

MICHAEL D. NADEAU

HE FLEXED HIS ARM AND LOOKED AROUND AT THE CARS FLYING by, hearing their soft purr as the glide systems carried them along. Slender buildings rose to the clouds, their lights bright against the ever-present twilight sky. Halloran Daer couldn't believe this was possible, yet here he was, making a fist for the first time in ten years. He sauntered down the street and smiled at others as they flitted by, too busy staring at the sights to notice him. He wasn't entirely sure if these people were like him or part of the dream sequence that this place was running. It all felt so lifelike.

As if fate had heard his thoughts, another person bumped into him, falling and taking him down in a heap of awkward limbs. "Oh gods, I'm so sorry," a female voice said as he tried to extricate himself from the tangle. Halloran finally stood, helping her up with both hands—something he never thought he would do again.

"Its fine, my dear. My name is Halloran, but people just call me Hal." He looked around, but most of the people going by didn't even seem to notice them.

"Thank you, Hal. My name is Natasha," she said, smoothing her dark red dress and fixing her tangled hair. She was beautiful in almost every way, from her bright blue eyes to her tangled auburn hair. The only awkward thing was the way she stood…like she hadn't done this before.

"First day with the new legs?" he quipped, using an old joke he used to hear from his grandfather. He tried to remember her from the crowd of others he had been with as they entered the tubes, but he just couldn't place her.

Natasha laughed at him, then twirled around, her dress flaring out as she did, showing off her pale legs for all passing by to see. The woman stumbled again but caught herself this time before she went down. She looked like a fawn just learning to stand. "I haven't spun like that in decades."

"I'm sorry. It was only a poor joke, and I never meant…" He knew full well the feeling she must be having. He had lost his arm two years ago in the Canadian Civil War of 2087 and hadn't been the same since. *Wait, decades?* he thought as he looked at her again. She seemed like she was only in her late twenties.

"No, it's fine," she said as she stopped and caught her breath on unsteady legs. "They said I would gain stability in a day or two as the program acclimates to our minds. Once it integrates with our synaptic patterns, it will be fine."

"Yeah, I heard. Are you here on the free trial or a subscription?" He had won a free trial through the military hospital he visited monthly after being discharged, but he knew they had subscriptions you could buy for more perks. Things like holopods for vacations and even a sim room for pleasure were big here in the dreamscape, yet they were expensive for people like him.

"Subscription," she answered as they both looked up to a roaring sound in the sky. A dragon, glimmering incandescent in the azure clouds drifted among the flying cars and roared its glee. The rider, barely discernible from here, must have had money to spare to afford a ride on that thing.

I can't believe we're all dreaming this, he thought as they walked in silence, *and at the same time!* It was the newest thing to come out of Aztechnology, Inc. They had perfected the dreamscape for one person four years ago and had done very well in the open markets. To insert yourself into a dream for recreation was the newest high, and everyone wanted in. It was limited, with very little interaction between people, but they had already begun trials for shared dream testing. If this went well, they could open it up for recreation and be on top of the industry.

The trials also opened up a new field as well: the perfect body. In the original dreamscape, you could insert yourself but with some changes, like in dreams. However, they weren't stable. People with impaired vision could sometimes see clearly, for example, but it wasn't reliable. Now with the new trials, you came in at the top physical condition allowed for your specifications. The retired football player with the bad knee? He'd be a superstar again. That cellist with the mangled hand? Playing a concert every night. It was all very chic, but Halloran just wanted to be whole again.

Natasha had a gleam in her eye as she turned her head, looking at him with an expression he hadn't seen in a very long time, not since his wife left him two years ago. "You know, they say that if they perfect this, you could stay here forever."

"Forever?" He ignored her look and concentrated on the sidewalk. "I'm not sure I would want to be here like that. I mean, it's only a dream."

"Exactly! I can do things here that I couldn't do back in the real world." She skipped ahead and turned to face him, stopping him in his tracks, her eyes dancing now. "There are things I have *never* done that are open to me in here. Things that I want *very* much to do right this minute." She came closer, throwing her arms around his neck and her hips against his body. "Want to go to the Sim rooms with me? My treat."

His mind was reeling at the implications, his dreamscape body reacting to the physical closeness as if she were really right next to him. He could hold her...touch her with both hands. He felt himself giving in, the thought of being with her so tantalizing, but something was wrong.

"Wait." His breath was labored now, his hand sweaty. He looked at his other hand, the one gained from the dreamscape, and it seemed to be translucent. "Why am I out of breath?" *This shouldn't be happening in this place.* A rumble shook the dreamscape, the dragon fading away as the rider plummeted down like a ragdoll.

"Warning, warning. Please proceed to the nearest portal gateway and exit the dreamscape. This is not a drill. Possible collapse and corruption of hosts imminent."

Halloran grabbed Natasha with his good hand and pulled her along. "Let's go!" He recoiled as she pulled back, her hand slipping away.

"No!" she said, shrinking away from him. "I can't go back out there…I won't!" She ran off, her steps halting and unsteady but determined.

Halloran turned back and reached out, his translucent arm fading away, but she was gone in the crowd of failing, static images. Real people were running now and calling for help. Halloran saw a man with no eyes fall to the ground, so he snatched him with his good arm. "I've got you." They stumbled to the portal gateway, the crowd pushing and shoving to get in and exit the collapsing reality around them.

His head pounding, probably from the dreamscape falling into ruin inside his brain, he pushed the blind man through first and squeezed in after him, the feeling of numbness spreading as he dematerialized away from crumbling paradise.

Halloran awoke with a gasp, drawing in stale air from his confining sleep tube. Lights and alarms sounded in the distance, as well as the screams and sobs of several people. The vertical tube opened, and he fell out, his legs numb from the stuff they gave him. A look at the clock showed only five minutes had passed, for what seemed like hours in the dreamscape.

Medics ran in, giving people blankets and shots to calm them down. They said the same thing over and over: "Everything will be fine." Except he knew everything was not fine. He stood as a medic threw a blanket around him, and he tried to push it off with his arm…the arm he only had inside the dreamscape. Cursing under his breath, Hal went from tube to tube, searching for Natasha. He counted at least four people that didn't make it out, their tubes still fused shut, red lights blinking steadily.

"Those people will be safe; don't worry," a voice said from behind him. It was a tall man with a clipboard, his right eye glowing, a mechanical replacement. He was rich indeed, to have that done. Cybernetics were only for the one percent of the upper crust that could afford it.

"Aren't they…I don't know, stuck?" Hal didn't know what had happened, but the word "corrupted" didn't make him feel warm and fuzzy inside.

"They are alive, but they can never come out of the dreamscape, sadly. However, they are in the best place possible." The man made notes on his clipboard and moved on to the next tube, checking off a page and shaking his head. "As long as they are in there, we have a chance to pull them out once we fix the dreamscape."

"How long will that take? I thought it had crashed."

"No, we stabilized it once you all came out—it was the number of people, apparently—though I'm not sure how long it will take. Is one of them family?"

"No, but a girl I met refused to come out," he said looking at the others as they filed out. "I don't seem to see her here. Her name was Natasha. Red hair, blue eyes…"

The man looked on his clipboard and flipped the page. "Ah, special cases room, down the hall to your left."

Hal walked quickly, entering the room and seeing bodies on the floor. They were all severely handicapped, including the eyeless man he had helped. He ignored them and went to the only pod blinking red. It wasn't standing like most of the tubes he had seen. In fact, it was the only one in the room on its side. He crept up and looked in, seeing the familiar red dress, yet horror filled him as he saw why she never wanted to come back out.

Natasha was missing *all* of her limbs, a quadriplegic laying there quietly dreaming of being whole. Her skin had chemical burns over the parts he could see, and half of her hair had fallen out, probably from rad poisoning.

"She was born that way," said a voice beside him full of emotion.

Hal turned and saw a short woman, clearly Natasha's mother, judging by the blue eyes and red hair. "She was?" he asked, backing up and giving her room to see her child. "And the burns? Was that from the war?"

"Yes to both. She has never walked, touched another, or even hugged someone. She's gone her whole life watching others do the things she's always dreamed of. It's no surprise she didn't evacuate," the woman said, hanging her head. "Then last year we got caught in one of the gas clouds getting out of Quebec. My husband died getting us safely out, but she still got burns as the gas leaked in through the ventilation system. We should've left when they first told us to, but we didn't want to leave our home." Then she turned and left, tears streaming down her face.

Halloran looked down once more, knowing that she was at least happy in the dreamscape. "When they fix it, I'll be back," he promised and walked out of the room, back to his normal, agonizing life. He opened the door with his one arm and walked out under the glaring red sky, an aftermath of the chemicals they used to win the war. He walked down the street, passed people, and tried to smile, but they all looked at him like he was some sort of freak.

His watch beeped, and he rolled his eyes. He was late for his therapy again, but he wasn't worried; his psychiatrist would get paid no matter what time he showed up. Halloran sighed as yet another person pushed by him, making him almost fall into the street. Thankfully, the piles of garbage kept him from getting hit by a bus as it sped by, but he still fell onto the pavement. Before he could get up, he was hit by some coins carelessly thrown at him, a couple of pennies clinking down the drain.

"Get a job, buddy," the man said, not even bothering to look back. The words hurt, more so because they were right. Yet what job could he get with one arm? He was a soldier, and that was all he knew. Oh sure, he could try and apply for the cleanup crews, sifting through the rubble of the ruined buildings for bodies, but they would pass him over because of his handicap. It was hard to believe that the war had been over for almost a year and there were still people unaccounted for, buried under collapsed buildings leveled by the bombs.

Getting to his feet, he thought again of that beautiful place he had been in. The clean air and tall buildings, nothing leveled by war. You were right, Natasha. *Forever in there wouldn't be so bad after all.*

Your vision momentarily fails you as the entire room seems to fill with pale, moving specks. If they remind you of falling snow, turn right for room 27 (page 351). Or if the effect seems closer to rising bubbles, proceed straight ahead to room 22.

22 Drifters

DAVID MICHAEL WILLIAMS

As a kid, Allison liked to expel her breath in a steady stream of bubbles and sink down to the lake's sandy floor.

Enveloped by silence in that murky void, she imagined she was floating in outer space or experiencing a new state of being entirely, bereft of her body. Freed from the burdens of physics, the distraction of sensation.

Stepping out of her dreams gave her that same feeling.

Allison closed her eyes to shut out the subconscious-built scenery and concentrated on the cool emptiness of that childhood lake. The dream, which had seemed as substantial as anything in the real world, melted away. The air around her grew heavier, or thicker. Wetter? But the cocoon of tranquil isolation embraced her for only a second before it was violently ripped away.

She held her breath, though she knew she wouldn't drown—*couldn't* drown—since she no longer had a mouth or lungs or a body at all. The idea of holding her breath was just a mental trick, an imaginary action that simulated what she would have done if any of it were real.

And how could she not compare the urgent pull of that invisible current to a raging river?

The first time she had wandered into this place—the space

between dreams—she had fought the current, thrashing and gasping and struggling until she finally realized she wasn't in danger. That was when she learned she could steer her formless self through the flow of not-air-and-not-water by thought alone.

Those first few weeks, she eagerly plunged into the nearest pocket of reality to escape the minimalist state of being. Somehow she had understood, even in the throes of panic, that the blurry, bubble-like shapes pouring past her were other dreams.

She didn't start to suspect they were *other people's* dreams until she penetrated the flimsy skin separating them from the storming emptiness and spent some time wandering the unfamiliar landscapes populated by strangers.

After a month of exploring those random dreams—testing how much she could control without drawing too much attention to herself and accidentally waking up the dreamer—she tested a new hypothesis:

With enough concentration and persistence, could she find a dream that belonged to someone she knew?

Eventually, with lots of trial and error, she found Matthew's dream.

Tonight, she once again focused on his kind eyes, the shaggy brown hair that had grown past his collar since he moved away, and the endearing white scar on his upper lip—a permanent memento from when he had fallen out of her treehouse.

Grasping that image tightly in her mind, the current tugged her in a new direction. She relented. Seconds later, she found herself racing toward a specific bubble and let the momentum sweep her into the dream.

Thanks to many nights of practice, she didn't fall from the sky. Instead, she approached slowly, allowing the dream to take shape around her. She kept to the edges, where details were sparse, where she could make sense of the setting stretched out before her.

Looks like a park. A big one. Central Park, maybe?

Allison scanned the pathways and grassy areas, but she couldn't see Matthew anywhere. She took a few steps forward and shivered. Whenever she entered someone else's dream, she was always wearing the same white T-shirt and jeans. She closed her eyes and pictured a gray sweatshirt to shield her bare arms from the crisp autumn air. When she opened them, the warm hoodie was there, zipped and hooded to hide her face.

She pushed her fists into her pockets and walked at a casual pace. It wouldn't take long to find him. While the fringes of every dream faded into nothingness, the center was the most vibrant, and that core always formed around whoever was having the dream in the first place. All she had to do was keep moving toward where the scenery was most vivid.

I wonder if he'll be dreaming about Bliss tonight.

She hoped not.

The ghosts of skyscrapers towered in the distance, but as she followed a paved walkway, the trees throughout the park began to transform, their dull gray leaves bursting into the colors of fall. A jogger passed by, steam puffing out of his mouth with every quick, shallow breath. To her right, two children kicked a soccer ball back and forth.

Allison kept walking. She had given up trying to determine whether these miscellaneous people—these extras— were based on people in the real world. They could have been acquaintances of Matthew's or strangers he glimpsed just once. Anyway, they never paid any attention to her, so why should—

Wait a second.

On her left, a bearded man in a brown sloping hat sat on a park bench, reading a newspaper. Only he *wasn't* reading it. The man smiled at her, and a spider web of wrinkles blossomed around his eyes. He nodded a greeting.

She gave him a tentative smile but kept walking.

I must be getting close to Matthew if this extra is real enough to interact with me.

Allison found her old friend lying on a blanket at the top of a small hill. Hands folded behind his head, Matthew stared up at the sky. A wave of relief washed over her when further examination of the area found no sign of the woman whose online name had been Bliss—that evil temptress who had lured Matthew to New York City and away from their wholesome hometown.

Matthew's eyes were open, which, she supposed, they would have to be. It wasn't as if he could sleep through his own dream. She inched closer to the red-and-white checkered blanket, which would have been at home at any picnic.

Except there was no basket, no food at all. And Matthew, who had always been a slim guy, definitely looked like he could have used a meal now. The topography of his ribs showed through his punk rock T-shirt.

As her shadow fell over him, he said, "You just have to find the right cloud."

"What?" She averted her face to keep the gray fabric of the hood between them.

When he didn't immediately answer, she stole another glance. Matthew continued to gaze straight up at the sky.

"If you find the perfect cloud, you can fly," he explained.

The voice was all Matthew's, but the words belonged to someone else. An imposter. New Matthew.

Reluctantly, Allison leaned over him. Thin ribbons of red crisscrossed his glassy eyes.

"Oh, Matthew…not again," she moaned.

He reached up, presumably to grab a cloud. Allison turned away, unwilling to watch sweet Matthew Karls's dream while under the influence of whatever drug had its hooks in him.

She wiped away a tear and then jerked in surprise when she saw the man from the park bench standing only a few feet away, newspaper tucked under one arm and watching her.

"I thought I might find you here again," he said.

Allison's reaction to the man's strange declaration

mimicked what she would have done in the real world: she ran.

A hundred questions assailed her as she put as much distance as possible between herself and the man with the newspaper. The details of the dream bled away around her. She sprinted into a fog that mirrored the haze obscuring her own thoughts.

How did he find Who is he and what does he Are there other people who can There must be because he said What if he's just part of Matthew's No He is real I could tell just by just by Oh God what's that up ahead?

She skidded to a stop. To her left and right were the faintest outlines of trees, light posts, and what might have been a garbage can. Directly in front of her was a solid shape that could only belong to a human being—a stark contrast to the white-gray nothing surrounding him.

"Please, Miss, I didn't mean to frighten you." The voice wafting from the fog grew louder as the silhouette drew nearer. "I was hoping you and I could have a chat."

Allison walked backwards, matching the man's pace. "Who…who are you?"

"My name is Milton." As he advanced further into the core of the dream—and she retreated back into it—more and more of his features manifested: a charcoal overcoat, the baggy brown hat, hands that he held out in front of him in a placating gesture. "Perhaps we can have a seat over there?"

With his left hand—which, she noted, no longer held a newspaper—he pointed past her at the empty park bench, perhaps the very one he had been sitting on when she first saw him.

"What do you want?" she asked, unable to hide her suspicion.

He chuckled, and deep wrinkles formed on either side of his mouth. He wasn't an old man, she thought, but he wasn't young either.

"Well, I'm not going to mug you if that's what you're worried about. As you likely know, this isn't really Central Park, and any valuables you carry on your person would vanish as soon as I woke."

She took a few more steps back but stopped when she saw the bench inexplicably beside her.

"Surely you have questions," Milton said. "I'd like to answer some of them, if I'm able."

There was kindness in those bright blue eyes of his, and there was something in the short-trimmed, salt-and-pepper beard and mustache—and the smile wedged between them— that reminded her of Grandpa Greene. She wanted to trust him.

Or maybe she was just desperate to know what the heck was happening to her.

Allison took a deep breath. "Okay, we can talk…but no funny business!"

The warm smile returned. "I wouldn't dream of it."

They sat down together, sitting at opposite ends of the bench and leaving plenty of space between them. Milton crossed his legs and turned to face her. She folded her hands in her lap and looked straight ahead, where people came and went in a silent, almost spectral manner. A flock of puffy clouds roamed the too-blue sky.

"If you find the perfect cloud, you can fly," Milton said.

She stiffened, drawing a breath across her teeth to produce a hiss, and then looked at the man.

"That's what he said, right?" Milton asked. "Your friend over there?"

Allison sighed and looked away. "He's high."

High and probably lying in some New York gutter, having the time of his life here in La La Land while his real life is ending one brain cell at a time. Oh Matthew, how did you end up like this? What could I have done to—

"He's wrong."

The statement brought her attention back to the stranger.

"You don't need the perfect cloud," Milton continued. "This is a dream. Anything is possible, including flight. However, traveling at the speed of thought is faster. That's how I was able to get ahead of you when you ran."

Allison nodded. "It's easy to forget that."

"Yes, it's all too easy for us drifters to forget what we're capable of, especially in dreams that so closely mimic the waking world."

"Drifters?"

Milton removed his hat and scratched the patch of scalp peeking through the black and silver strands. "That's what we call ourselves. Dream drifters. Oh, there are more technical names for what we do…dream telepathy…oneironautics…but 'dream drifting' rolls off the tongue so much easier."

He replaced the floppy brown hat on his head and asked, "What do you call it?"

"I don't know. I guess I just think of it as visiting a friend. I haven't told anyone about what I can do, so I didn't need a name for it. They'd just think I was crazy, right?"

"Or worse, they would believe you."

The statement took her aback, but she had other questions on her mind. "I first realized I could…*drift* a couple months ago. At first I thought I was losing my mind, or maybe the painkillers were messing with me. I had just had my appendix removed…"

She brought one knee up, tucked it under her, and swiveled to face him fully. "How long have *you* been a dream drifter?"

A faraway look washed over Milton, and his smile grew. "I've had lucid dreams for as long as I can remember. That is to say, I could control what was happening in my dreams. But I didn't *leave* my dreams until I was around your age… twenty-four or twenty-five."

Allison couldn't help but grin. Most people who met her assumed she was significantly younger than her twenty-two years—sometimes guessing as low as sixteen!—and here Milton actually estimated too high. She was liking him more and more.

However, her satisfaction quickly turned to suspicion.

What if he isn't guessing at all? What if he knows *who I am?*

"How did you find me?" she demanded.

Allison gasped as she, Milton, and the rest of Central Park were suddenly plunged into darkness. What little light was left stained her formerly gray sweatshirt a deep shade of purple. The clouds above were locked together in a solid, opaque canopy.

In the distance, someone cried out in terror.

"That hardly seems like the perfect cloud," Milton muttered.

"Matthew!" She jumped up, ready to run to him—her first love, her *lost* love—but Milton caught her arm. "Hey, what do you think you're doing?"

"He isn't in any danger, Miss."

His calm tone only amplified her panic. She pulled away, and he released her. Without looking back, she ran toward the hill. Matthew lay curled up in a ball, pulling the plaid tablecloth around himself like a safety blanket.

"No no no no no no no no no no no," he chanted, eyes clenched shut.

"Matthew, it's okay. I'm here. Nothing can—"

His eyes popped open, and Allison again saw the telltale capillaries intertwining like tiny red rivers. "It's *Him*, Allie. God! He's found me, and He's gonna…gonna…"

Matthew let out a wild shriek and started to scramble away but got tangled in the tablecloth. Allison spun around and nearly fell to the ground beside him when she saw a pair of gigantic, violet-black arms parting the clouds and reaching down toward them.

"I'm sorry!" Matthew yelled. "I'll never shoot up again! Oh God, nooooo!"

The colossal hands descended in slow motion. Simultaneously, the sky began to flash wildly as streams of colorless lightning snaked throughout the dense clouds. Something touched her shoulder, and she yanked away with a yelp, half expecting to find some avenging angel behind her.

It was only Milton. "Take a breath. This is a dream, remember?"

"It's a *nightmare*. I have to help him!"

Matthew moaned piteously, trembling inside his checkered cocoon.

"I'm afraid it's too late for that," Milton said. "That strobe effect means his mind is fighting the unreality of the situation. Do you see how little remains of the park?"

Allison looked around, and sure enough, the fog was engulfing them. All that remained was a shrinking island of grass around Matthew. Meanwhile, the lightning had spread from the purple clouds to the nothingness that surrounded them.

"The dream is ending," Milton said. "Take my hand, and we'll leave before we're forced out."

Allison had been ejected from dreams before. Remembering the terrifying undertow—like the earth was being pulled out from under her—she grasped Milton's hand, leaving Matthew and the darkness-bleeding fingers of the would-be deity behind.

One moment she was standing in Central Park at the stroke of Armageddon, and the next, speeding through the eternally gray currents. Up ahead, she saw the faint outline of Milton. If she concentrated too hard, she almost lost him, but when she relaxed, she caught him out of the corner of her eyes, and subtle details filled in.

The experience was almost as disorienting as the waterslide-fast velocity that sent a thousand dreams whizzing past her every second.

Allison lurched at the sudden appearance of a floor—not to mention her own two feet standing on it. Instinctively, she reached out to steady herself and grabbed ahold of the wooden table that stretched from one end of the room to the other.

As she studied the place, which was illuminated by a pair of candlesticks, she realized she was wrong to think of the room as a room. The ring of dense shadow surrounding them implied the space was much bigger than she could imagine. A wave of nausea compelled her to take a seat on one of the twin benches that framed the table.

"Ah, my apologies," said Milton, standing beside her. "I make the trip so routinely I sometimes forget how discombobulating it can be to traverse the dreamscape at such speeds." He gestured at the empty table. "You should take a drink."

Allison blinked, and a silver chalice materialized a few inches from her hand. It shouldn't have startled her, but it did. The impenetrable darkness, the medieval feel of the table and cup, Milton's knack for making the impossible possible—the entire situation was giving her a creepy *Phantom of the Opera* vibe.

"What…what is it?" she asked, resisting the urge to sniff the cup's contents.

Milton chuckled. "Water. Though you could make it something stronger if you prefer."

"Thanks, but I'm not thirsty." She wondered what would happen if she ran into the shadows or leaped straight up in the air to launch herself back into the gray current. Would he chase after her?

Milton sighed and took a seat across from her. "You'll have to forgive me. I haven't figured out the right way to do this. I can't blame you for being suspicious…Oh, don't deny it. You've been looking around like a caged animal ever since we arrived. But you're not trapped here. This is just another dream. You can leave at any time."

The temptation to flee came on strong, but her curiosity proved more powerful.

"You said you haven't figured out the right way to do this. To do what?"

"To introduce myself. To explain what we know about

dream drifting. To invite others to join our cause." His smile returned. "I'm something of a recruiter, you see."

How many other people can do what we do? How can we do what we do? Why have I never been able to do it before a few months ago? What's the point? How did you find me?

She had so many questions, but before she could ask any of them, she needed clarification on a bigger question. "What is your 'cause'?"

"Asking the tough one first, eh? Usually, people want to know the whys and wherefores of dream drifting, and I get to build up to the big proposal. Your shrewdness does you credit, I suppose. Some things I will not be able to tell you until you join, and even then, much of what we do isn't disclosed to all members."

"Is this a secret society or something?" she asked.

He sniffed in amusement. "Not in the way you might expect. We're sanctioned by the U.S. government, which has a penchant for keeping classified information…well…classified."

Taking in the ordinary man in the slouchy hat, she couldn't quite suppress a laugh of her own. "You're a secret agent?"

"I'm a *scientist*," he said. "I just happen to work for an agency that specializes in international security."

"Recruiting people like me?"

"That's one of my roles, yes."

"Recruit us to do what?"

Milton reached for a second silver goblet and took a sip. "My job is to find more consultants for this little project of ours. The more dream drifters we have in our ranks, the more we can learn about the phenomenon and the better we can prepare for any event in which a rogue drifter might make trouble in the dreamscape."

He took another drink and added, "That's my official mission. However, my chief interest is developing a community wherein we special few learn from one another in the spirit of scientific discovery and mutual benefit…for the greater good of mankind."

"Our perennial idealist," said a voice in the darkness.

Allison jumped. Cups weren't the only things appearing out of nowhere. At the opposite end of the table, a man wrapped in a long coat stepped out of the shadows. The top of the gray-green garment was trimmed with fur, and as he approached the table, the candlelight revealed the color of his eyes and cloak to be the same. She couldn't help but tense beneath his gaze.

"Sorry to interrupt," the newcomer added. "I didn't expect you would have company."

"That's part of my job, remember?" Milton replied. "I find *real* dream drifters…just in case you fail in your work."

The man in the cloak stiffened, his eyebrows arching higher on his considerable stretch of forehead. But just as quickly, his expression returned to a neutral state.

"I…I'm sorry. I don't know why I said that," Milton mumbled.

The stranger dismissed Milton's apology with a wave of his hand. "No offense taken. Just remember that you choose your level of involvement here, Borr. I understand that moral flexibility has been a challenge for you in the past. You can't pull away from the group and then accuse everyone from turning their backs on you."

Milton's eyes narrowed, and color flooded his cheeks. "This is nothing like my situation with the Lucid Dreaming Society, Earl. I—"

"Odin." The other man's voice was low, but it cut Milton off as effectively as a shout.

Milton blinked and followed the man's stare across the table—at *her.*

"Yes…yes, of course. How rude of me. I ought to make introductions." Milton gestured toward the man with the broad forehead and steely eyes. "This is Odin. His role within our organization is difficult to explain without additional context, but suffice it to say he is in a position of authority. Is your escort still about? I'm sure Baldr would love to meet our guest."

"She's a bit young, don't you think?" Odin asked.

Allison felt her own cheeks flush. "I'm not as young as I look. I'm twenty-two!"

"Nevertheless…"

"Is there something you came here for…other than insulting prospects, that is?" Milton asked.

Odin paused, cast a sidelong glance her way, and said, "We begin the trials with our first candidates tomorrow night. I would like to invite you to attend." Pause. "Unless, of course, you expect your other work will keep you occupied."

Milton sighed. "No, I will be there."

"Good night then." Odin turned and, without as much as a look at Allison, walked back into the shadows.

After several seconds of silence, she asked, "Is he gone?"

"Huh?" Milton looked from her to the far end of the table and back to her. "Odin? Oh, yes, he's left the Great Hall. He won't interrupt us again, though I can't figure out why he came here when he could have just…" He smiled at her. "Never mind. It's nothing that concerns you or our conversation. Where were we?"

"You called him 'Earl' at first but then 'Odin' after that," she prompted.

"Ah, you caught that, did you? We're supposed to use code names. Mine is Borr, but just about everyone calls me Milton. I'm not a big fan of secrets."

"Yet you're working for a secret government project."

Milton blinked in surprise, but he must have realized she was teasing him because he chuckled. "That's a long story, and I'm afraid it's getting late. I can't pretend to know when your alarm is set, but I'd better give you the highlights before either of us wakes up."

"All right."

She took a drink of the water in spite of herself. What was it about Milton that made her want to trust him? Because he was nice—or at least nicer than Odin? Because he reminded her of her grandpa, even though he probably wasn't much older than her dad?

Because he wasn't, as Odin put it, morally flexible?

Milton cleared his throat. "Very few people can do what we do. Some have elected to be a part of this project. As I said earlier, it's my job to find more not only because it increases our numbers, but also because it exposes more naturals to the code of conduct we've developed. There are those who would do great harm upon the unsuspecting dreamers out there. Intentionally or unintentionally."

"What do you mean?"

"At worst, a dream drifter can intrude and learn information about the host. In the arena of espionage, there could be dire consequences. But even in more casual situations, barging into another person's dreams uninvited is an invasion of privacy and, therefore, wrong."

The heat she felt on her face had nothing to do with the nearby candles. She wanted to point out that he had barged into Matthew's dream too. But she knew the only reason he had been there was because of her.

To stop her from doing it.

Tears stung the corner of her eyes. "He needs help."

"I know," Milton replied, "but you can't help him this way, not in the dreamscape. It's not fair to him."

She nodded and watched wax drip down one of the candlesticks. Milton wasn't telling her anything she didn't already know. She had been keeping guilt at bay by telling herself two wrongs made a right, but the truth was she hadn't been able to reach Matthew anyway.

"I don't know why God bestowed this gift on us, but he did," Milton continued. "It's our responsibility to protect those who can't protect themselves. That, first and foremost, is our mission at Project Valhalla."

"So if I joined, I wouldn't be allowed to go into Matthew's

dreams anymore?"

"Yes, we would insist on that."

The candles blurred as she blinked back tears. "And if I don't agree to join Project Valhalla, I'll be a rogue drifter?"

"Not necessarily, though if we thought you were up to anything malicious, we would try to stop you." Milton reached across the table and rested a hand on hers. She didn't pull away. "As much as I think you would benefit from our group…and vice versa…I can't force you to join."

She tried to focus as Milton spoke of fringe benefits and how her work for Project Valhalla wouldn't have to impact her life in the waking world. But even though a part of her was excited at the prospect of meeting other people who could dream drift and to learn more about her "gift," she couldn't help but consider what she'd be giving up.

And who she'd be giving up on.

"I have to think about it," she said at last.

"I understand." Milton stood up, wincing as he stretched out his legs. "See what I mean about how easy it is to forget this isn't real? There's no reason why I should have circulation problems here, but the mind defaults to a reality-based line of reasoning if we let it.

"Anyway, since I have plans tomorrow night, how about the night after next?" he asked.

Allison stood too. "Okay…but where? I'm not sure if I can find this place again."

Milton looked thoughtful for a moment. "You probably could, but Odin and the others wouldn't want me to tell you how. Not until after you agree to join. No, let's rendezvous the same place as last time."

"Matthew's dream? But I thought you said it was wrong to intrude."

"It is," Milton replied. "Think of it as a chance to say goodbye."

"But only if I join Project Valhalla," she pointed out.

Milton smiled that grandfatherly smile of his. "What can I say? I *am* an optimist."

Two nights later, Allison walked through the front door of a house she had visited many times in the real world.

The front hall and living room were almost as familiar as the one at her family's farm. Matthew's winter coat hung from the banister—despite the many times his mother told him to put it in the closet—and the large cross that hung opposite the door was slightly crooked. As she straightened it, Allison caught her reflection in the cross's silver surface.

The face looking back belonged to someone else.

She sighed, grateful she had maintained control of her disguise from one dream to another but also regretful that she was entering Matthew's old house as a stranger.

How many times did we used to play spy, using the old baby monitor as a listening device in order to foil your parents' nefarious schemes?

She started as the doorknob rattled behind her. Her smile faded a little when the man with the slouchy hat crossed the threshold instead of Matthew Karls.

"Hello again," Milton said.

"Hi."

They stood in awkward silence for a moment. The faint sound of chatter and clinking silverware came from farther inside, and Allison imagined the small dining room with its old pink carpet and needlepoint decor.

"Perhaps we should talk upstairs," Milton said, "so we don't disturb them."

As much as she wanted to sneak a peek at the scene in the dining room—to catch a glimpse of Matthew during happier times—she led the way up the creaky brown steps. Milton made far less noise as he followed.

Without thinking about it, she opened Matthew's bedroom door and walked in. The room was exactly as she remembered.

She wondered if it was her memory or Matthew's subconscious that rendered the football posters and model airplanes in such stark detail.

Although she had sat on the narrow bed so many times before, she chose to lean against the dresser, almost knocking over a picture of Matthew, her, and a bunch of other teens on a whitewater rafting trip.

"Soooo," she drawled, "How did your experiment go last night?"

The question appeared to take Milton by surprise because he hesitated after pulling out the chair at Matthew's desk, before sitting down. "Well, I suppose it was a success, but whether that's something to be celebrated or lamented is up for debate."

"Good for Odin but bad for you?" she pressed.

Milton's brow creased as he looked closely at her. "You seem different tonight... and not just because you've changed your face, though I suppose that is a statement in and of itself."

"Well, you gave me a lot to think about."

"And?"

"As I see it," Allison began, "if I work with you, I'll have the opportunity to learn more about my abilities. I'll get an inside scoop on what the government is doing with dream drifting. And I'll be helping people. If I say no, I'll be on my own, and you or someone else from Project Valhalla will probably shadow me to make sure I don't do anything you don't approve of."

She took a deep breath and glanced back at Matthew's smiling face in the photograph. "A yes means I can't see him anymore. A no means I can...unless you stop me."

Milton said nothing.

"I won't lie. I'm very curious about Project Valhalla. And... I think you're right...about Matthew, I mean. It's not right for me to come here and keep an eye on him. Even though I mean well. It's selfish."

"Does that mean you'll join?" Milton asked.

"On one condition."

Milton's eyebrows rose as he waited for her to go on.

"I get to keep my identity a secret. You all use code names anyway, right?"

"Yes…yes, that's true," he stammered. "But all of the other consultants have consented to give me their names. No one knows one another's real identities, however. That information is kept in my custody. But I'm afraid the CIA will insist on having your true identity on file."

"Then I guess it's a no," she said.

Milton frowned. "Can I ask why your anonymity is so important?"

She looked around the room at the replicas of Matthew's possessions, the snapshot of his life as it had once been. "Because it's an invasion of privacy. I'm hoping you can teach me how to keep other drifters out of my head, but small good that will do me if the CIA can find me in real life. I don't want to have to worry about agents tracking me down if I accidentally break some rule."

And I don't want that creepy Odin guy showing up on my doorstep just because he can.

Milton opened his mouth as if to reply, but he didn't speak for several seconds. "I understand your perspective, and I respect it. I'm just not sure…" He sighed. "If you're so distrustful of our organization, then why join at all?"

Allison mentally willed away the blush she felt coming. "It sounds like you believe God gave us these abilities for a reason. I'd like to figure that out with you…but I don't want to sell my soul to accomplish that."

Milton scratched his head, wrinkling his hat. "Well said. I'm…I'm just not sure…"

Then something hardened in his expression, and when his eyes met hers, she saw a strength there that belied his otherwise mild appearance. "Perhaps I can make an exception in your case."

"Really?" Allison couldn't hide her enthusiasm. It hadn't been a bluff—more like a longshot. She had fully expected Milton would refuse her terms.

"Granted, I don't know a lot about you, but from what little I've gathered, you have a good heart. Some might call me naive, but I don't see the harm in letting you keep your private life…well…private." A ghost of a smile tugged at his mouth. "Besides, I would like to think I haven't sold my soul either and that we always have a choice in the decisions set before us."

"Wow, that's awesome…Thank you, Milton!"

"Don't you mean 'Borr'?" he chided, but there was no weight behind his words. "You and I are opposites in this regard. I prefer people use my real name, though it drives Odin crazy. We'll have to come up with your code name quickly, and I'm afraid our options are limited to members of the Norse pantheon."

"Norse? I don't know anything about Viking gods," Allison confessed.

"The good news is only a couple of the goddesses' names have already been picked. The bad news is the goddesses tend not to be as popular as the gods, so you probably have never heard of most of them." Milton sighed. "Frankly, many of them aren't very pleasing to the ear. So…let me think…there's Sif."

Eh.

"Freyja."

No thanks.

"Nanna."

Yuck.

"Hnoss."

Double yuck.

"Syn."

Hmm…

"Syn?" Milton repeated, apparently seeing a change in her expression.

Matthew—in fact, all of her childhood friends and most

of her family—had called her "Allie" for as long as she could remember, never "Allison." It seemed only fitting that if she were turning a page in her life—and in some sense turning her back on Matthew and her old, ordinary existence—that she switch from the first syllable of her given name to the last.

Syn nodded.

"And am I going to have to get used to this new face of yours?" he asked.

She nodded again.

"A pity. I rather liked the freckles."

"So…what happens now?" she asked.

"We should proceed to the Great Hall and begin orientation," Milton said, "but I did promise you the chance to say goodbye to your friend downstairs."

Sparing a final glance at the rafting photo—at Matthew's happy-go-lucky grin—she said, "That's okay. He wouldn't recognize the new me anyway."

You're really starting to feel stuck in this maze, anxious to get out and return to your normal life, but you can't decide what it is about your life that you actually miss. If you think it might be a sense of community and belonging with other people, turn left for room 16 (page 199). Or if it's the mindless relaxation of activities like watching TV, proceed straight ahead to room 23.

23 Buffering

SHAUN ALLEN

THE BIRD WAS CIRCLING HIGH ABOVE ME. WATCHING. PERHAPS waiting.

I squinted at it, as if doing so would focus and zoom my sight to be able to pick out its species, instead of it just being a blob going around repeatedly. Buffering.

Surprisingly, the action did help, after a fashion. The bird was a seagull. I could make out its white body and black wing tips. As far as I was aware, gulls didn't circle like that. Did it think it was a buzzard and was counting on me to die and hand over my decaying carcass for its lunch?

It could continue to think that. It would be disappointed.

I turned my attention away from my airborne stalker. For a moment, I forgot what I was meant to be doing. I had a takeaway cup of coffee in my hand, with steam seeping out through the small drink hole. I shook it slightly. It was almost full, but I couldn't remember buying it. Looking around, I saw a coffee shop along the street and across the road.

I had something to do, some place I needed to be, but I couldn't think what or where. I was peering at my thoughts as if through a fog, and as such, when I turned the headlight of my mind onto them, all I got in return was the reflected glare. I looked up to see if the bird could answer my questions, or at least divert my attention so my mind could clear its mist. Seagulls weren't known for their helpful nature. It continued to fly in its buffering circle, so I mentally gave it a middle finger salute and returned to the matter at hand.

I was standing at the curb, as if waiting to cross the road. Good, that was a start. I had been on the other side, the side where the coffee shop was, so I'd already crossed once and was now ready to do so again. I'd let my body go where it wished. I'd be a passenger, drinking my drink, and let it drive itself. Companies were working on self-driving cars; I'd be a self-driving person, and hopefully not have a crash in the process. The road was busy, so it took a little time for me to be able to step out.

When I did, suddenly, all the drivers slammed on their brakes. The cars all stopped, except for one that hit the rear of the car ahead of it, that driver's reflexes not as good as everyone else's. I looked around to see what could have caused the abrupt halt but saw nothing. Besides, they were all staring at me, along with many of the pedestrians.

For some reason, the slow-reflexed driver didn't get out of his car to apologize or inspect the damage he'd caused. Nor did the owner on the receiving end. Both remained behind their wheels. Both were looking directly at me.

I looked down at myself. Nope. Not naked.

I wanted to ask someone what the problem was, but I felt as if someone had slapped a bull's eye on my back and everyone was waiting for their chance to take a shot. I couldn't step back onto the curb. That felt foolish. I had to continue on my unknown path and hope they'd all go about their business. I planned my course between the vehicles, then looked down at my cup to avoid making eye contact with anyone. The further I moved across the road, the more conscious I was that no one had yet looked away.

What had I done? What was their problem? They didn't look happy, so I wasn't going to ask. I just walked. Mounting the opposite curb was a massive relief—I'd crossed no man's land. I heard someone shout something I didn't catch, and as if a switch had been flipped, the world restarted. The pedestrians went back to their conversations or phones or window shopping, and the cars moved on.

I walked, keeping my head down and using the lower legs and feet of passers-by to ensure I didn't walk into anyone. Arriving at a corner, I was tempted to cross again, but felt a pull to the left. I let the impulse take me. Perhaps it would show me the way home, something I seemed to have forgotten along with the rest. The realization disturbed me, though it didn't feel out of the ordinary. I thought I should feel frantic. Worried. Lost. I didn't though. I no longer knew who I was, and it didn't entirely matter.

Had I *ever* had an identity? Was that why my reaction was so…minimal? No, that was ridiculous. Everyone was *someone*. Everyone had a name and a family. History. The more I thought about myself, the more I had the feeling I was someone else.

My name. It was…

Two names came to mind, pushing themselves through the fog, neither one stronger than the other. Ian Jackson. Harry Wolfing. I said them to myself quietly, feeling the way they felt on my lips or in my mind. Harry. Ian. Jackson. Wolfing. Jackson. Wolfing. Either one could be my name. I couldn't decide which. They both felt equally mine and alien. I checked my pockets and was relieved to find a wallet inside my jacket. There'd be a driving license in there. That would have my name and address. I could go home, and if I had any loved ones, they could fill in my blanks.

Opening the wallet, I knew where the license would be. My hands automatically went to a pocket behind the slots where my bank cards went. I could have pulled one of those out to see my name, but I wanted my license. My name, address, and the photo of me. I had no idea what I looked like.

I took out my license and read the name: Brian

Thomson. It sounded nothing like Ian Jackson or Harry Wolfing. At least *they* were familiar. Brian Thomson didn't sound like me. It didn't sound like it was a part of me. The photo I recognized; the face looking back at me was immediately familiar. That was me, though I seemed to think I had more gray hair now.

So, I knew my name. I saw what I looked like. The address may as well have been the arse end of nowhere for all the meaning it had for me. It didn't matter, I supposed. Once I'd done whatever I was supposed to be doing, a taxi would take me there.

The feeling of having a destination or some kind of purpose was still there. I wasn't walking aimlessly. At a corner, I took another left at the next junction. A couple of people stared at me, frowning. I frowned back, their expressions making me wonder if I was wearing something outlandish or hadn't tucked myself away and zipped myself up after visiting the toilet. I glanced down. No, all was as it should be. I hadn't stopped to ask why they were looking at me that way, and I didn't feel inclined to go back and do so. Let them be their judgmental selves at someone else. I, apparently, had somewhere to be.

The pull I was feeling increased, and I quickened my pace, stopping short of jogging. I needed to appear to be walking, not running. Why, I didn't know. Letting my feet and inclinations guide me, I could tell I wanted to hurry but had to hold back, just enough.

But enough for what?

Ahead of me, I could see the street I'd originally started on, where I'd purchased a coffee and stopped traffic. I was approaching the corner when a man stepped out, flanked by a woman in police uniform. They'd exited a large clothing store, and rather than walking on, both stopped dead in front of me.

I walked into the man, unprepared for his sudden halt. He stumbled forward, our feet tangling and sending us both down in a heap.

"Shit!" I muttered, then louder: "Sorry, mate. I wasn't expecting you to…"

I stopped as I saw his face. His hair was perfectly imperfect, as if it had been deliberately styled to make him look unkempt. He had a police badge attached to his belt, and a gun in a holster beneath his arm, partly obscured by his jacket. It wasn't the hair or badge or gun that gave me pause, however. It was…I recognized him.

As someone who seemed to have forgotten who they were and was letting instinct guide them in search of answers, to recognize a face sent a jolt through me. I gasped, staring.

"Sorry," he responded, standing and offering me a hand. "My bad. I shouldn't have just stopped like that."

"I should have watched where I was going," I said.

His voice was as familiar as his visage, but both wavered on the edge of actual knowledge. His name stayed tantalizingly in the shadows of my mind. It teased me, taking a step closer to the light, then backing up when I tried to make a grab for it.

He showed no reaction to me other than being apologetic. Surely, if I knew him, he'd know me, wouldn't he? Could he give me answers? The thing was, though he was obviously a police officer, that wasn't how I knew him. It didn't sit right with me. It wasn't the role his elusive memory would wish to step into.

But…who…?

He was saying something and must have noticed my look.

"You alright, mate? Are you hurt?"

"Erm…No…Yes…I mean, no, I'm fine. I just…I know your face."

"I've got one of those faces." He pulled back his jacket to show the badge I'd already noticed, but didn't move it enough to reveal his firearm. "Or maybe we've met in some other way?"

I laughed nervously at the inference, not actually knowing if it were true or not.

"No," I said. "It's definitely not that."

"Sir, we have to go." The woman in the uniform touched

his arm, and he looked at her warmly.

"Sure, Sue. Course." He turned to me. "Sorry, mate. Bad guys to catch."

The pair turned to leave, but I caught his arm. He stopped, looking angrily at me, but didn't pull his arm free.

"What?" he said, the anger in his face so far not working its way into his voice.

"I…I know you."

"Yeah, you said." He looked pointedly down at my hand, which I removed hesitantly. "So?"

"I…I think I've lost my memory. I can't remember who I am or where I live, but I know your face."

"Look, pal, you might know me, but I've no clue who you are. If you've lost your memory, I suggest you go find it. Stop hassling me."

Again, he turned to leave, and again I interrupted him.

"That's not what I expect from a policeman," I said. I didn't want to irritate him, but I was holding onto his attention like a rottweiler to a kitten, not letting go until my jaws were pried apart and my memory returned. "Aren't you supposed to care?"

"Look, You must be thinking of some other police. I've got a job to do, and I need to do it at the right time. You're delaying that. After I'm done, I'll sit and talk 'caring in the community' and such bullshit all you want, but right now, you're gonna leave me alone."

I opened my mouth to say something back—not really knowing what, but I'd find out when I said it—but then he pushed his jacket back to show his gun-filled holster. That did it. My jaws were pried, and I let him go. Releasing him and hoping his name would come to me at some point soon was more attractive than the small but fatal hole a bullet might make in my forehead. His colleague looked on, her face mainly unreadable, but the tightly pressed lips spoke for themselves.

"Okay," I said finally. "Sorry. I just thought you might be able to help me."

He hadn't waited for me to finish my apology. He was on his way, quickly followed by his partner. I let him go, watching his retreating figure with a sense of loss. His leaving, and taking with him a piece to my puzzle, left a cold space inside of me, one where a chill descended to fill the void. I shivered.

The drive I'd felt before had left me, or the man had picked it up and was carrying it off. I was suddenly cast adrift by his lack of concern. Had the pull I'd felt been directing me to him just for him to dismiss me out of hand? I understood he might have to be somewhere, but couldn't he have given me just a couple of minutes to maybe prompt something more than a vague recollection?

Apparently not. Now I'd lost the impetus, and didn't know which way to go. I decided to start again, and in the beginning, there was bad coffee.

As I'd almost come full circle, I wasn't far away from the coffee shop. The police officers had turned left, taking them onto the street where I'd almost been run down. I walked onto the same street but turned right instead. I resisted the urge to look back. What if he was keeping tabs on me, my attention raising his suspicions? He was after "bad guys," and I could potentially have been one of them, trying to divert him or give my accomplices time to escape. If he missed his appointment with them, unless it was actually a pedicure he was rushing to, he might come after me. Seeing me watching him could likely confirm any potential suspicions.

And, what if they were true? I couldn't remember anything, really, about who I was. How did I know I wasn't a bank robber or a serial killer? I could have been the country's most wanted criminal mastermind, and he had just let me go. He'd soon correct that mistake.

But I didn't *feel* like a criminal. I *felt* like a good person. I didn't, however, *know*.

I returned to the coffee shop. A couple at a table close to the entrance, in a place I wouldn't think to sit at because of the obvious draft that blew in whenever the door was opened, glanced up when I entered. They both went to return their attention to their mobile phones, but one did a double take, staring at me. Her friend, though a fraction slower, did the same. I held their gazes for a few steps. Maybe they recognized me. Someone must. The expression on their faces wasn't favorable, so I decided to keep my questions unasked.

I suddenly had the urge to turn and run. To be away from their accusational daggers.

Outside, my sense of direction—or sense of *a* direction—had abandoned me. There was nothing to guide me. No tug at the dusty caverns of my subconscious. No big, airborne arrow pointing as if Damocles had put his sword down and neglected to select a target. I was a spitball in a sea of saliva, with no sign of land offering a destination.

I stood for a moment, hoping inspiration would take me by the hand, leading me where it would like. I didn't care. I just needed a little help. Something to paint a picture on the canvas of my memory.

I could, of course, just go home. Sit out the absence of identity until it came back. *If* it came back. Any potential family could help, or take me to a hospital where *they* could help. That wouldn't really be of any assistance, though. There was something here that had called to me, albeit silently. I needed to…No, not needed. I *wanted* to find it. There was no driving need, simply a desire to know what the hell was going on. I could go home, yes. I could turn in the opposite direction and dismiss it all. But I wouldn't.

I figured if I retraced my steps, I could possibly find the thread that had pulled at me. I'd follow my initial route, this time not stopping to chat to random policemen. It was he and his colleague that had broken the spell.

What was his name? I *knew* him. He could be a clue.

No, leave him. First things first. Once again around the block, then maybe I'd search for him. Talk him into sparing just a few minutes of his clearly precious time.

There was no reason for me to cross the main road as I'd done previously, when the cars had angrily stopped. I only needed to go over the smaller side street on which I'd met the police officers. With luck, I'd pick up the trail of intent from before. The long building stretching from one street corner to the next held a single building divided into individual shops. A tailor stood next to a fast food outlet, which held hands with a vape and e-cig establishment also housing a currency exchange, offering the "best rates in town, ever!"

The first in the line, however, was a large clothing store. It was one that stood on many a town's high street. Though its tags and receipts didn't reach the lofty heights of being called a "designer" label, it was popular thanks to its reasonable pricing and wide range. I knew, somehow, that I'd bought clothes from this place on multiple occasions. I was probably, if I checked, wearing some now. It also had something I suddenly needed: a toilet.

I walked into the shop, enjoying the greeting of the air conditioning's blast as it cooled me. A sign on a column informed me I needed to be on the second floor. An escalator was close enough to carry me up.

The toilets were at the far end of the floor, which meant, of course, that I'd have to pass racks of strategically placed clothes and would potentially see something that took both my fancy and my money. Having no intention of buying anything, I passed the clothes without allowing them to distract me and pushed through the door to the gents'.

A large, long mirror hung on a wall over the wash basins. My reflection did what the clothes could not—it grabbed my attention. I looked tired. A tired stranger. Nothing of my appearance seemed even remotely familiar. The eyes were the wrong color, not that I knew what the correct color should be. The hair too, though the style, short and slightly spiked, did seem about what I'd imagined it would be. My build was decidedly average, both in height and stature. I was *ordinary*. I didn't mind ordinary; I was just hoping something would trigger a memory.

It didn't.

I heard movement behind me, in one of the stalls. It interrupted my reflecting on my reflection and reminded me my bladder needed attending to. I turned, and as I stepped forward, the only closed stall door opened. The policeman stepped out.

He nodded to me, though there was no sign of recognition from our interaction only a little while before. I didn't let it bother me. My bladder was forgotten again as I resolved once more to push this man for answers, even if it wasn't the done thing to strike up a conversation in the gents' toilet.

"How you doing?"

He didn't respond, probably thinking I was on my phone. I tried again.

"We bumped into each other outside. Did you catch your bad guys?"

He turned to face me, his expression puzzled. He didn't know me, and I was choosing this, of all places, to approach him.

"Huh?" he grunted.

"Sorry, I saw you outside. You were going to catch some criminals or something."

"Oh…right?"

"Yeah, I tried to tell you I'd lost my memory. You didn't give a shit."

I hadn't meant to sound aggressive, but his complete indifference to me had been emphasized by his not remembering me from just the length of time it took to walk around the block. How rude.

"Hey, no need for that," he said.

"Sorry, I'm having a bad day."

"Well, okay, but still. You say you've lost your memory?" I nodded. "Why haven't you gone to the hospital? They'd be able to help you. I'm just a cop."

"I haven't, not yet, but I…I know you from somewhere. I thought you might know me."

He looked at me, staring, as if our connection, if there was one, would mystically reveal itself. He shook his head.

"Yeah, I remember you…" he began. I felt my insides swell with anticipation. "…from outside. But I've no idea who you are otherwise."

The swell vanished abruptly, his words a pin to the balloon of hope. I felt my shoulders slump and didn't have the energy to lift them back up. "Are you sure? I mean, I don't even know my own face or recognize my own name."

"You know your name?"

"Yeah, only 'cause I checked my license."

"And? Maybe that'll give me something."

"Brian Thomson?" The name still felt odd to my tongue, as if I had spoken it in Klingon and my mouth was unsure how to voice the words.

He paused and screwed up his face, thinking. He shook his head, looking apologetic.

"Sorry mate, no idea."

I felt a sudden burst in my mind, fireworks zapping at my memory's synapses. Something about him had just triggered a recollection, but it was a shout in a cavern. Loud, but lost in the vastness of the space it attempted to fill. I needed to get closer. Have a repeat.

"Can you say that again?"

"No idea?"

"Yes, but the way you just did. With the face and everything."

He frowned. I imagined he felt trapped, cornered by a madman, and was looking for a way to escape. Until then, I'd hoped he would humor me.

"Sorry mate, no idea," he repeated, his face convulsing in the same way.

Then, I had it. I knew him. His face was front and center in my mind, with his voice saying that exact phrase.

He wasn't a cop at all! He never had been. The closest was when he'd played one in a television drama, where he'd been partnered with a younger, supposedly energetic new recruit who was actually the son of the drug dealer they were chasing. The recruit was trying to divert the investigation, even down to attempting to kill the man standing in front of me.

An actor.

Now…what was his name…?

John…No…James? Yes! James D…Dav…Donovan!

"James Donovan!"

"Sorry?"

"James. You're James Donovan," I said excitedly.

It was an actual, real memory. It meant, somewhere in my head, the rest of me must still exist. It might be locked away, but perhaps he was the key.

"I'm…? No, mate. You're confusing me with someone else. I'm Adam Carlise, and I'm a police officer, so if you don't mind letting me be so I can wash my hands, I'd appreciate it."

"Adam? Oh, is this a part you're playing?"

"A part? No, don't be stupid. I just needed to use the loo. I don't know you, and I'm not who you think I am. It must be your mind playing tricks. Look, I'd like to help, but I think you need to go to the hospital. See if they can do something."

He tried to turn away, to push past me, but I put my arm out.

"No, I know who you are. You're that actor!"

"I'm not an actor! I'm a cop! *Now let me pass!*"

So. Normally, I'd be a fairly easygoing individual. At least, that's how I imagined myself. I pictured a placid lake that might, occasionally, show a ripple and, once or twice, a wave. At that moment, however, a serpent rose out of the lake and snapped its jaws.

"Who the hell do you think you are?" I shouted, shoving him back. "I've told you I can't remember sod all! I finally recognize someone—*you*—and you tell me I'm a liar?"

He'd stumbled when I pushed him and knocked over a rubbish bin. The lid came off, and crumpled-up pieces of white paper towels scattered across the floor, running from my temper. He picked one up and threw it at me. Either from a lack of strength or effort, the missile fell short. But that was what he wanted, as I realized when I allowed my eyes to follow its course.

He was coming at me before I had time to react or ready myself. Colliding with me, his momentum threw us both back as I was rammed against the row of sinks beneath the mirror. The pain was sharp and severe in my hips and my head where one connected with the porcelain and the other the glass.

Why couldn't he just help me?

I brought my arm up then down as hard as I could, my elbow digging into the nape of his neck. He swore and broke free, moving away to prepare himself again. This time, he wasn't going to attack me. He had something else which would stop me much faster.

His gun.

His hand disappeared under his jacket and slipped the weapon easily free of its holster. He pointed it at me.

"Look," he said, panting. "I don't know your problem, but I suggest you just leave. Go to the hospital or a doctor and get yourself checked out. They might be able to help you. I can't."

I slumped and put my hands back to hold the edge of the sink. I shook my head.

"I'm sorry, okay?" I said, resignation in my voice. "I don't know what I'm doing. I was following a…an urge or something. I hoped it'd lead me somewhere that might trigger a memory. It led me to you, and I *knew* you. I just wanted your help."

"I've told you I can't give it. Just go. Let me get back to work."

"The TV series?"

"Collaring criminals, if they haven't already got away,

thanks to you."

Was he a method actor? Was he just fed up with autograph hunters and wanted to finish his scene? For all his protestations, I knew him. He had appeared in enough shows, both dramas and panel shows, for me to not be mistaken.

If that were the case, and I was correct (I knew I wasn't wrong), the gun was a prop, and he was just trying to scare me.

"Okay, fine," I said. "I'm sorry."

He relaxed, allowing the arm holding the gun to drop slightly. I leaned back and swung both legs up, swiftly kicking it from his grip. It flew away and hit a radiator, the unmistakable clang of metal on metal echoing around the room.

I didn't have time to wonder about that sound. Wouldn't prop guns be plastic or rubber? Surely not metal. Right? Such ideas stumbled at the edge of my stream of cognitive thought, falling by its shore before being swept up into the current and carried to the forefront of my mind.

No, not stumbled. Not just fallen.

Shot.

The gun bounced off the radiator and landed on the tiled floor. The sound of its discharge (something I didn't think possible with modern-day firearms) filled the room, echoing deafeningly, pressing upon my eardrums as if wanting to pierce them and drill into my brain. I winced, crying out with surprise, and ducked in a futile attempt to dodge the bullet's path.

I saw splinters of ceramic explode from their shattered home up near the ceiling. James—not Adam as he professed—glanced up too, then looked back down to where his gun had landed.

It lay between us, marking a halfway point with decided intent. Had it fallen deliberately, a challenge to the both of us? If this were dawn, we could have been in a field, dueling over the hand of a fair maiden. As it was, we were in the public toilet of a clothing store, and the maiden was my memories. Would I lay down my life for...my *life?*

It appeared so.

We both dived for the gun, neither of us, if we'd had a chance to think, knowing how a simple question had come to this. He was the fitter man, with the faster reactions due to his training. As an actor (or a cop), he would have put in many hours to ensure he could spring quickly into action when the occasion demanded. I was surprised, therefore, to find my hand on the butt of the gun a scant second before his would have landed. I pulled it back immediately, almost dropping the weapon in the process. With a shaky hand, I raised it toward him.

"Stand up. Don't try anything."

He would have been foolish to. If I'd never held a gun before, he didn't know it. For that matter, *I* didn't know! I could have been the surest shot, but even if not, our proximity would ensure my chances of missing him, should I pull the trigger, were minimal. I didn't want to shoot, as my trembling hand was all too willing to show. Whether I would if required remained to be seen.

I just wanted him to be honest with me! We were away from the cameras. Away from fans or a script or co-stars. He could be himself with no repercussions. No breaking of roles or rules. He could be James instead of Adam.

"Don't do anything you'll regret," he said, his eyes fixed on my hand. "You can still walk away from this. I won't report it."

"I just want you to admit I'm right. You're the actor. It's just one memory, that's all. Give me that and maybe the rest will come."

"Memory doesn't work like that. It's not a gate you can just open."

"How do you know that? I thought you were a cop. You a doctor now? Are you getting your films mixed up?"

"Look," he said. His voice was even, but his eyes showed the fear he was feeling. "I'm not a doctor, no. I'm just a cop. I just want to do my job. I don't know you. I really don't."

"No, I know you don't."

"Then..."

"I know you don't know me, but I know *you!*"

"You don't! Maybe I look like him or something. I've never heard of him, but maybe it's that. What was his name?"

"His name—*your* name—is James Donovan. You know it is. Why won't you just admit it? I won't tell anyone about this. I don't know if I have anyone to tell. I just want the truth!"

"I'm telling you the truth!"

"Bullshit!"

He took a step forward. I don't know if it was an unconscious move in response to my words or an attempt to better position himself, but either way, I didn't like it. I raised the gun.

"I told you not to try anything."

He lifted his hands, pushing the air down in front of him, as if trying to reduce the tension. I took a step back to keep the same distance between us. He took my step as a form of retreat and moved towards me again. I knew a repeat on my part would give him an advantage, both psychologically and physically. I'd have nowhere to maneuver, and he'd have the whole room. He wasn't getting that.

I took three steps forward, the tremble in my hand gone. I was close enough that the gun was almost touching his chest. He backed away, shaking his head.

"I'm sorry, really. I wish I could help. I just don't know what you're on about. Please, just let me go. Keep the gun, if you want. Just...just let me go."

"Of course I'll let you go," I told him. I meant it. I had nothing to gain from this. I only wanted the truth. I just wanted to know I was right. "Just admit it."

"Okay, okay. I'm James Davidson. You got it. I was just messing with you. Trying to keep in character. I'm sorry, mate. Just put the gun down, and we can both walk out of here."

"Don't give me that shit," I said angrily.

"What? I've admitted it! That's what you wanted!"

"Davidson? Who the hell is James Davidson? I said *Donovan!*"

"Donovan, Davidson, what difference does it make? I'll be both of them, if that's what you want!"

"What I want is for you to stop pissing about and tell me the truth!"

"The truth is, you're a bloody headcase and need taking back to whatever mental home you escaped from!"

I saw his face drop as he realized his outburst was entirely the wrong thing to say. Had I escaped an asylum? Was my lack of memory due to the amount of drugs they'd filled me with? No! No, absolutely not! My mind was clear, if I ignored the fog where my past should have been. This was real, I knew. He just had to tell me and *mean* it. Insults and lies were misplaced. I felt my anger build rapidly. It needed an outlet. That outlet was the gun. My finger was on the trigger. I felt it pulling, but at the last second, released it and swung.

The metal of a gun and a radiator makes a loud, echoing clang. The muzzle of that same gun hitting the side of a skull makes a much more subdued noise. It's more of a dull thud, one that holds back and leaves you wanting something more.

James dropped to the floor in a crumpled heap. I watched him fall, then looked at the gun. It suddenly felt alien in my hand. It burned without heat, the flames internal, running up my arm to my mind, where they filled the echoing chasm with shame.

I could drop the gun. I wanted to, but that would leave me at a disadvantage. I tucked it into the rear waistband of my jeans, a move I'd seen countless times in the shows James Donovan was known to star in. I just hoped it wouldn't go off and shoot me in my arse.

Quickly, I searched him. I wanted to find a wallet like mine. One that had his driver's license in it. One that would prove I was right. All he had was a badge. A police badge and accompanying ID. It said Adam Carlisle.

I felt sick and had to swallow back a rush of vomit that begged for release. No. It couldn't be. It was a prop. It must be a prop. These shows had to get the authenticity right. It made sense he wouldn't carry his own wallet around with him. If he pulled that out during a scene, it would be embarrassing.

I also found handcuffs. They were useful.

It took some effort, but I managed to pull him across the floor and into a stall. Putting the toilet lid down—I could still be courteous—I hauled his limp body up. He looked like an alcoholic who'd drunk too much in a pub and fallen asleep while going to relieve himself. The scene was familiar, and I wondered if he'd had another role where he'd done just that.

I used the handcuffs to fasten his wrist to the toilet paper dispenser. It was only screwed to the wall, so wouldn't hold up against any major amount of pulling, but it would suffice. I still had the gun, and he didn't know whether I would use it. Nor did I, but I suspected not. I hoped the threat would be enough.

I waited for him to wake up, with no idea how long a swipe to the temple with a gun would keep one out for. I could do nothing else. Luckily, no one else had yet decided to use the facilities. I hoped luck would remain with me. I had one hostage (there being no other word for him, really), and didn't want to add another into the fray.

It didn't take James long to recover. He lifted his head with a groan, eyes squeezed shut.

"What the hell have you done, you dick?!"

He moved his hand and realized it wasn't going where he wanted it to. That's when he opened his eyes. He pulled his arm a couple of times, testing how firmly he was trapped.

"You know this is only making things worse," he said. He was calm, much more so than I expected. "Why don't you just let me go?"

"I will. I didn't want this, remember. I just wanted the truth from you."

"I've told you the bloody truth! I've tried lying to appease you! You're not satisfied with either! What am I supposed to do?"

"You've told me a lie, then what you thought I wanted to hear—and you couldn't even do that right."

"You're sick. Sick in the head."

"That's what I've been trying to tell you! My memory is gone! I barely know who I am! All I asked for was a little help, and it's come to this! That's on you, not me."

"Me? Me? You really are…"

He saw me holding the gun, and his rant subsided quickly. It wouldn't do to anger me, he saw. I couldn't understand his reticence. Why not just admit it? Why be so obstinate?

I needed to apply more pressure. Push him. I just wanted to know. The tiniest piece of a puzzle. A starting point. That was all!

He had started yanking his arm, apparently seeing, as had I, that the dispenser wasn't secured to the wall very firmly. The gun placed gently against his forehead changed his mind. He let his arm slump, taking his shoulders with it.

"Please don't. Please, just don't. I'm sorry I'm not who you think I am. I wish I could be, I really do. I wish I could change things and be whoever you want me to be, but I can't. Please, don't shoot me."

I couldn't tell him I had no intention of doing so, as that would erase any chance I'd have of breaking him. He needed to think I was capable of pulling the trigger, or he'd tell me anything.

"You know what you've got to do. It's simple. I'll give you the count of ten. *Ten.*"

His eyes were fixed on the muzzle pressed against his forehead.

"*Nine.*"

He gulped, and I saw his Adam's apple bob as if we'd been transported to Halloween and he was one of the activities at the party.

"Eight."

A small whimper escaped his closed mouth, squeezing through his tightly pressed lips. It was almost a vocal fart. I wondered if his other end would echo the sound. He was in the right place.

"Seven."

"Come on, mate. Don't do this. Let's just go our separate ways. "We'll both forget it ever happened. We can do that, can't we? Yeah?"

"Six."

"Come on, please. Please! I've got a wife. Kids. Two kids. Three! Three kids! A baby! Don't do this!"

"Five."

"My baby! My wife! Don't do this! They don't deserve this!"

"Four."

"Come on! Oh, just *do* it! Pull the trigger! Why wait? Why drag it out? I can't tell you what you want to know! Just get it over with!"

"Three."

"You win. I don't know why I tried to lie. I was just involved in the part. I do that. I kinda lose myself. You were right. Now, you can let me go!"

I paused and looked into his eyes. Really looked. I saw past the tears. Past the bloodshot right one, evidence, perhaps, of my strike to that side of his head. Past the frantic, growing panic. I didn't like what I saw.

"Two."

"No! *No!* Don't do it!"

"W—"

A knock at the door stopped me from finishing the word. I turned, pushing slightly against his forehead. A warning.

"Yes?"

"That's a wrap guys. Great work. James, You might wanna get that eye looked at, though. Bri smacked you a bit hard. Go easy, Bri. He's an expensive mistake."

I blinked, and my breath seemed to get stuck on its way out of my body, creating a growing ball in my chest.

"What...?" The words dissolved as I tried to speak.

I looked down at my captive. I was right! I was right! More than that! They *knew* me! They knew my *name*! I was a part of it all!

"What the hell?" James pushed against the gun still on his forehead. "No! What? No! They...You...What?"

It seemed our roles had been suddenly reversed. Though my memories were still dust floating on a breeze of the past, it was James that was confused.

"I'm not James," he insisted. "I'm not! I'm Adam! Adam Carlisle! I'm a cop! A cop! A wrap? They...they were filming this? But...no! I'm Adam!" His voice faltered, the rising volume cracking then breaking. "I'm...I'm Adam."

"No, James," I said softly. "You're not."

He looked at me for a moment, and I returned the gaze. The gun wasn't needed now. Despite the shattered tile, it must have been a prop. I lowered my hand and shook my head.

"I tried to tell you."

"But..." He didn't finish the sentence. He had nothing to say. He didn't know what to think.

Music started, a tune I recognized but couldn't place. I couldn't tell its origin, and I could see James was having the same problem. It seemed to be coming from everywhere and nowhere. It was just there, as if every molecule of air had been transformed into a minute speaker. As the music grew in volume, the light seemed to recede. The lights above us were not dimming, but their glow wasn't quite reaching as far as it had, creating a creeping gloom.

I went to the door and pulled. It was stuck, not budging. I pulled harder, and still it refused to move. With a glance back at James, who hadn't moved and was just watching me, I carefully laid the gun on the floor, close enough to my foot for me to step on it and any hand that might try to grab it. I pulled the door again. Still it wouldn't move, so I ignored the instruction on the sign below the handle and pushed.

No go.

I pulled yet again, hard. Nothing had changed in the seconds since my last attempt. The door was stuck fast. It didn't feel locked, because then it would still have some give. It would have moved, even a fraction. The door could have been a part of the wall if it weren't for the gap around the frame and the fact it was, clearly, a door.

The music was louder now. I could feel its beat in my body, a pulse that thrummed in time to the tune. I looked over to James, and he shook his head. Any words would have been useless, lost in the whirlwind of noise that filled the room to bursting.

The gloom was growing, though the overhead strips were as bright as ever. There was a small window high on the wall where the bin had stood. I pulled the overturned bin back to its original place, leaving it on its side, and used it to stand on. It was unsteady, but bore my weight. I pushed the window open, then pulled myself up, looking out. The darkness was spreading outwards, rapidly taking in the world beyond the room we were in. The music, too, was filling the spaces where the light was pushed out.

I looked up, my gaze attracted by movement. I frowned, expecting to see the lights of a plane.

The bird was there, circling. Buffering. I fell back, slipping off the overturned bin and tripping over my own feet. The door stopped me from tumbling completely over.

"What is it?" James asked. "What did you see? What's out there?"

I didn't answer. I couldn't. I knew what I'd seen—other than the bird—but was unable to process it into words.

"Hey! Ba…Bri? Brian, is it? What's wrong? What did you see?"

"I…"

I didn't finish. I couldn't. The light had almost completely gone, to the point I could barely see him. The music was deafening, pressing down on my whole body rather than just my ears.

I could see them now. They'd descended to be visible through the window. Large and squared off and a bright white. The closer they came, the lower they fell, the more the world disappeared. I could see it encroaching into the room we occupied. The walls were disintegrating. Dissolving. The radiator was gone. The doors to the stalls, then the stall walls themselves. James's arm was released as the part of the handcuffs holding him disappeared. He then started to scream as his feet and right leg were eaten away by the darkness.

Without turning, my fumbling hands found the handle and pulled. It was of course futile. The door was no longer a door. It was now merely a series of marks and indents in a wall.

The night was reaching me. It was only a few feet away. James had completely gone, though I could still hear his screams, piercing through the music. Then it was upon me. Taking me. *Eating me.*

I look up. The window has gone. The room has gone. There is only me, or what is left of me. And them.

Them.

The credits.

It's probably just an auditory hallucination, but there seems to be music in the air. If it reminds you of an opera, turn right for room 26 (page 327). If you think it's something more like a carnival or a magic show, proceed straight ahead to room 24.

24
Thatcher Maugden and the Dream Witch

DEZ SCHWARTZ

THERE WAS NEVER REALLY A PREFERENTIAL DAY FOR A kidnapping, though the weather this time was much nicer than it had been during the last. More than just a comfort or excuse for banal general pleasantries, atmospheric conditions were extremely important when piloting a dream-skimmer. Just as necessary as tracking the phases of the moon, weather patterns could equally send you off course and into an unintended stream of the universal subconscious.

Thatcher Maugden had become a stickler for accurate weather reports and swore by almanacs over any religious texts, which—conversely—he viewed as nothing more than penny fiction. An audacious, but not entirely unfounded, claim for someone who had lived more than a third of their life in the dreamscape.

As for the business of kidnapping, he preferred to view it more as a redirection of a naive but, adorably, open-minded tourist. As of late, lucid dreaming had become wildly popular with those interested in the metaphysical. And while Thatcher enjoyed the sudden influx of regular company, he wouldn't mind having a few years of solitude again as he'd had for an era previously.

But his calling had rung in and the time for action was

now. Idle ventures would have to wait.

The craft of dream-skimming wasn't one that he was born into nor one he'd opted for by choice. He'd stumbled into the responsibility, which is by far one of the worst things someone can stumble into. Responsibility is a sticky substance from which one rarely gets out of alive.

This life-changing incident happened at the beginning of a budding career, when Thatcher entered a disappearing box on stage in London and found himself adequately—and irrevocably—vanished. A cheap illusion gone wrong, or perhaps wickedly right. The trick led him straight into the Dream World at the behest of a meddling Nightmare Demon, known to him now as Allucin.

Thatcher never reappeared from the box onstage.

He couldn't be sure if his surreal abduction was a random happenstance or if Allucin had specifically picked him out of some predetermined lineup of magicians. Surely, there were more interesting illusionists to choose from. Perhaps, his lack of fame was a selling point. Who would miss a vanished magician no one knew had disappeared? He was certain the audience had forgotten him as soon as they left the theater that night—a failed, unmemorable performance.

Either way, the dream-skimmer needed a new captain, and he'd come along at just the right moment for Allucin to assign him the job. How could he pass up such a wondrous opportunity? Though, later he realized that he'd never exactly been given an option. His eagerness was simply fortunate for a Nightmare Demon in need of a servant.

"You'd think keeping conscious minds out of the unconscious realm would be important enough to warrant expending some extra dream magic for upgrades! Whirl-gigging clunker!"

Mmm-hmmm! A round little ball, reminiscent of sparkling fairy floss, hovered above his shoulder and hummed in agreement. It had no mouth, nor eyes, nose, or any other facial features for that matter. Thatcher had no idea how it was able to communicate, or whether it was a figment of his imagination brought to life over the previous years of solitary living. He couldn't remember if it had traveled with him all along or just shown up one day to purr and hum in coaxes and arguments at him, but he'd named it Pixie anyway.

"Oh, don't pretend you're on my side about this, Pix," Thatcher said. "You could easily drop a little hint in Allucin's ear, but you never do. There's a name for people like you where I come from, and it involves kissing parts generally hidden from the sun."

Pixie squealed offense and floated to the other side of the cabin.

Thatcher slammed his fist on the dream-skimmer's dash, causing an atrocious whirring which finally straightened back into an even hum.

"There we have it! Now, coordinates, please."

When no answer came, he turned to see Pixie floating with little enthusiasm in the corner.

"Pix, there's no time for self-indulgent fits. Besides, I must've told you a hundred times: navigators don't sulk."

Sparkling light twinkled across the little cotton candy-like cloud as Pixie sighed and hovered its way back to his shoulder.

"Aha!" Thatcher spotted their target overlaying its life-force into the stream he'd managed to whirligig his way through. It was easy to tell when someone was lucid. The expanse of the Dream World looked like a vast universe of pulsating stars, each a synapse of an individual's dream. But when one was lucid, its dream glowed brighter than all the others and didn't engage in the usual rhythmic pulse of sleep. It shone like a beacon among a blanket of stars.

Thatcher veered the skimmer toward the light.

"Brace yourself!"

Pix braced. Or at least Thatcher assumed it had. It was just a ball of imaginary fluff, after all.

The dream-skimmer arrived in a short blip inside of a dream covered in stormy seas, save for one abstract stone structure which barely kept itself from being engulfed by the rising waters. Atop the stone was their dreamer.

She noticed them immediately and began to wave. Thatcher rarely received a warm welcome. Most lucid dreamers found his skimming vehicle menacing since it was nothing like any technology they'd ever been exposed to before. However, this young woman seemed to be relieved to see it.

Once they'd flown up next to her, Thatcher turned on his dream frequency communicator and called out, "It's time to wake up, Miss!"

"I'm so glad you showed up. No matter how hard I tried, I couldn't get the water to go away," she responded from directly behind him.

Surprised, Thatcher spun around.

The young woman stood comfortably in a modest nightgown. Her auburn hair cascaded over her shoulders, which peeked out under wide straps. When Thatcher met her eyes, he noticed they glinted with a pulsing blue starlight which he'd never seen before.

He addressed her with trepidation. "I see you've had experience with this."

"I've had a lot of careful preparation," she answered. "What is that?"

Thatcher looked over his shoulder to see Pixie, who was slowly floating to the ceiling. It had turned red and puffed out like a clown wig.

"Oh, that's just Pix," Thatcher said, offering no further explanation. "What are you doing inside my dream-skimmer?"

She looked around at it reverently before arching her eyebrows and showcasing an extremely charming grin. "Hoping that you'll use this marvelous vehicle to take me to the center of the Dream World."

Thatcher had to laugh at such an audacious and wildly dangerous proposition.

Once he realized she was completely serious, he stopped laughing.

He pursed his lips. "Uh, no."

"But you do know how to get there?" she pressed.

"I'm afraid this transport doesn't accept passengers. I'm not giving tours or offering cruises," Thatcher insisted. "This dream of yours is your last and only stop. I bid you adieu, madam. I need you to wake from this slumber, *tout suite!*"

She showed no signs of intending to comply. "I'm not technically asleep."

"Lucid dreaming is still a form of sleeping. Don't try technicalities on me, Miss. They're a sign of a weak debater."

"But I'm *not* asleep," she insisted. "This is part of a spell."

"Pardon?"

"Do you believe in magic?"

"I've had quite the fill of bunny hats in my life, thank you."

"I'm a Dream Witch."

This caught him off-guard.

"Well, technically, a Dream Traveler. A descendent of the original Sandman," she expounded. "Dream Witch is just an easier term for others to comprehend."

An internal alarm sounded for Thatcher, and then an external one.

Pix was shaking, pulsating a rainbow of bright lights, and emanating the most atrocious sound since the invention of the foghorn.

All for good reason.

Dream Witches had been explicitly banned from the Dream World, and Allucin had been very clear that Thatcher was supposed to turn them over to the appropriate cosmic authorities upon finding. In this case, to the Nightmare Demon himself.

This was the first time Thatcher had actually come across

a Dream Witch. He'd grown quite hopeful that he never would, thus ensuring his job as a sort of "dream policeman" would be rather laid-back. Now that he had met one, he regretted accepting the assignment. It would be difficult to bring himself to usher such a beautiful woman to her—most certain—doom.

Allucin was set on eradicating all Dream Witches. It was one of his less amiable qualities.

Thatcher quickly pulled off his jacket and wrapped it around Pix to muffle its blaring.

"I see you're both familiar with Dream Witches," she said, not looking nearly as concerned as she should be.

"You must go," Thatcher pleaded, lowering his voice. He held tight to Pix, who was now scrambling inside his jacket like a cat lost in laundry.

"Not until I visit the center of the Dream World."

"Your presence there is forbidden."

"Which is why I need an escort to sneak me in," she pressed.

Pix set the jacket on fire and broke free, causing Thatcher to shout at the minor burn to his hands. He dropped the blazing fabric and vigorously stomped out the flames.

Thatcher adorned each stomp with an equally emphatic rejection. "No! No! No!" Defeating the small blaze, he held up his hands in an effort to keep any more unwanted suggestions at bay. "Cosmic law states that—"

"Who mandated these laws?"

"Well, I suppose… I don't know. But that's not the point."

"Why would they make a law like that?"

"To prevent *this* from happening!"

"And what do you think 'this' is, exactly?"

"An attempt to alter the natural order of the universal subconscious?" Thatcher knew he didn't sound convinced of his own words.

"Allow me to try this again," the Dream Witch said calmly. "Hello, my name is Poppy, and I'm here to save the

Dream World."

Poppy reached out to shake his hand.

Flustered by the entire situation, Thatcher accepted her handshake out of gentlemanly habit.

"Thatcher Maugden." He tried his best to assess what karmic insult he must have committed in order to bring such terrible circumstances down upon himself.

"You're human," she pointed out.

"Yes. As are you?" he cautiously assessed her.

She simply offered a placating smile. "What if I told you that you could take me to the center of the Dream World and absolutely nothing bad would end up happening to either one of us?"

"I'd say you were quite misinformed and, very obviously, utterly mad."

"As men generally say to women who are, in fact, utterly brilliant," she sparred with a sly grin, which inspired Thatcher to trust her confidence.

He allowed himself to resign from the argument. "Save the Dream World from what, exactly?"

"From the Nightmare Demon who wishes to cut off access to all mortals, making this a realm of darkness, void of hope."

"Sounds bad." Thatcher bit his bottom lip, knowing exactly to whom she was referring.

"Very bad." She nodded.

He could see in her expression that she must suspect who he was working for.

"So, will you help me?"

Thatcher waved around the small space which only housed a captain's chair. "I'd offer you a seat, but this ship isn't really made for two. I suggest you find something to hang onto."

Without questioning, she grabbed onto the nearest protruding part of the skimmer to steady herself.

"I hope you're right about this. Otherwise, it's the last journey either of us will ever take." He sat down in front of the dash and closed his eyes. He had to will himself into a dream-within-a-dream state in order to pinpoint his heading. Once he was able to visualize it, he knew exactly where to guide them. Thatcher entered their coordinates and the skimmer took off.

"So, how did you end up trapped here?" Poppy asked, settling into the ride.

"Oh, I'm not trapped," Thatcher remarked without thinking.

"Aren't you?"

She was very astute. He was already growing fond of her, regardless of whether she was sending them to a certain death.

Poppy had been fairly open with him about who she was, so he chose to let his guard down and tell her his full story.

She absorbed it all in silence and then concluded when he'd finished, "So, you're a magician running on borrowed magic."

He wasn't sure he appreciated that assessment. "As long as we breathe, we are all running on borrowed magic. Are we not?"

Poppy was silent for the rest of the journey.

At first glance, the center of the Dream World was a vast expanse of forest terrain. It wasn't until they drew closer that it became clear that each plant, from bark to blade, was made entirely of cosmic dream dust.

As soon as they entered the realm, the dream-skimmer began to shake and drop.

Poppy gripped the wall with both hands, doing her best not to be knocked off her feet.

Realizing that skimming was no longer an option, Thatcher pulled a lever and tried to at least steer them into a decent landing.

The dream-skimmer hit the sparkling blue grass with a thud, pulling up the ground with it as it skidded to an abrupt stop right before hitting some alien tree on the edges of the forest.

"I thought you did this professionally," Poppy remarked as she rose to her feet. She'd failed to stay on them after all.

"Need I remind you that trespassing—and all that comes with it—was your idea?" Thatcher countered. He turned off the dream-skimmer, hoping that their haphazard arrival hadn't alerted any of the locals. "We're in restricted territory, meaning this skimmer and any other dream device I might have has been rendered utterly useless. Only natural dream creatures have any power here."

He spun around in his chair to face her. "So, you're in the lead now, Dream Witch."

"Where's your fluffy friend?" she asked.

Thatcher immediately looked around the cabin of the skimmer. "Pix! Pix! Are you all right?"

"Oh, there they are!" Poppy pointed to the window at the dream fluff floating outside. "How did they get out so quickly?"

"Fluffs are ideas." Thatcher scratched his mustache while he explained. "Ideas can't be contained."

To demonstrate the difference, he immediately opened a door on the side of the skimmer so that they could join Pix outside.

Placing his hands on his hips, he turned to Poppy. "All right. I brought you here. What now?"

Poppy offered an apologetic look. "I need you to leave."

Thatcher scoffed and motioned to the dream-skimmer. "Not very likely."

"Then hide," she insisted.

"This is the center of the Dream World. You can't hide here," he said.

Her troubled expression made him worry that whatever plan she had was already falling apart.

"I'm going to die here, aren't I?" Thatcher shook his head and began to pace. He should have followed his gut. He knew the dangers. But...

He *had* followed his gut. His intuition told him to trust her.

"Like I said, you're not going to die," Poppy reassured him. "This will just be easier if I do it alone."

"What do you need to do?"

"I need to defeat the Nightmare Demon in charge," she said, stoically.

"Wait. You mean you're going to *kill* my Nightmare Demon?"

"I don't think he belongs to you."

A sinister, disembodied, voice echoed across the expanse, bouncing from every direction. "I belong to no one. Least of all a traitor."

Thatcher moved in closer to Poppy to protect her. How he planned to do that, he had no idea. She was the magical one. With his dream-skimmer crashed, he was just a man lost in a dimension where he was no longer welcome.

Poppy shouted back, "The only traitor here is you!"

"Okay, so we're just jumping right into aggressive confrontation then?" Thatcher mumbled quietly, aware that he was simply a bystander with a target on his back now.

Allucin's voice echoed again. "The Dream World belongs to me!"

"Lies!" Poppy was incensed. "You are a false king! The Dream World will forever be the domain of the Sandman."

"The Sandman is *dead*!" Allucin's voice didn't echo this time but was as loud as a crack of thunder.

"He lives on in the veins of all Dream Witches!" Poppy dared. "Show yourself, lesser-demon!"

Silence filled the expanse. Thatcher waited. Heart pounding. It felt like ages since he'd met Allucin face-to-face, and it was a visage he would rather go the rest of his life without seeing again, especially on bad terms.

Poppy stood tall, alert to their surroundings and waiting for any sign that the creature might show its face.

Suddenly, a flurry of nightmarish bats descended from the skyline. Thousands of them wove a concave blur of terror as they flew directly for Poppy and Thatcher.

Poppy extended both hands. Her arms emanated a blue starlight which pulsed visibly through her veins. Out of her palms, she produced a shield of energy to protect them from the attack.

Thatcher shouted, "What is that?"

"Dream energy," she said, holding her ground against the incessant smacks of hundreds of flapping wings against her barrier.

"Impressive!" But he worried how much longer she'd be able to keep it up. The nightmarish creatures seemed to have endless energy.

Suddenly, a large cotton-candy-like cloud began to expand and swirl over them. Pix was turning into a massive funnel, effectively sucking up every last bat.

When it seemed safe, Poppy let her shield down. "What is *that?*" she parroted.

Thatcher smiled proudly at Pix. "An idea unbound."

Poppy frowned. "Helpful, but it won't be enough to hold him while he's still on his own turf."

Thatcher wondered what her plan could possibly be then.

Poppy commanded the brewing storm inside of the Pix-cloud, "Show me your true form, you coward!"

"Can you at least bring back the shield thing first?" Thatcher suggested.

Poppy did, but this time she created a small force-field around only Thatcher to keep him safe. Or perhaps, just to keep him quiet.

A dark, rotating, smoke poured out from the cloud and reshaped before Poppy into a gruesome beast comprised of pure nightmare energy. Allucin's body was part humanoid and part like the bats he'd emanated before. He had wings and legs protruding at grotesque angles. His head was faceless, aside from the oversized mouth that curved into a wide, feral grin.

"Is this his true form?" Poppy asked.

Thatcher quipped, "Handsome, fellow. Isn't he?" A half-hearted joke to distract himself from the fact that they would surely be dead in moments.

The demon unhinged its jaw in an unsettling, serpentine manner. The more its mouth widened, the less sound seemed to carry through the Dream World. Perhaps the momentary deafness was a side effect of fear, Thatcher reasoned.

Poppy summoned her magic once more. Her entire body radiated with sparkling blue starlight, which she funneled into her palms. This time, it slowly condensed into an orb of pure dream energy in her hands.

Thatcher pleaded, "Whatever glorious thing you're doing, please do it faster."

The orb expanded until it was so much larger than the both of them that Poppy and Thatcher had to step back in order not to be engulfed in it.

Poppy threw herself forward. The momentum of her spell pitched the orb directly into the Nightmare Demon.

Thatcher wondered if the creature would explode. Instead, it was sucked inside the swirling iridescent mass.

Sound returned to the Dream World in the form of menacing shrieks as Allucin was sealed in his supernatural prison.

The orb, along with the entrapped demon, shrunk until Poppy could hold it in her palms once more. She sent it floating up into the vast galaxy which hovered above them until it disappeared from sight.

Catching his wits, Thatcher demanded, "What just happened? You let him go! Will he be able to come back?"

Poppy placed her hands on her hips and turned to face him with pride.

"He's trapped inside a dreamscape now. He won't be back unless one of my kind finds him and sets him free. And I seriously doubt that will be happening anytime soon."

Thatcher was relieved, but admittedly still confused.

Best not to question it and just thank your lucky stars, he counseled himself.

"Come on, Mr. Maugden. Let's get you back home." She took both of his hands in hers.

"Call me Thatcher, dear." He glanced toward the crashed dream-skimmer. "But I'm afraid we won't be going anywhere."

"Trust me. I know a quicker way home."

"Home. I don't believe I have one of those anymore," he admitted.

She pondered this for a moment. He witnessed her eyes soften the longer she considered him, until her lips finally turned up into a welcoming smile.

"I might have use for an illusionist, if you'd like to stay with me," she offered.

Pix hummed happily, and Thatcher took it as a sign of approval.

He'd never been one to refuse a surreal opportunity before. He accepted her invitation with a grateful nod.

"Close your eyes," Poppy gently instructed.

Thatcher did so. And with a calming breath, he ventured back to the Waking World, for a chance at a life filled with more magic than he could have ever dreamed.

All of a sudden, you're feeling desperately lonely. To allow yourself a quick escape into fantasy, turn left to return to room 1 (page 13). Or if you vow to get out of this alive and make a real connection with someone special, proceed straight ahead to room 25.

MIRRORMAZE

The Dragon's Nest

THOMAS FORTENBERRY

Do the dead dream? Or more to the point, do their dreams ever die?

But I'm getting off track, as I often do in these cases. Let me explain.

It was raining. I overslept. But it wasn't a real concern. Work had been slow of late. When I don't have enough busy work to distract my processors, the downtime tends to lead to neural snarls. I had taken to watching dramas throughout the night to distract myself as I could not sleep well—because when I was in this state, my twisted mind would provide all-night rerun war thrillers. Traumatic stress exhaustion was costly.

So, I was up until daylight, but then the morning dragged. At some point, I obviously dozed off. Now awake, yet still groggy, I put on tea, showered, and dressed. Took my time browsing the news. It was one of those lazy, rainy days in the pre-monsoon season, where the weather was still pleasant, and the soft susurrus of rain made everything hazy and calm. I suppose in retrospect it was a calm before the storm.

I rubbed some oils across the half-bald skin, half-chrome plate of my head. The human-ZENN interface tended to itch and flake if I didn't. I grabbed my hat and took a carriage to the office. I worked in an odd partnership with Sharlokh, a private detective of some note on Carnon. This big planet, spinning in a sprawling seventeen-world system tucked away in the Imran Cluster on the edge of Humanspace, was home now. Or where I hid. But this cluster lay officially beyond the reach of foreign empires and human states, beyond their politics in general and wars in particular, which was just the way I liked it.

I called Sharlokh to let him know I was on my way. His deep, reptilian voice burred in my ear. The subsonics of his species always messed with the speaker in my earlobe.

"You are late, Doctor. I am on my way out. We have a case."

A new case? The ZENN triggered, and my mind instantly sharpened.

Sharlokh's thickly accented voice continued, "I need a partner who is actually available when the work arrives. I can always find another AI. You can wait for me at the office until I return."

Sharlokh was a bit gruff. I am not sure if it was a Koror trait or just him. But, I was used to it. All of his species lack human emotions. Coldly reptilian, as critics put it. Besides, I had known quite a few human bastards from my years in the Galactic War. Often the very ones I was stitching back together would curse me out the worst. According to some of them, the medics were the worst, because we weren't frontline fodder. We got to sit back in the hospital ships and salvage the damaged in complete safety. Of course, they never realized that all of us "soft" medics were also the ones that had to go to the front unarmed and extract the wounded in the middle of firefights in order to get them back to the safety of the hospital ships. And occasionally, like me, you got blown to hell and became one of the wounded soldiers. Whatever. You grew a thick skin in the Planetines. I knew my worth.

I parried Sharlokh with, "You won't find one like me. There are very few ZENN-cyborg doctors and fewer still who would put up with a former enemy. You might say I'm one of a kind. I'm on my way already. I will pick you up and we'll go direct. Be out front."

He grunted on disconnect.

I looked out the window at the trees lining the sidewalks. Green leaves glistened everywhere, and trunks passed by like pickets. It had been raining all night. Water flowed through the plastcrete streets like a river. Vanceville was a city near the equator on the curled, green continent of Marakata. Its meandering streets and warrens of buildings sprawled down out of the Ageddon foothills and across the rain-soaked delta of the Robeson River. It lined the shore of Ochama Bay, a quiet nook of the broader Madhyamara Sea. Vanceville was home to hundreds of millions, but still managed to pull off the atmosphere of a sleepy little seaside village. Temperate weather. Quiet people. This was exactly why I chose to live here.

The carriage arrived minutes later at our office. Sharlokh stood like a tree on the sidewalk. He was two-and-a-quarter meters of gaunt, brown lizard. Except that they were tailless, his race resembled nothing more than bipedal crocodiles. The Koror were one of the most formidable races in the galaxy. They were once our fiercest enemy, but if there had been a silver lining to the horrors of the universe on fire, it had been when the Humans and Koror finally became allies. Our union had driven back the Ashvani tide and probably, realistically, saved Humanity from extinction. At least it saved our civilization from complete ruin and ended the nightmare of the Galactic War.

"Admit passenger," I ordered. The carriage door opened with a hiss, water cascading down the curve of the door.

Sharlokh entered and sat facing me.

The carriage door sealed. "Destination?" the carriage AI asked.

I raised an eyebrow and stared into his impassive red eyes. I would say he was grinning back at me, but Koror always displayed a snout full of sharp teeth.

He provided an address, which I instantly looked up. It was on the waterfront, in the dockyards, on the edge of the Koror

Sector. I whistled. "Now we know why they called you in for an opinion."

"Perhaps." There was a long pause, and then he shocked me with, "I can tell by the haggardness of your face that you have had a rough night. I presume the usual. If you do not feel up to working on a case today—"

"No, I'm fine," I interrupted. I knew he was attempting a pleasantry, but he actively disliked laziness, illness, complaints, and anything else he construed as a sign of weakness. Koror did not appreciate weakness. Even though my injuries and experiences in the War granted me all the legitimate excuses in the world, I tried to never show a weakness around Sharlokh. I was his partner, albeit junior, and acted as the human half of the detective agency. Though I began as a helper—more of an assistant, secretary, and recorder of his cases—I had more than earned my keep and proved my worth. Though he had been a Koror military policeman in the Galactic War and had far more experience in this field than I, he still needed a diplomatic go-between for human society. Besides, the ZENN implant granted me computer-like efficiency in recording, accessing, and processing data.

I am a cyborg. I used to really hate this metal, AI-powered replacement for the half of my body that the Ashvani blew off, but I have acclimated. The Zygopleural Encephalopathic Neural Net embedded in my skull causes me headaches—literally and figuratively—but it also gives me fantastic abilities.

"Very well," Sharlokh continued. "Detective Alden contacted me. A human was found last night. Annahilge Lim. Female. Approximately twenty-six years old. Apparent suicide."

"If Alden called, it isn't a suicide."

"Correct. There are discrepancies."

We met Detective Alden in front of a massive warehouse. The sort of man who looked exactly like a cop should look, he was a large, wide man, built somewhat the opposite of me, with a thick shock of curly, brown hair and bushy, graying mutton chops. He was part of the homicide division of the Vanceville Police Department. We had worked with him on numerous cases before.

The carriage pod let us out and then the oblate sphere slowly drove away, its AI idling until it received another ride order. We walked over and greeted Alden.

"Dr. Watt-ZENN," Detective Alden said, shaking my hand. And then extending his hand toward my partner, "Sharlokh."

Ignoring the human greeting, Sharlokh began bluntly, "You called about discrepancies in your case. You weren't satisfied with the initial ruling. What are the problems?"

"And a good morning to you." He waggled his eyebrows at me in exasperation. "Sometimes I wonder why I call you, Sharlokh."

"You need my help."

"True," Alden sighed.

"Show me," Sharlokh ordered.

Alden waved an arm. "Back this way. Around the side. Alley behind this building." We trudged after him. The wall of this warehouse had "KAMAN ULTRA" emblazoned on the side in thirty-foot red letters. When we reached the designated garbage area, Alden pointed out the giant square metal bin. "Found right here in this garbage receptacle. On her side. Against this sidewall."

Detective Alden flipped open his notecom and pulled up a picture of the body. He held it up to Sharlokh and then showed me. It was the same tragedy I had seen a thousand times.

We took a minute looking at the scene. There were no traces of blood, no writings, no scratches or dents—other than the usual damage on such a receptacle—or other obvious signs of struggle.

"Now, back to the problems," Sharlokh said.

Detective Alden flipped through his screens. "The victim was a human female. Annahilge Lim. Twenty-six years of age.

College graduate. Unmarried. Employee of Rowang Segosh Corporation. Shipping secretary. No criminal record."

"Family?" I asked.

"Parents live on the other side of Marakata. They were notified. Said they have not seen her in several years, but that they talked periodically every few months. They were unaware of any current relationship she had. They didn't even know her current job. Didn't seem particularly close. Nevertheless, I will be interviewing them later."

"Why is this being treated as a suicide?"

"Cause of death, according to the onsight toxscan, is an overdose of gawgaw."

"Oooh," I whispered. "Gator lockjaw."

"Exactly." Detective Alden glanced at Sharlokh to see if the slang bothered him. I knew nothing ever really bothered Sharlokh.

Sharlokh ignored it. "Too early to determine if she is an addict?"

"Correct. We'll know shortly when they do the autopsy."

"So, if she was a clean, innocent secretary," I asked, "why was she on an alien drug?"

Alden pointed at me in agreement.

Sharlokh continued, "Who found the body? Workers?"

"No. She was found in the garbage receptacle early this morning by a teen."

"Human?" Sharlokh inquired.

"Yes, a human teen. Name's, um…" he flipped through several screens, "Charles Huber. A nobody. Clean tox. No record."

I raised a hand. "Care to explain why he was looking through the trash behind a Koror warehouse early this morning?"

"He said the trash-diving is better here. He gets more exotic items. He resells stuff. Makes some kind of bullshit jewelry. Says alien junk is a lot more valuable than human."

Sharlokh looked down at Alden. "So, you have a body

found behind a warehouse. An overdose victim. Why am I here?"

"This Koror company and the first responders are pushing for a quick resolve. Suicide. Ms. Lim was fired from work yesterday. She left a note." Alden consulted his notecom again. "Quote: 'I am so sad. I can't take it anymore. I am sorry.' That's it. The note was printed, in her pocket. The owners of this warehouse are calling it an accident. They say they have no cameras back here, hence no security video of the crime scene. But they state no suspicious activities or people have even been reported back here. They say this girl just wandered up here after a night out in a club somewhere and OD'd. They claim it was an accidental death, that she probably didn't even mean to die. The street cop took their word for it. But then we found the note, so he is ready for me to rule it a suicide. I'm not. Not yet. Something doesn't feel right. Not for a suicide."

"I don't work on feelings. What is the problem? There are no apparent signs of foul play."

"I know."

"Then what is the problem? You called me."

Detective Alden flipped back through his photos. "Of course, we haven't done an autopsy, but I searched her body for any signs of foul play. Look."

He showed us a picture of the young woman's body laid out, with the shirt open exposing her torso. On her left side, on the ribs below her breast, was a semicircle of scars appearing like dashes. He pushed the pic, and the video ran while they turned her body. The circle of scars continued onto her back.

Sharlokh said nothing. Detective Alden said nothing. I looked from one to the other and finally asked, "What is that? A tribal marking? A new fad? If it were some kind of normal surgical procedure, the scars would have been removed."

"Correct, Doctor. That's not surgical scarring," Alden said. "But, I used to work vice. You know what that is, right?" He looked up at the scaled face of Sharlokh.

"*Hrrast,*" Sharlokh said in his native tongue, the subsonic R making a growled snarl in his throat.

I ran the term on my Xothikad translator. "A bite mark? This is a Koror bite mark?"

Detective Alden nodded. "Exactly."

I looked at Sharlokh's long snout and giant teeth. A chill ran down my spine. I was seeing the reptilian side of the Koror in a way I hadn't since the Galactic War.

Sharlokh explained: "It is an ancient tradition used by Koror lovers to mark territory. In some sexual deviants who prefer to use mammalian species, they will mark their property in this way. It is like playing with a mouse."

I blinked and swallowed, processing that image. "So you mean…she had a Koror lover?"

"Yes, except probably not a 'lover.' I think this is what Alden is intimating."

Detective Alden nodded. "I worked vice for years and ran into this long ago. There is prostitution between races. Some reptilians prefer mammals. 'Fur traders,' we used to call the Koror johns, and we called the prostitutes 'snake-eaters'— well, that was for the simple street prostitutes. We called the high-end club escorts 'gator gals.' It's kind of like any other underworld activity. Hidden. Sometimes private individuals, but many times run out of casinos or by organized syndicates. There are special high-end clubs for executives and the like who indulge in all kinds of wild fantasies, including interspecies sex. The gator gals we brought in used to have these bite marks. Some of those girls choose that lifestyle, but some of them are forced into sexual slavery, you know."

"Property marks," I said. "Like brands. Like brands on slaves."

Alden rubbed his head. "Yeah, kind of."

"Because, in the clubs, customers would know which prostitutes served only Koror," Sharlokh explained. "This does reveal the young secretary in a whole new light."

I agreed. "Not an innocent college grad worker bee at all."

Sharlokh stepped back into the wider alley. "Where is the Rowang Segosh building? This is the Kaman Ultra warehouse."

I ran the address. "Serroles Street. Other end of the District."

"Thus, she worked for the Rowang Segosh corporation, a Koror shipping firm," Sharlokh stated, "was fired yesterday, writes a note that she is depressed, and then commits suicide by taking a Koror drug forty blocks away behind a random warehouse."

Detective Alden nodded. He closed up his notecom and put it in his jacket pocket. "You see why I called you."

Sharlokh looked down at the detective. "I see that there is indeed a problem with this death."

Alden pulled at his mutton chops in frustration. "Now, you see the crux of my problem. The company wants no bad press. They probably aren't involved at all. The parents may not care too much, so the pressure will be on by the department to just sweep and go. We have no budget, time, or resources to waste on a nobody like this. They will autopsy today just as a recording formality and then cremate. I know there is a definite Koror connection. But, that doesn't help me much. We're looking for a needle in a—what is the xenopopulation?—a millions-of-Koror-high haystack. That's a hell of a search."

Sharlokh raised his hand. "We will narrow the focus. We should not waste any time on this. The girl is unimportant on the scale of things. Your department, the corporations, even her family do not care. But, we should care.

"First, we have probably discovered a recurrent solution to a problem these criminals have. That is, disposing of these prostitutes after their usefulness has expired, or their accidental deaths, or they have threatened to expose certain individuals or organizations that wish to remain hidden.

"Second, if it is such a murder, we can expose the criminal parties, while exonerating the innocent employees here at Kaman Ultra, along with her friends and family.

"Third, we must act extremely fast before you cremate the only evidence we have, the young woman. Let us get immediately to work." With that, Sharlokh walked off.

We followed him back around the warehouse to the main street.

Alden was hurrying to keep up with Sharlokh's long strides. I was used to the way the Koror walked. The detective grunted, "Okay, I know you often work by leaps of logic and like to cut to the chase, but what are we doing? Where are we starting?"

Sharlokh inquired, "Do you know of the local sex clubs that cater to Koror?"

"Yes," answered Detective Alden.

"We will need one that is directly connected to the management of Rowang Segosh. Those clubs are expensive, so we can probably dispense with the lower-level employees and any of her immediate colleagues. Her department heads or the chief executives will suffice to start. Her extracurricular activities were with them. Can you cross reference the company executives with their bank statements and pinpoint a club?"

"I should be able to do so."

"Very good. Send me the data, and I will go interview the proper Koror at the proper club. It will be better if I speak with my own kind than if a human detective barges in asking questions. You will get no answers."

"Okay," Alden agreed.

"But, most importantly of all, I am sending Dr. Watt-ZENN to the autopsy. You must grant him permission to do a brainjack."

Detective Alden and I stopped.

"Seriously?" I asked.

Detective Alden stuttered, "W-wait. You mean like a—" he glanced at me, at the chromium side of my face.

"Yes, that's exactly what he means," I answered. My stomach tightened. Brainjacks were rough.

Alden whooshed out a breath, walked in a circle, and then stopped. "But, she's dead! What the hell, Sharlokh?"

"There is a process that we can do on the recently deceased. It is a bit extreme. If the brain hasn't deteriorated over time or been severely damaged by a massive head trauma, we can pass an electrical current through the organ, thus temporarily reactivating regions of the brain. We can thus access memories."

"By 'we,' Sharlokh means me," I pointed out, my voice sounding suddenly like gravel.

"I'll be a son of a—" Detective Alden paced back and forth. He was staring at me with a kind of horror. Then, as if the feeling came over him, he rubbed the back of his neck exactly in the spot where I had my brainstem port. "Holy hell, Doctor. I knew you could jack into a com, or read a datasystem or whatever, but I never knew you could jack into a person— much less a dead person…"

"Yeah, well, it isn't something you should really be doing." I was staring at Sharlokh.

He stared back. No emotion on his lizard face. Red eyes cold as always. "We have little choice. Now, I understand that you would like to sit around and mull this over for hours on end, savoring each angst-ridden emotion that overwhelms you—just as you do at night instead of sleeping. However, they will cremate that girl within an hour or two. The record of the crime will be lost. You have no time to waste. Go there and perform a brainscan."

I gritted my teeth. Sometimes Sharlokh could be a real asshole. "Jacking into another person's brain is nothing like a simple mainframe scan. I am not browsing a system, searching for a few nifty entries."

"There is nothing simple about it. I understand."

"You have no idea!"

"You have no choice. Time is against us. If you can access her memory, you can identify the murderer for me. Then relay the data, and I can capture the proper suspect at the proper club."

"Just like that?" Detective Alden asked.

"Yes," Sharlokh said. "If you want to solve a murder, you have to actually work at it. This case will be solved by this evening if we all do our parts." He signaled for a taxi on the Net.

I looked at the two of them in disbelief.

A carriage approached from blocks away and slowed to a stop.

Sharlokh stepped inside. "Send me the proper club address, Alden. Watt, call me the moment you access the information."

The door cycled closed, and the carriage moved away.

A dead silence descended. I don't know how long I stood there looking down the empty street after he had gone. Eventually, I felt Alden's hand on my shoulder.

"Let me give you a ride to the morgue, Doctor."

This is the really hard part. I record and publish these reports of our cases per Sharlokh's desire. He is a student of alien cultures and criminology. Sharlokh loves solving mysteries more than anything else. I think his experiences in the War burned away any excess interests and left him with this insatiable drive to understand crimes, and to solve them so people can live better, safer lives. He has experienced enough suffering and death. Sharlokh wants an accurate record of these events for future reference. This is why I was originally hired. My writings are a valuable resource for future investigators, as well as those morbidly curious about crime in general.

However, it is extremely difficult to convey the thoughts of another person. Brainjacks are very complex—not because of the physical process but because of the union of thoughts. To physically plug into someone else's brain is fairly simple. It is much better with a living person, if they are willing, because your brains then work together to share memories and perceptions. It can be very difficult if they are unwilling and resisting. I did that several times during the war. Every thought along the way can be a proverbial fistfight.

A dead person has zero resistance, so it is easier in that sense, but it is far worse on a personal level because the actual consciousness that is always there in someone's mind is just absent. Just as you have a cold brain full of inert neurons, you have a massive pile of dead knowledge, and you can feel death all around you. It is similar to dissection. You can peel apart all the layers of the body, cut away flesh, pull apart muscles, open organs, and trace veins, but the flesh is cold, inert, lifeless. Not like operating on a living patient. I have done both. The brainjack of a corpse is a sickening autopsy of someone's dead thoughts lying in the coffin of their brain.

Furthermore, I cannot accurately convey the experience. It is like a dreamscape, or perhaps a nightmare, made exponentially worse because you are sharing the thoughts of an outsider. I am already used to this Other feeling since my butchered brain is linked to a neural net implant. I already have two systems of thoughts in one brain. This is why most neural cyborgs don't survive. The result is usually a severe psychosis like schizophrenia or utterly debilitating insanity. That's why the nasty old term "psycho-cyborgs" came about. But I survived, and I'm used to the craziness of having outside thoughts rammed into my brain.

Still, I find it difficult to describe a mindmeld. Sharlokh wishes me to try.

It is like falling through darkened space. You feel motion but cannot see anything. As the minds approach, flashes of colors, shapes, and sounds begin to occur. At first, it is like lightning in an approaching storm. You see brief flashes of illuminated thought, and then they vanish. But like a storm, they become more frequent, stronger, last longer, until they pummel and overwhelm you. Then you are at risk of being destroyed, as if by a tornado. Thoughts and sounds pound at you like rain. Memories howl, faces loom, geometric designs form and oscillate; buildings like old houses erect themselves and then deconstruct; friends and animals leap up at you; favorite movies play, and remembered books confuse whose tale and which character you are experiencing. Whole conversations blast your ears, and the wild actions of entire days run before your eyes, making your legs run and arms wave. You can just maybe grab their oldest friend or dearest relative, laugh at their favorite joke, make love to their spouse—all while every shred of your own essence is being stripped away.

It is utter madness.

The secret is to hang on and survive the storm. You have to focus and find the calm center, like the eye of a hurricane. From the center of knowledge, you can peek out to witness the storm of thoughts and slowly, every so carefully, begin to tease them apart and process them.

For me, I often see the thoughts of others in a symbolic way. People will appear as if they were cartoons or avatars. Like Sharlokh may appear to me as a towering brown streak that stretches infinitely into the sky. Or an inquisitive alligator with a magnifying glass who is pointing to some detail for me to study more intently. Thoughts are sometimes geometric shapes, which I can pick up and handle, and if I work at it, I can solve them like odd three-dimensional puzzles and open them to find what lies inside.

Nevertheless, to witness murder within my own mind is… *murder.*

I witnessed Annahilge Lim die over and over as I pulled apart her memories. I felt it, heard it, tasted it. I kept having to feel the black-streaked lavender of this act over and over. I had to run it forward and backward. I had to trace back strands of memories to see who she had met, why they had met, when they had met, and figure out what connections they had, if any, to her death. I climbed around her mind like a spider on a vast network of webs.

Of course, she made it more difficult. It wasn't her fault. She had been poisoned, so the closer to the last moments I got, the more confused and bizarre her memories became. The gawgaw had hallucinogenic properties that wrecked her trains of thought. As she died she remembered her past, her family, her friends, and all sorts of little moments in a life cut short. The fear was also overwhelming. Emotions were like tidal waves. They came crashing in sometimes and would disrupt everything. I would have to regain my position and go back into her thoughts. My ZENN helped me process the mountains of overwhelming data. At times, I clung to my AI like a rock in the middle of a violent ocean and cried while the waves battered me. Without ZENN, I probably would have been lost.

I unfolded her memory like origami. When I pulled it open, I found a dragon nesting inside. Green, powerful, hideous. It squatted at the center of this event hoarding the memory. It opened its mouth, fangs dripping with the poison that took her life. Then the dragon reared at me, snapping those venomous jaws. I flinched, falling backwards. It was a reflex. The dragon couldn't truly hurt me because it wasn't real; it wasn't now. It was then, replaying. I was outside looking in. This was memory, not reality. Her memories, not mine. It took a moment to process that and recover. Nevertheless, her memories were real to her, and horrifying.

But like Sigurd or some other ancient Terran knight, I returned to the dragon's lair. I waited, observed it, studied the dragon's movements and the treasure it hoarded. The ill-gotten gains, the contraband being shipped in from other systems. I saw the dragon scrolls, the manifests, times, amounts, where all the gold coins and jewels were hidden. Annahilge Lim had unfortunately discovered this dragon and his hoard. This particular crime lord, this particular monster. That knowledge had cost her life. I witnessed her making love to this monster. Witnessed the dragon attack and kill her. I felt the fear and horror well up inside, threaten to drown me. I shuddered, sickened, as I watched this tragedy play out.

For her sake, I raised my torch high and lit this memory

on fire. I flushed the dragon out; it rose on emerald-hued wings and flew from the nest. Pulling down the electric sky, I captured the dragon in my neural net.

Eventually—nanoseconds to infinity—the long soul-night was over. The storm passed in that bleak, abandoned land of the dead, and I eased my way back into the daylight world of the living. I had dragged a dragon across that wasteland. I was exhausted. Being lost inside of another mind feels like forever, but often only seconds have passed. But those moments inside are soul-wrecking. I felt an exhaustion overwhelming me as if I had run a marathon.

But I had the data. I knew the face of the murderer, his name, the place and time. I had recorded it all.

Weak, my hands were trembling as I disconnected the brainjack.

"Are you okay, Doctor?" the Medical Examiner said, rushing forward to help me. I waved him back.

"Contact Sharlokh. I recovered the data."

I sat up on the gurney in the sterile cavern of the morgue. Annahilge Lim lay quietly on the table beside me. My legs almost gave out as I stood and leaned over the examination table. I looked down at her quiet form. Was it my imagination or did she seem more content, more at peace? I felt sure she was.

"Rest easy, Annahilge. I did it. No, *you* did it."

Annahilge Lim had just helped us find her killer. She had slain the dragon and earned herself justice from beyond the grave.

You're having a hard time telling memories from reveries from reality. If you'd like to rid yourself of such intrusive imaginings, turn left for room 28 (page 359). Or if you find that you're actually enjoying them, proceed straight ahead to room 26.

26 *Somnium*

JEB R. SHERRILL

SOMNIUM RAKED THE TABLE WITH SAVAGE STROKES OF RAGE. Papers and pens, water and glass crashed to the floor of his dimly lit music room. The woman in his mind had stopped singing. *Damn her,* she'd stopped singing. Her mouth lay open, shrieking nothing; not a line, verse, or note. She just stood there before the black palette of his imagination, a darkness which until moments ago had spread across his mental mock-up of the Casn Theater from end to end.

A great red sun had adorned the stage, the kind born from the horizon and murdered at the end of day. It had bled into the blackness, seeping over the cobalt columns and emerald arches, gracing the stage with a set only a bad dream could devise. It would have been reproduced by royal artisans, would have filled thousands with the longing dread and dark sadness of the woman and her song. But the set was gone, with even the memory fading. And the woman, her mouth still a bottomless pit, singing nothing, stood like a lifeless statue, her phantom arms growing more transparent by the moment. Her body melded back into the darkness until the open mouth was one with the walls of his mind.

Damn. Scattered papers weren't enough. He flipped the table itself end over end. The paper-thin, marble top shattered shards of stone over the glass tiles like angry atoms. The dim light was gone now, his tiny, novelty lamp, sharing the same fate as a glass pitcher, two crystal tumblers, and of course the table itself.

Unquelled anger drove him to find the next breakable object, but a splintered, acrylic chair brought him to the ground, jabbing the bone of his right shin. The shards of marble met him, taking sweet revenge on his hand. Warm blood ran down his arm as he lifted his hands. He pounded the floor with the same damaged fist only to cut himself again.

"Lights! Damn it, *lights!*" The room instantly illuminated, glow strobes blasting harsh radiance through the smooth, glass walls, beamed from invisible hiding places beyond. Somnium shrieked and clapped an arm over his eyes. "Dim, *dim,*" he shouted, and then, "dimmer, *dimmer!*" The walls obeyed, but only after more precise instructions did they reach an acceptable level.

Somnium glared across the room at the fallen pages of an unfinished opera, covering the floor with white leaves of ripe failure. Black ink pooled around its broken bottle, and his favorite quill, the one he used only for operas, lay silent but unharmed amid a shower of transparent, colored pens.

He didn't feel like picking it up. Instead, Somnium slunk to his bedroom and fell onto the bed, not bothering to dress his wound. He couldn't believe it: a nightmare like that and he couldn't remember long enough to write it down. He tried to think of the images again even as he lay staring at the ceiling. A thin sheet of color-changing water rolled over his head in gentle waves, down the walls and back up again.

The image wouldn't come. The alien columns and arches were just word memories in his shead. So was the woman. Tears of rage trembled at the edge of his vision as he pulled an empty glass vial from the floating nightstand. He shoved the small table away. It bounced off the wall and roamed aimlessly about the room.

Nothing left in the vial, even the last drops sucked out. He drew his hand back to shatter it against the wall, but suddenly he didn't care. The anger had worn him out, and like a marionette whose strings had suddenly been clipped, he fell into the satin sheets.

He soon fell asleep to the gentle waves of his ceiling but woke again minutes later. Nothing. Not an image. Not a sound.

Without bothering to dress in anything better than the rancid clothes he'd been wearing for days, Somnium stumbled out the door and into the city streets. *It must be three in the morning*, he thought, but that was good. The suns wouldn't be up for hours, and the streets were empty, save a horse-drawn carriage thundering over the black-slate cobblestones, rushing hot-cold wind as it passed.

Mammoth horses, white-maned beasts of the Outer Planes hauled it into the distance, leaving him in peace. *Peace?* Well, it left him in silence.

Musa never closed his shop for anything, and to the best of his knowledge, never slept.

Musa's black market "House of Sleep" looked more like a hole in the side of a building than a proper shop, but that was part of the point. He entered, coughing at the thick odor of Soma-scented incense used to cover the even worse smell of foul concoctions. If you couldn't smell anything, or notice the filthy floors and counters, the place looked like a kaleidoscopic phantasmagoria.

The walls of the tiny shop were filled with rows of slim vials, strung along the shelves from ceiling to floor like endless strands of DNA, light reflecting off and through the sticks of glowing color. Red, then blue, then three or four green, then pink and orange and a row of eight or ten deep purple. These two-inch vials held one dream each.

Red carried simple love and lust. Beautiful women, brawny men from the covers of romance videos, any dream of ecstasy anyone could ever desire.

Blue held all dreams of flying and breathless swimming. Green triggered memories of lost loves and played them out in the best of circumstances.

Pink gave you the fluffy dreams of wonderful places: gray castles in the sky, plush meadows in the mountains, seas begging to be crossed by ship or dolphin fin, or your own fins as a mermaid or sea-dragon or other aquatic beast of legend-history.

If you needed a victory, a day to stand a hero, acceptance by the throngs, then orange was your best choice. You'd wake exhilarated and passionate, with adrenaline pumping in your brain, success breathing down your throat and knocking down your door.

Purple brought the purity of fantasy, the wonder of myth and realities beyond reality. It was the choice of sages and mystics, children and fools.

They could all be mixed in various ways by the skillful hands of the Fel Night Traders, or by your own hands if you dared.

The Namor Council banned dreams, but the trade still flourished as long as Night Traders like Musa kept their shops hidden, their arts a secret, and the local soldier-police well paid.

Musa himself stood behind the dusty counter, leaning on his spindly elbows and grinning at Somnium through razor teeth. He looked the same as he'd always looked: the crumpled top hat, the ancient tailed jacket and vest, the pointed ears and long, sharp nails. "Ssssssomnium," he hissed, whispering loudly in the slow lisp of a wounded serpent.

Somnium approached the counter, frowning at the thought of conversation.

The impish face leaned towards him. "Ssso sssoon." Musa rapped his razor nails against the worm-eaten wood. "Dreamerss alwayss need more dreamss, don't they?"

Somnium said nothing. He was too tired for Musa's spiel.

"I'd ssay you look heavy tonight. Heavy as lead, I'd ssay. Perhaps ssome flight might do you good." His round frog eyes glistened as he rummaged beneath the counter and drew out a tall, slim blue vial—dark blue, almost navy. The puck manipulated the glass with amazing ease, passing it from hand to hand and flipping it end for end between his nimble talons. "A special mix I dreamt up just today." He held it to the light and stared deep into the dark, nebulous liquid. "I see the world of Kandra, and you flying as a pulse of tantric light. You've always had the eyes of a wonderer, the aura of a monk, and the scent of an animal, dear Composer."

Somnium stared into the yellow eyes, so big now they might have exploded. He leaned across the counter. "You know what I want."

Musa grinned, sliding the vial through a slot in the wall. "Why won't you dream of beauty, Somnium? You never try my lovelies anymore."

Somnium gave a heavy sigh. "I have enough money," he said, drawing a handful of gems from his pocket and heaping them before the bulbous, ever-growing eyes.

"Enough money?" Musa looked hurt. "My boy, I just want your happiness. Take a dream of fancy."

Somnium held his impatience. "Keep your fancy. Sell them to the children who want to dream of bubblegum and fairies. Sell them to everyone craving happiness, relief, ignorance." He narrowed his eyes and gripped the counter tight. "Give me what you *won't* sell them."

Musa grimaced. "You should be dead already," he said motioning to the door which locked itself and covered its own window with a rolling shade, "or insane."

"Who says I'm not?"

Musa twitched his goblin nose and reached beneath the counter to the secret cabinet Somnium knew lay just beneath the surface, in a space-box, a small hole in time that led somewhere *else*. His twig fingers withdrew a stand-up tray holding six larger vials, ten times the size and dreams of the smaller ones, and Somnium knew the mixes to be far more potent. Each contained liquid as thick and red as blood. Musa popped the corked one and ran the smoking mouth under his nose. "Lust, lad, as even you have never known. I smell a woman. A woman baked inside a cherry pie the size of a king's bed." He sniffed again. "She stands, tearing the membrane crust as if born from it, just for you. She steps from the dish, red with thick glaze and dripping cherries and stares at you like a lioness in heat and…" Musa paused and stared deep into Somnium's eyes, "you'll wake, drenched in sweat, unable to move. You'll spend the rest of your life looking for her, longing for her with a pain so harsh, your veins will burst and your heart will shatter. You'll make love to a thousand women, trying to recapture that moment. You love pain. It's your poison."

Somnium closed his eyes and shook his head. "You know what I need. I have to write. I need an opera for the Crown."

"But love is a beautiful—"

"That's not love," Somnium barked and pushed the gems toward the demon hands. "You have the pain I want."

Musa licked his lips. "I deal in dreams, lad. Nightmares are a black trade."

Was the impish merchant testing him or trying to drive him mad?

"Those, *I* cannot even make. Only the Marsachs of the Outer Shades concoct such madness. To be caught with a drop of it is death."

Somnium pushed the gems closer.

Musa exaggerated another sigh, slid the red vials back beneath the counter, and pulled out a wooden lock-box. "This is all I have. I'm a fool to have kept it this long. And truth be told, it's the worst I've ever smelled, and therefore a collector's item for me. I never intended to sell it, not even to the Black Monks for their sacrifices." The clasp on the box fell open with a wave of his hand, and the silver top opened like the lid of a casket. "It could kill you with one dream."

Somnium removed the vial of thick liquid. A pewter

design encircled the glass, a shining ruby sunk deep into the bulk of metal, centering the intricate swirls. "What is it?," he asked, tipping the contents back and forth, watching the black sludge flow like thin tar from side to side.

Musa's wicked grin slipped away and he became darkly serious. "I don't know. I don't even want to look or smell. The Marsach that traded it to me said the base liquid came from the belly of a Coiks Lizard. I can only imagine what they must have added, and can't even guess the potency, or the number of nightmares it contains. Everything else aside, you're one of my best customers, and I'd hate to lose you, boy." His eyes grew narrow. "Does the Crown really demand such pain?"

"*I* demand it," Somnium said, replacing the vial and closing the box. "The Crown can go to Hell. And keep the change; I may not need it."

The night seemed a little brighter as he left the shop and he sensed first dawn advancing on him. He walked faster than normal, avoiding the few pedestrians invading the street mazes of the city before work. The crisp air, chilly beneath his loose shirt, drove him faster.

His home looked colder than ever tonight: its glass triangles like prisms jutting out against the dark sky. He entered at a slow stagger, the sleepless nights of sweat and toil catching up to him and mixing with the frigid air.

No sleep now. There wouldn't be enough time for any dreaming or composing. *Sanguineous*, his latest opera, opened that night, and dreams like the one in the bottle could last for days.

Somnium stood before the far wall of his bedroom. With a touch, the rushing, streaming water turned calm and clear as a still mirror-pool. He wore a ruffled white shirt beneath a black velvet suit, long strands of his dark, stringy hair dangling past his chin and mingling with the soft fabric of the ruffles. His mismatched eyes—one magenta, one green—looked darker than usual. Others would be wearing the Pierrot clown faces so popular at operas: a glossy black tear dripping down the right cheek for men, down the left for women, and one down each cheek for the androgynous whores who serviced the temple altars.

His skin was already the sickly pale of soured milk, removing any need for makeup. This crossed with the dark lines etched into his thin flesh by sharp bones gave him a look that was both unique and beyond fashion.

With the tip of his slender finger, Somnium brushed hair from his face and examined the deep purple beneath his eyes. The pupils stared into themselves for a moment, and then he blinked. He pulled the ruffled cuffs from the arms of his jacket and smoothed them back across the sleeves. He struck a pose with both hands as if conducting a vast orchestra and smiled at the absurdity.

They hadn't allowed him to conduct in years. Ever since the night he broke down on the dais, crying and screaming at the singers and musicians. The doctors said it was the nightmares driving him mad. The truth was the fools had pushed him too far on a bad night, by taunting him with misrepresentations of his work. The chorus had sung the wrong harmony. The sonics played half notes off. They'd done it on purpose.

Only the Emperor kept him out of prison when they discovered he'd been dreaming, and doctors didn't dare check ever since. No one really cared how he did what he did, so long as the operas continued. So long as he brought the nightmares to stage, and gave the people the pain and terror they craved to alleviate the boredom of the two-hundred year peace with the Sluag Kingdoms. Sometimes the only reason for continuing was the distant hope that one day one of his operas would give the Emperor a heart attack, or perhaps his witch of a queen, or the bastard prince, spawned with a harlot from the Edge Provinces. He shuddered thinking of the psychotic six-year-old princess, who was rumored to kill her own playmates.

Both arms slunk back down to his sides. He knew it didn't matter. The fact remained that he'd probably die if he ever stopped. Only the art itself sustained him. But it would kill him too.

He chose a smoked glass cane from his collection, one with a tip as sharp as an ice-pick, and headed for opening night. Just before leaving, he checked his precious nightmare. The murky blackness rested peacefully within its glass and silver coffin, locked behind a hidden panel which could only be opened when the wall-water rushed towards the ceiling.

A carriage already waited for him on the slate cobbles, the royal crest (two silver eagles with the head and tail of snakes) adorning the side door like a brand—a brand that might just as well have been burned into his chest.

Sitting in the driver's seat, an animated suit of glass armor motioned with crackling digits for the door to open and the onyx steps to descend. Somnium got in as if entering a hearse. He leaned against the leather cushions and heard the door seal shut. The air inside quickly cooled to the customary sixty degrees.

"The Royal Casn Theater," the glass man announced, his voice sounded like electric bells. His whip cracked, and the white-maned beasts started off. They stormed the streets without regard for vehicle or man, exercising the right of royal transportation.

A child screamed and fell to the side holding his leg. Somnium closed his eyes and tried to imagine life before peacetime.

The blue-skinned doormen bowed low as Somnium entered. For a moment he felt almost alive as people whispered his name and children tossed silk roses onto the green carpet path. Tonight, although the Emperor and his accursed family would be attending, the people were there to see *his* opera. They were there for him, not the master wielding his leash.

Two men, in matching white Victorian suits and purple court wigs bowed low. Their pet peacocks, dyed red, screeched almost human screams as they writhed at the ends of silver cords, bound about the men's wrists to gaudy bracelets of many-colored gems. "Luck to your piece tonight," said one, giving a snide smile through his color-inverted Pierrot face, black with a white tear.

"Yes, luck, Somnium," said the other, giving another exaggerated bow. "I hear it is a masterpiece."

He ignored them. They were composers (of a sort), but nowhere near his caliber, and they hated him for it. Tomorrow the few reviewers they had in their pockets would do all they could to thrash *Sanguineous*. It mattered little. The Emperor's reviewers would praise him as the rival of Orpheus and swear that on his death, he would be placed among the stars to conduct the heavens in their obits, or some such rubbish.

The crowds parted and bowed like one great wave falling and cresting down the long hall. It was the Emperor coming. His bald head shone with a crystal skull-cap that glowed, shifting from one color to the next as if red and yellow were trying to mate with blue and green.

As the great bald man approached, Somnium bowed low, acknowledging the ravishing queen—her black tear so large it covered her left cheek—the tall prince—his nose and eyes pointed at some spot on the ceiling high above Somnium's head—and of course the Emperor himself. The little princess was not showing tonight. The crystal-headed man smiled like a pig with gas and gestured toward Somnium. "Somnium," he bellowed, not so much to the composer as to the crowd, "I hear *Sanguineous* will be the greatest opera ever to grace the Casn Theater."

Somnium bowed again. "I pray it will, my Lord. Like all before, it is but a humble gift to amuse Your Majesty and his subjects."

The big man smiled again, and together they entered the Royal Box, which stood high against the wall opposite the stage so that they towered over the mezzanines. The box extended forty feet over the crowd, casting the shadow of a pyramid over the Common Seats of the floor.

Leidous, Pope of the Black Order sat down several seats from Somnium, adjusting the cowl of the flowing pitch robe which denoted his order. He turned and eyed Somnium with a piercing stare as if searching for something. The Pope, who knew more about the dreams and nightmares used in his monks' sacrifices than even the monks did, turned away muttering under his breath. "…and he's not dead?" was all Somnium could make out as the sourceless light of the walls dimmed. The wall of angled obsidian that rose from the front edge of the stage to the ceiling shone like a smoked mirror.

The crowd hushed as the dim lights became nothing, and the orchestra warned the room with a volley of staccato notes.

A column of light rose slowly from the Music Pit dais. Upon the platform stood a man, his head hung, his wild hair a mass of struggling vines. *Estous*. The fool would be conducting his opera. A fool who hardly knew what a sonic baton was for. A fool who could no more compose than brush his hair.

Estous's head and arms rose in a dramatic gesture as the drums thundered. He flicked the needle-sharp instrument through the air with rapid jerks and exaggerated sweeps. A pulsing pin-laser emanated from the baton's tip and danced to the beat of Somnium's opus. The beam of light cut through the thin fog which burst from the dais as the strings began. It guided the winds and reeds and petal tubes into the tricky melding of sharp soprano cellos and high violins, along with the thumping drone of the oracle horns and glass tubas.

It wasn't right. At least, it wasn't perfect. The crystal snares had started a beat too soon, and the light flutes hadn't started at all, choosing just now to join suddenly over the softer mourn of the ghost horns and electric chimes. Nevertheless, Somnium closed his eyes and drank his own notes in, savoring the distant terror that would come at the end of the deceptive intro.

His eyes opened again as Estous's baton cast a sudden arch in the air and the column of light shifted harshly from sky blue to blood red. All but the thundering drums stopped, and the banshee pipes screeched over the top. The obsidian wall-curtain lit up with hideous shapes too vague to be made out but just crisp enough to invoke dread of ancient astral beasts lying dormant in distant race memories—the astral beasts from which Somnium knew many of his nightmares had once been stolen.

Just as the crowd—screaming as if falling down a shaft toward a bed of razor spikes—seemed about to acclimate to the freakish images, the wall began to melt. It melted from the ceiling down and then from the bottom up and then from the sides, revealing a host of actors frozen in place against the scarlet backdrop and glowing scrims, shifting like water.

Each actor wore an upside-down mask, depicting mythic creatures of legend-history. Some bore noses two feet long, twisting at awkward angles, painted with shadows and highlights that matched the theme of their own unique costumes. Several women hooked together formed serpents, writhing up to the gray and silver towers that shone only when the roving spotlights crossed them. The green demons, known well from the *Moon Myths of the Outer Boundaries*, with variations Somnium took from the nightmares he knew to be more truth than legend-history, twisted around columns of bubbling, yellow sand. Their long fingers and snakelike nails, spiraled up into black voids, which the spotlights never crossed.

Somnium smiled as the Pope's eyes narrowed at the depictions of monsters born of the Cilohtac Church's own holy books. Could it be he disapproved of the variations, or was he frightened of their closeness to the truth? Whatever the case, so long as the Church remained angry with him, the people would flock to his operas for the controversy, and of course the Emperor loved nothing more than antagonizing the religious leaders with one hand and supporting their law and ceremony with the other.

Somnium turned back, just as the lead vocalist, dressed in scarlet tights and a matching upside-down demon mask, transformed into the same-colored likeness of Selucreh, the many-time hero of Namor legend-history. Selucreh's arms twisted and writhed in contortions so strange it took the audience several minutes to realize the singer beneath the suit faced the rear of the stage, his outfit worn backwards. The misshapen mask dipped to the ground. Its crooked nose, now slim and shapely, almost reached his navel as the singer threw back his head and launched a single high note to the ceiling. The shrill sound refused to ebb, bouncing around the room and turning back on itself as one by one the other singers transformed into likenesses of Selucreh's warriors and joined in, heads flung back as well. Each note was different, each purposely out of harmony. They continued for more than three minutes, blistering the audience with a wall of sound until all at once, the many-colored characters, like so many arched trees, crumbled to the ground and fell silent.

Somnium savored the effect. Around him, faces shone pale, even through their makeup. The Pope himself shuddered and drew back into his dark cowl. The Emperor bit his knuckle but giggled with the sick delight only a true masochist could exhibit. Somnium narrowed his eyes and folded his arms.

Just as the audience seemed on the verge of recovering, the singers leapt to their feet and began to sing, each one a different song in a different ancient tongue. As they sang, colored smoke matching their various costumes spewed from their mouths in a steady stream, billowing into the Common Seats.

Several women screamed. Seats clattered. The front section scrambled for the door until armored soldier-police returned them to their seats. The Emperor found this particularly amusing and nodded to Somnium, his fishlike eyes wet with glee.

Arms outspread, the singers began to float. Still singing.

Still spewing smoke. The background scrims changed, undulating between drips of crimson, waves of silvery black, and the crackling patterns of cosmic storms. Shadows flying battle steeds rode the rippling scrims, which bore ancient knights of the *Pre-Legend-History Wars*. Drums rolled as the wind of their fearsome wings blew against the audience and their battle cry, a thunder of coral shrieks, tore into everyone's soft eardrums.

Selucreh and his Warriors drew sapphire ocarinas, steel lyres, and crystal flutes from their belts. Together, they lashed out with staccato notes, driving the shadows back. But only for a short time. The shadows rallied, prism-holograms projecting the hideous beasts as translucent shapes against the torrent of scrims.

Selucreh and his Warriors fought with all their might, stinging their attackers with quarter notes and razor-thin eighth notes. Steeds fell, their riders bleeding black water against the scrims. A stray arrow struck the mighty Selucreh. His song quailed. His lyre shattered against the stage. The warriors crashed beside him, one by one, as wavering swords cut them down. Shadows shrieked louder as the songs rotted to silence and the stage floor turned red.

The audience held their breath, awaiting the fallen to at least be borne to heaven. But the shimmering figures of the ancient gods appeared one by one against the flowing scrims, and each, as they appeared, turned their backs upon the mighty warriors; the colored troubadours of Tane, last of the fledgling champions.

Selucreh sank into the floor, as did his men. The harsh earth sucked them down to the mewing of silver harps, and while they vanished, the redness of the stage seeped away until it shone glistening obsidian. And the great stone curtain melted up to the ceiling.

The music ceased.

The crowd sat quaking.

The Emperor appeared overcome with emotion. His eyes quivered, horrified and transfixed, but still the giggling sadomasochist. He rose from his chair and applauded. Still glassy-eyed, the remaining members of the Royal Box stood and applauded with him. It felt like no more than a programmed response, and Somnium could see their knees trembling, their makeup running with tears of dread. The drone of their dutiful applause contrasted with the Emperor's enthusiastic clapping. The rest of the theater joined them in a growing wave until the entire room was standing and applauding, all eyes on Somnium.

He let both hands lay still by his sides. Only his head moved as he returned slight bows to the thundering applause.

Bowing to his left, he noticed the Pope. The cheerless face lay scowling inside its hood. No terror to the creased features. Only anger. For a moment, Somnium's own fear rose, but he pushed it down and turned back to the grinning Emperor. His Majesty made grand gestures towards the young composer with his fat arms.

The Emperor appeared far more pleased than ever before. As usual, the opera's true meaning was lost on the bald dictator, but Somnium smiled as if in appreciation.

The Emperor raised an arm high above his head, and all the theater ceased its clapping. He motioned to Somnium and then to the floor. Somnium hesitated but knelt before his master, head hung down. "Somnium," the Emperor said with the same grand voice. "Somnium, opera has never been opera before this night. Singers have never sung. Poets have never spoken…"

Somnium watched from beneath his strands of dangling black hair. The Emperor fell silent, closed his eyes, and rocked his head back sand forth toward the ceiling in ecstasy. "Somnium, Somnium," he moaned. Curling his hands into fists, he opened his eyes and looked down again. "The court has found a voice tonight, and it is you." With that, he removed the cresnium mantle from his neck. Thousands of tiny woven jewels sparkled between the silver threads. He placed it over Somnium's head and let it conform to his narrow shoulders.

The bald man made him stand, and there was an explosion of applause. "I have never named a Royal *Master* Composer," he said as if to Somnium, but he shouted it to the crowd. "However, tonight the title is yours."

Somnium thought of the nightmare back at home, calling him to bed. Calling him to create. Wishing the Emperor would be silent and let him leave.

"I will throw every other composer in the land to the Beasts of Preidox if you but ask," the fat man continued. He turned to the two composers from the hall. "Somnium may dine on those scarlet peacocks if he wishes." Then to Somnium, "All the composers. You may have their wives for your slaves and their children as lovers."

I just want to dream, thought Somnium, but he bowed lower.

The Emperor continued. Somnium heard only a monotone drone. He nodded graciously and smiled, thinking of the vial of black dream lying quietly behind its secret panel.

As the Emperor turned to gather his family, the crowd rushed at Somnium with shouts, nods, and glass roses of shallow congratulations. The other composers prostrated themselves, offering him bribes in the form of exorbitantly priced music lessons for their children, which he would never actually have to show up for. Some offered their wives and offspring as slaves, hoping to save themselves.

Somnium brushed them away. *As if I'd want any of them.* He tried to be pleasant to the other people, however. Most were devoted fans, and though he might despise them for their lack of true understanding, he had to praise their taste.

A black carriage waited for him outside. It didn't bear the Emperor's seal, but he leapt aboard regardless, glad to escape the throngs. A taxi was a taxi.

The glass driver crackled as he whipped the great steeds.

They pounded down the street much faster than regulation speed.

"Somnium."

Somnium twisted. He hadn't noticed the form lying against the shadows of the carriage's corner. It was just a mass of shimmering highlights, but it solidified into the tangible shape of a cloaked priest. Somnium cursed his haste and snapped his gaze to the opposite seat. Another priest peeled himself from the cushion shadows and held up a gloved hand. The tight leather fingers glowed with green, pulsing energy.

Somnium couldn't move. His throat tightened. His body felt like wood.

The priest across from him pulled back his hood, exposing a Pierrot clown face. Somnium recognized him as one of the Pope's personal guard. The priest tore the white face off in one piece like a mask of flesh, exposing twisted features almost as pale as the Pierrot skin. "You like to sleep, Somnium." The fingers glowed red. "So sleep."

Somnium awoke to walls of shifting lights and a ceiling that looked like a long, writhing serpent. At least twenty hooded figures stood around him. He still couldn't move. A thin web of fleshy gauze held him to a raised platform. The priests murmured in their secret language from the dark recesses of their hoods.

"Somnium." *The Pope.* Somnium couldn't see him, but the voice was unmistakable. "We found this in your home." A gloved hand moved over his face, a vial of black liquid held tight in its grasp. "What is this?"

Somnium couldn't speak. The web locked his jaw and head in place.

"You have no business with such crafts, Composer. Even *I* have never seen such potent dream."

Somnium closed his eyes. They would kill him now.

Possession of dreams was immediate death if the church got a hold of you, and a nightmare like this wouldn't even require a trial. Only the priests could even *speak* of nightmares.

The black hoods murmured, but the Pope's voice silenced them. "No sacrifice would live to tell the tale. Few could survive one measure of this." Leather fingers flexed around the vial. He bent down into Somnium's face. "I could kill you for possessing this, but mere death would not be enough."

The web loosened beneath Somnium's chin, and several metal instruments were pushed between his teeth. The priests pried his jaw apart while the Pope himself uncorked the vial. "Your final dream, dear Somnium." The Pope's small eyes blazed. "Savor it."

Somnium gurgled as the entire vial poured down his throat. The web tightened again, and there was nothing but silent stillness.

He lay in a desert, covered with blades of sand that swayed in the tempest wind. They broke and grew again beneath him. Unlike dreams and nightmares before, the world felt far more crisp and clear than even his waking life. It was as if he were *more there* than before, though the world itself seemed much stranger than ever. The air whispered and quarreled with the wind in ancient languages he recognized and even *knew* in a way, but he still couldn't translate the words.

The wind blew into the sand, picking it up and swirling it up to the clouds, leaving pockets of open space around him where the ground should have been. Sky and earth merged and then separated, merged and separated again as if uncertain of their own form. The wind began to scream, and the still air screeched back. The sand struggled to remain whole, and the clouds turned brown as dust touched them and became white again as the dust receded.

Somnium shivered in the warm air. This wasn't like any

of the others. No strange beasts or mythic battles. No archaic architecture, gem mountains, sea animals, or colors of any kind for that matter. Only the desert and sky, and desert/sky, and the air around. Its very simplicity frightened him more than any nightmare before.

The sand settled again, hardening itself against the ever-increasing wind. Clouds turned dark and began to move. They rolled like waves, crashing and banking and ebbing and swirling. They rumbled and thundered, and webs of sapphire electricity rode the waves' building crests.

It was as if the sky were the sea, but upside-down, and he feared falling up into it. He dropped to his knees and dug his hands into the dirt, anchoring himself to the sky, as it were.

From the waves came cloud-galleons bigger than mountains. They rode the thundering storm, dipping into the waves and out again, riding the tidal clouds up toward him and back down to the vacuum of space. Ships of another design, similar but from another nation, raced in from the opposite direction. As they met, the sky seemed to shatter with a deafening crack of thunder. Instead of ship wreckage, it rained glass chess pieces like hail. All around him, kings and bishops fell, rooks and pawns and queens. A great knight landed at his feet and shattered into a pool of blood. All the pieces shattered and bled. Soon the desert was red, and the sky was red, and the air rushed to keep them apart this time, as they fought to leak into each other.

"Ssssomium," came a voice from beyond the air and the sky and the blood. The rumble of it seemed to stay all movement, and the desert returned to rolling, flowing dunes, the sky to a mass of cotton white.

"I know you," Somnium shouted into the void. "Musa!"

The voice paused. "I have no name."

Somnium looked for a face to grow out of the sand or clouds, or to take shape in the air, but nothing did. "You are one of the ancient beasts, the ones these dreams are stolen from.

Do you sell your own dreams?"

"Sell?" The voice gave a sort of giggle, a familiar laugh he knew too well. "The beasts you speak of will not be born for eons."

"Do not lie to me, demon. I know you, Musa."

The air and land and sky swirled as one, as if considering something. "Perhaps one day I will be thiss Mussa, but he is no ssimple beassst. One day, when the world is more solid and there are individual men and beasstss, but not here. Not now. Your race is not even thought of, nor that which preceded you, nor the one before, or before that, or that, or that. Your world does not even exisst. The universse iss sstill young and ssoft. Look around: your mind does not even know enough to conssider what it iss sseeing. You only hear a voice, becausse you need to, becausse you musst hear it to sspeak to me."

Somnium tried to stand firm against the increasing gusts of wind. "Then you are one of the Elder Gods that formed my world."

Everything around him seemed to shrug. "Elder Gods? No, look." As the voice spoke, dust forms rose up from the sand and floated a man's height from the desert floor, as if spread across invisible tables. They lay great and muscular and nude and silent. Dead perhaps, or sleeping, or dreaming, or all three. "One day thesse will be the Elder Gods you sspoke of, but not before they are a great many other things. They are not even yet concepts or ideas, or even the dust from which an idea might be formed. You sstand in a place so long ago that it iss not a place, and not a time. The universse iss sso ssoft you could not sstand in it if you were not who and what you are."

"And that is?"

Again the presence seemed to shrug. "A sserofvant of sssorts."

"A servant to whom?"

"Him, for one," the voice replied, seeming to regard one of the floating forms. "That is what will one day be a note, and then a ssong, and then a poem, and then an idea, and eventually a god. You will call him Art, and you will know him in ways no one ever has."

"Not art. Music," Somnium shouted.

"What you call dreams," the voice continued, "are but a time to reengage with birth. Most never travel beyond their own lifetime, and none have ever traveled beyond the age of their own world."

"And what am I?"

"A dream? A thought?" The voice seemed to consider again. "Nightmare iss another word for prophecy. You are bound to thiss primal god, and to me, or thisss," it said, seeming to mean the whole dream, "or whatever you wish to call it."

Somnium felt reality close in on him. The very air became thick around his limbs.

"You cannot free yoursself from your own passt, and therefore you cannot free yoursself from the future. Your world iss ending. It has become too ssolid. That iss why dreams are rare. It will continue to ssolidify, until it stopss, turnss back on itsself, and ssoftens again, and universse beginss anew."

"How long do we have?" Somnium asked as he struggled against the thickening sand that crept up his legs.

"You know more than mosst," the voice said. "Your operas have foretold more than anyone knowss. None but your priestss even guess at their true meaning. It's why they ssacrifice sslaves to the black waters of nightmare. They wish to learn even a page of the books you've written in ssong."

"They hate me."

The voice seemed amused. "They have watched you all your life, hoping to undersstand what they will never ssee, for they can do no more than interpret. They are but priesstss, not prophetss. They learn little from their ssacrifices, becausse most die before divulging more than a broken poem. But you are natural to it. You are a child *of* it. A shaper. A shaped. A sseer.

A sseen. An idea. A god. You unlike most men have a sspirit born from thesse very ssands, and therefore you can never be sseparated from the past or the future. You are both the island and the river. The land and the water."

Somnium shuddered. "Then this very moment is a prophecy of doom. Will I even live?" Somnium thought better of the question. "Will I even wake?"

"That dependss on how well your mind copes. If you fight, it may kill you. If you accept it, you may live."

"Then, I'm a pawn."

"Pawn. Knight. King. You ssee the future becausse you ssee the past, and all that happenss now happenss then."

Somnium's mind clouded. He was having more trouble concentrating, as if the sands had sifted into his head. But he spoke through the mental haze. "Then peacetime is over soon. Those ships. The shattering knights. The blood of my other dreams. The wars of gods and demons and heroes and beasts. My nation will fall."

Reality itself seemed frustrated, and the clouds and sands rolled with irritation. "Your nation iss but a sspeck of ssand. Yess, it will ssoon end for you and your time, but ssoon after, all will soften and end. You will help form the next beginning."

"All is lost."

"Nothing iss ever losst, you fool. Each sspeck of reality iss…" The voice fell silent.

Somnium looked around. Looked to the floating forms for answers. Looked to the sky for meaning. The desert for hope. The wind for words. "Am I to even wake?" Somnium screamed. Nothing. The whispers were silent. The sands lay motionless, and the sky leveled to a cotton curtain of thick mist. His skin numbed. He felt himself bleeding into the sand as it swirled around his body and engulfed his thinking. Somnium's hands began to fade. Bits of him were blowing away as fine particles of dust.

He was nothing but a part of *their* sleep. Little more than a fleck of sand in something else's dream. He was a slave, a pawn, a simple teller of tales. The universe was using him, and at any moment, some great dreamer might awake, and even these gods would be word memories in the mind of that other being.

"Noooo!" Somnium screamed, clenching his fists and willing his body back into solid existence. "*No.* I am Somnium, and this is *my* dream," he shouted to the voice which had abandoned him. "You are a voice in *my* head, in a land *I* paint. These gods are *my* creations, and their will is my will. This is *my* dream!" he screamed once again.

In a moment the wind whispered, "As you wish, Composer."

Somnium woke to sweat and pain. His muscles throbbed, as did his head.

A nurse dabbed water on his brow. He opened one eye, and then the other. He tried to speak but could hardly croak through his dry throat.

"You're in the Emperor's private clinic," she said responding to the question he didn't ask. "You've been unconscious for over two weeks." She re-moistened the wet towel and adjusted the life support systems. "The Royal Guard rescued you from the priests the same night you were taken."

The Pope, what about that bastard? He thought.

She read his eyes again. "They arrested several bishops and a few priests for high treason against the Royal Master Composer."

Somnium gave a heavy sigh. The Emperor couldn't touch the Pope, so several scapegoats (probably the ones present) had been offered up. It wasn't enough, but he hoped they'd hang.

"You need sleep," the nurse said. "I'll bring you food after a while." She smiled, stroked his forehead, and was gone.

For the first time in years, Somnium relaxed. The Empire had little time left, and for that matter, the Pope and the Emperor. Prophecies of doom were unfolding in his mind even now. He knew truths remembered from the grains of sand, the color of the sky, and the unopened eyes of the sleeping gods.

Doom for the empire was peace for him. Now he would sleep and not dream. There was time to eat, and to sip warm wine. Time to write one final opera.

This room has an old-fashioned television set in one corner. You try turning it on, but it appears to be broken. If you see only your own reflection in the curved glass screen, turn right for room 23 (page 273). If you think you can make out a faint miasma of static fuzz, proceed straight ahead to room 27.

27
Visual Snow

L.B. SHIMAIRA

To me, darkness isn't just dark.

It's alive.

It moves.

Because of visual snow.

If you don't know what that is, I don't blame you. I have it, yet I didn't know it was a thing until a year ago. I always thought everyone saw this old TV static covering their vision. Turns out that nope, they don't.

I see it in the light but also in the dark. Hell, especially in the dark. Bright light tends to hurt and screw with my vision, temporarily blinding me in part. If I stare at the bright blue sky, I'll see stuff move as if there are tiny little flies whisking about. But in the dark? In the dark, the static sometimes seems to coalesce.

Is it really just static I'm looking at, or is there some kind of entity observing me in return?

I used to enjoy staring into the darkness, and I wanted the darkness to stare back at me. I actually wanted it to reach out.

"Reach out and touch me."

Yes, I was a fool.

I've tried certain drugs in the past—legal ones, mind you, in my country at least. I hoped they might be able to expand my mind, truly bring that darkness to life. But alas, it seems I can get a better trip from just staring at a wall without any drugs—or alcohol for that matter—in my system.

So, that's what I tried instead: just staring at stuff until my pupils began to dilate and contract all on their own, making the room pulsate with dimming and brightening lights. Do this while staring at something with a pattern and be prepared for quite the trip!

But the other night, my sober trip felt very much like I was surely using some psychedelic drug.

I was in the bath and staring at the tiles. The room was already pulsating, and the visual snow was breathing life into the pattern on the wall. It moved, it grew, it flooded into the water. I remained calm, knowing it would all vanish the moment I'd so much as blink too fast. But when the pattern touched my skin...It tingled.

I jerked and blinked, but that brief moment of darkness that you get when you blink didn't go away. I was certain I'd merely blinked, but everything had gone dark.

Except for the static. The visual snow is always there.

I knew I was still in the bath; the sensation of tepid water against my skin confirmed that. My fingers searched for my eyes, checking if my lids were indeed as open as I thought they were.

They weren't.

I plucked and peeled at my lids. They seemed glued shut, and I was beginning to panic when finally a small strip of light appeared in the static as I managed to pry my eyes open.

Then, as suddenly as the world had vanished, it returned. Despite what had happened just moments before, I blinked several times—thankfully, the world remained. Yet the visual snow was more prevalent than how I remembered it. Even with the dim bathroom lights on, the mere air seemed alive.

Moving.

Little flies of static light shot left and right, only to vanish.

I shook my head and turned back to my bath, wanting to

unplug it. My breath hitched as I saw that the pattern of the tiles was still visible on the water, like some kind of oil spill. It expanded and compressed while the opalescent colors shimmered and reflected the light.

Confused, I blinked and rubbed my eyes.

The water was back to normal. The static in the air was not.

I unplugged the bath, and a loud ringing started in my ears. The sheer volume took me by surprise; it left me as good as deaf on both sides. While tinnitus wasn't unknown to me, I was used to it being only in one ear at a time and not as loud as I was hearing it now.

I got out, holding onto the radiator for support, and slipped into my bathrobe. My gaze fell on the mirror, and I nearly lost my balance, light-headedness overwhelming me. I had to take a seat on the toilet, not taking my sight off the—what would normally be—reflective surface.

The full face of the mirror was an amalgamation of iridescent pixels, flickering snowy static in no color I could name. The surface no longer seemed flat as visual snow danced in a neat rectangle, both in front of and behind where the glass used to be.

My heart pounded heavily in my chest, and I kept blinking, thinking it was just some weird hallucination from low blood pressure or the tinnitus that still rung in both my ears.

But the mirror remained a portal of prismatic static that pulsated and swirled before my eyes.

After staring at it for what must have been a good several minutes, I slowly rose to my feet. My curiosity had become stronger than my fear. I stepped closer to the mirror, and the tinnitus finally decided to decrease in volume. Biting my lip and holding my breath, I did something I knew was foolish: I reached out toward the static.

As my fingers came closer to it, my skin began to tingle—just like how my leg had in the bath when the pattern had touched it.

I pulled my hand back. Gaze dropping to the various items scattered along the sink, I reached for my hairbrush but then decided to grab a hair tie instead. With a sly smile, I tossed the thing toward the mirror.

For a moment, I thought it had vanished into the static. But no, I had merely missed it fall. When I looked down, it lay right next to the tap. I wrinkled my nose, grabbed the hairbrush, and slowly brought it toward the mirror. My skin didn't tingle, but the moment the plastic made contact with the static, the tinnitus ceased.

The sudden silence took me by surprise. I froze, my arm with the brush still outstretched. Then I took a deep breath and leaned forward. The brush went further into the static. My gaze shifted to the wall. The thing should be touching the mirror by now.

Yet I was still able to lean further toward the mirror without feeling any resistance on the plastic hairbrush. My hand was getting rather close to the static now, the strange pixels making my fingers tingle whenever they got out far enough to touch me.

I wanted to pull away, but the brush was stuck. Recoiling, I released it and jumped back. The black handle remained stuck in the air before it was pulled into the static and vanished. Without thinking, I blurted out, "Hey, give it back!"

I felt silly the moment those words had crossed my lips. As if whatever had taken it would listen.

But, it did. The brush reappeared at the bottom of the mirror as it was gently slid right next to the tap, pushing the hair tie into the sink.

A part of me wanted to bolt out of the bathroom.

Another part of me wanted to get a broom and see how far it would go into the former mirror.

I stood nailed to the floor for a while, just staring at the static. Mesmerised. Whatever was on the other side of that wall of static could hear me. That, or it simply hated foreign objects being prodded at it.

I couldn't help a crooked smile appearing on my face. This was all sorts of weird and fucked up, but it was also an experience. Something to record and share with my closest friends. But I'd need proof.

"Hell, I need to document this," I muttered. "Don't go anywhere!"

I didn't know if whatever was on the other side had heard or could even understand me, but I left the bathroom, rushed into the study, grabbed a pen, and tore out several pages from a notebook. With the paper and pen in hand, I stepped back into the dimly lit bathroom, a part of me fearing the mirror would just be a plain old mirror again.

It wasn't.

From the door opening, the field of static seemed even more alive than it had when I'd been standing in front of it mere moments ago. I returned to my previous position. I held the paper slightly curved between three fingers, placed the pen in the hollow this created, and took a deep breath.

"Do you want to try and talk to me?"

I moved the paper toward the static, then tilted it slightly so the pen would slide in. The moment it had vanished, I pushed the paper further in. The snow was almost licking my skin again when I felt a slight tug. I released the sheets, and something pulled them into my former mirror.

Excited and anxious for what would happen next, I took a step back. My gaze was fixated on the area by the sink, waiting for the paper to reappear. Instead, something caught my attention higher up: One of the sheets had reappeared in the middle of the static. I couldn't see what was keeping it there—its edges were surrounded by the iridescent static.

The words on the page were small, and I took a step closer to read it. The handwriting was quite neat, almost as if someone had printed the text:

"What are you?"

The question took me by surprise. I'd thought of several possible scenarios as to how the interaction could have gone, but this…This had not been one of them.

"I'm…human," I answered hesitantly, not sure if that was what the static wanted to hear.

The paper vanished back into the iridescent snow only to reappear a second later. New words had been added below the previous question in the same immaculate handwriting: *"How can you see us?"*

I frowned. "I—I don't know. Can I? I just see static. What are *you?*"

The sheet was pulled back again and reappeared with a new message. *"We are conscious."*

"What does that mean? I'm conscious too. Or, I think I am…" I was starting to doubt that now. "I mean, I could be dreaming."

New words were added: *"Dreaming is something all who are conscious have in common."*

Confused, I asked, "But what are you then?"

The paper seemed to merely flicker as it returned swiftly with a new message: *"What are you?"*

I frowned. "You're not really making this easy. Are you human too? Am I dreaming, or is this real?"

"We are conscious. Dreams are real."

Getting annoyed, I crossed my arms. "Am I awake, or did I fall asleep?"

"Why do you ask us about the state of your mind?"

I opened my mouth to counter, but what could I say? I took a moment to think of a reply: "What is your definition of *real?*"

"Everything a consciousness experiences. Actively or passively."

A chill went up my spine. I wanted to counter how dreams weren't real…But nightmares do have real effects. If you're hurt in a dream and you feel it, how is the memory of that pain any different from a memory of pain felt in the real world?

The subject was making my head spin.

"Where are you? Are you from some other dimension?"

The paper was gone longer this time. *"We are everywhere and nowhere. We are conscious. We exist. You wouldn't be able to understand if we tried to explain further."*

I huffed. "Try me."

"We want to ask questions now. Why do you see us?"

"You already asked me that—and I still don't know why I'm seeing you, or even *what* I'm seeing." Without thinking, I reached toward the mirror to touch the ever-moving static. The tingling sensation rippled through my fingers as the opalescent pixels made contact with my skin.

Black. White. Red. Yellow. Electric blue.

The tinnitus hit me hard again and I fell forward, trying to catch myself on the sink. Instead, the static flowed out of the mirror and engulfed me. Deaf and blind now, I grasped the sink tightly. The feeling of the cool surface, along with my bare feet on the stone tiles, grounded me as my head swam in static and high-pitched noise.

Go away. Go away. Go away.

I kept repeating those words, hoping it would dispel whatever was happening. After several minutes—or was it hours?—the tinnitus began to fade, and I opened my eyes.

My reflection stared back at me.

I sighed in relief, straightened up, and rubbed my eyes. What had happened? My gaze dropped to the tap, and goosebumps erupted all over my body. A hair tie lay in the sink. A hairbrush and a pen were next to the tap. A single sheet of paper appeared to be stuck against the glass.

But I had given multiple sheets…

With trembling fingers, I peeled the paper from the mirror. In neat handwriting, there was but one sentence written on it.

"We will be watching you."

I shuddered and dropped the piece of paper into the sink. I kept my gaze low, refusing to look at my reflection. What if it did something different from me?

Shaking my head, as if that could erase the strange experience I had just been through, I walked out of the bathroom and into the darkness of the hall. The visual snow seemed more present than it normally did.

The darkness more alive.

I closed my eyes, but doing that just makes the snow all the more visible. The static never had an actual shape. It sometimes appeared to want to have a shape, but it didn't—not really.

But it's different now.

I said I wanted the darkness to reach out. Well, it did. And it touched me all right. Or, I touched it.

I must have fallen asleep then. I don't remember much of what happened after I went into my bedroom. But this morning, when I stumbled into the bathroom, the sheet of paper still lay in the sink. The words on it were gone, however.

Did I dream? Did I hallucinate?

You tell me.

The visual snow is thicker now than it used to be, and the tinnitus—when it hits—is more intense. When I close my eyes, I swear I can see things move through the static.

What is real?

I don't know anymore.

The lights flicker off for a moment, and your imagination takes over. For the space of maybe two seconds, you feel as if you're still in the woods, no abandoned carnival, no mirrored labyrinth. You know your head isn't right, but which is the dream, and which is reality? If you think you might prefer the dream, turn right for room 21 (page 245). Or if you'd rather it come to an end once and for all, proceed straight ahead to room 28.

Nightmare's End

ALEX PILALIS

TONIGHT WILL BE DIFFERENT.

The thought plays over and over in my head, to the point where I realize I've stopped listening to Martin on the phone.

"So, your date went well?" I say, trying to get back on track with the conversation. I balance the phone between my shoulder and ear while I fold an old T-shirt and place it in a drawer beside my bed.

"Well, she got in that taxi pretty quickly," Martin says. "But there was also that long kiss. So, who knows? It did feel a little odd though, being out on a date while there were kids running around trick-or-treating."

"Well that's one way to spend a Halloween," I tell him. While others were out partying in costume or knocking on doors asking for treats, I had my own plan for the night. "See how she sounds when you speak to her next."

"Yeah, true," Martin says thoughtfully. "Anyway, dude." His voice takes a strange, harder tone. "I should get going. It's getting late."

Oh, that's why he sounds weird, I think to myself. I sigh and say, "I'll be fine. You don't have to worry about me every time I go to sleep."

Pacing my bedroom, my bare feet slapping on the wooden

floor, I come to a stop as I wait for his response. Complete darkness shows from the two roof windows of my loft room.

"I know," Martin finally says. "But it seems like you have those nightmares every night, these days."

I shake my head, despite the truth in his words. I should've been talking to Amy about this. If she would talk to me, that is.

"It's never as bad as it sounds," I lie, trying to sound casual. "Sleep paralysis is a common problem for loads of people."

"And sleep apnea, yeah. But that doesn't mean it's not a serious issue. I mean, it could…"

"It can be fatal," I finish what he can't say. "I know, dude. Look, you should get off the phone, in case that girl calls you for a post-date chat."

"It's not the nineties anymore," Martin says, slightly irritated. "Phones can tell us if someone rings when we're on a call."

I chuckle. "Okay, then just get off the phone. It's sleepy dreamtime."

Martin laughs at the reference to an old joke we have. "Okay, I'll leave you to it, Lee. Have a good, and safe, sleep."

A part of me shudders at his words. We shouldn't have to wish people safe sleep. At almost twenty years old, I shouldn't have to worry about going to sleep—worried that the boogie man would get me. "Thanks, man. Speak later."

"And Lee," Martin adds. "Happy Halloween."

I smile weakly. "And to you."

We hang up, and I remain holding the phone against my chest. My new clock ticks loudly in the quiet room. A shiver runs over me. Okay, time to do this.

At the windowsill, I light the stubby candles lined up, as well as the candles on my bedside table and on top of the drawers at the foot of my bed. A warm, vanilla scent wafts over the room—the smell reminds me of church when I was a kid.

I drop down and start doing push-ups. Both my mind and my body need to be strong for what I'm going to do. I soon become lost in the routine—I can do over thirty reps now.

Breaking free from the demons of sleep can take a terrible toll on the body.

Those were the words of the old Filipino man who told me how to stop the nightmares. It took me weeks to find him online and longer to research several websites and forums to find out that he was as legit as he claimed.

To end my sleep paralysis nightmares, I need to follow his every word.

As I begin my sit-up routine, my mind wanders to Amy. I wish I could call her tonight, to speak to her one last time before I go through with this. But she's made it clear she doesn't want to speak to me, not after our last argument. *If I make it through tonight, she'll be the first person I call in the morning. I'll make everything right. Everything will be better after tonight.*

I stretch and shake my tense muscles. It feels like I'm about to run a marathon, rather than the nice, relaxing sleep I should be having.

I turn off the bedroom light, and the candles fight the darkness with their dull, yellow glow. I watch the shadows wavering over the room as I run through my checklist. All the windows are closed; the blinds are now up. My door is closed but not locked. The candles are burning. The new clock I bought continues to tick loudly.

Fuck, what if this goes wrong? I shake the chilling thought away as I climb into bed. Somehow, I feel like every action I'm taking now will lead to the end. I pull the covers up and keep my arms over the duvet as I lie on my back, legs straight and close together. The way the Filipino man told me to.

A sheet of light appears under my door, lighting the opposite wall. The bathroom door closes downstairs. My dad washing up before bed.

God, I hope I see them again, I think as I lie in the gloomy darkness. With my sister married and out of the country, I'm the only one left to look after my elderly parents, who had me late in life. Mum wasn't doing so well these days, and I don't know what Dad would do without me, or her.

Closing my eyes, I focus on my breathing as I start counting backwards from one hundred. I have to do this right, for them. For Amy. For myself.

I hear the downstairs light flick off and my dad going to his room as my heartbeat slowly relaxes. I begin to feel the onset of sleep. *Sixty-eight. Sixty-seven.*

Sixty-six.

At some point I become vaguely aware of no longer counting. Have I fallen asleep?

A floorboard softly creaks in my room.

The sound immediately quickens my heart. *Oh God, it's happening.*

Keeping still—not that I could move, anyway—I slowly, very slowly, inch my eyes open, keeping them mostly pressed together. Through the dim light and my blurry, limited vision, I see the shadow in my room.

The shadow man is standing silently near the far corner, mostly obscured by the real shadows around him. While it would be hard to see him, two dull red orbs fill the space where his eyes should be, giving him away. Two red lights in the darkness, staring at me.

Rather than moving closer, he remains still. Which only means one thing.

He's just here to watch. And that means he isn't my true tormentor tonight. The thought sends a cold shiver over me.

When the shadow man doesn't try to reach for me or drag me out of bed, it means he'll just stand there, waiting for something else to appear. Something worse.

The hairs on my arms tingle as I press my eyes shut, trying to steady my breathing. I'm asleep. I have to act like I'm asleep. Even if I'm aware of everything. That's the thing about sleep paralysis: you're caught in between asleep and awake, locked in a world where nightmares are very real, your mind fully awake while your body is trapped on the other side.

No matter what, do not let them know you are awake, the Filipino man told me. Despite having only spoken to him online, I hear his voice as an old, wise mentor, like from a martial arts film.

Concentrating on my breathing, I focus on the vanilla scent of the candles and the ticking clock—the links tying me to the real world.

Something presses down on my bed, near my feet. Then another pressure point shifts the mattress, tilting my legs a little. At first it reminds me of a small animal walking over my bed, like when I used to stay over at my cousin's house and their cat would come into my room and walk on my bed. But I know this isn't a cat...

The points of pressure move closer to my chest, under my exposed arm. The bed creaks from the movement. I keep my eyes firmly shut, my face as relaxed as I can make it despite the fear coursing through me. I'm sleeping; they can't get to me. Sweat builds up. My face grows hot.

A light wind brushes over my arm. No—a whispery cloth; something tangible.

Oh God, it's her.

It's her.

Focus on the ticking clock. Smell the candles. Don't let them—

A heavy weight presses down against my chest. For a moment, my breath is taken, before I fight through the pressure and try to maintain a steady heart rate. *She can't affect me; I'm asleep. She hasn't seen me wake up.*

I hope to God the old man was right about all this.

People say that these are just nightmares, that I can't actually be hurt, but...fuck me, it feels so real. I can't deny the weight on my chest, the feel of cloth against my bare arms, and that rancid, decaying odor coming from her.

I don't need to open my eyes to know what's sitting on me. I've seen her enough times before. If I looked up, I would see a dark, squat form—a tangled mess of hair over tattered black robes. The witch.

Close to my face, a light, crackly voice says, "I know you're awake." The sound is so sharp it's like an airhorn in the silence.

Oh God, oh God.

I'm asleep. She can't get to me. Usually they would see me peeking, or the pained grimace on my face told them I was awake. When they grabbed me, I would always attempt to scream, despite having no voice in these nightmares. But not tonight. Tonight, I was dead to the world. I had to stay asleep at all costs, according to the old man.

My floorboards creak again as a throbbing sensation builds up in my ears. The shadow man is getting closer; I can feel it.

Sweat drips down my face, the beads tingling and itching my temples. I want so badly to rub my face and clear the itching sensation.

Concentrating on my feet, I tense and attempt to wiggle my toes. The witch won't see if they move, and at this point I don't care if the shadow man notices. My toes shift. I focus on the movement. Yes, they can move. I'm not fully paralyzed.

The pressure on my chest shifts slightly and the harsh stench increases. *Focus on the candles. Keep the plan in mind,* I remind myself. *It's almost time.*

Cold fingers slowly curl around my throat. The grip tightens as both hands take hold.

A numbing shiver runs through me as my breath catches. *No, no, don't…*

It takes everything I have not to gasp, not to open my eyes or show any signs of distress. Heat flushes my face as I silently fight for breath, unable to move or do anything to stop her.

Now is the time. It has to be. Please, let it be time.

Her fingers tighten over my throat, and I can't stop a slight gasp escaping.

"Come to me, Lee." Her gravelly voice is close, her rank breath on me.

I fight against the throbbing sensation burning my face and try to move my arm. The mattress shifts and my arm drops, falling free as if a hole has just opened next to me. A heavy wind blows over my dangling arm. *It's not real.* My body shifts towards the hole in my bed, like I can fall through it. And maybe I can.

The clock seems to tick louder, as if fighting against the demons in my room. *Keep your heart rate in line with the ticking clock,* I was told.

I try and move my hand, focusing everything I have on my fingers.

What strength and willpower I can feel within me starts to ebb, my focus waning. Despite my eyes being closed, I feel a dizzy, spinning sensation, and the urge to vomit.

The duvet moves by my feet. The air changes as my feet become exposed—something lifting the covers.

Cold ringlets of wet hair brush against my shins, causing ripples of shivers over me. The hair brings an incredible itching sensation and the instinct to kick my legs out, but I can't. I *can't.*

Fuck. What the fuck is this?

A quiet gasp escapes me, my dry lips shifting only slightly, but I keep my eyes firmly shut. The witch squeezes my throat tighter, cutting off my breath.

Something large and warm moves against my legs, under the covers, going further up the bed. My arm remains dangling in empty air, my body sinking even more towards the hole beside me.

Oh God, oh God. It's now or never.

The ticking spurs me on. The incense gives me focus.

Willing myself into action, I open my eyes. I spring to life, lifting my torso and bringing my arms together as I scream, releasing every last drop of energy I have.

I blink through the blurriness and darkness. I'm sitting up in my bed, breathing heavily and gasping for air. Sweat is dripping down my shirt and beading on my hot face.

I'm alone in the room. My arms are in front of me as if I've just tried to catch air. No witch, no shadow man, and nothing under the covers. My sputtering breaths are the only sound.

Holy shit...I did it. I'm awake. I beat them.

I caught them in their own world.

I can smell the glowing candles and hear the clock. Does the ticking sound different? Muted?

I look over the room as I carefully crawl out of bed. Everything is in place, but something doesn't feel right. *I'm definitely awake*, I tell myself.

I did it. I can see Amy again. I can still take care of my parents. My shoulders sag as relief washes over me.

I turn back to my bed and see myself there.

My heart jumps at the sight. There I am, still in bed, in the same position in which I'd fallen asleep.

What the...

My stomach tightens as I take a shaky step closer, my foot pressing against the cold floor. Sweat drips from my face as I look upon myself. *If I'm there...*

No, no, no.

I shake my head. No, this can't be. I'm still dreaming. But I did everything the old man said. I beat the demons. I...

Rimmed by the blinds on the windows, I see the sky is lighter outside. A cool blue rather than a deep black. I move towards the window and lift the blind up with a sense of dread. My street is the same, but different. A cold shade of blue tints the world, like the early dawn light. Except it's still the middle of the night.

I look back over my room, noticing how blue the room is also, even with the yellow candlelight. This isn't right. The world isn't right. I'm...

My floorboard creaks. I spin toward the sound, my pulse pounding in my ears. I see the shadow man in the corner. His flaming red eyes are on me.

"Welcome," he says, grinning.

As you enter this room, a pale shape on the floor wriggles quickly out of sight. If you think it was probably a snake, turn left for room 25 (page 311). Or if it looked more like a large worm, proceed straight ahead to room 29.

MIRROR MAZE

29 So Long

CLIFF JONES JR.

I'VE BEEN STUCK IN THIS DREAM FOR SO LONG. I KEEP THINKING I've woken up, but there's always another layer. I got a dream journal for my birthday. *Who was that from?* I keep thinking that I'm writing in it. I'll be on a roll, remembering absurd little details and making some mind-blowing connections, but then just when I've finally got something good scribbled down, I wake up again. *Ha.*

So I start all over, scrambling to remember what I've just finished writing. The most interesting threads become memories of memories, so far removed from my actual experience that they may as well be fiction. *As well, or better even.* Can I even trust my memories inside of a dream? Maybe I only *think* I've been waking and writing, waking and writing, waking and writing…

Acorns the size of chicken eggs lie scattered all around the front yard of my childhood home. I crack one open to get to the fruit inside, something between a blackberry and a lychee. It tastes exactly as I imagined it would—which makes perfect sense because actually, I am imagining all of this. *Right?* At least, some part of me is.

But what does that even mean if it's a part of me that I can't control, can't experience directly…It may as well be somebody else. *It may as well be you.*

I open up a second acorn, but this one looks like it's been partly eaten. No. It's being eaten right now. Some invisible worm works its way through the fleshy fruit as I look on in horror. I can see little bits of lychee-blackberry meat being pulled away from the rest of the fruit and quickly dissolving into nothing.

I should just drop the thing, but I can't move a muscle. I'm frozen in place staring at this fruit in my hand as it's slowly devoured. Somehow, I know that when only the shell remains, my hand will be next.

"Wake me up!" I try to say, but my lips don't move. I struggle with everything I've got, but nothing works. *Wake me up!* The last bit of fruit disappears. I can feel the constricting pull of my sheet, the sweat on my pillow. *Wake me up!* I hear myself groan in pain as the tip of my left index finger begins to dissolve.

I open my eyes and gasp in relief. *Wow, that was weird. I should write it down.* I grab the dream journal from the mess on my bedside table. Finally, I'll get some use out of it. I open it to the first page and get to scribbling.

I have the strangest sense of deja vu.

I've been stuck in this game for so long. It's lonely here despite the crowds. Never mind the endless variety of player-to-player interaction that's possible these days. *The sports, the gangs, the hive parties…*It's meaningless. No one here stays attached for long. Why would they?

I miss you. Is it possible we've met in-game without even realizing it? Maybe. *Not likely.* I miss the *real* you. If you're still out there. *If you ever actually were.*

Time goes by so quickly in this invented world. At the speed of REM sleep, or of thought. Sometimes I go for days without a reminder to eat or drink or have a bathroom break. In-game days, of course. They fly by. Or at least it feels that way in retrospect. *At least, that's the way I remember it.* I work inside the game. I get more done that way, make more money. *Ha.* And I sleep—when I do sleep—in tune with the cycles of the game.

There used to be a point to all of this, back when the game first started. It wasn't always about wringing out every last drop of productivity from the players; it was actually *fun.* You could run around picking fights and exploring the environment all day if you wanted to, finding loot here and there as you went. Valuable items would just be lying around for the taking: gold, potions, clothing, amulets…*other players…*

It's still the same basic game now, but you have to *work* for everything. I write clickbait articles designed to catch and hold your attention long enough for advertisers to descend on you like flies. You can bat them away, sure, but they'll always come back to lay their eggs. After a while, you give up. You get used to them. The larvae hatch and worm their way into you— slowly, relentlessly eating you alive. *Invisible worms dissolving you into nothing.*

What's happening to me outside of this digital world? How old am I now? I'm sure I know these things when I'm disconnected, but in here, it's all a fog. I imagine it all comes flooding back whenever I exit the game. I can almost remember the feeling of waking up, unhooking all my gear…*breathing.* I crave that feeling. *I need it.*

But for one reason or another, I always come back to the game. *I hate myself for that.* There has to be a better way.

I've been stuck on this trip for so long. I should have come down by now. *Right?* How long has it been? It feels like eons. I'm caught in an infinite regress as my time-sense dilates further and further. What used to be an hour becomes a day. What used to be a day becomes a year. If I keep halving the time remaining until the drug wears off, I'll never get to the end of it. *Like Achilles and the Hare.*

I stare into the spectral void, watching it fracture and constellate into my little clockwork friends, my smiling tormentors, the elves. *Wait, what?* If you've never encountered them yourself, then you probably think this sounds ridiculous. *Elves?* On the other hand, if you've already climbed that death rope, then you *know* just how ridiculous it is. But that's how they like it. It's all a joke to them, even the tragic parts. Especially the tragic parts. *It's all a game.*

The elves are particularly interested in *you*, actually. They want to see you through my eyes. We're all so separate from each other compared to them, locked in our own minds. *Safe from uncertainty, from awareness.* We are of divided minds, but for the part of us that takes action—the part of us that *lives*—practically everything we do is an effort to claw through our ego barriers and merge back into one. Naturally, we're drawn to merge with some more than others, which leads to all those little tragedies they love so much. *Ha.*

I'm sitting on my couch next to a being who calls herself Elisa. The name sounds female, so I think of her that way. Somewhere in this is a joke at my expense. *Or at the expense of humanity in general.*

Elisa leans back and flips her hair so it spreads out along the back of the sofa. We've stopped talking. *This has happened before!* Cautiously, carefully, I lay my own head back. I feel an electric buzz as the strands of our hair mingle and intertwine.

Wait. What's happening? Elisa's hair is actually *moving*. Its delicate tendrils writhe like long, translucent worms, slowly winding their way toward me. I'm frozen in terror as one by one they burrow under my scalp, through my skull, and into my brain. *It tastes like something between a blackberry and a lychee.* We're connected now by invisible strands of burning agony. I want to run. I want to scream, but every bit of me has turned to stone. It's not even *me* anymore, just a shell.

I see my entire life broken down moment by moment. I relive every bad decision I've ever made and feel their effects ripple through the fractal fabric of the universe. The guilt is overpowering for a while. And then finally, after countless ages of anguish, it breaks me. *I'm done.* Now I pity my former self right along with all the people I've hurt. If only I'd known back then what I know now. I hope I can hold onto some of this when I eventually do come down. *Whenever that may be.*

I ask myself, *Is this eternity?*

It's always eternity in the moment, you answer. *Until it's over.* Only in retrospect can you hope to gauge how much time has passed, using the reference points of what came before and what came after. But what if nothing comes after? That really *would* be eternity. If I died.

I wonder if that's what happened.

I've been stuck in this trance for so long. Hovering between life and death, between fantasy and reality. It wasn't supposed to go this way. I thought I could bring you back with me. *My Persephone.* I thought you'd just climb inside my head, settling into the folds of my brain.

Now all I'm hoping for is to find my way to my own pineal body so I can slip back in before it's too late. *How long can a body survive without a soul?* I had no idea the astral plane would be so crowded. I thought it would be more like a fog, or an ocean. It's like a tangled ball of Christmas lights that just goes on forever, invisible wires twisting and writhing into eternity. *Abandon all hope, ye who enter here.* I've learned my lesson: Necromancy is not for dabblers.

The really strange thing is that each of these lights is a different person…but I can't tell if they're *really* different people or just different versions of myself. Each soul I sample, it feels like *me* while I'm there. All the memories feel like my own, and there are no others. But then I step away, and I forget. If I found you here, what would that make you? *Dead.*

Oh, my lost darling. *My Euridyce.* What were we to each

other? Was it you who gave me the journal? It was! For Christmas, I remember now. But where did you go after that? There was something I needed to tell you. Something I wish you'd known before—

No, that's not it. I know you from the game. *My Sophia.* You were one of the founding architects, but you never let on, not with anyone but me. You could have been running that place if you wanted. You were a legend. You were a goddess. We all loved you so much. Why did you have to leave us like that?

But none of that was real. Not like that night when I held you on the couch and you fell asleep in my arms. *That was us, wasn't it?* I remember the evocative scent of your hair. *My Elisa.* Earlier that night, you had told me why we'd never work as a couple. Incompatible. Star-crossed. Tangled up in knots. *Ha.* You called that one. But I never told you…I didn't care.

I shout into the void: "Elisa, wake me up!" *No response.* "Wake me up!!!" I feel a hand on my shoulder.

"Who's Elisa?"

I've been stuck in this life for so long. This can't be all there is. Day after day, I keep borrowing and spending, doing as I'm told and waiting for that direct deposit to keep me afloat another couple of weeks. I can't complain; I'm doing all right most days. Better than most. *God help us.*

I keep thinking about my first job, back when I was still in high school. I was an all-purpose coder at Kismet Software Group, a small tech company that did a lot of simple websites and cheesy 3D animation. I was only an intern, so they didn't even have to pay me minimum wage. Half the company was interns, which should tell you something. The boss liked to save money. *Ha.*

Nick Diangelo. Kismet was such a tiny company that we all reported directly to him. The whole place was like an extension of his personality, his idea of what a tech company looked like. *A caricature of a caricature.* He was so proud of our little standalone office building, all metal and black paint. It must have been some kind of barn originally. The entryway looked normal enough, but the back room where we all worked (except for Nick) had a really high ceiling and no windows at all. It was perpetually dark in there, and every time Nick gave potential clients a tour, he made sure to tell them, "We call this room 'the Cave.'" We never actually did, but it made the tour more interesting, I guess.

Working there for a little over a year, I gradually came to see that nobody was making much money, not even the full-timers. Everybody had their own particular reasons to settle for Kismet instead of moving on to bigger and better things. Not me though; I was going to college. Once I got that degree, I'd be pulling down the big bucks, calling the shots, living the good life. *Working for pay instead of "experience."*

On my last day, Nick took us out to lunch at that burger place where you put it together yourself. *Fuddy-Duddy's? Dumptruckers?* We carpooled, and I'll never forget what he told me afterwards as we were pulling back up to the office: "Now, remember…This isn't 'goodbye,' just 'so long.'"

I didn't know what to say. He was trying to be nice, letting me know there was always a place for me at Kismet if I wanted it. After I got done with this college thing. I couldn't help but feel a little insulted.

Five years and a small fortune later, I found myself jobless with barely any work experience and a new family to support. I applied all over town, but I couldn't even manage to get an interview. Eventually, I had to swallow my pride and see if Kismet would hire me back.

For all his talk, Nick was reluctant. I guess he was worried he couldn't afford the new "educated" me. He was right to worry. As soon as I find something that pays better, I'll put in my notice and move on. Nothing disloyal in that. I've got to follow the money. *Right?* I've got to be responsible. *Mouths to feed and all that.*

I fell asleep at the wheel the other day. It was just for a second, but it really got my attention. Ever since then, I can't shake the feeling that none of this is real—that I'm lying in a hospital bed somewhere, or worse. I mean, honestly, how would I know?

I feel like there's something I'm missing, but I can't quite remember what it is. Something important.

Oh.

It's *you*, isn't it? You should be here.

I keep trying to move, but my body doesn't respond. It just chugs along on its own like a machine, day after day. Somewhere along the way, so gradually I never even noticed, I got hijacked—taken over by invisible parasites worming their way into my heart, consuming my free will. I've been absorbed into something that repulses me to my core, and *I want out.*

What am I without my ability to say no? Do I even exist? Do *you?* Some days, I don't feel like I've *ever* really existed, like it's all just false memories. I see myself in the mirror, and something isn't right. That's not *me.* Just a shell.

What is all this anyway? A dream? A game? A trip? Does it ever actually end? *Does anything?*

I open my eyes. Everything that seemed so important a moment ago fades from memory as I start to get my bearings.

I have the strangest sense of deja vu.

This room does not offer any forking paths. Proceed straight ahead and climb down the ladder to freedom.

Epilogue

You've done it. You've found your way through the maze of mirrors and returned once more to the world you left behind.

But of course, you know that can't be true. In your brief absence, the world has changed, as it always does. Like a river composed of flowing water, you cannot enter the same world twice. There is no going back.

So what will you do?

To consider your options and ruminate awhile longer, climb back up the ladder to room 1 (page 13). To forge ahead into uncharted territory, close the book, take a breath, and open your eyes.

About the Authors

Cliff Jones Jr.

Cliff has several irons in the fire and more than a few bees in his bonnet. He can't be satisfied with just one life, as evidenced by his degrees in linguistics, career in software development, and obsession with dreampunk fiction. Therefore, he places a high value on dreams and other alternative modes of experience. He's been happily married his entire adult life and is the father of both a toddler and a teenager. Someday, he hopes to own a cat. Find him online at *CliffJonesJr.com*.

Elizabeth Roderick

Elizabeth Roderick is the author of *Love and Money*, *Hoodlum Army*, the *Other Place* series, and the *Tales from Purgatory* series, as well as many short stories in various anthologies. She is a musician and runs a small, diversified farm in eastern Washington State, where she lives with her daughter and far too many animals. You can find her at *TalesFromPurgatory.com*.

Ragnar Martinson

Ragnar was born 1,000 years too late to be a proper Viking and 1,000 years too early to command the Galactic Space Fleet. Instead he lives in the south of Germany, where he writes code by day and stories by night. His various creative endeavors can be found at *Advantarium.com*.

Courtney LoCicero

Courtney LoCicero writes, teaches, and dreams up scenarios for her carousel of colorful muses. She publishes works of young and new adult fantasy across digital storytelling platforms. Find her on Wattpad and Patreon as *@CocoNichole*.

Jeb R. Sherrill

Jeb Sherrill is a novelist, musician, and ex-magician who's been writing dreampunk since long before it was officially a genre. His liquid psychotropic style bends the fine line between the real and the surreal. His debut novel *Storm Dreams* is available in print and audio.

Steven R. Brandt

Steven R. Brandt has a Ph.D. from the University of Illinois for performing the first numerical simulations of rotating black hole spacetimes. Currently, he works in computer science at Louisiana State University. As a writer, he's able to use his computer and physics powers to listen to true stories from nearby spacetimes.

J.R.R.R. (Jim) Hardison

J.R.R.R. (Jim) Hardison has worked as an animator, film director, screenwriter, graphic novelist, and regular-old novelist. Writing is the dream job from which he hopes to never wake. He currently resides in Portland, Oregon, with his lovely wife, two amazing kids, one smart dog, and one stupid dog. Visit *jimhardison.com* for more.

Yelena Calavera

Yelena Calavera was part of the first wave of dreampunk, and she describes her writing as "poetic realism." She loves the poetry of Pablo Neruda, the writing of Robert Jordan, the psychology of Jung and Arnold Mindell, and the storytelling of Studio Ghibli. Her stories draw from her unusual childhood spent traveling around rural South Africa, from the Dreaming, and from the Tao that cannot be named. See more at *YelenaCalavera.co.*

David Pierre

David Pierre is a Spanish fantasy writer. He has published *De Brujas y Gigantas* (Cerbero, 2019) and *Proyecto Ficción* (Caligrama, 2018), in addition to some short stories in different media. In 2020, he co-edited the science fiction and horror anthology *Vínculos Oscuros* (Literup). He co-directs the literary project Café Librería and the publishing services company Tiburón Letra and runs a small book and art supply shop.

Alex Pilalis

Alex Pilalis is an internationally bestselling author of multiple genres and has been writing, editing, and critiquing for over ten years. His main career is in 3D animation, where he has worked in the television and games industries, and he enjoys his passion for writing in his spare time. He can usually be found in a coffee shop in London writing on his laptop. You can find out more about him at *Linktr.ee/Alecc0.*

Anna Tizard

Anna Tizard's deeply weird fiction is an ode to the strangeness of the human mind and imagines what our thoughts and inner worlds might look like if they were places, creatures, or objects come alive. Her current project is an emerging collection of weird tales called *The Book of Exquisite Corpse,* inspired by the surrealist word game of the same name. Anna lives in Brighton, UK, and can be found sharing stories at *AnnaTizard.com.*

Stephen Coghlan

Stephen Coghlan is an ever-expanding indie author who has already knit together a few forays through the looking glass. Feel free to share his tapestries on *SCoghlan.com*.

M. Crane Hana

M. Crane Hana lives in Central Arizona, where she makes weird fiber art that ends up in museums, writes weird space fantasy books that no one reads, launches liberal political rants on her blog and Twitter that apparently everyone reads (keep those death threats coming!), and welds very tiny circuits. If you want to stalk her, start with *CraneHanaBooks.com*.

Catherine Dufour

Catherine Dufour is a French author of short fiction and novels. She is also a computer engineer. Since 2001, she's published several books of light fantasy, science fiction, and mainstream literature, and won several awards. Since 2016, she has been involved in a multi-faceted reflection on the society of tomorrow, *Extricating Our Future*, within the Zanzibar science fiction collective. More on *CatherineDufour.net*.

Charles C. Mitchell

Charles C. Mitchell is a writer and culinary artist from rural Mississippi. He swears that he knows you from one of his incarnations, but he's not sure if he's lived it yet.

Tessa B. Dick

Tessa Dick and her cat share the belief that mirrors possess a special kind of magic, but they suspect that the magic of the mirror might not be completely benevolent. After all, the cat in the mirror keeps poking her nose into their food. Discover more at *PKDMemoir.BlogSpot.com*.

Thomas Fortenberry

Thomas Fortenberry is an award-winning author/editor who has also judged many literary contests, including the Georgia Author of the Year Awards and the Robert Penn Warren Prize For Fiction. A favorite character amongst the genres he writes, he has explored the mystery of Sherlock Holmes in a number of ways, including tales in *An Improbable Truth: The Paranormal Adventures of Sherlock Holmes, Sherlock Holmes: Adventures Beyond the Canon,* and *Sherlock Holmes in the Realm of Steampunk.* Check out his website *ThomasFortenberry.net* for more details.

L.B. Shimaira

L.B. Shimaira tends to write short stories based on dreams and nightmares, but the story included here was inspired by her actually having visual snow syndrome and wanting more people to learn about its existence. However, as far as she knows, no strange entities have contacted her through mirrors. If you wish to connect with her or discover her other dark fiction works, you can visit *Shimaira.com.*